PJ Gronam

A Lifetime of

Betrayal

A McKinney Brothers Novel
Book 5

PD House Books

Copyright © 2013 by P. J. Grondin

Published by P.D. House Holdings. Second Edition

Library of Congress Control Number: 2019931179

www.pjgrondin.com

ISBN 978-1-7370004-6-4

A Lifetime of

Betrayal

PROLOGUE
1997

The yelp of pain followed a puff of light colored smoke by a fraction of a second. From Harold Trent's vantage point nearly 700 yards away, Colonel Milton Chester's howl sounded like rubber tires briefly screeching on a paved road.

Trent watched two men; Colonel Chester seated at a picnic table under a pavilion covered with a sheet metal roof, and Ace Glover, a young, blond-haired man with a slight build standing about ten feet from the colonel. The pavilion stood next to a small, concrete building that had once housed the elevator down to the control room for one of the United States' long range Patriot missile silos outside of Grand Forks Air Force Base in eastern North Dakota.

Through powerful binoculars, Trent clearly saw the scene under the pavilion, despite the heat waves that rose from the acres of prairie grass. He licked his dry lips, feeling several days' growth of stubble at the base of his lower lip. A salty taste filled his mouth from the accumulation of dried sweat. He smelled his own stench, the result of three continuous days on the road following the young blond man standing under the pavilion. Now, as his excitement grew, he all but forgot about his lack of hygiene.

After a moment, he saw another puff of smoke. Chester jerked his arm back and let out another scream, muted by the hot, dry breeze. The shot had hit its mark, confirmed by the dark spot expanding on his arm.

Ace, standing on the other side of the table, held the source of the puffs of smoke. Trent couldn't make out the type of gun, but it was definitely a pistol with a silencer, explaining the lack of a report.

The hot, dry wind blew across the grassy plain, sucking moisture from everything. The late afternoon sun bore down from an angle slightly behind Trent, making it difficult for anyone looking his way to see him crouched down in the high prairie grass. He had been sitting in this grassy field for nearly half an hour before Chester had pulled up to the deserted missile silo in his dark military issue sedan. The colonel had confidently strolled out to the pavilion to meet Glover, who had preceded his arrival by some fifteen minutes. How the kid had managed to get the colonel, the Commanding Officer of Grand Forks Air Force Base, to meet him at this site was a mystery, but it didn't matter. He was here.

Moments before, Chester had been confident, almost cocky in his attitude. Before any of the current drama had unfolded, he had stood and said something to the kid, then turned as if to leave. As he started towards his car, Glover pulled the gun from the back of his waistband and convinced the colonel to stay. Holding his hands up in an expression that seemed to say, 'Wait a minute, let's calm down,' the colonel slowly, carefully turned back to the picnic table and sat. That had probably been a mistake, though, in all likelihood, it wouldn't have mattered. A man with a gun can be very convincing and bullets travel much faster than a fleeing human, no matter how fast they run. In this case, the man with the gun was only nineteen, a fact Trent knew with certainty.

The colonel's demeanor changed from cocky to cautious. The kid motioned at the officer to look at something on the table, held there against the hot breeze by a rock. Chester picked up a piece of paper and when he read the document his facial expression went from disbelief to shock, then to fear. Even at this distance, Trent saw Chester's body tense as he slowly looked from the papers to Glover's face. Chester's eyes were wide, his mouth agape. It was as if he'd seen hell approaching and there was nothing he could do about it.

Trent said out loud, though no one could hear him, "That's right, you prick. You were her father and you didn't even know it. You put her mother through hell. I wish your old man was alive to see this." If anyone could have heard him they would have wondered who "she" was, but that didn't matter. He knew. And now the colonel knew. He continued to look through the binoculars, unconsciously pressing the eye piece tight against his eyes. "Do it, Ace. Do it now!"

That's when he saw those first telltale signs that the kid meant business, when the first two shots were fired. They were merely meant to coerce the colonel to action, but the warning shots, even though they struck the colonel in the left hand and left arm, apparently didn't work. That's when Ace threw something on the picnic table. Whatever it was, the colonel's face turned to pure terror. He bolted and tried to run. There was another puff of smoke. Trent saw Chester's left leg jerk backwards as the slug hit its mark. This time, Chester fell to the concrete floor of the pavilion. The colonel turned over and looked up as Ace eased around the picnic table, pacing himself, knowing that his wounded prey had no means of escape.

Trent held his breath and gritted his teeth for what seemed like several minutes, but in reality was just a few seconds. He leaned forward in anticipation as Ace, masked in rage and a sinister smile, stopped and stood over his victim. Trent had often wished he would be the one to carry out this grisly act. At least he could watch the execution, decreed by the kid's own mother.

Chester's mouth and eyes were wide open. He frantically pushed back using his good arm, kicking with one foot. His left leg was limp, incapacitated by the third shot. Dust stirred as the colonel scrambled trying to get traction to escape his pursuer. In quick succession, three more puffs of smoke rose from the gun. No more sounds of pain came from the colonel lying motionless on the dusty concrete floor of the pavilion.

Ace casually placed the gun on the picnic table, then picked up what looked like a pen. He leaned over the colonel's dead body and placed the tip of the pen on the colonel's chest. Trent frowned for a moment, trying to see what he was doing.

With a pen in one hand and what looked like a notepad in the other, Ace appeared to make a quick note in the pad. He threw the pen aside, put the notebook in his pocket, picked up the gun and the papers from the picnic table, then walked slowly to a white Dodge Sebring.

Trent froze for a moment as the kid stood by the car and scanned the area around the missile silo and picnic pavilion. He stopped and seemed to stare in Trent's direction. After several long seconds, Ace broke off his stare and opened the car door. The car started then did a U-turn around the government issued sedan and headed for State Route 20. He appeared not to be in any hurry, even though he'd just murdered a military officer in cold blood.

Harold Trent waited for another five minutes before heading back to his beat-up pick-up truck. Pulling the dry grass away from the vehicle, he opened the windows and waited for the heat that had built up to dissipate. He also headed for State Route 20. It had been a very satisfying day.

***

After ten more minutes, another car started and left the murder scene from the opposite side of the pavilion. A rented Ford Taurus headed towards State Route 20, stopping as William "Hatch" Hatcher looked east then west for any oncoming traffic on the sparsely traveled road. Nothing was coming in either direction. Wiping his hands over his face, then back over his short, bristly hair, he moved his head in a circle, working out the tension that had built up as he had watched another human murdered in cold, vengeful, blood.

He had followed Ace Glover from a parking lot in eastern Virginia, where Ace's half sister and his mother were gunned-down by a team of federal agents, to this desolate field in North Dakota expecting that there would be a violent confrontation. He was still surprised by the cold and calculated manner in which Ace Glover had delivered his version of justice. He was also taken aback that there was another witness to the carnage.

In a southern drawl that was far out of place in the northern plains, he asked himself, "Well, wudn't that sumthin'?"

Chapter 1
June 30, 1999

Ace Glover's thoughts were back in Savannah, Georgia as he traveled south on Interstate 95 just east of Kingsland, Georgia, heading for Jacksonville, Florida. It was just after 3:00 AM and he needed some shut-eye before continuing on to St. Augustine later in the day. It had been a long night. He had driven the winding back-roads along the Atlantic coast prior to jumping on the interstate south of Brunswick, Georgia and fatigue was setting in. He feared that he'd fall asleep at the wheel and end up in one of the roadside ditches or a salt marsh in this rural section of the state.

But Ace's mind wandered from more than just the grueling drive. He was thinking about women, two in particular. He would probably never see one of them again. He was certain that he'd never see the other.

He smiled as the bright reflectors in between the white lines in the center of the road passed in a hypnotic rhythm. He thought about Angelina Valentine's platinum-blonde hair draped across her left shoulder. It had flowed onto her chest like a silky smooth waterfall as she sat in the corner of her over-stuffed couch. The too-blonde color contrasted with the short, shiny black robe draped across her ample breasts. The nails on her hands and toes were painted a high gloss black to match the evening's night wear, a sexy black negligee and matching panties. Her legs were tucked up under her rear end, a wine glass sat within easy reach, nearly empty on the modern art deco end table. The entire room smelled faintly of her perfume. She was already in the mood for a long night with her man.

He remembered her yell to him in a southern drawl, "Ace, be a dear and fix me another glass of wine. And put another bottle on ice. I'm sure we'll need it before the evening is through."

The beautiful woman's southern belle, over-the-top accent was hard to swallow, but it was her condescending attitude that had made the hair on the back of Ace's neck stand up. He had lived with Angelina Valentine in her Savannah, Georgia home for the past year. The longer he had stayed, the more he had hated the terms of their agreement. He felt like a caged animal, as if he had to do circus tricks at the behest of the ring master, all the while looking for a way to escape. Now the gate had been left open and he'd made his move.

Ace hadn't always loathed his situation. Over the last year it had been a good reciprocal arrangement. When Ace had met Angelina in the grocery section of the local Trader Joe's, she'd been widowed for just over two months. She had been in the produce aisle and had dropped a bag of kiwi fruit. Being the gentleman that he was raised to be, Ace bent down, picked up the bag and handed it to her. They started a casual conversation about the trials and tribulations of their respective lives.

Ace told her the story of a life on the road with his poor, single mother who had lost her husband, Ace's father, before he was born. He told her of the meager existence of his childhood and how there were times when he went to bed hungry only to wake up to no breakfast. He said his mother took two and three part-time jobs just to make ends meet. He had to start work at the age of ten to help pay the bills, but they always ended up getting evicted from one trashy, dingy apartment or an old, beat-up trailer for non-payment of rent.

It was a sad story, very convincing, and mostly contrived. He'd had a lot of practice over the years, perfecting the lines with a false sincerity that would win over the greatest skeptic. The tall tale was delivered to his audience in a manner that pulled heavily on their heart strings. It was close enough to the truth that Ace felt no guilt in the telling.

Angelina bought it, hook, line, and sinker. Besides being a convincing storyteller, Ace was also a good listener. In short order, Ace became Angelina's new tenant with exceptional fringe benefits.

Angelina Valentine's wealthy sixty-year old husband had been killed in a car accident on Interstate 16 just south of Dublin, Georgia. He had been to a sales convention in Atlanta where he closed a multi-million dollar textile contract. His commission was substantial. His newly widowed wife was the beneficiary of the sale. That chunk of change paled in comparison to the fortune he'd already amassed, and that didn't count the mid-six figure life insurance policy payoff that she'd received. Though Angelina did grieve, her mourning period was tempered by her sudden marital and financial freedom.

Many of her husband's friends were appalled at her quick emotional recovery. They were even more stunned when she allowed a young, blond "housekeeper" to take up residence in her "husband's house" in the exclusive Whitemarsh Island neighborhood. Her husband's body was barely cold, the grass not even mature over his grave. Worse, she barely hid the fact that Ace was much more than hired help. At forty-one, she was over twice Ace's age. She frequently used hair coloring to hide the gray and she covered up her deepening facial lines with the most expensive skin care products on the market. No one could argue with the results. Angelina Valentine was still a beautiful woman. With Ace in her home and in her bed, she felt alive, vibrant, and sexy again.

For his part, Ace did everything he could to keep his new lover happy. She provided him with a roof over his head, great food, clothing, a generous allowance, and all the sex he could possibly want or need. The home was a mini-mansion with nearly ten thousand square-feet of living space, a swimming pool, four-car garage, and tennis court. There was enough room for several families. But Angelina had the estate all to herself. Through a chance meeting, Ace had the good fortune to share the estate with her...at least until now.

The arrangement had been heading south for many months, at least from Ace's perspective. Sex wasn't the issue. Ace was more than happy to keep her satisfied, regardless of the sometimes odd sexual games she wanted to play. She had a penchant for playing rough. Sometimes, she wanted to be the victim, other times, the aggressor. Either way, Ace enjoyed most of the sexual acrobatics.

The problem wasn't even that she expected to be waited on, hand and foot. After all, it was Angelina's money, or more accurately, her dead husband's, that paid for everything. All Ace had to do was put up with her. Up until now, it hadn't been too difficult.

When Angelina wanted to talk, he was there to listen, but she'd started to ask probing questions about topics for which he had no good answers. When she asked for specifics about his past, he'd try to deflect her questions and change the subject, but when her inquiries grew persistent, he'd simply lied. In that department, he was a pro. He'd had a great teacher, his late mother, Abigail Glover.

As time passed, Angelina continued to press for more details about his tough family life. Where he was born? What schools he'd attended? Did he have any friends? As with all liars, he started to forget the stories he'd previously told her. But he could tell by her expressions that she knew he was lying. Ace wondered how much she really knew. *If she starts asking the right questions of the right people, this could become a problem.*

Besides, even though the arrangement was good financially and the fringe benefits were great, Ace had grown tired of the role of Angelina's play toy. And he had a job to do that had nothing to do with Angelina Valentine or Savannah, Georgia.

Several months before, he'd put a plan in motion that he'd hoped would help him accumulate cash more quickly. Part of it was to be in a position to make off with a large amount of Angelina's money. He certainly wouldn't try to rob her blind. Far from it. It was more like he planned to take a sum that was in keeping with the work he did around Angelina's estate, in addition to being her personal play-thing. Ace's financial needs were not nearly as significant as his host's. But he did need enough cash to make a clean get away from Angelina and Savannah.

Ace planned on heading to Norfolk, Virginia, King's Bay, Georgia and several stops in Florida where some unfinished business required his attention. He was getting anxious, even excited to take the next steps in his plan, which he figured would require about two hundred thousand dollars. Acquiring that much money from a single source, and not get caught in the act would be difficult. So he decided to venture out in search of other sources of easy money.

Ace possessed natural good looks, and even at the tender age of twenty, honed skills that made meeting and wooing women easy. His handsome narrow face and square jaw, fit and trim body, and disarming charm attracted stares and interest from women as soon as he walked into a bar, restaurant, or grocery store. That's what had attracted Angelina.

And that's what had been the problem of late. Angelina was extremely possessive.

He couldn't get out alone in the evening. She rarely left the house and constantly demanded his services, either in bed or as a servant boy. Ace had thought long and hard, trying to figure out a solution to his problem.

One day while he read the paper and Angelina slept on the couch, he thought, "If only she was a heavier sleeper." A light in his brain came on. The solution was simple.

Rohypnol. Roofies. One of the popular date rape drugs, Ace knew that he could slip Angelina a roofie in her drink most any time since he was always waiting on her, fixing dinner and drinks. Getting a supply of Rohypnol was easy, too.

And it worked like a charm.

Ace would fix dinner, then spike one of her after dinner glasses of wine and *voila*, instant freedom. Angelina would be out for long hours, giving Ace free reign to hop the local bars in search of another easy target.

In the first few weeks he'd drop into a downtown nightclub where the cover charge was twenty dollars, which, in Savannah, was pretty steep. The result was that only wealthy kids with hefty financial support from Mommy and Daddy made it through the doors. The ratio of young women to men was nearly three to one, especially on "ladies night." For Ace, it was like shooting fish in a barrel. He was actually only twenty, but his fake ID and the manner in which he carried himself made him appear much older. When the young girls would guess his age, they'd say mid to late twenties. Some would even say thirty-ish, which gave him a little self satisfaction, since his mom had always referred to him as her little boy. *Your little boy's all grown up now, Momma.*

Ace moved quickly with his new dates. He was amazed at how easily women appeared to believe his line of bullshit. He used two basic storylines. In the first and most convincing story, he was an ex-marine just back from Iraq. When asked what it was like "over there," he would tell tales of raids north of Baghdad, but his tales were never about the horrors of war. He always spoke solemnly of finding an orphaned little girl or boy and how he and other members of his squad helped to feed these children and find them new families. The tales were laced with such emotion that it sometimes brought tears to his eyes, making the story seem more authentic to unsuspecting women.

After the orphan story, he told the tale of his poor mother who was about to lose her house because she had cancer and was unable to work. "I'm leaving this weekend to head home and try my best to help her." Of course, Wall Street bankers were the greedy villains stealing his mother's home in her most desperate time of need. The woman was ill, for God's sake. All she needed was a couple thousand dollars to save her house. Ace had some money, but unless he could raise more cash quickly, he wouldn't have enough to save the family home.

Between the alcohol and Ace's convincing manner, these young women were in a trance by the time Ace was through spinning his web. They were like putty in his hands.

Without bills and any other financial responsibility, his financial stash grew quickly. He was rapidly approaching his goal and his plan appeared to be on track.

Then he screwed up in a big way.

Angelina was fast asleep on the couch after a nice dinner followed by a spiked cocktail. Ace was at the *Jazz'd* lounge working his magic when Gloria Mason, a wealthy socialite and close friend of Angelina listened in while Ace told his tale of life in Iraq. After a time, she struck up a conversation with Ace. At first, he didn't recognize her, but once he did, he knew his plans were out the window. Gloria would surely tell Angelina of his exploits. He couldn't allow that to happen. His time in Savannah was history.

***

Angelina awoke sometime after 2:40 AM, still lying on the couch. Her head felt like it was stuffed with cotton, her vision still blurred. She felt groggy, as if drugged, unable to shake off the feeling that gripped her. *This is getting to be a habit. Why am I always so tired?* Getting off the couch was a chore. She didn't bother to straighten out her nightgown. Unsteadily, she headed to the foot of the stairway, flipping on lights as she went. Something wasn't right. Ace was always there. Why did the house seem so empty?

In a deep southern drawl and a drunken-sounding slur, she called out to him, "Ace? Where are you, dear?"

The silence engulfed her for the first time since Ace had moved in. She started up the stairs using the handrail far more than should be necessary. But in her disoriented state, she needed the support.

She continued calling Ace's name, but when she got to the bedroom, the realization hit her. He was gone. His dresser drawer was emptied; his suitcase was missing. She looked in her walk-in closet and noticed her safe was ajar. Peering in, Angelina saw that over one hundred twenty-seven thousand dollars in cash that had been stacked in the huge safe was gone. She smiled a sad smile. She then went to her jewelry box. It was still locked and looked undisturbed, but she checked the contents anyway. Not one piece was missing. *So all he wanted was cash. He should have just asked. Oh, well. It was fun while it lasted.*

The phone rang. Normally, it would have startled her, but in her state, it was a dull, muffled tone. *It's nearly 3:00. It must be Ace. Maybe he's calling to apologize.* She picked up the receiver.

In a voice that still sounded as if she were a bit tipsy she said, "Hello."

A man with a deep, heavy southern drawl asked, "Mrs. Valentine?"

"Yes."

"This is Deputy Dewayne Arnold with the Chatham County Sheriff's office. First, I must apologize for calling at this hour."

That got her attention, but in her drugged state of mind she said with a slur. "That's alright...what did you say your name was?"

"Dewayne Arnold, ma'am."

"Alright, Dewayne. Is this about Ace Glover? Because he really isn't a bad person."

Deputy Arnold hesitated for a moment. "No ma'am. Why would you suspect that I'm calling about Ace...what was his name?"

"Glover. Ace Glover. He took some money from me and I thought that you might have caught him with it."

"Sorry, ma'am, but that's not my department." A pause. "Did you know a Miss Gloria Mason?"

There was a long pause. Even in her foggy state of mind, the past tense wasn't lost on Angelina. She shook her head, trying to clear out the stuffy feeling. Her voice stammered when she replied, "Y-yes, I do. What do you mean 'Did I know her?' And what department are you in?"

He ignored her question. "She was reported missing earlier by a friend. When was the last time you saw or spoke with Miss Mason?"

"We had dinner yesterday evening...no, the evening before last...around seven-thirty at Noble Fare, then we went shopping until about 10:00. We said our good-byes in the parking lot as the stores were closing. Is Gloria alright?"

"I'm sorry, Mrs. Valentine. Miss Mason's body was found out in the water near Fort Pulaski about half an hour ago."

The receiver hit the carpet with a thud as Angelina Valentine passed out.

Chapter 2

"Can you believe how hot it is already?"

Sitting at a patio table under the shade of their lanai, Diane McKinney looked up from her *Ladies Home Journal* article and glanced at her husband, Pat. She wasn't sure saying what was on her mind was the best response to his silly question. It was just before noon in Dunnellon, Florida on June 30. There wasn't a cloud in the brilliantly blue sky and the sun beat down, reflecting off the surface of the pool. Pat and Diane's children, eight-year old Sean and six-year old Anna, were in the pool splashing away at each other. The temperature was in the low nineties and the humidity made sitting in the sun unbearable, unless you were in the pool. It was a sure bet that clouds would form in a couple of hours and the mid-afternoon showers would soak everything. Then the sun would come out and dry the streets, sidewalks, and driveways, and raise the humidity another ten percent.

Pat sat on a lounge chair just outside of the shade of their covered patio. It was a good thing Diane had lathered him up with lotion before he volunteered to watch their children play in the new pool. Pat picked up a tall glass and sipped sweet iced tea, also courtesy of his dear wife.

The pool had just been completed and filled three weeks earlier. Pat and Diane had been swimming only three times, but Sean and Anna hadn't missed a single day, except the previous Saturday when rain drenched the entire state from dusk to dawn. Even then Sean had wanted to take a swim; until a bolt of lightning had struck a tree some two hundred yards behind their house. He had quickly changed his mind and decided it would be a good day to stay indoors.

Getting the pool installed was somewhat of a controversy between Pat and Diane. They both thought it might be a good idea, but the closer it came to actually making a decision to have the large, in-ground pool installed, the more nervous Pat became. He'd always been a bit uneasy about having a pool in the back yard. Their children were still young and accidents happen. But Diane pushed the plan, stating that nearly every one of their neighbors had a pool. If the kids didn't swim at their home, they'd swim at their friends' houses. Diane stressed that if *they* had a pool, they'd at least be able to keep an eye on the kids. At a neighbor's house, you had no idea if any adults were supervising the kids or if they were on their own.

Pat relented, but he was still a bit wary. So to calm his nerves, he stayed vigilant, watching Sean and Anna as they played and splashed each other.

When the pool was finished, Sean was at first hesitant to jump in, reluctant even to take the first steps into the shallow end. But he quickly learned to swim, thanks to his Aunt Lisa and Uncle Joe. Together, they taught Sean how to use different strokes to swim on and under the water. His final test was to first jump, then dive from the diving board into the deep end of the pool while they remained close by. Now he wasn't even afraid to dive and swim in the deep end on his own. He'd dive in to retrieve pool toys and coins, coming up from a dive with a handful of multi-colored rings, a bright smile on his face. From then on, Sean wanted to go in the pool every day. It wasn't long and he was splashing around like a dolphin. Diane had to get him three new swimsuits so that he'd have a dry suit each day. To Pat and Diane, his smile made the pool worth every penny.

In the first week, he got a nasty sunburn even though Diane made sure he was coated with suntan lotion with a thirty SPF. Now his skin was a dark tan.

Until the pool had been installed, Sean had been the most serious little boy anyone had ever known. He rarely smiled and always appeared to have something heavy weighing on his mind. He worried about everything, from his parents' health to his sister's safety, to his dad possibly going away again on a submarine. He was convinced that Pat was going to get recalled to active duty even after Pat had explained to him that it couldn't happen. Sean had replied that 'Uncle Joe got called back to the Marines, so they could make you go in the Navy.' He finally, reluctantly believed his dad's explanation that Uncle Joe had been in the Marine Reserves, but that he was completely out of the Navy. Even that took reassurances from Diane that his father was telling the truth.

Since getting the pool, the biggest change was in Sean's personality. The young, serious boy who'd been trying to grow up too fast turned into a smiling, playful eight-year old. Pat and Diane couldn't believe the complete about-face in his moods. It was as if expending all his energy in the pool left him little desire to contemplate more serious matters.

The real proof was on paper. Sean's grandmother had given him a journal as a gift the previous year. She told her grandson that he should write down his thoughts and feelings or what he did during the day, or just anything that came to mind. Grandma McKinney thought it would be a good way for him to express himself, to unload some of that serious energy. She'd checked with Pat and Diane to make sure they were okay with her gift and they had both approved.

At the time, Sean wasn't sure he liked the idea. He'd said, 'Girls keep diaries.' His grandmother agreed with him that only girls kept diaries, but that what he was doing was like writing a book. She assured him he didn't have to write something every day, just when he felt like it. Without a smile, he nodded his approval.

Apparently, he liked the idea because he wrote in his journal nearly every day. Occasionally, when Sean was at school, Diane would read the journal. She wasn't horrified, but some of his thoughts caused her genuine concern. Sean wrote about having to learn how to defend his family from "the bad people." In several entries, he stated that he was going to have his Uncle Joe teach him how to use a gun. He was afraid that, when his father was away, something might happen to his mom and sister. *'I don't want my family to get hurt like what happened to Uncle Hatch's family.'*

When William Hatcher had been out to sea on the USS *Nevada*, his entire family had been murdered. None of the adults had ever openly discussed the horrific crime, but somehow Sean knew. Diane had no idea how he had learned of the brutal murders of Pat's best friend's mother, father, and little sister, but the crime was spelled out in his journal with just enough detail for her to know that Sean knew what had happened.

When I think about Uncle Hatch, it makes me sad that his little sister is gone. And his mom and dad. That must make him sad, too. He doesn't seem sad when he's here with us, but it must be hard living at the swamp all alone. I know when I'm alone in my room, I think about what it would be like to live in our house without Anna and Mom and Dad. I know I would be scared and sad. That's why I want Uncle Joe to teach me how to use a gun because I need to be able to help Dad protect Anna and Mom. I know Dad thinks he can take care of us but he isn't home all the time. When he's away, I'm the only man in the house. What if bad people come to the house to hurt us while he's away? I feel like I can't help Dad if I don't know how a gun works. I know it isn't as easy to use a gun as it is on TV. Uncle Joe told me so. But he said he'd help me learn when I was older and Mom and Dad said its okay. I hope they do it soon. I'm afraid if they wait, it will be too late.

Diane had cried for several minutes after reading Sean's plea for help. He was truly afraid. Boogey men were all around him, but they weren't really, were they? She believed that these "bad guys" were invading the very impressionable mind of an eight-year old.

She didn't tell Pat about the entry. She was afraid that he'd go right to their son and try talking with him about it. That would violate their agreement with Sean that his journal would be private; that only he could grant permission for anyone to read his private thoughts. And yet, Diane had done just that. Without her son's approval, she'd read his deepest, most private thoughts, as if she'd tapped a direct line to his brain. But it was her duty, wasn't it, to protect her son any way she could? Or was it a violation of his privacy that, if discovered, would destroy any trust between them? She'd hoped his intense feelings would temper over time.

But with the installation of the new pool, Sean had seemed to be transformed almost overnight. Diane was cautiously optimistic that her son was becoming a happy, well adjusted eight-year old and that the old, too serious Sean would fade into the past. At least until he was older and better equipped to handle life's curveballs. Growing up was tough enough without trying to carry the weight of the world on such young shoulders.

While Sean and Anna played, Diane padded over to where Pat sat. She carried her glass of iced tea with her. When she was close enough, she let several drops from the cold, sweating glass drop on his back.

He tensed and arched his back as the drips hit between his shoulder blades. "Holy crap, honey! That's freezing...but it feels pretty good."

"Why don't you jump in the pool with the kids and cool off?"

"I'll tell you what, I will if you do."

Diane recognized that sly smile. She could tell he had something more than a swim in mind. Pat stood, looked briefly at the kids in the pool, then moved up behind Diane, slipped his arms around her waist and lightly kissed her neck. Tightening his arms around her waist, he quickly lifted her and carried her towards the pool.

Diane screamed, "Put me down! No, Pat! Don't you dare! I mean...ahhhh!"

The splash of them both hitting the water drowned out her scream. Pat held on tight as they broke the surface of the water after being under for a few seconds. Diane did her best to break free of his grip while he held on for dear life.

Both Sean and Anna laughed hysterically at their mom and dad. Diane couldn't help but smile, seeing her children having such fun, especially Sean. Finally, she broke down and laughed, assuring her husband that she wouldn't beat him up if he let her go. He asked twice if she promised. And twice she said yes, all the while crossing her fingers where the kids could see, but Pat couldn't. When he let go, Diane spun around and jumped on Pat, pushing his head under water. They splashed and fought playfully in the pool for several minutes before settling into an easy hug.

Pat and Diane stayed that way, relaxing in each other's arms until they heard Sean yell, "Aunt Lisa, Uncle Joe, Danielle!"

Joe emerged through the back patio door into the lanai, followed by Lisa and Danielle. Little one-year old Danielle walked next to Lisa, her legs a bit wobbly as she held her mother's hand. But she was making her way through the patio door. When she made it to the lanai she stopped and smiled. Her hair pulled back in two little pigtails tied with white ribbons, she wore a pretty white sun dress that matched her mom's.

Joe said, "Hey, kids. Weren't you in the pool the last time I was here?"

Both Sean and Anna said in unison, "Yeah."

Sean, wanting to show off his swimming skills, said, "Hey, Uncle Joe, watch this." Before Joe could say anything, Sean turned and dove underwater. He glided with smooth strokes along the bottom of the pool into the deep end where he stopped for a moment, then moved to another spot and stopped again. After another twenty seconds, Sean headed back to the shallow end of the pool, still under water. His head finally popped above the surface of the water and he showed Joe a fistful of multi-colored diving rings. Sean's smile was as broad as any of them had ever seen. It nearly brought tears to Diane's eyes.

"I've been practicing my swimming underwater and holding my breath. I can hold my breath for over a minute now. Cool, huh?"

"Very cool, Sean. But remember what I told you. Never swim alone and always watch out for your swim partner, right?"

"Right. Anna is always in the pool with me. Right, Anna?"

Anna nodded her head. "I like swimming. It's fun, even with Sean." She splashed water at her brother who splashed her back. They both laughed.

The adults smiled. Then Joe turned towards Pat and Diane, "So I see you guys like swimming, too. But shouldn't you be wearing your suits?"

From the edge of the pool closest to Joe and Lisa, Diane replied, "Your brother decided we didn't need suits today. He just threw me in. He broke one of his own rules; something about horseplay around the pool?"

She gave Pat a look that said *You're in trouble now*.

"I didn't throw her in. We just jumped in together." He turned to Sean. "Right, son?"

"You're on your own, Dad."

Joe and Lisa laughed. Joe said, "Smart move, Sean. You don't want any part of that."

Diane, thinking about when her daughter Anna had just started walking, smiled at Danielle. "Aren't you a pretty girl? You look like your cousin did at that age."

Diane wanted to have another child, but she and Pat had already decided that Anna would be their last. With Pat's penchant for finding danger, they both felt two children was the limit. They were good, healthy kids, one boy, one girl. Why upset the balance?

She looked at her husband. "I'm getting into some dry clothes. Someone's got to make lunch."

"I guess I'll get out, too. But I'll wait to change. Heck, in this heat, my clothes will be dry in no time."

Lisa asked, "Is there anything I can do to help?"

"Sure," Diane said. "We're having burgers and dogs, so if you want to get out the buns and plates, stuff like that. Pat should be starting the grill any minute now." She glanced at her husband as she made her way to the steps in the shallow end of the pool. "Right, dear?"

"Right, uh, I was just planning on that."

Joe shook his head and smiled.

Chapter 3

"Damn it to hell!"

Detective William Banks swore as hot coffee spilled over the file that he'd been flipping through for what seemed like the hundredth time. He jumped up from his wooden relic of a chair, his 6-foot-1, 210-pound frame nearly knocking it over in his haste to avoid getting a lap full of the hot brew. He quickly grabbed for a handful of paper towels that he kept at his desk. Usually they were used as napkins for lunch or wipes for the whiteboard that hung behind his desk. Now they served as the emergency coffee cleanup kit.

As Banks worked to contain the flow of java, his phone rang. Both of his hands were wet and still held coffee-soaked paper towels. It would have been a real challenge to get to the phone without getting his white dress shirt or tie doused with the dark brown brew.

Reid Hansen said, "Keep cleaning up. I'll get that."

Banks nodded at his partner, his face cocked in a half-smile as he soaked up more coffee, then tossed the dripping paper towels into the heavy plastic trash can. He threw down more dry paper towels on top of the thick folder and noticed that some of the ink on the top pages had started to run. *Damn!*

It wasn't a real big deal; just an inconvenience if they had to be replaced. Each page of the two-year-old file was already scanned and stored on the Grand Forks Police Department's server. It was one of the new features that came with the renovation of the building after the great flood of 1997. The police department building had fared better than many of the buildings downtown, but it hadn't completely escaped the damaging waters of the Red River as it reached record levels.

Hansen's and Banks' desks faced each other in the tradition of an old squad room. They shared file cabinets and guest chairs. For Hansen, at 6-foot-5, reaching across his desk to Banks' phone was easy.

Banks heard his partner say, "Grand Forks Police Department, Detective Hansen."

Hansen smiled, glancing at Banks as he listened to the caller. Banks went back to cleaning up the mess on his desk when Hansen responded to something the caller said. "No ma'am, we haven't identified the source of the loud noises over on Seventh Avenue."

A pause.

Hansen said again. "No, ma'am, we haven't given up. We understand that it's waking you up at 3:30 AM. We have just two officers on at that hour, but they are patrolling the area of the noise around that time."

Another pause.

"Yes, ma'am. I'll be sure that the officers get this information."

After a few more "Yes, ma'ams," Hansen hung the phone up. He shrugged and said, "Old Mrs. Iverson. She's hearing things again."

Banks smiled. He would have to make a point to stop by and see her. She called at least once each week with some imagined emergency. She was probably calling just to chat. At ninety-two years old, she lived alone but still managed to get around town in her 1982 Crown Victoria, though Banks felt her time behind the wheel was coming to a close.

The desk cleanup was as good as it was going to get so Banks sat back down and started flipping through the pages in the Milton Chester murder file again. The top two pages on the right side of the folder had taken the brunt of the spill. They were stained brown and still damp, but most of the file escaped unscathed. He leaned back in his chair, which creaked in protest. He stared up at the ceiling, feeling the futility of the effort of combing through the file again.

The file on Colonel Milton Chester was nearly two inches thick. The folder was dark tan, heavy cardboard and had a two-hole clamp at the top of each side of the folder's interior. On the left side was a page with a picture of the late Colonel Chester. It was free of any coffee stains from Banks' blunder. The picture was from mid-chest up. It had been supplied by the military and was most likely taken during his tenure at Grand Forks Air Force Base, where he was the base Commanding Officer. The rest of the page had personal information, including birth date, height, sex (as if anyone viewing the file couldn't tell by the picture), hair color, and race. In a separate section of the form, "Married" was checked for Marital Status, along with his wife's name; Vivian Ashton Chester. They apparently had no children. The page also listed his former address, occupation, and other facts about his military history. He was not a highly decorated war hero. On the contrary, his medals, awards, and achievements were slim for someone commanding a military base. Banks did recall that the colonel's father, Alton Chester, retired as a Brigadier General, which may have helped the younger Chester's career.

The right side of the folder contained all the forms that had been completed during the investigation. The pages were arranged in chronological order as more data was discovered and recorded. The most recent information was on top, the oldest on the bottom. So when Banks spilled his coffee, the newest page took the brunt of the spill.

That didn't bother him. Even the newest information was relatively old and most of that was mundane and of little value. Besides, for the most part, he had the folder committed to memory.

He continued to stare at the ceiling, picturing the crime scene from two years ago. It was a difficult case, occurring less than three months after another unsolved murder in Grand Forks County. There was a definite connection between the two cases. During the investigation, it was discovered that a woman who had been married to the first murder victim, Kevin Reardon, was killed in Norfolk, Virginia. Becky Reardon had been shot, used as a human shield by her panicked boyfriend, as they were about to be arrested for extorting money from the federal government.

Banks remembered the two NCIS agents, a man and a woman, who had investigated the extortion case. They were both Marines, though the guy was a reservist who'd been called up to active duty. Their task was to investigate a rash of extortion cases against young soldiers and sailors. The agents, Nancy Brown and Joe McKinney, tracked down the woman in the case, Becky Reardon. Ms. Reardon had a number of aliases, including Tanya Brush, Charlene Wilson, and Rebecca Lippus. It was believed that her real name was Rebecca Lippert, but she had been illegally married so many times that her real name was still in question. All the information gathered on Ms. Lippert during the investigation was a dead end, literally.

Her boyfriend was another story. Robert Garrett had been a Yeoman in the Navy. His file said he was something of a hothead. Garrett's history included beating his father nearly to death when the elder Garrett announced to Bobby's mother that he was leaving her for a much younger woman. Garrett was just seventeen when that happened. For that incident, he spent time in juvenile detention.

During his incarceration, one of his handlers noticed that Bobby was a stickler for detail, was highly organized, and had beautiful handwriting. Taking an interest in Garrett, the handler contacted a Navy Recruiter to see if they were interested in talking with Garrett about opportunities with the Navy. Just as Garrett was about to be released, the recruiter approached him with the promise of a great career as a Yeoman. His natural abilities were a perfect match for the position, so he enlisted for a six year hitch.

His Naval career progressed smoothly and he was promoted rapidly. He loved his job, the men and women with whom he worked, and the travel. His division officer liked him and thought he had the potential to become an officer. His career seemed to be right on course until his temper got the best of him again.

He and two other shipmates were in a bar fight where Bobby couldn't control his temper. He was arrested, spent the night in jail, and missed muster the next day. That little problem cost him a stripe, half a month's pay for two months, and confinement for a period of time.

During his time in the brig, Bobby studied the various forms used by the military for all sorts of things. Two forms in particular caught his interest. One identified military personnel who had been killed in action. The other form approved the distribution of life insurance premiums to a beneficiary. Once Bobby learned how to get these forms into the pipeline, he hatched his plan.

His secret weapon was Becky Lippert. Together, they scammed numerous young soldiers and sailors out of their life savings. Then they scammed the federal government out of hundreds of thousands of dollars in life insurance money.

It worked until Joe McKinney and Nancy Brown tracked the couple down in Norfolk. But that wasn't the end of the story.

An older woman, believed to be Becky Lippert's mother, was also killed that early morning at the apartment where the couple was trying to retrieve one of the life insurance checks. She literally charged the agents who were carrying out the raid and started shooting at the apprehension team and was shot dead.

That would have been the end of it, but it turned out that the woman, identified as Abigail Glover, had another child, a boy named Ace Glover. Ace was never apprehended. The team in Norfolk surmised that he had escaped the scene at the apartment complex where his mother, sister, and Bobby Garrett were killed.

Three days after the bloody shootout in Norfolk, Colonel Milton Chester was gunned down. Everyone involved in the investigation wondered whether the shooter was Ace Glover, but no one believed that Ace could have escaped the scene in Norfolk and traveled across the country to North

Dakota in just three days. Then there was the fact that the colonel had been lured to an abandoned missile site.

Banks shook his head. *How could a nineteen year old kid trick a full bird colonel into making that trip? It just isn't likely.*

But it was possible.

All of the physical, forensic evidence from the Milton Chester murder matched the evidence from several murders that occurred along the southeast coast of the United States in the vicinity of military bases. At the scene of the murder of Colonel Chester a cheap *Bic* pen was found with the colonel's blood coating the pen's tip. A similar pen was found at murder scenes for several servicemen, the tip covered with the blood of each murder victim. Other links between the murders were identified, such as bloody shoe prints from a few of the murder scenes that matched each other. Witnesses spotted a similar vehicle leaving the scene of several of the murders. Could it have been a copy-cat? Perhaps, but it was more likely that the same person killed Milton Chester and all of those young soldiers and sailors.

The clincher in Bank's mind was that nearly all of the murder victims along the Southeast Coast were "married" to Becky Lippert when they were shot to death.

Bill Banks rubbed his eyes with the palms of his hands, then swept back his salt and pepper hair with his right hand. *I need a haircut.* Without thinking, he reached for a pack of *Marlboros* near his desk phone. When he picked up the pack and tapped to free one of the cancer sticks, coffee dripped from the opening on to the surface of the Milton Chester file. The combined odor of cold coffee and wet tobacco assaulted his nose. Banks frowned, threw the pack in the trash, and wiped up the coffee drops with a paper towel.

He recalled the difficult circumstances of the investigation. The entire Grand Forks Police Department had been in temporary quarters outside the flood zone as thousands of people worked to clean up the downtown area of Grand Forks. The April 1997 flood had submerged the town under flood waters that reached a peak of nearly fifty-five feet, some twenty-seven feet above flood stage for the Red River. Attention was divided between the murders and the recovery of the town. The murder investigation lost priority to getting the city back to normal.

To make matters worse, communication with the Naval Criminal Investigative Service's team that had been in charge of the military's arm of the investigation evaporated. NCIS' job was declared a success with the deaths of Bobby Garrett and Rebecca Lippert.

Shortly after the flood waters of the Red River receded, the investigation into the murder of Milton Chester was left high and dry. William Banks and Reid Hansen were assigned new cases. Over time, the flow of information on the murder of Milton Chester ground to a halt.

Banks thought for a moment. *Maybe it's time to go back to the base and shake a few trees. Something's bound to fall out.*

Chapter 4

"So do you guys have your bags packed yet?"

Retired Air Force Colonel Richard Aims chuckled over the conference line as he gave his colleagues, General Adam Wesley and Retired Colonel Carl Dempsey, a good-natured ribbing. It was time for their annual golf outing and it was Aims' turn to plan the itinerary for the event. He leaned back in his overstuffed office chair behind the massive mahogany desk in his home office. He tapped the ashes from the Cuban cigar then put it back between his lips. Cradling the receiver between his left shoulder and jaw, he reached for his *Macallan* on the rocks and swapped the fine cigar for a sip of the top shelf Irish whiskey. After savoring the smooth taste, he swallowed, feeling the cold liquor slide down his throat. He set the tumbler back on the ceramic coaster and returned the cigar to his mouth for another puff.

The three men had gotten together each year since graduating from the Air Force Academy in Colorado Springs for a week of golf, booze, and partying. Up until two years ago, the threesome had been a foursome. That ended when Milton Chester was found murdered in North Dakota. This was to be the second outing with just the three remaining academy buddies.

Richard "Dick" Aims had been the first in the group to retire. His papers had already been submitted when he received Adam Wesley's call with the grim news of his friend's murder. At first, Aims had been shocked. Then he thought about the way Milt Chester had treated people over the years and realized that the list of possible suspects might be difficult to whittle down.

The topic of who shot and killed their friend and colleague had never come up between the remaining three, though it seemed to be festering on the tips of their tongues during last year's trip. Each man seemed to be weighing the importance of a promise that they'd made to each other, a promise of silence about one incident in particular. So far, that promise remained intact. Aims thought that, maybe this year, the silence would be...no, should be broken. Maybe if they talked about their friend and possible suspects they could help the police solve his murder. *Not now, though, not over the phone, not during our planning session. Maybe while we're out on the back nine at Slammer and Squires.*

The tradition included a rotation of responsibility to host the outing. This year would have been Milt Chester's turn on the rotation, but Aims, being next in line after Chester, had stepped up to do the honors. Duties included selecting the golf courses, setting up the tee times, arranging for dinner, and the evening entertainment. There was talk of replacing the now deceased colonel, but they hadn't found anyone yet that fit in well with the remaining three friends. Chester had been the leader of the group, in a manner of speaking, even though Adam Wesley, a Brigadier General, had officially outranked the colonel.

When Milton Chester had been the host of the annual event, the men had always enjoyed the entertainment portion of the trip. The colonel would book several nights at a gentleman's club and Milton knew how to pick them. The women were always beautiful, friendly, and discrete. To the best of their collective knowledge, news of their strip club adventures never made it back to their wives. Now, with their friend tragically murdered, they weren't too sure about continuing that part of the tradition. They had gone to one strip club during the previous year's outing and it had been just okay. The three men were much more subdued without Milt Chester there to loosen up their moods.

Aims thought that they might be over the grim circumstances of their friend's death and able to enjoy the club hopping segment of their trip. So he planned to set three nights aside at different clubs, two in Daytona, and one in

Jacksonville. Since he lived in Santa Rosa Beach, Florida, near Eglin Air Force Base, there was little chance that his wife would find out. He figured that he was the perfect husband fifty-one weeks out of the year. One week to let loose wasn't too much to ask, was it?

Adam Wesley, the now-retired Brigadier General piped up. "Real funny, Rich. I guess your old lady doesn't rummage through your bags looking for condoms and porn flicks like mine does."

The three men chuckled, keeping the conversation light as they worked on the specifics of their golden getaway week agenda. Each day included at least eighteen holes of golf at a championship course followed by dinner and drinks. St. Augustine boasted several challenging courses from which to choose so that part of the agenda would be easy.

Richard Aims had retired from the Air Force as a colonel. He was still a young man, forty-four years old, six-feet tall, with hair the color of a rusted tin can, now sprinkled with a bit of gray. When much younger, he'd sported a face full of freckles. He smiled most of the time and cracked jokes at times that were deemed inappropriate. Many found it hard to take him seriously even when the topic of conversation was dead serious. He decided to retire after being passed over for Brigadier General. It wasn't that he had less than satisfactory performance appraisals. In fact, they were quite positive. The main problem was that he'd had very few challenging assignments. Early in his career, he was simply overlooked for the cherry projects that allowed an officer to shine. His friends believed that his penchant towards using humor at the wrong moments around senior officers may have been his downfall. As years passed, his superiors began to notice the lack of any real accomplishments and it was assumed that he didn't have the talent or the ambition to advance to a command position.

So Aims knew without much prompting that his career had reached its zenith. His next logical move was a life of leisure. He had every intention of enjoying that life both with his wife of twenty-two years and on his annual trips with his best friends.

He loved his wife and they got along well, but they decided early in their marriage that they both needed a little space on occasion. His wife was planning a getaway with her friends during the same week as his trip, but her trips were not with Air Force wives. She traveled with a group of friends from her college days. Like her husband's getaways, they were a great way to catch up with her friends and unwind.

***

As Aims relayed his plans for the coming week, Carl Dempsey listened without making a sound. He was the most serious member of the group, and he missed Milton Chester's presence in their outings the most of the remaining three. Chester knew how to bring Dempsey out of his serious shell and get him to loosen up.

Dempsey was tall, slender, with square shoulders and a pointed jaw. He had perpetually dark stubble on his face which also had a number of large pock marks from a serious case of childhood acne. His hair was thick and black on top with just a hint of gray at the closely trimmed sideburns. He had just retired from the Air Force in the past month. The opposite of Richard Aims, he hardly ever smiled, his face stuck in a stone-cold expression. Most people who met him thought he was angry, but he was just an outwardly serious man.

As the conference call continued, Dempsey tuned out a bit and thought about his friend Milton Chester. Why had he been murdered and why in such a remote location? The three men hadn't been apprised of the details of the murder, except for what was in the papers and the *Air Force Times*. There was a general warning issued for service men and women to be aware of anyone trying to lure personnel away from bases or trying to isolate them from a group. There was little in the way of details or any mention of serious suspects. Carl had a notion that he should start his own investigation but his wife told him in no uncertain terms that he should leave the investigation to the professionals. He'd countered that the professionals hadn't appeared to have made any progress. She was adamant that he drop the idea. It never came up again in conversation, but it never left the forefront of his thoughts.

Three months after his friend's murder, Dempsey called the Grand Forks Police Department asking about any progress on the case, but he was told that it was an ongoing investigation and they could not release details of the crime. At that time, the department was also in the midst of efforts to clean up the city of Grand Forks after the flood. They referred him to a spokesperson for NCIS, the Naval Criminal Investigative Service, the organization that supposedly had handled the military end of the investigation, but Dempsey knew better than to call. The last thing he wanted was to get his name officially tied to Milton Chester. No need to shine the spotlight unnecessarily in his direction. So he bypassed all official lines of communications and instead called Major Shawnda Hull, the base Commander's Executive Assistant at Grand Forks Air Force Base.

The conversation with Major Hull had been strained. She was shocked that her boss had been killed. She had spoken to him before he left for the day. He'd mentioned that he had a meeting with "some young kid," but he hadn't told her the name of the person, the location of the meeting, or the purpose. Major Hull was also distressed because she was told by NCIS investigators, the Air Force Office of Special Investigations, and the local police not to discuss the details of the case with anyone. She had been unsure of what she could, or should, say to Colonel Dempsey. He hadn't wanted to push her. At the time, she was clearly distraught and tense. He wondered if there had been a personal relationship between his friend, Milt, and the major. It wouldn't have been the first time that he'd had a lapse of judgment.

"Hey, Carl, are you with us?"

The question brought Carl Dempsey out of his trance. "Yeah. Sorry, I was distracted. What did you say?"

Adam Wesley said, "We were hoping that you could get a couple bottles of that scotch that you brought last year. That was some good booze."

Dempsey smiled to himself. He said, "Yeah, I can bring a couple more bottles of *Macallan 17*. I still have a few left."

In reality, he had a couple cases left. He had bought three cases several years back and he only cracked open a bottle for very special occasions. He figured an outing with his friends fit the bill.

Wesley said, "Great Carl. We can toast Milt when we crack the first bottle."

After he said it, silence filled the phone. Each man immediately thought about the murder and how little they actually knew about what had happened to their friend.

And there it was on the tips of each of their tongues; the question that they needed to ask. But not one of them would be the first to break the silence. They would continue to ask the same question of themselves: *Did Milton Chester's murder have anything to do with Colorado Springs?*

Would they ever know the truth? Or would the question remain out there, gnawing at their conscience and rotting their souls?

Chapter 5

The air was thick and foul, the stench of body odor rising with each passing minute. Joe McKinney was in the attic of his home in Winter Garden, Florida. The central air conditioning unit had failed earlier in the day and Joe was trying to find the problem. His white, Marine Corps tee-shirt was soaked with sweat, as was the front of his green cargo shorts. Even his socks felt wet and slippery. In the high humidity, heavy beads of sweat oozed out of the pores on the top of his head then rolled down over his close cropped hair, onto his temples, then to his cheeks. The sweat stung his eyes as it flowed over his eyebrows. Pink fiberglass insulation stuck to his wet legs and socks as he maneuvered around the tight space.

Unfortunately for Joe, he had little training on how the unit functioned. He had called the nearest heating, cooling, and air conditioning company, but they were booked solid for at least a week. Joe was relying on information from his brother, Pat, on how home air conditioners worked. So far he had checked the circuit breaker, the main cutoff switch, the fuses, and the electrical connections, and the various safety sensors along the ductwork. He had also checked that the blower would run in manual, and the thermostat appeared to be working. None of the easily fixed components were the problem. Since all the electrical components appeared to be working, the next step was something that was beyond his capabilities. Pat had said that the refrigerant might be low or have leaked out altogether. If that was the case, he was screwed. He had no idea how to check for leaks and he knew nothing about recharging the unit. Pat said he'd come over and help, but he couldn't make it for a couple days. Joe was learning the hard way that nothing was easy about home ownership.

After he finished the check of the last override relay in the circuit, he was beat. He figured that he needed a break and a tall glass of water. Dragging the fluorescent drop light and cable behind him, he made his way back to the access hatch that led down to the walk-in closet in the master bedroom. He'd just reached the bottom rung on the pull-down ladder when the house phone rang. As he headed into the bedroom where the nearest phone rested on a nightstand, he pulled up his tee shirt to wipe the sweat from his face, but stopped when he remembered that it was probably covered with fiberglass. Had he wiped his face, it would itch for a week.

The phone stopped ringing. Apparently Lisa had answered it on the extension in the kitchen. He took the opportunity to wipe his face with a towel from the bathroom. It helped that the ceiling fan moved the air around a bit. It was a mere ninety-three degrees in the bedroom compared to nearly one hundred thirty degrees in the attic. That temperature difference, combined with the fan, made it seem relatively cool.

Lisa hollered to him from near the kitchen as she walked towards him down the hall. "Honey, can you take a call?"

Her shout grew louder as she approached the bedroom. As she reached the door, he gave her an appreciative look up and down. She was wearing loose fitting silk shorts and a matching tank top. She was sweating, too, but nothing like Joe. "How do you look so cool in this heat?"

She smiled, still holding the phone, "Just comes natural, I guess." She noticed his bright red face and soaking wet shirt. "You look beat. I'll get you a glass of water."

"I am. Thanks, sweetie. Who's on the phone?"

She handed him the phone as she said, "Some detective. I didn't get a name."

He raised an eyebrow as he took the phone and pressed it to his ear. The earpiece was immediately soaked with sweat. "Joe McKinney."

"Sergeant McKinney, Bill Banks here. I'm with the Grand Forks Police Department."

Joe recognized the voice and name instantly. He remembered the detectives from Grand Forks, Banks and his partner, Reid Hansen. They were big guys who took their jobs seriously and they were both very professional. Banks was the older of the two. His dark eyes bore crow's feet from years of stress on the force. The wrinkles that extended down from the corners of his mouth framed his chin like a pair of parentheses.

His blond-haired partner, Hansen, was a former Marine and Vietnam Veteran. Hansen's hair was trimmed so close that he could still pass inspection in any Marine Corps unit.

Joe had liked them both from the moment he met them. They were his kind of men when it came to taking care of business.

"Sure, Detective, I remember you. Call me Joe, please. I'm not active duty now."

"Okay, Joe. Call me Bill."

There was a pause, then Banks came right to the point. "We're looking into two unsolved murders, the Milton Chester murder and the Kevin Reardon murder. We're reaching out to anyone who had any involvement to see if we can get new information about the cases. Sometimes details pop up over time that didn't seem important back then. So would you have time for a couple of questions?"

Joe looked back at the closet door before answering. He could either answer Banks' questions or head back up to the attic and stare at duct work and electrical interlocks in 130 degree heat for the next hour. This was a no-brainer.

"I've got plenty of time, Bill. Fire away."

There was another moment of quiet. Joe figured Banks was either reading some notes or gathering his thoughts. "As I said, I'm calling about the Milton Chester and Kevin Reardon murders because we know there's a link to several murders of military personnel along the southeast coast. We just can't seem to make the connection with any law enforcement folks down there. It seems like any investigation into the murders has been shelved. We were hoping that someone in the military might still have an active interest."

Joe's face tightened into a frown as he listened. He always believed that NCIS should have continued the investigations. But since Bobby Garrett and Rebecca Lippert, the persons that the military believed to be responsible for the deaths, were also deceased, there was no reason for NCIS to continue working the cases. There were a lot of other hot potatoes to pursue and like any organization run by the government, money was tight. The only thing more scarce was resources. There just weren't enough people to devote to cases that were cold and getting colder by the day. In the opinion of the Navy brass, these cases were closed. If the Air Force wished to investigate the murder of Milton Chester and Kevin Reardon further, that was their call. As far as Joe knew, military involvement in the investigations was non-existent. Since he had been officially placed back on inactive reserve immediately after being debriefed about the Robert Garrett and Rebecca Lippert case, he had no official stake in any cases involving NCIS and no official need to know.

In a serious, but business-like voice Joe said, "It's been over two years since the murders." He paused. "Have you hit up anyone at the base?"

Joe meant Grand Forks Air Force Base where both Milton Chester and Kevin Reardon had been stationed. He hadn't thought too much about their murders in recent months, but there were a few things that had bothered him about the cases.

"We're planning to question the staff at the base up here to see if they remember anything. We didn't get the sense they were being very cooperative at the time. Maybe the new base commander will be inclined to let his staff talk to us. After all, his predecessor was murdered and the killer was never found. You'd think he would want to assist in tracking down the shooter."

"Yeah, you would."

Joe wiped the sweat from his face again. He tried to remember the various staff members that he and Captain Nancy Brown had interviewed. The problem was that when the NCIS team was in Grand Forks, they had been investigating the murder of Staff Sergeant Kevin R. Reardon. They hadn't returned to Grand Forks to complete that investigation and were never called upon to investigate the murder of the colonel.

Lisa walked in and handed Joe a tall glass of ice water, then turned to leave. He took a quick drink of cold water then said, "I'll tell you what, Bill, I can provide you with the list of personnel that we interviewed along with my notes. We didn't get very far in the investigation because we were called back to the east coast after just a few days. I heard through the grapevine that you guys didn't get much cooperation from the base or the AFOSI."

The Air Force Office of Special Investigations at Grand Forks didn't give Nancy Brown or Joe much cooperation while they were in Grand Forks, so Joe knew exactly what Banks and Hansen had dealt with back in 1997.

Banks said, "We did find two sets of tire tracks out near the missile site where the colonel was killed. One set was about seven hundred yards from the spot, the pavilion, where the colonel was murdered. The other set was a bit closer but on the opposite side of the pavilion. We found several cigarette butts at one site along with some good shoe prints. We tried to get a DNA sample from the butts. No luck. It was obvious that, whoever was at both locations, they were keeping an eye on the action at the pavilion. We have good reason to believe that they, whoever they are, witnessed the murder."

"What makes you think that the tire tracks are related to the murder? I mean, they could have been there before the murder. Or maybe someone wanted to get a look at the action at the silo while you guys were responding to the scene."

"When we arrived on the scene, there were two county sheriff's cars at the pavilion with their flashers on. It was still light enough so that we could see across the prairie. There were no rubber-neckers at that time. They had the scene roped off and the surrounding area secured within twenty-five minutes. No one made their way up the paths to where the tire marks, foot prints, and cigarette butts were found."

Joe thought, *Now, there's a Navy man, or he knows one*. "Is it unusual for anyone to be at one of those sites?"

"Once in a while kids from town go out there and start a fire and drink. But it's not normal to have a bunch of flashing lights at these sites. They're abandoned."

Joe looked again at the walk-in closet. Banks was running out of questions and Joe was out of excuses to put off heading back up into the attic.

"Bill, let me chew on this a bit. Do you remember my brother, Pat, from the Kevin Reardon investigation?"

"Yeah. I don't think I ever met him but I do recall you talking about him. Why?"

"Do you mind if I run some of this past him? He looks at things differently. It might help, it might not, but it sure can't hurt."

"Sure Joe. Whatever you can do to help us out would be appreciated. Do you have my number?"

Joe thought for a moment then remembered he had Bank's and Hansen's business cards in his office. He relayed that information, talked for a few more minutes, then ended the call.

Now the house wasn't the only thing heating up.

Chapter 6

In his dream, Ace Glover's vision faded in and out. One moment, his sight was as clear as day then a heavy fog moved in, obscuring furniture and fixtures no further than a few feet in front of his face. A chill ran down his spine and spread throughout his arms and legs. Goose-bumps rose along the surface of his skin. He couldn't catch his breath, which came in short, shallow bursts. Then, as if a weight had been lifted from his chest, he could breathe again, inhaling and exhaling in a smooth, rhythmic flow, his body relaxed. A strong scent of pine filled the room as if it had just been cleaned, or a real Christmas tree was present, but none was in sight.

Then the chill was back, building slowly from the base of his spine, like someone running sharp fingernails lightly across the small of his back. The sensation rode along his spine to his neck then spread out to his arms, hands, fingers, legs, feet, and toes. Even the roots of his scalp tingled as his view of the room grew crystal clear once more.

Ace glanced around the grand parlor of a stately home. Dark red walls, the color of drying blood, were in vivid contrast to the white brick and dark mahogany mantel of the fireplace. In the yawning opening of the fireplace, embers glowed, but no flames were in view and no heat emanated, the fire all but extinguished. He recognized the home, the picture over the mantel, the ornate ceiling molding so perfect that no human could have carved the precise designs by hand. The pressed metal ceiling tiles looked new, not painted over and ruined. Ace had been in just a few historic homes when he had accompanied Angelina to her friends' houses. None of them were in such pristine condition.

His dream became nostalgic. Was this his childhood home? He couldn't remember such a home from his past, but his visions were convoluted. He couldn't square what he now saw before him with the images ingrained in his mind. His memories were of ancient trailer parks with old, run-down trailers. He remembered musty smelling carpet, walls stained yellow by cigarette smoke, and neighbors so close you could hear them arguing, night after miserable night. The things he'd heard as a child in those trailer parks stayed with him even now. He'd hidden in the closet, covering his ears, trying to block out the screams, the slaps, the swearing and cursing. The names the men called these women…such vile names. He'd thought about going over and confronting them, but what could a young child do against grown men? His plans had seemed clear and wise, even fool-proof, but he'd remained in the closet, covering his ears, wishing the noise would stop.

The next morning he'd see the women heading off to work or wherever they went, the bruises evident even though hidden behind heavy makeup and sunglasses. At the end of the week they'd bring home their pay and turn it over to their men only to endure a beating for not bringing home enough to cover their gambling and booze.

Ace learned to hate the abusers. How could one human treat another that way? He couldn't understand why the women stayed. The realization hit him that, if he tried to take revenge on these men, he wouldn't be doing it for these women, but for his own satisfaction. He vowed to never treat a woman like that.

Once, he'd made the mistake of using one of those nasty words in front of his mother. He called one of the women who lived near them a bitch. Abigail Glover turned on her son, her face bright red with anger. She started to raise her hand as if to slap young Ace, but she regained control, her face turning from anger to shame then to sorrow. Sitting down cross-legged in front of Ace, she began to cry in deep sobs, all the while hugging her son, telling him how sorry she was for raising her hand in anger to him. After regaining her composure she explained to her son that he should never, ever speak badly of a woman.

She'd said, "If you treat a woman like a princess, she will grow to be your queen. If you treat her like a dog, she will someday turn on you and bite you when you least expect it."

Ace had barely understood what his mother had said back when he was five years old, but her words stuck with him all his life. They became the guiding light in his quest to make sure that if bad men didn't see the errors of their ways, they saw the wrath that he unleashed on them for treating their women badly. Once Ace turned fourteen, he was big and strong enough to take on many grown men in a fight. When he saw a woman being mistreated by her boyfriend, he wrote their names in his notebook.

In three of the trailer parks where he and his mother had lived, a young woman's boyfriend or husband "disappeared." No one suspected that Ace, the handsome, young teenage boy, caused the disappearances. It was Ace's first taste of killing, and it made him feel good that he was protecting these poor women.

At first, it surprised him to see the women actually cry in despair when their men didn't return. He thought he was doing them a favor. It would be years before he would stop trying to understand their crazy emotions. One day they were punching bags for the worst kind of men, and the next day they were in despair because the 'love of their life' was gone.

Ace wasn't in one place long enough to worry about what became of any of these women. When he wasn't in a trailer park, he was in a van on the road to a new city, following his momma's latest boyfriend. As the years rolled by and his momma chased after her boyfriend who'd treated her like the men at the trailer parks, he began to believe all women were like that. They must want to be treated like door mats. Otherwise, why would they stay? What makes a woman want to endure not only the pain, but the humiliation of being seen in public with the visible scars of an abusive relationship? The physical pain had to be horrendous, but Ace believed the mental pain from the verbal abuse had to be even worse, at least in some perverse way. But the trailer park women, just like his momma, always went back for more. The need for love, or what they were getting as a substitute for love, was greater than their physical pain and mental anguish. Since his momma's boyfriend was treating her like a dog, he wondered when she would turn on her abuser, but it never happened.

He looked around the room again, ignoring his thoughts about the past. He smiled at some distant familiarity, some sense that he belonged here in this room. He took in the look, the feel, the smell. As he walked around the room with the pinewood flooring creaking with each step, he was touched by an overwhelming sense that he was home.

As he looked up at the chandelier, the light brightened, the crystals sparkled as the candlelight pierced the cut angles of the clear glass. It lifted his spirits momentarily. Then the image faded and the walls took on a grimy, worn appearance.

He looked down again as an image began to form across the room. The image had no detail but it buzzed as if it were alive, like a thick, swirling cloud of mosquitoes, a million individual insects making up a single entity. For a moment, Ace feared the cloud would come at him, surround him, and consume him. It stayed across the room, not stationary, but not advancing or retreating. As he watched, the cloud slowly transformed, taking the shape of a human. He saw the head followed by arms, legs, and a torso. As the face continued to evolve and take on more detail, Ace realized that he knew the man. The face staring back at him smiled...no, not a smile...a smirk. It was a look he remembered all too well. His vision and his mood darkened again. It was his mother's old boyfriend.

Bobby fricking Garrett.

Ace hated many things about his life. He hated the trailer parks, the years on the road, the fact that he had no true, lifelong friends. He hated the abusive men that were his mother's neighbors. He hated that the women didn't realize that they weren't being loved, but were simply being used. He hated moving around from town to town. All that hatred combined didn't come close to how much he loathed Bobby Garrett.

Bobby Garrett had only been around for a few years when Ace was growing up. He didn't treat his mother badly at first. In fact, he treated her well. But one day all that changed.

His mother found out a bit of news that made her very happy. She told Bobby of the news and he appeared pleased, too. Whatever the news was, they had to move again. They moved to Florida close to a home with lots of kids. It was an unusual family. Many of the children were the same age. Some were black, some Hispanic, still others were white. One was of mixed race. His mother had said it was a foster home and there was a special child in that home. Ace didn't understand what was so special about this child back then. It would be many years before he learned the truth.

After only a few months of living in their new neighborhood, Ace's mother ran into his room in a panic. The special child, a young girl about eight years older than Ace, had run away from the foster home. The parents had no idea where she'd gone. But they weren't worried. This girl knew how to fend for herself. Still, Abigail Glover insisted that she, Ace, and Bobby Garrett look for the girl. And they did.

Hours turned into days. Days turned into weeks and weeks to months. There was no sign of the girl. Abbie called the agency in charge of foster care and pretended to be the home's mother. She asked if they knew where the girl had gone or if she'd been found. After weeks of calling and pleading, crying both real and fake tears, Abbie was rewarded. The agency found the girl. She was no longer in foster care, but they knew where she was. That was all Abbie needed and they were on the road in search of the special girl.

Then they settled again. Ace finally got a look at the girl who so fascinated his mother. She was a pretty blonde haired girl, like his mother. In a strange way, she looked familiar, but Ace knew that he'd never met her. Of that he was certain. He would have remembered this girl – young woman, actually. She was only fourteen then, but Ace thought she was at least nineteen because her face wore the burden of someone who, out of necessity, had grown up fast. His momma called her Rebecca, though he had no idea how she knew her name.

It was about two years later, after they'd arrived at the apartment in Key West, Florida. Ace's momma would watch out the apartment window to get a glimpse of the young woman any time she left the neighboring apartment. Bobby Garrett would tease her and ask why she didn't just go out and introduce herself.

She replied, "I've got my reasons. Why don't you? You've seen that she can take care of herself. I'll bet you're scared. Maybe you could convince her to join us."

Garrett would shrug his shoulders and turn back to watching television. He seemed indifferent to Ace's mother's infatuation with this girl.

Then one day when his mom was out shopping, Bobby Garrett left the apartment when he thought Ace was sleeping. Ace moved to the window facing the young woman's apartment, pulled back the curtains just a crack so he could get a good view. He watched as Rebecca left her apartment and headed for the beach. Garrett followed her, keeping a good distance between them. Rebecca rounded the corner of the apartment on the path that led to the beach. She was out of sight. A moment later, Garrett disappeared. After that day Bobby Garrett was a changed man. He started treating Ace's mother badly, calling her names like the trailer park men did their women. Bobby also disappeared often, sometimes not coming home overnight. Garrett and his mother would argue, but she would always give in to his demands.

Then one day when his mother was out, Bobby Garrett packed his clothes and left for good. The bastard had left his mother for the very young Rebecca Lippert when Ace was only eight years old. Ace's mother had unwittingly made this young woman easy prey for Garrett. It would be years later when Abbie Glover would find out where Bobby Garret and Rebecca Lippert were staying.

Bobby fricking Garrett.

Ace saw his face clearly now. When the cloud first appeared and Garrett's body took shape, Ace had moved across the room, or the cloud had come closer, he couldn't be sure which. All he knew was that Garrett was standing right in front of him, so close he could see the tiny veins in the whites of his dark eyes and feel the heat and stench of his breath. His own blood began to boil, the temperature of his face rising with each passing second. He was about to pull his gun and blow Garrett away for what he'd done to his mother. Then the vision of Garrett disappeared.

In a fit of anger, Ace looked around the room, trying to see where he had gone. The room seemed empty and dark. There was no color. Everything he saw was some shade of gray. There was just a faint light coming through the window as if it was dusk outside. He had no idea of the time, no clue whether it was morning, afternoon, or evening. He felt a chill in the air, not from the temperature, but as if a burst of cold air from an open freezer had hit him. The hair on his arms and the back of his neck stood erect.

He sat bolt upright in bed, awakened from his deep sleep by the image of a man who was already dead. Sweat soaked the bed. He wanted to shout at the top of his lungs, but he remembered he was in a hotel room. It came back to him, slowly at first, then with a flood of thoughts and images. He'd escaped the possessive stranglehold of Angelina Valentine. The nightmare about the man he'd hated most in the world brought his plan into focus. The bastards who had killed his mother and those who had abused his sister would pay, and Ace was the bill collector.

Chapter 7

"So, do you remember the detectives from Grand Forks?"

Joe McKinney's question caught his brother, Pat, by surprise. He had expected Joe's telephone call to be about fixing his central air conditioning. *Why on earth is he asking about a couple of guys from half way across the country?* Pat had all but forgotten about the special assignment to which Joe, and a female Marine Captain named Nancy Brown, had been assigned. The majority of their time had been spent between Norfolk, Virginia and Kings Bay, Georgia. Much of the investigation had them chasing down a couple of scammers who were ripping off young soldiers and sailors of their life savings, Bobby Garrett and Rebecca Lippert. The whole affair had started in North Dakota after the body of Kevin Reardon was discovered in an empty house in Grand Forks. The chain of events that followed had dramatically changed Joe McKinney's life, at least for several months. He had been called back to active duty by his former boss to assist in the investigation, much to the dismay of his fiancé.

Pat had believed that the investigation was ancient history and the books closed on that chapter of their lives. Now his brother was asking about the two key detectives in the case. His brain immediately went on alert.

"Yeah, I remember them, at least, I remember you talking about them. You and Nancy both said they were good cops." Pat paused for a moment then asked the million dollar question. "Why are you asking?"

"I just got off the phone with the lead on the case, Bill Banks. I guess things are slow in Grand Forks and he's looking into the Milton Chester murder again. He wants to question everyone that had any connection with the case."

Pat sat at the dinner table watching his wife load the dishwasher. Their daughter, six year old Anna, helped. Diane rinsed the plates and handed them to Anna who placed them in the bottom rack. Pat smiled at the scene. The aroma of a late breakfast still hung in the air and Pat reached for his coffee cup to enjoy the last few sips of brew.

"Did Detective Banks say why they were reopening the case? I remember they were trying to get us all excited about Colonel Chester's murder, but that wasn't part of your marching orders, if I recall correctly."

"That's right. Our bosses at NCIS shut down our participation in the case after the shootout in Virginia. That always bothered me. You know, we were told to stand down before Ace killed the colonel in North Dakota. That's how quick they pulled the plug."

"Yeah, but you sure made Lisa happy. They did you a favor by cutting the investigation off when they did." There was a pause. "So what did Banks say?"

"Banks told me a few things about the case. They received absolutely no cooperation from the brass at the base. The interim commander was no help at all. They flew in a full bird colonel from California. According to Banks, all he cared about was making sure that things were back to some semblance of normal as quickly as possible so he could get back to his real job on the left coast. When his permanent replacement arrived, he left North Dakota in a flash. He never looked back and never returned a single call from Banks or Hansen. The new commander was even less interested in finding the killer. He put out what amounted to a gag order and turned the whole affair over to the Air Force Office of Special Investigations. No one was to talk with the civilian detectives without prior approval of his office."

"Wow, I'd have thought they would want the killer caught. Wouldn't you?"

"Yeah. That's a no brainer. But Banks and Hansen think the Air Force wanted to catch the killer and grab the glory. Either that or they knew who the killer was and wanted to cover it up." Joe paused for a long moment.

Joe said, "Sorry, Lisa and Danielle are on their way to the pool. Lisa's in her new bathing suit. Anyway, with all the delays by the military and then recovering from the flood, the investigation by the Grand Forks PD ground to a halt. Banks and Hansen were pulled into policing the flood areas. Then every public official helped with restoration of the town. That left no time for their investigation."

"I guess things are back to normal now and they want to pick up where they left off."

"It seems that way. Banks told me some stuff about the crime scene and the vicinity. He thinks that there might have been witnesses to the murder."

Pat asked, "You mean accomplices?"

"No. According to Banks, the witnesses were away from the spot where Chester was shot, like maybe several hundred yards."

Pat frowned. The wheels in his head turned faster as he processed what Joe had just told him. "From that distance, they wouldn't be very good witnesses. What was it, some kids partying at the abandoned site?"

Pat heard the playful screams of his niece, Danielle, over the phone. "I take it Lisa just put Danielle in the pool."

"Yeah. She loves it. Can you tell?"

Pat smiled, waiting while he let Joe enjoy the moment.

After a few seconds Pat asked, "Hey Joe, you still there?"

"Yep. I'm watching Danielle and Lisa in the pool. There's nothing like being a dad."

Pat had to smile as he replied, "Nope. Nothing like it in the entire world."

"Anyway, where were we? Oh, yeah. Banks said he believes the two witnesses were watching from different locations away from the pavilion. They could have been together or not. No way to know without talking with them.

Who knows, they could have been lookouts for the killer, but Banks thinks that's not the case."

Pat frowned. "Why is that?"

"Because nearly all the footprints in both locations faced the pavilion. If they were lookouts, they'd have been facing the road. He said they found some cigarette butts at one of the sites but the other site was clean."

There was silence on the line for several seconds as the brothers processed everything Joe said. Finally Pat asked, "Do they have a clue about who the witnesses might be?"

"No, not at all. There wasn't much else to go on at the witness sites. At the pavilion there were a few clues. One, the pen with the bloody tip and a few hairs stuck in spider webs, but those could have come from anybody. The pavilion is used as a party spot sometimes. There were a few tire tracks that were determined to be new and they did castings. The killer left the shell casings, too. Semi-automatic pistol, 9 mm. So it wasn't a total wash."

Pat took a deep breath then asked, "So, have they been able to get any information at all from any of the staff at the base?"

"There was this one enlisted guy, Airman Goff, who was assigned to help Nancy and me with logistics, stuff like setting up the office, getting phone lines, computers, office supplies, stuff like that. He actually called Banks and offered some information up, as long as he could remain anonymous."

"So, if he was anonymous, how do you know this?"

"I guess Banks figures that I'm half a country away, that it won't get back to Goff. Anyway, Airman Goff tells Banks that Colonel Chester's staff was questioned at length by the new commander, the permanent replacement guy."

"And…"

"Patience, Grasshopper. Seems he asked a lot of pointed questions about the Colonel's behavior towards the females on the staff. Apparently there had been some allegations of sexual misconduct from his previous command, but no charges were ever brought against the colonel. Goff told

Banks that Chester at times made some borderline remarks to his assistant, Major Hull. He said she wouldn't even bat an eye. It didn't appear to faze her."

"Interesting. Maybe he was a player and Major Hull wasn't interested. Maybe the colonel was trying to put the moves on the wrong woman?"

"That's possible. One other interesting development that may or may not be related is Major Hull went AWOL. No one knows where she went."

Pat's eyebrows went up on that bit of information. *Coincidence?* Not likely. A young woman with a good career and a bright future just didn't pull up stakes and throw it all away without a very good reason.

"Did Goff know Major Hull well?"

"From what Banks said, he knew her quite well. They worked close together for about two years. The Major was about to be transferred to the Air Force Academy in Colorado Springs. It was to be a big move for her."

Pat heard Lisa yell to Joe from the pool in a child's voice, "Hi, Daddy. Come on in, the water's great!"

Pat said, "I better let you go. Sounds like you have some family time to enjoy."

"One more thing before you hang up. Banks wanted to get in touch with Hatch and Nancy. Would it be okay to give him Hatch's cell phone number?"

Pat thought for a moment. Something lurked in the back of his brain, but he couldn't get the thought straight. He knew it had to do with Hatch and his involvement in the case of Bobby Garrett and Rebecca Lippert. It had been two years since the close of the NCIS investigation and Pat couldn't remember how much Banks and Hansen knew about Hatch. He said, "Why don't you give me Bank's direct line and I'll ask Hatch to call him."

Joe replied, "That'll work."

* * *

William "Hatch" Hatcher had been stationed onboard the USS *Nevada*, a ballistic missile submarine based in King's Bay,

Georgia. One of his shipmates, Wilson Brush, asked for his help in finding his wayward bride, one Tanya Brush, *aka* Rebecca Lippert.

Wilson had met Becky Lippert in a bar near the base and fell hard for her. She was beautiful and charming and sweet, and she'd said and done everything right, making him believe that she was his soul-mate, the woman he would love and live with forever. Shortly after they tied the knot, Wilson was deployed for several months on the *Nevada*. When he returned, his wife was gone along with all his personal belongings and the money in his savings and investment accounts. Expecting the continuation of the wedded bliss that he'd felt before his deployment, he was crushed by her betrayal.

Hatch felt bad for his shipmate, though Wilson's actions were foolhardy. But he understood that love is blind and sometimes naïve, too. Hatch knew a couple of guys that could help Wilson. That's when he called Pat McKinney, hoping that he and his brother Joe could help him track down this heartless woman.

***

After the call, Pat tried to piece his thoughts together on why he was worried about Hatch and any connection to North Dakota. He knew that Hatch had disappeared for about a week after Bobby Garrett, Becky Lippert, and Abbie Glover were killed and Hatch never told anyone where he'd gone. At the time, Pat wondered about his friend's disappearing act, but he wasn't too concerned. Hatch did that from time to time. When Pat would ask what he did during those periods, Hatch would dismiss his inquiries with a shoulder shrug or a polite, "Y'alls being a bit nosey today." That was always followed with a good-natured smile. But the message was clear. *It ain't none of y'alls business.*

Pat heard his wife tell Anna that she could go in the pool as long as Sean went with her.

Pat offered, "I'll go in, too. I could use a good swim."

Diane's surprised look was followed by a smile. Then she added, "Me, too."

Chapter 8

The morning sun was just above the horizon in the cloudless sky over the Slammer and Squire Country Club northwest of St. Augustine, Florida. The course looked unnaturally perfect with vividly contrasting colors. The sapphire-blue sky, bright green, carpet-perfect fairways, and the dark green of the pine trees lining the course seemed like something out of a movie set. Even the light mist that hung in the air over the small lakes bordering the fairways looked as if it was painted on canvas.

At just after 7:00 AM in the clubhouse and the pro shop, elderly men in ugly, plaid shorts and poorly matched Izod golf shirts milled about searching for new putters, drivers, and the latest, most favored golf balls. The conversations varied. Some spoke of incredible rounds of golf the previous day. Others were about investments and the poor returns they were getting on their money market CDs. A younger man, possibly the club pro, was coaching a man, who had to be in his eighties, on how he could correct his slice by simply changing his grip on the club. The elderly gent seemed pleased that such a simple adjustment would improve his game so dramatically.

Ace avoided contact with the crowd as best he could, keeping his hat low, moving away from anyone who moved towards him. The racks of golf shoes and shirts, and expensive golf equipment from clubs, bags, and umbrellas to the latest in interactive training videos didn't interest him. He was pleased that no one approached him with questions about his golf game, because he wasn't sure he would have known how to answer even the most basic question.

While Ace wasn't a golfer, he had studied the game on the internet. He needed to look natural, like a seasoned golfer, like he fit in with the regulars who knew the appearance and the lingo. Among all these seniors, though, he felt uncomfortable. He hadn't anticipated he'd be the youngest person at Slammer and Squire on a Tuesday morning. The only people his age were the cart runners and concessionaires. But as he moved about the pro shop, he began to relax.

Ace was there for one purpose that had nothing to do with golf. Three men, two retired military officers and one still active duty, had a 7:40 AM tee time. They needed to check in, pay, get whatever supplies they needed for their round, retrieve their carts and get in line at the first hole. To do all that and not miss their tee time, they needed to arrive soon.

He moved down an aisle near the back of the shop where one wall was filled with brightly colored golf shirts and wind breakers. He looked at the price tags on a bright green shirt with alligator logos. The price took him by surprise, $89.00 for a single shirt. The shock on his face was immediate and involuntary. *Come on Ace, get it together. You're acting like trailer trash. You're a grown man who can afford anything, now start playing the part and keep your cool.* After three slow, deliberate deep breaths, his heart rate slowed. The look of indifference to the merchandise all around him returned to his face. He continued walking around the shop, looking at price tags, pulling clubs from their racks, looking the club heads over as if looking for the answer to why one club or another drove a little white ball further down the fairway. Then it crossed his mind that a driver could be used as a powerful weapon and the slightest smile crossed his lips.

As Ace turned to look at a rack with new putters, three men walked into the shop. His smile grew just a bit more. As he turned back to the rack still holding the driver, an image appeared in his mind. He hadn't summoned the image, it just appeared. The evil smile was replaced by a soft, loving smile. There was a young, teenage girl laughing. At what, Ace had no idea. The young girl stood in the living room of an apartment. Her face was clear in the vision, but everything around her was obscured by a mist. She looked familiar, with sandy blonde hair, a thin nose and cheeks, concave like a model's. She wore a white tank top and tight blue-jean cutoff shorts. The tumbler in her hand had an amber liquid with ice cubes that rattled every time she laughed. The sound of the cubes grew louder with each passing second, like an alarm bell going off. His own smile slowly disappeared. Something was wrong. He wanted to yell at the girl. *Stop drinking and get out of there. You're in danger!*

The girl in his vision looked right at him. She giggled. "You're ruining my party. Go away."

Then she turned to the side and a young man appeared. The face was still in the mist, but the man was at least a head taller than the pretty girl. The mist drifted away from the two people in his vision. Ace saw the man more clearly now and he scowled, his blood beginning to boil. He recognized the face, Milton Chester. As his anger continued to grow, three more men came into his vision. He recognized them all.

As he watched, each man reached out and touched the teen girl. At first, their hands patted her arms then lightly stroked her hair. Soon, they all had their hands on her, stroking her back, her arms, her face, then on to more intimate areas. Their intentions became clear. She tried to get away but each time she moved in one direction or another, one of the men blocked her path. The fear on her face was clear. She knew what was about to happen.

The men at first were smiling. Then the façade slowly slipped away as they became a pack of hunters, driven by a primitive sexual hunger. Lust filled their eyes. Ace heard a chorus of low moans as desire began to override common sense and the conscience that distinguishes right from wrong.

They closed in on her and began to remove her tank top. They moved slowly and gently at first, but quickly became more aggressive when the young girl wouldn't cooperate and give in to their advances. She was near panic. When she screamed, Milton Chester covered her mouth and warned her to not scream again or they would kill her. Then Milton Chester looked right at Ace and said, "Wait until you see what we're going to do to her."

Ace swung the driver he was holding. He hit the very young Milton Chester, but the club passed right through his body, making contact with a hanging rack of golf shirts.

The crack of the oversized head of the driver against the metal rack snapped Ace out of his trance. The shirts were strewn across the floor in the aisle. He still held the driver like a baseball bat.

For a long moment he stood still, trying to piece together what had just happened. One minute, he was in an apartment with a young woman and four other men. They were going to rape the girl. He knew that because he knew the girl and the four men. It was a nightmare he had many times, but this was the first time he'd had the vision while he was awake. Hoping that, somehow, he would be alone in the pro shop, he slowly turned, lowering the club.

Dropping the club, he headed for the door. It was only about thirty feet, but to Ace, it seemed like a mile. He passed the line of floor displays for new sets of golf clubs then skirted a bin with at least twenty new golf bags. After what seemed like long minutes, he reached for the door and pushed. He nearly ran into the club pro who was headed back into the shop.

"Did you get everything you needed, son?"

Ace didn't reply. He kept his head down with the bill of his hat covering his face and continued to walk, picking up the pace as he put distance between him, the shop, and the people heading towards the first tee.

Once outside, he moved down the path in the direction of the parking lot towards the Pro Golf Hall of Fame. He needed to get away from all human contact to clear his head. Then it dawned on him the three men had paid for their round and were now waiting in line to tee off. That didn't matter. He had plenty of time before they reached the tee at the eighth hole. It was going to be a killer round.

***

The sun was on the rise, but it was still cool compared to a typical Florida morning. The air was clear in most areas, except by the many lakes and ponds on the magnificent course. There, a light mist hung like miniature clouds.

Harold Trent had been sitting in his pickup since 6:30 AM, waiting on three men. It had been a long wait, but he was a patient man. He had waited for years for this day.

His body had been tense all morning. His back ached from sleeping in the pickup truck in the rest area on Interstate 95. He'd been awakened by the sound of semi-trucks heading out of the rest area accelerating towards the interstate. He'd wiped the sleep from his eyes, yawned, felt the stubble on his chin then headed into the rest room to clean up as best he could.

That was nearly two hours ago. He hadn't had a shower, brushed his teeth, or changed his clothes in nearly three full days. The accumulated funk was becoming gross. He knew it was bad because he could hardly stand the scent of himself. Adjusting the rearview mirror, he looked at his own image. It was as bad as he thought. Now, sitting in a beat up seven-year-old *Ford F-150* pickup truck in the parking lot of Slammer and Squire, he stood out like a sore thumb. There was no time to be concerned about that now. He had business that couldn't wait.

Finally, they'd appeared, all of them laughing, joking about the early hour for a couple of old, retired guys. The jovial mood of the threesome had the opposite effect on Trent. Seeing the three having such a good time darkened his spirits.

He caught sight of Ace through his binoculars. He'd been worried Ace would duck out of the pro shop from a different door and be lost from sight. He knew exactly why Ace was here and it sure wasn't to get in a good round of golf.

Ace emerged from the pro shop, moving quickly at first then slowing. After moving up the walk, away from the shop, he stopped completely. He looked around for a moment then headed towards the first tee.

Trent said in a quiet monotone, "What are you doing, Ace?"

He continued to watch, his full attention on the young blond man walking slowly towards the first tee. The sound of a two-way radio crackling very close to the pickup startled him.

Then a deep, almost manly woman's voice spoke into the radio, "Heading to meet the Sheldon party now."

The woman walked past, glancing suspiciously at him in the pickup truck. She lifted her radio again as she reached a service cart that was set up to collect and deliver golf clubs for guests from the bag drop area to the tees and back again. As she sat in the cart and drove off, she spoke into the radio, glancing in his direction again.

It was decision time. If he continued to sit in the parking lot and monitor Ace, he was in danger of having to face resort security. If he left, he might lose track of Ace. That was not an acceptable option. Just as he was about to leave his pickup truck and head over to the first tee, Ace started coming back towards the parking lot. He was moving quickly and Trent had no time to start the pickup and move.

It didn't matter. Ace moved past him without a glance. He got into a white, non-descript Chevrolet and quickly drove off.

***

A little over two hours later, just after 10:00 AM, Ace stood next to the refreshment cart, property of the Slammer and Squire Golf Club. The sun was climbing in the morning sky, the heat and humidity building. The young man who was supposed to be operating the cart was now unconscious behind a stand of trees about two hundred yards from the eighth tee. He would have a headache when he came to, but he'd have no long term side effects from the powerful sedative Ace had injected into him when he'd turned his back to retrieve the beer Ace had requested.

After donning the young man's shirt, Ace removed the silenced 9mm Glock from the waistband at the small of his back. He checked the weapon, ensured that a round was chambered, and placed it back in the waistband. As he moved to the driver's seat he heard the crack of a driver slapping a golf ball down the eighth fairway.

Showtime.

***

General Adam Wesley had just hit his tee shot about two hundred eighty yards down the fairway. It rolled to a stop in a relatively good position, shy of the cart path that crossed the fairway approximately halfway to the green.

He turned, smiled, and remarked to his companions, "You guys can go ahead and give me the skin for this hole now. It'll save us time."

Richard Aims and Carl Dempsey both chuckled. Aims said, "Right. Did your wife teach you how to drive the ball like that?"

Wesley replied, "Okay, tough guy. You're up. Let's see you top that."

Richard Aims walked up on the grassy mound and teed up his ball a little higher than usual. He hoped to put a little more height and distance on the drive to show up his friend. Now, standing behind his ball, looking down the fairway, the sound of an approaching cart distracted him. He turned to see the concessions cart headed in their direction.

He said to his partners, "Hey, when he gets here grab me a couple of *Bud Lights*."

They acknowledged his request, turning their attention to the approaching cart. Aims turned to address his ball, standing up straight, holding his club out and away from his body, looking down the fairway.

Adam Wesley and Carl Dempsey heard the loud crack that didn't sound anything like a driver striking a ball. They turned in time to see their friend fall back, away from the ball which still sat on the tee, untouched. As Aims hit the ground, his shoulder hit the left tee marker, forcing his body to twist so that his chest was visible to them from fifteen feet away. They saw the stain on his shirt growing, but it didn't register to either man what had happened. Wesley took three steps towards his fallen friend, but another loud crack sounded. He felt the thud on the right side of his chest which spun him around, knocking the breath out of him. Then a burning sensation and immense pain wracked his body as he fell, face first, into the soft grass.

Panic seized Carl Dempsey. He froze. Then he finally realized the loud reports were gun shots. He dropped to the ground, keeping his head up to try and locate the shooter. Noticing a small plume of smoke coming from the woods a mere sixty feet away, he spotted a man holding a rifle. It was pointed in his direction. The last thing he saw was a puff of smoke. The last thing he heard was the report of a rifle shot. The bullet struck his forehead as he craned his neck for a better look.

***

Ace heard the shots and saw the three men fall in succession. He didn't bother to stop and check for a pulse. As he turned the cart around to head back to where he'd left the cart vendor, he caught a glimpse of a man in the woods heading away from the eighth tee. His first thought was to head in that direction. But there was little precious time for him to flee the area. There were three men behind him, all shot, possibly dead, and he had a hijacked snack cart with a silenced pistol. It was time to head for safety. He could sort out the rest later.

Chapter 9

Friday, July 2, was supposed to be a long, busy day for Detectives Bill Banks and Reid Hansen. The morning started early as they pulled their black sedan into the headquarters parking lot at Grand Forks Air Force Base. Hansen found plenty of parking spaces available for visitors. Actually, there was plenty of parking in general. Banks figured many of the base's personnel took a few extra days of leave over the July fourth holiday weekend. That might pose a problem for their plans to interview as many of those personnel as possible about the Milton Chester murder. They had about a dozen names on their list, fully expecting that a few of those people had been transferred or discharged over the past two years. No sense worrying about them. If needed, they would interview them by phone.

But telephone interviews weren't as effective as those conducted face-to-face. When you sit across from a person, you can watch their expressions as you ask the questions. Little things such as nervous twitches, defensive postures, or abrupt changes in mood can be detected by a seasoned interviewer. Those signs can point the suspicion meter in one direction or another. They can provide some indication of when a person is telling the truth or lying. Other, more subtle reactions such as eye movement or the pupils changing size are all signs that, just maybe, the interviewee knows something they aren't telling. Banks and Hansen were both veterans at interviewing crime suspects, witnesses, and wannabees, those folks who claim to have seen a crime, but in reality are just seeking their fifteen minutes of fame.

The early morning temperature was a chilly fifty-eight degrees, but the sky was clear and bright blue. It was expected that the day would top out at a comfortable eighty-five. As the detectives approached the headquarters building Banks asked Hansen if he ever missed his days in the military.

Hansen, without missing a beat said, "I was in 'Nam in some real hell holes. I saw a lot of my buddies die horrible, painful deaths. For those of us lucky to get back from 'Nam alive and in one piece, there were no parades and no celebrations; nothing like the guys returning from previous wars or wars since. They called us murderers, baby killers, and criminals. The government pretty much abandoned us. But the Marine Corps is a brotherhood. We helped each other out as best we could, even without the government's help." He paused, but Banks didn't respond because he knew that what Hansen described was true.

Hansen continued with a smile, "So, no, I don't miss the military at all." He paused again then said, "But I did get the best military training in the world. That's how I ended up here in Paradise, North Dakota."

Banks smiled at Hansen's sarcastic comment on Grand Forks. He knew Hansen's wife's family was from Grand Forks, so he knew the real story on why Hansen was here "in Paradise, North Dakota."

When they checked into the headquarters building, they were directed to a waiting area just off the main entrance. Before they had time to sit in the pee-green, faux leather chairs, a young man in an Air Force uniform stepped into the room. He was a captain, but he appeared to have just graduated from high school.

In a rather high pitched voice he welcomed the detectives to Grand Forks Air Force Base. "Detectives, if you'll follow me please?"

Banks grumbled towards Hansen, "Man, do I feel old."

They were escorted down the pale green hall with ultra-high-gloss polished floors. They thought they might slip on the surface with each step. The baby-faced Captain didn't say another word as they continued their walk down the long hallway, their steps echoing with each click of the heels of their shoes. The only décor on the walls were pictures of missiles from various stages of the cold war and numerous KC-135 refueling tankers performing in-flight refueling operations.

The captain stopped abruptly, extending his arm towards an open door on their right. The captain squeaked, "Please be seated in the chairs in front of the major's desk. She'll be with you in a moment."

The men nodded and entered the office. They heard the loud, echoing click of the captain's shoes heading back in the direction of the headquarters entrance, the sound fading as he walked down the hall. Then there was silence.

There was a metal desk, the kind purchased in bulk by government agencies. The chairs where they sat were identical to those they saw in the guest room near the building's entrance. The detectives tried getting comfortable in the chairs. It wasn't possible.

The desk was clean and clear of any paperwork except a small thin folder in a plastic inbox on the front-right side of the desk. There was no outbox. Apparently, paperwork didn't sit long in this office. A telephone with multiple line capability was the only other object on the desk, except for a name placard. *Major Blaine Sanders.*

The office was lit by two sets of fluorescent fixtures, each containing two eight-foot bulbs. Between the bright lights and the highly polished floors, the detectives were sure they would get cataracts before exiting the building.

Both men noticed an open door at the back left side of the office. A light was on in that office, but there were no sounds indicating that it was occupied. For a few seconds neither detective said a word. Banks felt like they were in a library and the librarian would scold them if they said anything above a whisper.

Hansen turned his way and said in a tone almost too soft to hear, "I feel like I'm in the principal's office."

Banks smiled and was about to reply when they both heard the click of shoes coming down the hall. Banks thought that the shoes sounded heavier than those of the captain who guided them to the office, but the clicking sound had a manly cadence. The two men's breathing slowed in anticipation. When the sound walked right past the office and entered a room across the hall, they both took a deep breath.

Hansen smiled. "I told you we're in trouble."

Banks' smile was the slightest curl of his lips. Then he heard the rustling of papers from the inner-office followed by the distinct sound of a man clearing his throat. The men looked at each other, Banks eyebrows raised. The sound of heels clicking on the glossy, hallway floor drew their attention once again. A young woman entered the office from the hall and stopped next to their chairs. As they stood to greet her, in a rather deep, manly voice, she said, "Hello Detectives. I'm Major Blaine Sanders, Assistant to Colonel Templeton."

Banks and Hansen extended their hands and shook the Major's hand, introducing themselves as they did. Her grip was firm, but not manly.

Blaine Sanders was a tall woman with a slender body devoid of any feminine features. She had square, rather muscular shoulders, well toned arms, and straight hips. Her facial features were also more masculine than feminine with a square jaw, complete with a dimple in the middle of her chin and the slightest hint of facial hair above her lip.

"Please, be seated."

Once they were seated again Major Sanders began by apologizing. "I'm sorry to say that your trip here may be less than fruitful."

Banks eyebrows rose at the remark as the major continued. "I received the list of personnel that you'd like to interview, but I'm afraid that there are only a handful of them left on base, three to be exact. The rest are either on leave, transferred, or have left the service. I've circled the three individuals that are here today. We made certain their schedules were adjusted so they were available this morning."

She handed Banks the list. Three names were highlighted in yellow with times listed next to them, Captain Jeffrey Halliday, Airman's Kelvin Johnson and Adam Goff. The only name that Banks recognized was Airman Goff who had been assigned to assist Nancy Brown and Joe McKinney when they were at Grand Forks investigating the Kevin Reardon murder. He remembered Goff as a big guy, very personable and talkative.

Banks handed the list to Hansen then addressed Major Sanders. "When we investigated Colonel Chester's murder two years ago the assistant to the base commander was Major Shawnda Hull. Has she been recently transferred or discharged?"

It was one of those moments in face to face interviews that caused the interviewer's radar to kick in. Major Sanders facial expression didn't change, her hands and arms remained steady, unmoving, but the telltale was there. Her eyes darted just once from Banks to Hansen and back to Banks again. Something was up with Major Hull and Sanders didn't want the detectives to know about it.

After the slightest pause, in her deep voice, Major Sanders said, "Major Hull is no longer at this base. Her transfer papers were sent through about eighteen months ago. I replaced her at that time."

Banks' expression also did not change though he started to get the feeling that the day would not be entirely wasted. He didn't know why yet, but he figured that they needed to know more about Shawnda Hull.

"Where was Major Hull transferred?"

The confident front had returned to the Major. She looked straight at Banks. "Her transfer was to the Air Force Academy. Her appointment was as the assistant to Colonel Melinda Barnes, the Base Commander."

Hansen spoke up for the first time since the major entered the office. "Great. So you can supply us with her number and we can do the interview by phone."

That threw Sanders a curve. But she recovered nicely by saying, "It's getting close to your first interview. Why don't you conduct the interviews and I'll get that number for you before you leave."

With that, she stood. "Let me show you to the interview room. I'll have Captain Joyce make sure the interviewees are on time."

***

The detectives were just completing their third interview of the morning. It had been with Airman Goff. They'd expected Goff would be the easy going, talkative young man they both remembered, but they were disappointed. At one point during the interview, Banks asked Goff if there was a problem that was causing him to be so nervous. The young man responded with a simple *No, sir*. Most of Goff's answers were short and to the point, with very little substance, so the session went by quickly. It had been the same for the first two interviews as well, short answers in both time and detail.

Once Goff left the interview room, Banks and Hansen stood to stretch and gather their sparse notes. The irritation was clear on Banks face. Hansen's expression was neutral. Before they finished tucking their notes away, Captain Joyce was there, offering to escort them to the front door of the headquarters.

Banks said, "I'd like to speak with the base commander."

Joyce's face turned ashen. "I'll check with Major Sanders to see if Colonel Templeton is available, sir."

Banks didn't wait for the escort. He walked right past the young captain and headed straight for Major Sander's desk. When he strode into the office, Major Sanders stood.

"So, did your interviews go well?"

Banks wasn't deterred. In a rather insistent voice he said, "I need to speak with Colonel Templeton. It'll take just a few minutes of his time."

Sanders didn't bat an eye. She looked directly at Banks, "The colonel's schedule is very full today. I'm sure he doesn't have the time to-"

As Hansen entered the office behind him, Banks raised his hand and cut her off saying in a rather forceful tone, "There have been two homicides involving Air Force personnel from this base. One was the Commanding Officer, the other a mid-level non-com. He can take the time to-"

The distinct sound of a man clearing his throat came from the back of the Major's office. A man, about 5 foot-4 with a squat body, and close cut salt and pepper hair, stood in the doorway to the inner office. He looked like an accountant or a financial advisor instead of a military officer. He said in a deep, radio announcer voice, "Major, I'll speak with the detectives."

Colonel Eugene Templeton, Commander, Grand Forks Air Force Base, turned to Banks and Hansen. "Gentlemen, please come in. I can give you ten minutes. Major, please hold all calls."

The detectives followed the colonel into his office. The door closed behind them.

Colonel Templeton's office was just slightly bigger than the Major's, but there was another room, paneled in handsome oak, behind his office. From what the detectives could see, it appeared to be a conference room, complete with conference table and chairs that looked much more comfortable than the ones in which they now sat, a whiteboard, and a projector mounted from the ceiling.

The commander wasted no time. "There's not much I can tell you about either murder."

Apparently, the commander wasn't planning on answering any questions, but he probably hoped to control the flow of information. Banks was not going to allow that to happen.

"Colonel Templeton, why were your personnel directed to not cooperate with our investigation?"

***

Banks and Hansen spent exactly nine minutes with the commander. It was time well spent. They also had the phone number for Major Shawnda Hull's new command.

As they were driving off base, a car fell in behind them and followed them all the way back to Grand Forks when the car's lights began to flash on and off.

Banks pulled into the nearest parking lot as the car pulled up beside them. It was Airman Goff. They spoke for only a short period of time. Goff was nervous and didn't want to be seen talking with the detectives, but the conversation was well worth the risk.

***

When they arrived back at their desks, Banks' phone rang. He picked it up on the third ring.

"Banks."

A man's voice with a southern accent said, "Hatch."

"Pardon me?"

"This is William Hatcher. Joe McKinney asked me to call you."

"Yes, Mr. Hatcher. Thanks for calling."

"Detective Banks, please call me Hatch. Mr. Hatcher was my father. Now, what can I do for y'all?"

Banks gave Hatch the spiel on how they were starting up the investigation into Milton Chester and Kevin Reardon's murder again and he wondered if Hatch remembered anything from when he, the McKinney's, and Nancy Brown talked a few years ago.

Hatch said that he hadn't but would call the detectives if he did.

***

Nancy Brown came into the large open room in Hatch's cabin and asked, "Who was that?"

"Well, Miss Nancy, that was Detective Bill Banks. He wanted to know if I remembered anything about the Kevin Reardon or Milton Chester murders."

"I hope you didn't tell him that you witnessed Milton Chester's murder."

"Nancy dear, I was born at night, but it wudn't yesterday."

She smiled, shook her head and said, "That's not how the saying goes." She kissed him. "I have to get back home. My boss called a team meeting tomorrow and I have to be there."

"Well I'll miss ya. Want me to come along for the ride? I ain't real busy these days."

"I'll be back quick. I need a vacation, so we'll have plenty of time together."

Hatch rubbed his hands together and smiled. "Well, alright."

Chapter 10

The air was clean and fresh west of Lake George in the Ocala National Forest in Northern Florida. Pine trees lined the sandy road that ran to a circular clearing nearly seventeen miles from the nearest state highway and several miles from any homes or trailers. Birds chattering and a hot, humid breeze rustling through the trees were the only sounds that could be heard. A small lake was visible through the trees, the surface a deep green from the reflection of the trees on the far shore.

The white, two-door Chevy sat in the shade of the pines on the south side of the clearing with both doors and the trunk wide open. Multiple sets of older tire tracks could be seen in the sand, though none had been recently left. Cans and bottles littered the perimeter of the circle, evidence this was a popular night-time party spot for teens and young adults. Several pine trees had crudely carved initials and plus signs in the center of a heart, a testament of young love. The lovers must have believed that by desecrating these trees with their declarations, their love would conquer all and stand the test of time.

Ace's attention was miles away, on a golf course in St. Augustine. He'd nearly lost control of the Chevy several times on his way to this clearing as his mind wandered and his rage grew. The first incident was when he nearly ran a stop sign at a busy intersection of state routes. The blaring horn of an eighteen wheeler racing through the intersection snapped Ace out of his trance. Had the driver not sounded his horn, Ace would have plowed right into the side of the big rig. No doubt, the results would have been catastrophic.

The second incident involved a curve on a narrow, two-lane county road. In Ace's mind, he drove a food cart on a golf course towards three golfers. The cart raced over the lush green grass, his concentration, a laser-like focus on his prey. He saw each man standing on the mound of the tee, preparing for their first shots on the eighth hole. He pressed the pedal of the gas power cart to the floor, trying to get every bit of speed possible out of the cart. He willed it to go faster, but the accelerator would go no further. He leaned over the steering wheel, nearly leaving his seat. As the cart closed the gap to the golfers, Ace reached back with his right hand to grab the pistol from the back of his waistband when he heard the first shot. He snapped to when the passenger side tires of his car caught the lip of the blacktop and began to pull hard to the right. Ace corrected to the left and nearly clipped a four wheel drive pickup truck that was heading east.

Ace pulled over and took several deep breaths. He quickly realized that he could have been killed. As he sat on the side of the road trying to regain his composure, the pickup returned, pulling up next to him. The passenger window rolled down.

Ace had his face in his hands, thinking about what had happened on the golf course. A loud bang on the driver side window brought him out of his intense daydream. He looked over at the side of the truck. The open passenger window of the truck was high above the driver side door of the Chevy. When Ace looked up, he saw a man with a brown, scruffy beard covering wide, fat cheeks, dark eyes, and a pock-marked forehead. The driver of the truck had moved over to the passenger seat and leaned out the window. He'd thrown an empty beer can at Ace's car to get his attention. His camouflaged ball cap had a salty sweat stain line on the sides and bill. His face wore his best 'I'm a bad-ass' look. Ace guessed he was in his mid-thirties. The man gestured with his hand for Ace to roll the car window down.

Ace was annoyed that this hick was bothering him while he tried to collect himself. What did the guy want? He hadn't hit his truck or forced him off the road. Why couldn't he just move on and mind his own business. As he reached for the button to lower the window, the man threw another beer can. This one hit just above the window and bounced onto the hood of Ace's car. Ace took a deep breath, working hard to contain his growing anger, the red rising in his face, his blood beginning a slow boil.

He pressed the button. The slow glide of the window made a whirring sound. As he looked up, the man in the truck spit out a stream of chewing tobacco juice that hit the door of the Chevy, just missing Ace.

In a gravelly smoker's voice with a strong southern accent, the man shouted, "Hey kid, y'all got a death wish or somethin'?"

Ace didn't say a word. As he stared back at the man, he slowly reached between the driver and passenger seats and felt for the hand grip on his pistol.

Again, the man shouted, "Hey, punk, I'm talkin' to you. Are you frickin' high on something?"

Ace said nothing, but his rage continued to grow. The pistol's safety was off. All he had to do was pull the weapon up straight. It would be hidden by his body. He could plug the guy between his eyes before he had a chance to move.

The man apparently saw something in Ace's eyes. Ace saw the change in his expression, from confidence to uncertainty then to…fear? Maybe, but whatever it was, the man said, "Look, man, if you're drunk or high or somethin', just get off the damn road 'fore you kill somebody."

With that, he slid over to the driver's side of the truck, did a u-turn and peeled off in the direction he was originally headed, leaving a strip of burned rubber in his wake.

Ace sat for a few more minutes, getting his temper under control. His first thought had been to chase after the man and teach him some manners. Then he thought about his mission. It was time to get back on track. So he had headed off to a place he knew in the Ocala National Forest.

Now he sat in the clearing, confused, angry, depressed, alone…dangerous. He'd gone to St. Augustine intending to make sure three men were killed, and they were, but not as he had planned. It was his justice. He was supposed to be the judge, jury, and yes, the executioner. These men had violated his mother in the most heinous way, yet they lived lavish lives while she was tossed out like garbage. At least he'd been able to get the ring leader, the instigator, Milton Chester.

He wasn't supposed to know about any of this, but long ago he'd heard his mother talking with Bobby Garrett, another bastard, about the party in Colorado Springs. At the time, he didn't really understand what they were talking about, but over the years, as he learned about such things, he figured out what rape was and how brutally they had treated his mother. Maybe that was a point in her life where she felt like she deserved to be treated that way. He'd found out about his half-sister, Becky and how she'd been abused much the same as their mother. The last straw had been when his mother and half-sister were murdered, gunned down by government agents.

And yet, here he sat, far from civilization, far from any of the perpetrators. And now someone else had stolen his power.

He had a new mission; find out who had killed these men and why. Then take back the justice that was rightfully his.

Again, his anger rose. He looked at the hearts and initials carved into the trees, wondering what it was like to be truly in love with another human being. He longed for more than the physical touch of a woman. His handsome appearance and natural charm, along with his ability to spin a most believable yarn afforded him easy access to beautiful and sexy women. That kind of love came natural to him.

The only person he could honestly say that he truly loved was his mother, Abbie Glover, but that was different. The strong emotional bond that they shared was that of a mother and son; a love that grew stronger from being together through tough times. They'd been through many lean years when the basic necessities had been difficult to come by. At times, meals were slim and even a roof over their heads was an old car or van. Near the end, just before his mother was gunned down, it appeared that their plan was coming together, that they would finally be able to work together to build a future. But that plan and the future that it promised was blown away with his mother's last dying breath. Now Ace had to build that future on his own.

What good is a strong financial future if you have no one to share it with? That question made its way into Ace's brain and would not let go. *Why can't I feel love? I've never been able to feel the bonding of my soul to another. It seems I can't open my feelings up to a woman.*

The more Ace thought about it, the more rooted in his brain the idea became that he would be alone for the rest of his life. At first, he was sad. His soul was hollowed out and there was nothing to fill the void, to take root and grow. And he knew why his soul was empty. Others had drained it.

When he was growing up, all he'd ever wanted was to be like other kids, though he hardly ever knew any kids his age. He was always around adults, friends of his mom. Most of them were her lovers. They would come in and out of their lives so quickly, and sometimes, so violently, that he hardly knew them. Only a handful stuck around longer than a few weeks, like Bobby Garrett. He'd liked Bobby, but it was Bobby who had indirectly caused his mother's death. But Bobby Garrett was dead and someone had to pay for his mother's murder.

What about his sister, the sister that he didn't know existed until he was an adult? She was murdered, too. Who was going to pay for that crime?

The more Ace sat in the clearing surrounded by nothing but trees, chirping birds, and unseen wildlife, the angrier he became. He started to bite his nails. When he pulled a nail out with his teeth and tore a piece of flesh from deep along his cuticle, the finger bled. Not too badly, but it hurt. He licked the blood from his nail then wiped his finger on his pants, but the blood kept coming.

The chirping of the birds grew louder. The trees swayed, the breeze making the leaves rustle, adding to the chaos in his overloaded brain. He jumped up, putting his hands over his ears, the tension rising as he thought about all the death that seemed to surround him. The forest started to spin. He desperately needed something to grasp, something to stop the spinning. He grabbed the open trunk lid of the car. Looking down in the trunk he saw his Glock. The silencer was removed. Grabbing the pistol with one hand, still hanging onto the trunk with the other, he searched for a target.

The first thing that came into view was a heart carved into the bark of pine trees about thirty feet away. It was a symbol of the love that Ace could never have. *If I can't have it, neither can you.* He took aim at the nearest pledge and fired a round.

It hit the tree, but missed the heart low and to the right. Ace's anger grew. At this close range he should have hit a bull's eye. He took aim and fired again. Another miss, this time high and to the right. Another shot, another miss.

Ace became angrier with each attempt. He fired in rapid succession, swearing after each round missed its mark. When the clip emptied and the slide locked in the full back position, he threw the gun into the trunk and pulled out an AR15 with a modification that changed the weapon to fully automatic. He took aim with the assault rifle and fired a single shot. When it also missed he switched the weapon to fully automatic and fired, emptying the magazine.

The noise was deafening, the smoke from the gunpowder rising into the trees.

As the smoke cleared, Ace smiled. The heart was obliterated, pieces of splintered pine strewn all about.

He pulled a small note pad from his pants pocket. He flipped the cover open to the first page. There were nine names on the page. One was crossed off with a dark, rust colored, coarse line. Milton Chester. Under Milton Chester were the names of Adam Wesley, Richard Aims, and Carl Dempsey. He couldn't cross them off in blood, but he pulled out a pen and put a check mark next to each. He placed the tip of the pen on the next name on his list. Dean Gray. *Time for a change of plan. Norfolk, Virginia sounds nice this time of year.* Before he flipped the pad closed, he added a word to the bottom of the list, the bastard who'd stolen his plan.

Shooter.

Chapter 11

Airman Adam Goff's job as a glorified gopher at Grand Forks Air Force Base headquarters wasn't his only talent. A self-taught computer geek, he knew several program languages and developed a knack for hacking into what most people would consider secure databases. A close friend, Airman William Sherrod, worked for the Air Force Office of Special Investigations in the IT department. They spoke on the phone several times each week, chatting about what innocent hacks each had performed since their last call. When Goff asked Sherrod for a major favor, the techie at first balked. He was reluctant to put his career on the line, even for a good friend and a good cause. But he knew Goff wouldn't have asked if it wasn't important.

Goff wanted to help Major Shawnda Hull, but he didn't know how. When she fled Grand Forks in search of someone or something, he had to find out why. One thing he did know, at the time Major Hull went AWOL, she was pregnant with Colonel Milton Chester's child. Goff had a not-so-secret crush on Hull even though he knew she wouldn't reciprocate, but that didn't change his heart and how he felt about her. He needed to find out why Colonel Chester ran out of the office for the unscheduled meeting which led to his untimely death. He had just one name – Ace Glover.

Two years ago during the police investigation of the colonel's murder, Goff was tasked with setting up the meeting room where base personnel were questioned by the Grand Forks Police Detectives. Goff added some special touches of his own that weren't in the instructions for room preparation. He added several electronic listening devices in strategic locations so that he could hear the interviews. During Major Hull's interview, out of the blue, Detective Banks had asked her if she knew a young man named Ace Glover. When she had said "no" they moved right on to the next question. Goff knew right away that whoever Ace Glover was, he was a person of interest in the investigation.

Along with his friend, Airman Sherrod, Goff began his internet search for Ace Glover. It turned out that Glover was easy to track down, mainly because his name was somewhat uncommon. After eliminating all other possibilities, they determined that he lived in the home of Angelina Valentine in Savannah, Georgia. Local gossip columns named Glover as the new love interest for the recently widowed Valentine. It was a local scandal in the social circles of Savannah's upper crust.

The next step was a bit more difficult. They had to physically locate Glover and determine a means of tracking his movements. Airman Sherrod provided the answer – GPS tracking. He had been the technical lead during an Air Force project that used satellites to track small electronic devices. The team determined that passive Radio Frequency Identity Devices, RFIDs for short, could be attached by magnet, glue, or simply dropped into a pocket, and the satellite could then detect the device from hundreds of miles in space.

The bigger issue was how to get one or more devices in Ace Glover's possession such that he would always have one with him wherever he traveled. That meant putting a device on or in his car, in his clothing or his wallet. Since Goff was in Grand Forks, North Dakota and Sherrod was at Wright-Patterson Air Force Base in Dayton, Ohio, getting the devices planted was a challenge.

Goff solved the problem by calling Savage Investigative Consultants. The owner, Peden Savage, was a Marine Corps veteran and a former FBI agent. Goff knew one of Savage's techies through a gaming club. With the help of Peden Savage and his team, several RFID chips were planted in Glover's car, his duffle bag, and his shoes. When Goff asked how they'd done it, Lee Sparks, Savage's technical guy said, "If I told you, I'd have to kill you. But I sent you the tracking program. Instructions for download are in your inbox. Call me if you need help with the download."

The program installed on Goff's personal computer without a hitch. Within seconds of activating the program he could see "pins" on a street level map of Savannah, Georgia. The electronic pins were labeled with a word description of the location of each device. For over a year, the pins stayed within a few miles of the historic district. Then on June 30, 1999, the pins on the map headed south.

**

Each time Major Shawnda Hull started to hit the speed dial on her cell phone, she stopped short. Her heart pounded, her hands shook and her mouth went dry. She looked around the small, dingy motel room for a place to hide…from what, she didn't know. All she knew was that she had to make the call to let her parents know she was okay. No ill had befallen her. No psychopathic killer had grabbed her and dragged her into an alley. She was fine…well, not exactly fine. Physically fine, yes. Mentally? That was another story.

She backed away from the old, beat up desk with the uneven legs. The nylon pad had broken off the bottom of one of the legs. Instead of fixing the desk by putting a new pad on the leg, motel "management" put a pack of matches under the offending leg. Shawnda was amazed someone hadn't pushed the lone desk drawer closed causing enough friction to light the pack and send the entire motel complex up in flames. But after this evening, that wouldn't be her problem. Someone else could worry about this valuable piece of real estate. Whoever owned the land would probably welcome an "accidental" fire that took out the run-down rat trap.

Two years ago she would never even have entered such a low class, flea-bag joint. She would have been afraid to touch anything in the room for fear of catching something you couldn't wash off. Times, and fortunes, had changed.

The greasy burger and fries hadn't been the best choice for dinner, but she didn't want to travel far from the source of her reason for being here. As she stood behind the chair, she began to feel sick to her stomach. She ran to the sink and leaned over as waves of nausea rippled through her mid-section. Closing her eyes, trying to think pleasant thoughts, she fought to keep her dinner down. For the time being, it worked. She reached for the lukewarm half-empty water bottle, took a quick swallow, and hoped the water would calm her stomach and with it, her nerves.

Straightening, she caught her image in the mirror over the sink. The thick glass of the ancient mirror had a crack running diagonally from top left to lower right. Lead colored blotches covered much of its surface, clouding out the reflection of the young woman staring back at her. She didn't like the image. It looked like her mother or her mother's sister, Aunt Sheila. Certainly, it couldn't be her own reflection unless she'd aged fifteen years since the last time she'd looked into a mirror.

"He's killing you and he doesn't even know you," she said out loud to the image staring back at her. "Get yourself together and call home. Now!"

One deep breath led to another. Her stomach calmed. Her nerves steadied, though they had a ways to go. Closing her eyes so that the old woman in the mirror no longer stared back at her, Shawnda took another deep breath, then thought of the one thing that always made her smile.

She walked across the stiff, stained carpet to her purse, pulled out a small folder, and flipped up the cover. There he was. Trevor Jason Hull. Seeing his face nearly tore her to pieces. Her heart leapt into her throat, nearly choking off her breath.

There were two pictures. In the bottom photo he was just fourteen months old, wearing dark blue shorts and a light blue tee shirt covered by a large bib. His pudgy face and the bib were red with the juice from a melting popsicle. What was left of the icy treat covered his left hand in red, sticky juice. She smiled even as tears welled up in her eyes. Joy mixed with feelings of longing, wishing she was with her child now. She wiped the tears away with the back of her free hand.

In the glossy picture on top, he was a newborn infant in the tiniest diaper; helpless, hands and feet still curled as if unable to unfurl from the confinement of the womb. Her arms and chest felt cold. She wished she could hold him close to her now and forever.

She noticed the hands that held her son, his grandfather's hands, her father's hands. Only the hands and a small part of his left arm were visible. She loved her father dearly, but he was a hard man to love. Even her mother said he was demanding throughout their marriage. But he was a military man. It was in his blood. Her mother had said it was one of the traits that had attracted her to him in the first place.

Shawnda knew exactly what her mother must have felt and why she fell for her father because she, too, had been in love with a military man. She looked at the pictures of her son and tried to imagine him as a young man. Even at fourteen months, she could see his father's facial features. It was the only part of her child's father she would ever have. Her eyes watered again as her heart ached.

That was the hell of it. Her only connection to the man she loved was the little miracle in these two pictures, her son. So far, everything else had been a nightmare.

When she finished her business here in Florida, she would go home to her parent's house. Only then could she get her life back on track. Without a doubt, it was going to be hell. No amount of explaining to her superiors would save her from substantial punishment. But she would take her lumps, no matter how severe.

She kissed each picture then held the folder close to her chest and closed her eyes trying to extract some warmth from her son's photographs. Reciting a silent prayer that her son remained safe, happy, and healthy while she was away, she wiped the remaining tears off her cheeks, closed the folder and placed it back in her purse. The room stopped pulsating. Her heart slowly returned to a normal rhythm and her nausea disappeared. She was ready.

Her concentration back, she focused on the task at hand. For most people, a call home to their parents was second nature, but her relationship with her parents was strained. Blocking out the squalid conditions of the motel room, she opened her cell phone and hit the speed-dial button for her parent's number.

Her mother picked up the phone before the second ring. "Hello."

"Hi, Mom."

In a voice nearly shrill with anxiety, Clara Hull said, "Oh, Shawnda, dear, where are you? We've been worried sick about you."

She heard her mother cover the receiver and yell to her father that she was on the phone. She imagined the look on her father's face. His brow would furl, his lips tighten, then he'd grab the arms of his favorite lounge chair. He'd be torn between grabbing the other phone extension and walking out on the back porch of their turn of the century home to light a cigarette to ease the tension.

Her mother came back on the line. "Your father will be on in a moment, dear. Tell me where you are, and why haven't you called? It's been nearly a week!"

"I'm sorry, Mom. I've got some things that I have to sort out. It won't be long and I'll be home."

"Oh, honey, what could be more important than your child? What you're doing, whatever it is, it can wait. Please-"

"Mom!" She needed to change the subject. In a voice barely louder than a whisper, she asked, "How's my baby boy doing?"

Her mother's reply took on a more conciliatory tone, the voice of a proud grandmother coming through. "I'll tell you one thing, he's just like you were at that age. He's into everything he can get his hands on. I expect we'll find him on top of the refrigerator one day soon."

Shawnda smiled. "Is he still awake? Can you put him on?"

Shawnda heard a distinct click on the line. Her mother replied, "Let me see if he's still awake. Last I saw, he was trying to climb out of his crib."

Almost as soon as her mother finished, a clear, deep voice filled the receiver. "Shawnda, are you safe?"

"Yes, sir."

"Do you need any money?"

"No, sir."

An awkward pause ensued. To Shawnda, it seemed like an eternity. She wished her mother would hurry back with her Trevor, but it was taking forever.

Shawnda broke the silence. "Dad, I know I screwed up and I know you can't possibly approve of what I've done, but when I get home I'll tell you everything." She paused, hoping he would say something, but he remained silent. "After I come home to see Trevor, I'm going to turn myself in."

Again, an uncomfortable silence followed. Then her father said something that she never expected. "We'll get you a good lawyer, the best we can afford. It may not do any good, but I know you had to have a damn good reason to throw away your career."

Major Shawnda Hull looked around the motel room, her throat constricting as she tried to choke back the tears threatening to escape. A retired colonel, Jason Vincent Hull had never before said or done anything to go against the United States Air Force. He'd been a decorated Vietnam era pilot and was extremely proud when his daughter had graduated from the Air Force Academy near the top of her class. She'd also wanted to fly fighter jets, but color blindness disqualified her.

She was about to try and tell her father that she loved him when a little voice came over the phone. Her heart pounded in her chest once more. The joy of hearing her son say "Momma" brought tears streaming from her eyes.

***

Shawnda sat on the edge of the bed in the rundown motel room, thinking of the call to her parents, and hearing her son for the first time in over a week. It had been a call filled with anxiety.

She'd been overwhelmed with emotion for nearly an hour before she realized she had to get down to business. She had high hopes of ending her year-long crusade and heading home to her parents house. Then she could start the next difficult chapter of her life.

It had been a simple plan. Track Ace Glover, the bastard son of that whore, Abbie Glover, until he did something criminal. Videotape him in the act, then turn the tape over to the local law enforcement agency. It didn't matter where he was when he screwed up; if it happened in a back woods, hick town in the south where the cops were less worried about the civil rights of their prisoners, so much the better. Maybe he'd end up in a cell with a couple muscle bound rednecks. Ace had such a pretty face. With his blond hair and light complexion, the gangs in lock up would be fighting over him. He wouldn't last a week.

Shawnda set the hand-held video camera on the motel room table and opened the miniature screen. She turned the camera on and pressed play. She shook her head, disappointed that she hadn't captured the majority of Ace's exploits at the golf course. When Ace had assaulted the snack cart guy at the golf course and left him tied up, she was so nervous that she thought the camera was recording, when it was actually on *Play*. By the time she realized her mistake and hit *Record* she'd missed anything that would incriminate Ace in the shooting. In fact, it showed that Ace was not the shooter, but instead, was a witness. Her plan went out the window.

The first thing she saw on the video was Ace driving the cart towards the three men on the tee. The video clearly showed he hadn't drawn the silenced gun as he approached. She could hear her own labored breathing on the audio, then the reports from the gunshots rang out. Two of the three men collapsed to the ground, the third dove to the ground before looking up trying to identify the source of the gunfire. In the video, another shot rang out and the man's head snapped back.

Ace was visibly upset, but the way he reacted was off. He clearly wasn't afraid of the shooter. As he turned the cart to flee, he seemed angry, not afraid. The big question was *Why?*

She wondered if Wesley, Richards, or Aims had survived the attack and were now in the hospital describing the events. Maybe one of them saw her with the video camera when they'd been attacked. *Oh, God. Could it be?*

Shawnda quickly turned off the video camera, turned on the television, and flipped through channels looking for a local station. There was a tag line across the bottom in red. She caught the tail end of the sentence which said "shot dead." But who was dead? She watched the channel for another twenty minutes before the news anchor announced the murder of three men on a St. Augustine golf course.

The good news was there were no witnesses who would report her filming to the police. The bad news was that Ace Glover wasn't the killer and she had no idea who was.

Chapter 12

The day after the murder of three Air Force officers, news stations from across the country had converged on the Slammer and Squire Golf Course north of St. Augustine, Florida. The reporters were disappointed when the St. Johns County sheriff and prosecutor made very few comments, mostly stating they could not release any details of the crime, including whether there was any solid evidence, persons of interest, or suspects. They had no idea why these military officers were the target of an apparent assassination. The only information they released was that each man was shot with the same weapon from approximately sixty feet.

Several members of Congress were grandstanding on national television, calling the murder of three Air Force Officers a terrorist attack and an act of war. The national media uncovered much of the officers' backgrounds, including their military careers, duty stations, and service medals. Most of the stations reports were similar. On the second evening following the murders, the stations honed in on their family lives. Overall, they were Air Force Officers, one active duty and two retired, with very little claim to genuine distinction in their careers. The two retired men were not involved in any major projects or campaigns even during their active duty years. General Wesley was the only one of the three still on active duty at the time of the murders, but even his career was mediocre by comparison to most of his counterparts.

For some reason, the congressmen's ranting and repeated claims was gaining traction in the news media and in barrooms, workplaces, and schools across the country. Newspaper editorials asked leading questions, pointing towards Al Queda or the new leadership in Iran as the mastermind behind the plot. They asked *Who's Next?*

In Colonel Warner's mind, all this information begged the question; what makes these men so special they would be singled out for murder by terrorists? The other tell-tale sign that the congressmen's rants were unfounded was that no organization claimed responsibility for the attack. All of the agencies tasked with monitoring voice traffic of known terror organizations reported the airwaves were quiet, except for some who openly spoke of the foolish leaders and naïve citizens of the United States and how easily they were being led astray.

***

Nancy Brown received a call from her boss, Colonel Shelia Warner, head of the Marine Corps Anti-Terror Unit, with orders to report to the colonel's office to meet with her and other members of the unit. Nancy made the drive from her new home near Reston, Virginia in just under an hour driving the back roads outside of the beltway. Since arriving at the conference room next to the colonel's office, Nancy had read the file on the murders, including the background investigation on the victims. Other members of the unit were scheduled to arrive within the next hour, so Nancy had the room to herself. She tried very hard to see all angles of the crime, from a possible terror attack to a random robbery, and everything in between. She'd come to her conclusion rather quickly, but read through the entire report before deciding that her original thoughts were well founded.

Colonel Warner walked in and sat at the head of the conference table. "So, Nancy, what do you think now that you've had a chance to review the file?"

Nancy looked directly at her and with no emotion stated, "The killings were clearly an assassination, but not by terrorists."

Colonel Warner's facial expression didn't change. She gave away nothing in her body language.

"What makes you so sure?"

Nancy spent the next twenty-five minutes detailing her analysis of the murders, including the crime scene photos, the relatively insignificant careers of the victims, and the lack of claim of responsibility by any terror group. She mentioned other minor observations, such as the location of the murders and the lack of any attempt at mass destruction. She also mentioned the kidnapping of the concessions cart operator. He stated he was assaulted by a blond-haired kid about twenty to twenty-five years old. The kid was an American and spoke with a Midwestern accent. He was most likely involved in some way, if not the actual killer. The final point that sealed it early for Nancy was that sheriff's deputies combing the area for evidence found a spent shell casing near the most likely point from where the shots were fired. The shell casing was for a 7.62x55 bullet for an American made assault rifle. Terrorists favor Russian made AK47s.

Finally, the Colonel's lips curled in the slightest of smiles. "Now that we know it's not any terror group, who are our killers?"

Nancy's right eyebrow rose slightly. "Killers? As in more than one?"

"That's just a possibility, but I think we may be looking for more than one killer. Remember what you said about the kid who was driving the concessions cart. Some blond kid attacked him and drugged him. He didn't say anything about an assault rifle. In fact, the kid said the guy didn't even have a golf bag with him. He was on a golf cart when he approached, but had no golf equipment. It only dawned on him just before he blacked out."

Nancy rose, then walked to the table and poured a cup of coffee. The steaming brew was black, the way the colonel liked it. She took a sip before returning to her seat and setting the cup on the conference table.

"If there were two assailants, why did all the shots come from a single weapon?"

The colonel considered Nancy's comments. "Maybe there were supposed to be two weapons used and one jammed or one of the assailants was delayed or spotted before they could get into place."

Nancy had already dismissed the likelihood of two gunmen. The fact that a single weapon was used led Nancy to believe that only one gunman was involved. When you can effectively take out three moving targets with three shots, why would you need a second gunman? She didn't want to dismiss the possibility outright, but to Nancy, it didn't make sense.

Nancy stood and walked over to a white board and picked up a green dry erasable marker. She drew a rough outline of the tee area of the eighth hole, then filled in green circles for the trees that lined the tee some sixty feet away. Trading for a black marker, she drew a stick figure behind the trees where the shell casing was found. On the opposite side of the tee there were no trees, but there was a pond, which Nancy added using a blue marker. Then she picked up a red marker and stepped to the side. She pointed to the area where the shell casing was found.

"If this is anywhere near a realistic view of the murder scene, there are a couple points that become clear. First, the vantage point used by our gunman was the closest point to the tee that had any concealment. They wanted to be certain they had a good, clear shot, but they also did not want to be seen. Also, if there were two or more gunmen, then there's no other place for a second gunman to hide. And the trees wrap along the fairway." Nancy pointed to where the trees appeared to move away from the tee as the fairway widened almost immediately beyond the front of the tee mound. "The way the tree line is set back from the fairway not only increases the distance from the tee, it also provides a poor angle for a clear shot."

Colonel Warner nodded. "So we're back to the question. Who killed these three and why? They must have really pissed somebody off."

"How do these guys know each other, aside from that they were in the Air Force? I mean, they must have known each other for some time. Maybe they had a duty station together and stayed close."

"It's better than that. They graduated from the academy in Colorado Springs together. We're still looking into that connection. It'll be tough to get anything of value from that long ago, but we've sent an inquiry to the commanding officer. We should know something soon."

***

The official inquiry went to the Office of the Commander of the Air Force Academy in Colorado Springs, Colorado. It was hand delivered by Major Maurice Alexander, the Commander of the 10th Security Forces Squadron. Major Alexander, a tall, slender man with a shaved, bald head and dark black skin, was in charge of security and law enforcement at the academy. Before delivering the inquiry to the commander's office, he read it, and had his assistant make a working copy so he could get a head start on the pending investigation. He was angry that these men were murdered in cold blood after they spent their careers in the military defending their country. He was surprised when he received a direct call from Academy Commander, Colonel Melinda Barnes, directing him to hold off on any investigative work.

"Major, my office will handle this inquiry. It's a simple matter of compiling some information on these officers and their years here. You have more important things on your plate."

"Ma'am, if I may . . ."

"No, Major, you may not. Consider this an order. My office will handle this matter." There was a long, uncomfortable silence before Colonel Barnes asked in a tone that held no ambiguity. "Is that clear?"

Major Alexander paused for as long as he dared before saying, "Yes, Ma'am, perfectly."

The major expected Colonel Barnes to say more, but before he knew it, he was listening to a dial tone. He eased the receiver back in its cradle. The copy of the four page inquiry sat on his desk. What on earth would cause a full bird colonel to want to keep a simple inquiry off the radar? He picked up the pages and walked to the shredder behind his desk. Slowly, he leaned over to destroy the copies. The papers were within a centimeter of the automatic switch on the shredder when a knock on the door stopped him.

In a booming voice he said, "Enter."

"Major?" It was his administrative assistant, a petite, middle-aged black woman, Technical Sergeant Asiamarie Vance. "Your eight o'clock appointment is here, sir."

"Show them in please."

Vance returned with the parents of an academy cadet who had been caught with marijuana in his room. He was going to do a brief stint in the brig, then receive a dishonorable discharge. His parents were undoubtedly here to plead his case. As they entered his office, he asked them to take a seat. Turning back to the shredder, he hesitated, then plunged the pages into the machine and listened as it reduced the document to confetti. But as soon as he heard the blades of the machine start to grind, the feeling swept over him that he should have kept his copy.

Chapter 13

The red and green lines of the stock market graph jumped off the screen of the three week old *TerraSlim Wafer*, the newest, fastest, sleekest notepad computer on the market. Compared to Dean Gray's old laptop, this machine was lightning fast. Exactly what he needed to make his stock trades in a rapidly moving market. The green and red bars pulsated slightly, indicating fractional movements in the price of selected stocks. Share prices and price movement percentages were displayed below the bars as the level and rate of change was measured and displayed as close to real time as an unlicensed trader could get. That gave Dean an advantage over other less-skilled stock traders. Equipment was one thing, but knowledge and experience were what really counted.

Dean had been a sailor on the aircraft carrier USS *Nimitz*. After serving just two years, he'd been recently discharged at the convenience of the Navy. According to some obscure regulation, conducting training sessions on board ship on how to become a stock market day trader was against the rules.

Initially, there had been no major problems with Dean's classes. The students seemed to learn well and they were making money. They were doing so well that a number of the sailors were getting to their watch-stations late or not showing up at all. Then the market took a turn south and several of the young traders didn't recognize the warning signs Dean had tried to teach them. They lost all their investment money and then some. Their wives called the command office and complained their husbands had bankrupted them. The commander of the carrier group contacted the commanding officer of the *Nimitz* and demanded to know what the hell was going on. All fingers pointed to Dean, who was given an immediate discharge and helicopter ride off the great ship. That had suited Dean just fine.

Sitting alone in the makeshift office in his apartment, he watched the flow of stocks and money from his computer. He made several quick buys in a company that he'd sold just two days ago, before the company announced that it had lost a major client which accounted for approximately eighteen percent of their revenue. The stock had immediately tanked nearly twenty percent. Now at a market bottom, Dean had just purchased a new stake in the company anticipating they would get several new accounts replacing and surpassing the revenue lost from the previous account. He would know within a few days if his instincts paid off.

He leaned back from his computer, rubbing his hands and smiling. Life was grand now that he was out of the canoe club. He made more money in one month than he had the entire previous year from his Navy pay. One other advantage of being out of the Navy was that he no longer had to worry about his personal belongings and his finances. That had been a real problem shortly after he got out of boot camp two years ago. It was a lesson that he would never forget.

Dean thought about the young woman who'd stolen his heart…and a lot more. He'd been out of boot camp for just one day and had been out with some of his friends to celebrate. They were at a local bar that catered to sailors who liked southern rock and roll. Sitting alone at a table nearby, Julie Lippus looked his way until he caught her eyes. Then she shyly looked away. But her beautiful gaze returned along with an amazing smile. He was hooked before he took a single step in her direction. By the end of the evening, Julie Lippus had Dean Gray wrapped around her little finger. Within two weeks, just before he was deployed on his first cruise on the USS *Nimitz*, they were married.

Being locked up in boot camp, not seeing a woman for seven weeks, and being relatively naïve when it came to women, Dean had never anticipated what came next. When the Executive Officer of the *Nimitz* called Petty Officer Gray into his office, Gray thought he was being reprimanded for stock trading from personal computers on the ship. When Dean found out he was being flown by helicopter to Norfolk Navy Base, he didn't understand why until he was met by his father and stepmother. They explained to Dean his marriage was a sham and that his Julie Lippus had stolen nearly all of his belongings. Lucky for him, her boyfriend had been unable to access his stock brokerage account or Dean would have been wiped out.

At that time, he was still in love with her even after hearing what she'd done. When his father told him that his cheating, thieving, two-timing, scamming wife was killed, he was devastated. After all, he had only seen and experienced her good side. It would be weeks before he finally came to his senses and realized how lucky he'd been. He learned of other servicemen and members of their families who weren't so lucky and were murdered in cold blood. The last bit of information that cleansed his mind and heart of any feelings for her was when he learned her real name was Rebecca Lippert; that she had stolen the name Julie Lippus from a young girl who had died years earlier from leukemia. He wondered how the same woman who had lured him into marriage with apparently genuine feelings of love could be so cold as to steal an innocent dead girl's identity.

From that day forward, his heart went cold and he immersed himself in the art of making money from the stock market. It would now take a very special woman for Dean Gray to expose his heart to such torture again.

Something broke into his daydream. He couldn't place it, but he sat up and looked at the green and red colors on the screen. It looked like there may be another buying opportunity approaching on a stock that he'd been mapping for several weeks now. He rubbed his hands together as the red continued to dominate the stock's movement. It was near a month low despite indications that a series of new orders were imminent.

There it was again. It sounded like a knock at his apartment door. That was odd. He wasn't expecting anyone.

Dean hated to leave his computer screen as a buying opportunity approached so he waited, hoping whoever was at his door would simply go away. He was poised over the keyboard, planning to place a buy order of 5000 shares when the knock came again, this time louder and more persistent than before. Now completely distracted and annoyed, Dean pushed his office chair back and stood. Should he just continue to ignore the intrusion? Maybe there was a problem in the apartment complex. It could be a neighbor or a rescue worker warning the tenants of a danger.

He took one last look at his computer screen. The buying opportunity was still available but it would soon pass. *But there are others. I better see what the noise is all about.*

Making his was out of the office through the combined dining and living room to the front door, Dean stopped at a mirror to make sure he was minimally presentable. He rubbed his right hand over his hair, shrugged his shoulders as if to say, *What the heck?* As he did, the knock at the door returned, this time shaking the door on its hinges. Now Dean was perturbed. Unless the building was on fire, and he didn't smell any smoke, there was no good reason for the assault on his door.

His anger rising, Dean grabbed the door handle, quickly slipped off the safety chain and, without checking in the peep hole, yanked the door open wide.

He never saw the gun. All he saw was a middle-aged man's scruffy face before the deafening noise of the report briefly rang in his ears. After a split second, everything went black.

*** *

As Ace turned the corner into the entrance of the Arbor Arms Apartments in Norfolk, Virginia, he had a feeling of dread. This was the last place where he had seen his mother alive. He felt shame that he hadn't reacted and followed his mother in her unilateral assault on over half a dozen agents who were closing in on her daughter, Ace's half-sister. He'd watched from the safety of a car in the back of the parking lot as the entire drama unfolded. There were fewer than a dozen shots in all, but at least three were fatal. One killed Bobby Garrett, his mother's former lover, *the bastard*. Another had ripped through his sister's neck, severing her carotid artery, causing her to bleed to death while the NCIS agents stood around, watching her die.

The last bullet was the one that Ace felt he should have taken instead of his mother. He sat in the car, petrified with fear as his mother raced towards the apartment, firing at the NCIS agents until they returned fire and shot her dead. He knew as soon as she fell that the shot was fatal. It hit her in the center of the chest, knocking her straight backwards. When he saw her hit the ground, he climbed into the driver's seat and slowly drove off without even turning on the lights, even though it was in the dark hours before dawn.

Now, he approached the same parking lot, driving past the same parking spot where he and his mother had sat, waiting for Bobby Garrett and Becky Lippert to arrive and collect an insurance check. This time, it was in the middle of the day, just after lunch with a temperature in the mid-eighties. The parking lot for the complex had few trees but those were mature and had large canopies. They threw a good spread of shade. Ace hadn't noticed the large trees on his previous visit, mainly because it had been dark the entire time that he and his mother sat waiting in their rental car. Now he looked for an open spot to park within sixty feet of Dean Gray's apartment, but still in the shade. It didn't matter too much because Ace planned to be in Dean's apartment for only a short period of time. He would say that friends of his told him about Dean being a wizard in trading stocks and that for a small fee he was willing to teach others what he knew. Ace had done his homework. Dean was from Iowa and was trusting to a fault, though he was somewhat more reserved since his whole marriage fiasco. Stock trading was his weakness. If you started talking stocks, he lowered his defenses. *Like shooting fish in a barrel.*

Ace parked the car and lowered the windows to allow the shaded air to pass through. He'd need some air flow to help minimize the smell of cordite once he finished his business with Dean Gray. He pulled the small flip notebook from his pants pocket. It was worn from years of handling. Whenever he thought of his sister, he looked through the notebook at the names of the men that his mother, Abbie, had said had abused her. She made Ace promise her that he wouldn't let their deeds go unpunished. He was only fifteen years old when he assured Abbie Glover that, if she was unable to make the bastards pay, he would carry out her wishes.

He believed that he was on track to complete his mission when he killed Colonel Chester, but when his next three targets were killed right before his eyes, he felt cheated. There was nothing he could do now except move on to the next target on his list.

He opened the center console and pulled out his Glock 9mm, then pulled out the silencer and began to screw the tube into the barrel. He stopped.

Off in the distance, the faint sound of sirens drifted into the car. They were too far away to be a concern, so he finished attaching the silencer and began to check the gun. *Safety's off, round in the chamber. Ready to go.*

The multiple sirens grew louder. Ace began to get nervous and looked around the complex for any signs of a problem. He looked over at the common area in front of Dean Gray's apartment. A woman was standing there looking past Ace's car towards the entrance to the complex. Now the sirens were loud, seemingly around the corner.

It was too much of a coincidence. Ace steadily, but quickly, removed the silencer from the pistol and placed both in the center console. He started the engine and backed out of the space. Just as he reached the stop sign before the turn near the exit, two Norfolk Police cars raced into the parking lot with their lights on and their sirens blaring. They both flew past Ace. He breathed a sigh of relief. Then a third police car pulled in and stopped directly in front of Ace's car, blocking his exit. Ace froze. The officer driving the car exited with his gun drawn. He pointed it at Ace and told him to keep his hands where they could be seen.

Ace's mind raced. Should he try to draw his gun and fire? That was a fool's move. He'd be dead before he could open the lid to the console. He could step on the gas and try to run the cop over. Again, that would be too slow. Besides, the other officers would see him make his move and come to their fellow officer's aid. Ace figured his best move was to be still and try to explain his way out of the situation.

The woman who had been at the entry to Dean Gray's apartment shouted to the officer. With his windows opened, he heard her loud and clear.

"No, it's not him. It was an older man. He had on a security guard's uniform. He was driving an old pickup truck. I saw him leave just a few minutes before you got here."

After a few moments hesitation, the officer holstered his weapon and waved Ace around his car. Ace pulled out into traffic wondering what he had just witnessed. Who had worn a security guard's uniform and what had they done to merit such a speedy response from the Norfolk Police?

***

Two hours later in his hotel room, Ace learned that Dean Gray, former US Navy sailor was shot and killed in his apartment in an apparent robbery attempt. But he knew better. The only thievery going on was that someone was stealing his plan and denying him his chance to even the score.

The damn shooter.

Chapter 14

It had been a full week since the murders of General Wesley and retired Colonels Aims and Dempsey. The political rhetoric about a possible terrorist attack had died down. Apparently, members of congress realized they had nothing to gain if they persisted in making accusations of a terrorist plot. Word of the murders all but disappeared from the national news. Only the local television stations in St. Augustine and Jacksonville, Florida continued updates on the story. Even those became fewer and farther between.

Nancy Brown decided now was a good time for a two week vacation from the Anti-Terror Unit. Her boss agreed since there was little in the way of a genuine terror threat on the horizon.

Sitting on the front porch of William "Hatch" Hatcher's log cabin north of Moniac, Georgia, Nancy sipped at her long neck beer. She was relaxing, enjoying the view of the giant cypress trees with their long, flowing Spanish moss in the Okefenokee Swamp. It was an eerily beautiful sight, thin streams of sunlight pouring through the trees at a steep, late-morning angle. The temperature in the shade hit eighty-two degrees with the prospect of exceeding ninety by early afternoon.

She and Hatch sat in the hanging swing, leaning into each other and enjoying the sounds of the morning; crickets, bull frogs, a number of birds and their varied calls, and the occasional growl of an alligator. There was no traffic noise; no cars, buses, or horn-blaring trucks. The air wasn't pure, not with the ever present scent of vegetative decay and a slight odor of dead fish; but there was no engine exhaust and no stench from dumpsters that hadn't been emptied in nearly a week.

Virtually no invasion of humanity made it into the landscape that was Hatch's childhood home.

Nancy and Hatch hadn't seen each other in nearly two months, but they had made up for that last night.

As they sat relaxing, an alligator growled. The gator couldn't have been more than one hundred feet from the cabin. Nancy tensed. A chill raced up her spine, her skin instantly covered with rising goose-bumps.

"How can you stand to live here with the gators and snakes?"

Hatch again smiled at her. "I've lived here my whole life. I know most of them gators by name. Well, actually, I named 'em all. The gators and me have an understandin' that goes back a long ways. Now, the snakes still worry me at times. You have to be careful where you walk and where you sit. I usually check out the rafters on the porch when I walk out here in the mornin' cause they can climb. But the gators just want to eat fish and birds and lay in the sun. If you don't mess with 'em, they generally won't mess with you."

"Generally? That's encouraging." Nancy rubbed her arm hard, trying to get rid of the bumps. She always thought she'd fall for an Ivy League type, or a clean-cut Marine like Joe McKinney. While she had enjoyed working with Joe on the Lippert-Garrett case, she'd found him far too intense for her taste. His personality was too much like hers. To her surprise, she'd found William Hatcher much more to her liking. He grounded her with his humor and logical thinking. He was serious when needed, but at the same time charming and witty. She found that he was one of the brightest people she'd ever met. She figured it was a combination of his accent and his misuse of the English language.

When Nancy had first met Hatch she wasn't sure if it was an act or if he used his southern drawl for effect, to put people off guard. Now, she realized it was just his normal, easy going manner coupled with his lack of concern for what others thought about him. When Hatch cranked up the southern charm, he was just playing to the audience.

One thing was certain; she'd fallen for Hatch in a big way. It hadn't caused any conflict with her job yet, but at some point they would have to talk about their relationship. She worked at the Quantico Marine Corps Base and lived in Reston, Virginia. He lived in a swamp in the southeastern-most corner of Georgia. Would he ever consider moving to Washington, D.C.? Would she give up a job she loved, chasing terrorists; a job someone needed to do to protect the nation? So far, their arrangement was working, but the weeks and months between visits were lonely. Plus, Nancy's biological clock was ticking. She wasn't sure she wanted children and she didn't know if Hatch did or not. She knew about his family, though she hadn't heard the story from him. She wondered how the murder of his family would weigh on his decision to have a family of his own.

Nancy hadn't wanted to spoil their reunion with talk of murder and mayhem. But she knew by the look in his eyes that the time had come to get down to business and dig into the topic they both knew was the second reason for Nancy's visit.

She looked him in the eyes. "Go ahead. What's on your mind?"

He asked in his slow southern drawl, "I hate to talk shop, but are there any leads on the St. Augustine murders?"

"We sent an inquiry to the Air Force Academy and another to the Bureau of Personnel for the Air Force. We wanted to see where these men's careers crossed paths. It turns out they were all in the same academy graduating class. All of the official information we got back from Colorado Springs was routine. Names, grades, scholastic information, stuff like that. Nothing of consequence."

"What about the 'unofficial' stuff?"

Nancy grinned. "That's where things get interesting. We didn't get all of the information we requested, but the assistant to the Commander of the security squadron at the academy called me."

"And...?"

Nancy paused just to tease Hatch. "She spoke to me on the condition that she remain anonymous."

"And   ?"

"Well, if I tell you everything then she won't remain anonymous." She smiled. "Okay. This 'anonymous source' said the three men were not only in the same graduating class, they were roommates all the way through the academy."

Nancy sipped her beer. A tree limb snapped and fell into the swamp some two hundred feet away. She turned towards Hatch who was grinning at her attempt to get under his skin. He could wait her out for however long she wanted to play this game.

She took a deep breath and continued. "So, that was pretty interesting news, not astonishing, but interesting. What is astonishing is that they had another roommate."

"So what's so astonishing that a tree limb fallin' can distract you?" Hatch took a swig of his beer which was nearly empty.

Nancy turned and faced him directly. He had a look on his face, like he already knew the answer. "You already know."

"You mean that their other roommate was Milton Chester? I had no idea."

Nancy shook her head. "How did you know?"

In his best southern drawl Hatch said, "Just a wild guess."

***

The call from Nancy Brown surprised Detective Bill Banks. He hadn't heard from Joe McKinney or anyone else from the military for several days. Her news that the murders of Milton Chester and the three Air Force Officers in Florida were connected was an interesting new piece of the slowly evolving puzzle. Except for the fact that the men were roommates at the academy, their murders had little in common. Milton Chester had been gunned down at close range by a 9mm. The murders in Florida were by a high powered assault rifle.

Banks thought about the connection between the murders of the young military men along the Southeast. The same gun used in the murder of the Colonel Chester, Kevin Reardon, and the murders in the southeast. Now, though the new murders were linked to Milton Chester, was there a link between all the murders? It didn't seem likely. But the one thing that could tie them together was Milton Chester. He seemed to be the center link in this weak chain.

Then there was the information provided by Airman Goff, the big creampuff of a guy who'd been assigned to assist Nancy Brown and Joe McKinney while they were at Grand Forks Air Force Base. Goff had followed Detective Banks and Hansen when they left the base a few days before. What he told the detectives off base had been much more informative than what he'd been allowed to say during his scheduled interview.

Even though he was married, it turned out Colonel Milton Chester was quite the player. The trysts were supposed to be secret, but according to Goff, there were so many of them, and Grand Forks was such a small community, that the colonel and his 'dates' would run into base personnel with some regularity. The colonel would make some lame comment about the rendezvous being work related, but nobody believed him, especially when he was caught with young enlisted women. That was strictly against regulations.

The biggest revelation from Goff was about his last assistant, Major Shawnda Hull. When the colonel was found dead, she had a breakdown and was hospitalized for nearly two weeks. That's when the rumors started to fly. According to a couple of Goff's sources in the Air Force grapevine, Major Hull was pregnant and the only man she'd ever been with was one Colonel Milton Chester.

Chapter 15

The vision stayed clear in his mind, as if he was still over there in that godforsaken country. *I was only doing my job, for chrissake.*

The back room of the tan house was dark except for the narrow stream of light coming through the open window. The sun was high overhead and beat down on the packed dirt and sand that surrounded the small town for as far as the eyes could see. Outside, the temperature hovered around ninety-two degrees. The bright sunlight that surrounded the three-room hut shared by eleven family members made the sand radiate, the heat waves making the distant mountains wave like a picture on a giant flag in the breeze.

Sergeant David Wallace ordered most of the family who lived in the hut into in the main room, huddled on the floor, facing away from the back room. He and Private Perez, a young soldier from southern California were in the back room interrogating two members of the family; a young man, probably in his middle teens, and a girl who appeared to be about ten.

Wallace and Perez were in full desert BDUs, the battle dress uniform with light brown, tan, and black patterns designed to help the soldier blend in with the desert sand. They carried minimal gear since they were close to their base, but even with only a water thermos, extra clips for their weapons, goggles, and a knife or two, the extra weight was a constant drag on their energy, especially in the desert heat. To the young Iraqis, they looked like giants.

The girl was tiny, frail-looking to the point that she appeared to be malnourished. Her hair was a dark chestnut, her skin dark tan. She sat on the floor to the left of Sergeant Wallace with her legs drawn to her chest, nervously rocking back and forth, whimpering, looking down at her feet. Tears tracked down her face, though she was too frightened to cry out loud. The constant movement and whining grated on the two soldiers' nerves.

Her brother stood tall and defiant. His features were similar to his younger sister's though more rugged. With square shoulders on a slim frame, his muscle tone was refined as if he'd been working out. Even barefoot, he stood nearly as tall as Sergeant Wallace and several inches taller than Perez. A scar graced his right cheek, possibly from a knife. His hands also had numerous scars and calluses. Wallace thought he may have been sixteen, but no older. The teen stared straight into the eyes of the soldier, the leader of the platoon that had taken over his family's home.

That was alright with David Wallace. He hoped the kid would try something stupid. It would give him all the excuse he needed to use the M-16 he held across his chest to put a bullet in the kid's head.

Sergeant Wallace's job had been to gather intelligence from the local villagers about any insurgent activity in the small town northwest of Najaf. His orders were to make friends with the villagers, to work closely with them and bribe them with food, water, and the local currency, if that's what it took to get their cooperation. That, according to his command, would gain their trust and confidence. They would be willing to open up and turn in those invaders who were taking over their country and forcing them to convert to their strict Islamic doctrine, Shari'ah law. The military command, backed by intelligence reports from the government of the United States, assured the commanders in the field that the people of Iraq would be happy to help them find these insurgents and drive them from their country.

David Wallace hadn't believed a word of their propaganda. He had planned to get the information his way. Private Perez was his interpreter. Without taking his eyes off the teen he told Perez, "Ask Haji here if there's any al-Qaeda in the village."

Perez relayed the question in his best Iraqi Aravic, which was passable, and waited for a response. The kid just stared at Wallace, his eyes steady, unblinking.

Without taking his eyes off of the youth, he nodded and motioned with his hand, telling Perez to ask the question again. He did. It netted the same results.

"Ask him his name."

Perez did. Nothing. Just the same steady, cold stare.

Sergeant Wallace took a deep breath, then a slow, purposeful step closer to the young man. The M-16 across his chest was so close to the young man that he could have leaned forward and touched the youth with it. Their eyes were nearly on the same level, locked on each other, searching for some advantage, some way to show who was the more macho as the standoff continued. Wallace felt the young man's breath, a sour odor; the breath of one who had never brushed. Tiny beads of sweat were visible on the bridge of the young man's nose and forehead, but he still had not changed his expression, his steel eyes still steady.

Wallace's M-16 was pointed downward in the general direction of the little girl. He purposely tensed his muscles, his left hand on the top of the barrel of the weapon, his right hand on the pistol grip, trigger finger outside the trigger guard. In a quick, nervous like motion, his finger moved inside the guard and now rested on the trigger.

The move was not lost on the young Iraqi. His pupils grew larger, his eyes opened just the slightest bit, but they did not stray. His arms remained at his side with his fists clenched.

Wallace thought for a moment about how to gain the upper hand. His lips curled almost imperceptibly. He said to Perez, "Ask him his sister's name."

Perez hesitated, then, in a loud voice, asked the question. They waited, but there was no response from the young man.

From the front room, family members of the two youths must have heard Perez's question. They began to protest, though Wallace couldn't understand what they were saying.

Finally, he was getting a response, just not from the kid. He dared not smile outwardly. That would have ruined the advantage he had just established.

"Tell him I will kill the girl if he doesn't answer my questions."

Wallace noticed Perez's disbelieving look.

Wallace said, "Do it now!"

Perez replied, "Sarge, you can't be serious."

Without hesitation, David Wallace pulled the trigger on his M-16 and fired a round. The report was deafening in the small room. The girl shrieked and rolled over onto her side. The round hit the dirt floor of the room sending bits of hardened sand into the air. The weapon emitted smoke and the unmistakable odor of burned powder.

Startled, Perez jumped back and away from his sergeant and the young man. "What the..."

Two soldiers from the front room ran into the back to see what had happened. As they entered the room, the young man jumped at Wallace, grabbing at the M-16, trying to move the barrel away from his sister. Wallace squeezed the trigger again. The teen pushed on the gun and forced Wallace back. The sergeant went down, falling on his back, his gun still against his chest.

Perez and the two soldiers in the doorway raised their weapons at the young man. Seeing the hopelessness in his actions, he stopped and raised his arms in the universal sign of surrender. The three soldiers kept their weapons trained on the young man.

From his back, Sergeant Wallace aimed his weapon at the Iraqi boy and pulled the trigger. The round that struck the center of the young man's chest propelled his body into the wall. His head and shoulders hit hard against the wall, then he fell, face first into the center of the room. His head was just inches from the bottom of Sergeant Wallace's boots. Wallace lowered his smoking weapon to his chest and took a deep breath, then smiled.

He stood and looked around the room. The little girl no longer whimpered, a slowly expanding pool of red visible under her motionless body.

***

David Wallace signaled the bartender for another shot of *Jack Daniels Black Label* and a beer chaser. He'd already told his story to two people this evening, but they weren't interested in his whining about how the Army was screwing him over. *All I was trying to do was what I was ordered, gather intelligence. Who cares if a couple of stinkin' rag hats got killed? He sided with the insurgents. It was obvious. That the little girl was killed, well, she was collateral damage. He shouldn't have grabbed for my weapon.*

The story sounded plausible, except for the fact that his platoon wouldn't back him up. They'd warned their CO that Sergeant Wallace was a 'loose cannon' ever since he'd come back to Iraq from the states. That was when he'd learned his father had been murdered, his mother died from a stroke, and his 'wife' had left him, all in the same week. A series of events like that would take its toll on any man, but it had sent David Wallace over the edge. He taunted the villagers, trying to provoke them with insults to their country, their village, even their family. He called the women whores in front of their husbands and sons, accusing them of all kinds of vile behavior.

On more than one occasion the men had lunged at the sergeant trying to get their hands on him. It was only a matter of time before he did or said something to get himself or one of the platoon killed for no good reason. When it finally happened, none of the men stood up for him.

Now he was back in Columbia, South Carolina at Fort Jackson awaiting his fate. He wasn't confined to base, but his movements were restricted. He had to report to the duty officer twice daily, once at 0900 hours and again at 1600 hours, even on days when he didn't have duty.

Mirrors Lounge, where he sat at the bar nursing his ego and fueling his private pity party, was just outside Fort Jackson on Percival Road. It was just past 2230 hours and the bar traffic was slim with just twelve patrons, most of them active duty Army. All of them, except Wallace, sat at tables. It was a diverse mix of three women and nine men. Two of the soldiers were black, one man and one woman. Another of the men was Hispanic.

Glancing at the mirror behind the bar, Wallace noted one man sitting alone at a table about twenty feet away in a position that afforded him a view of the entire bar. The man appeared to be looking in his direction; that irritated Wallace. He picked up his shot glass, raised it in a mock salute to the man in the mirror and downed it. He followed the whiskey with a long pull on a *Budweiser* long neck.

The man at the table stood and approached the bar. "Mind if I join you?"

"Free country. Suit yourself."

The man gestured to the bartender to set up another round.

He turned to Wallace. "Name's Trent."

"Dave Wallace."

When the bartender left the two men alone, the man raised his shot glass towards Wallace and said, "Dave, here's to killin' raghats. I heard you talking about your troubles in Iraq. Man, are they screwing you or what?"

Wallace turned to the man who had a few days growth of beard. His face looked sallow and wrinkled. He looked about fifty-five, but may have been younger. Wallace couldn't say. Regardless of his age, it appeared the man had been through some rough times. He raised his glass, and said with a smirk, "I'll drink to that."

They sat at the bar for another forty-five minutes, doing Boilermakers and talking about war, the hardships of being a soldier, and how people stab you in the back when the going gets tough. Trent told his own tales about two tours in Iraq in the early days of Desert Storm and how he'd personally killed dozens of those 'Iraqi bastards.' It didn't matter to him if they were fighting men, old men, women, or children. They were all terrorists as far as he was concerned. When Wallace asked him where in Iraq he'd served, Trent could only name Baghdad. As Trent carried on with his account of his tours of duty, Wallace started to doubt that Trent had ever been in the country. He played along because Trent kept buying the rounds. What did he care if this guy was a fraud?

Then Trent said, "Hey, I know a great place to get the best wings and pizza in the south. It's just about a ten minute drive. You game? I'm buyin'."

Sergeant Wallace checked his watch. It was just before midnight. He had to check in by 0900 hours the next morning, but he didn't have duty. All he had to do was check in wearing the uniform of the day then head back to the barracks. He could hit the rack and catch up on his sleep then.

In a voice slurred from too much alcohol he said, "Sure. I'm game. I just got to take a leak."

"Okay. I'll drive. I'm parked at the far end of the lot. Go out the back exit here and head straight to my truck. I'll be waiting."

Wallace finished in the restroom, then headed out into the dimly lit parking lot. He spotted the pickup truck at the edge of the lot. When he got to it, he tried the passenger door but it was locked. No one was inside.

He yelled, "Hey, Trent, where are you?"

From the wooded area beyond the parking lot a voice said, "I'm over here, man. I think I hurt myself."

David Wallace was pissed. He didn't even know this guy, but he was on his side in this whole court martial thing and he had bought the drinks over the last couple of hours. The least he could do was help this guy out.

"Okay, man, I'll be right there. Keep talking so I can find you."

He staggered into the woods, pushing branches aside, feeling the cob webs across his face.

"Over here, man."

"Okay, okay. I'm almost there."

A flashlight came on, pointed directly into his eyes. David raised his hands as a shield so he could see Trent. Why was he shining that light in his face?

Then Trent said, "This is for Rebecca."

"Get that flashlight out of my eyes. And who the hell is Rebecca?"

"She was my stepdaughter. You knew her better as Charlene."

A loud report and bright flash erupted before his eyes. A vision of a naked Charlene flashed in his mind just before he lost consciousness for the last time.

Chapter 16

Finding Wallace's whereabouts was easier than Ace expected. He called Fort Jackson's general number and said he was looking for his brother-in-law, Sergeant David Wallace, who had just returned from a tour of duty in Iraq. After being transferred from operator to operator for several minutes, he was finally connected to the Personnel Support Office. The young male clerk asked a few questions about the nature of his inquiry to which Ace replied his brother-in-law had called saying that if he was in the area to look him up and they'd get together. Without further questions, the clerk gave him Wallace's quarters' address and phone number.

Around 11:30 PM, he dialed the number for Wallace's quarters. On the fourth ring, Ace was about to hang up when a man with a gravelly, sleepy voice answered.

"Hello?"

Ace hesitated slightly, then said, "Dave Wallace?"

"No, Dave's gone out."

"I was supposed to meet him for a drink. Any idea where he went?"

"Yeah. Same place he's been going every night; *Mirrors Lounge*. Hey, when you see him, tell that ass-wipe to try and not get too smashed tonight. I have duty at 0600 hours and I don't want to be kept awake listening to his sob stories all frickin' night."

Ace smiled. If all went well, no one would have to listen to David Wallace ever again.

***

It was less than a ten minute drive from Ace's room at the *Econo Lodge* to *Mirrors Lounge* on Percival Road.

Ace parked in the lot near the road so he could exit onto Percival Road quickly. He tucked his Glock 9mm into the waistband at the small of his back and pulled the light-weight wind breaker down so the gun was out of sight.

He saw half a dozen vehicles in the dimly lit parking lot, most between four and eight years old, only one from an American manufacturer. The rest were foreign jobs, Toyota, Mitsubishi, or Honda. He didn't waste time trying to figure out what kind of car Wallace was driving. An old beat-up pickup truck parked at the back of the lot in the shadow of the interstate caught his eye, mostly because it was so out of place parked away from the other cars. As he walked to the entrance, he noticed a man walking away from the building, heading in the direction of the pickup. He was alone and pretty steady on his feet. *Must not have been in there too long.*

As Ace approached the front door, a couple walked out, arm-in-arm, smiling at each other, talking about heading back to his place to watch a movie. He paid them no mind and continued into the bar.

Once inside the door, Ace took note of every individual in the single room bar. Even though none of the patrons were in uniform, it was easy to see most folks in the bar were off-duty soldiers. The jukebox played a song by *Brian Purcer and the Hot Licks*. It wasn't turned up as loud as he'd heard it played at other bars, which suited Ace just fine. He needed to concentrate on the task at hand.

The lighting was low. Most of the illumination came from the fluorescent bulbs that were the backdrop for the bottles of booze lined up on a glass shelf behind the bar. The mirror that ran behind the liquor helped distribute the limited lighting throughout the room, picking up the hue of the colors of the booze bottles or the booze itself. Even with the limited lighting, it was easy to see that David Wallace was not seated at the bar or at any of the tables.

To the right of the bar, Ace noticed a hallway above which was a restroom sign and an exit sign. In the subdued lighting he couldn't see much beyond the opening.

It was just turning midnight. Maybe Ace had missed him altogether and Wallace had gone to another bar, or even headed back to the base. Ace figured it wouldn't hurt to sit and have a beer. If his target was in the restroom he would most likely be back any minute. Or Wallace could have gone to another joint first and would end up here before closing time. He walked up to the bar and hopped on a stool.

A deep voice with a strong southern accent asked, "What can I get ya?"

Ace was startled by the bartender as his gaze was still on the hallway to the restroom. He turned to face the man. He was about five-foot-eight, with a buzz cut showing just stubbles of gray hair. He had large, highly tattooed biceps and a beer gut that put a serious strain on his *Mirrors Lounge* tee shirt. His tattoos were a mixture of patriotic slogans, American Flags, and naked women, all of which were old and fading to a pale blue.

Ace said, "Bottle of *Bud*."

In a flash, the bartender opened a cooler just under the bar, pulled out a *Bud*, twisted the top off and put it on the bar. "Want to run a tab?"

"Nah. What do I owe ya?"

"Buck an' a half."

Ace threw a couple one dollar bills on the bar and waved off the change. He took a long pull from the beer, then set the bottle back down on the polished wood of the bar. He turned his attention back to the hallway entrance.

The bartender asked, "You waitin' fer somebody? I noticed ya lookin' 'round."

Ace wondered if describing David Wallace to the bartender might be a bad idea. Then he thought, *What could it hurt?*

"Yeah. I was hoping to meet a friend here. Guy's name is Dave. Dave Wallace. He's a good sized guy, Sergeant in the Army, has sort of a surly disposition at times."

"Is this guy about six foot even, stocky, big chest, and just got back from a tour in Iraq?"

"Sounds like him." Taking a page from Wallace's roommate, Ace said, "He's been complaining about being railroaded on some charge. Seems to want to tell everybody about it. I just want to calm him down, get him to shut his mouth before he gets himself in deeper shit."

"Yep, that's yer boy. He's been cryin' to anyone who sits anywhere near him. He bends their ear 'til they get tired of it. He was in here 'bout five minutes ago. Left with some homeless lookin' guy. They was talkin' 'bout getting' some food, wings I think."

Ace cursed, then thought about the guy walking towards the pickup truck. "Did you notice if they left by the side door?"

"I didn't take notice. I was in the back cleanin' some glasses when they left. Like I said, it weren't but 'bout five minutes ago. The guy yer' talkin' 'bout's been in here ever' night fer the last two weeks. He's havin' himself one heck of a pity party. I don't necessarily disagree with him. Hell, them raghats would kill all of us if they had the chance, but when a guy whines like this guy, he's pretty much pleadin' guilty, if ya' ask me."

Ace took another long hit on his beer. "Did they say where they were headed?"

"Not that I heard. There's only a couple wing joints 'round here though. One of 'ems down the road on Fort Jackson Boulevard, the other's in a plaza 'bout ten mile from here."

Ace emptied his beer and thanked the bartender, then headed for the door. As he left, the pickup truck sped past him, kicking up gravel. The truck was misfiring some but picked up speed as it hit Percival Road. It backfired once, causing Ace to jump.

Under his breath, he said, "Damn. Get that thing tuned up, would you?"

***

After an hour of searching for Wallace in the two wing joints and one other bar to the north, Ace decided to head back to the *Econo Lodge*. As he got onto Interstate 77 on Exit 15 heading south, he noticed a large number of flashing lights just off the highway. As he got closer, he counted at least a half dozen police cars and a rescue vehicle. He almost ran onto the shoulder when the rumble from the warning grooves got his attention to get back into his lane. He wondered about the cause of all the commotion. As his car passed, the flashers reflecting off his face, he noticed the action was in the parking lot of *Mirrors Lounge.*

Maybe there was a fight. But that's a lot of police for a barroom fight. Hell, there weren't that many people in the bar when I left.

Ace opened the center counsel, saw his Glock 9mm, silencer removed, and closed the compartment again. It was time to get back to his room. He wouldn't find that bastard this evening. Maybe tomorrow would net better results.

***

The problem with waiting was that too many things can happen while you sit around and decide what to do next. Indecision, procrastination, inaction, all had cost Ace the opportunity to square up the score in St. Augustine, Florida and Norfolk, Virginia.

The slight, musty odor in his hotel room was screwing up his sinuses. His eyes were watery and his nose was starting to run. He blew his nose as he flipped through the channels on the TV. He had a bad feeling and it wasn't because he was catching a cold. He found a channel with late night news. After watching for less than five minutes, there they were, the flashing lights in the background, a news reporter, a young man with a microphone, pointing over his shoulder at a wooded area near the interstate.

That's right, Wilma. The body of a US Army sergeant was found this evening around 1:30 AM by a bar patron whose headlights flashed on what he thought was a dead animal as he pulled into the parking lot. He went to inspect with a flashlight and found the soldier, dead from several gunshot wounds. The name of the soldier is being withheld pending notification of next of kin.

Ken, do the police have any suspects, motive, or evidence at this time?

If they do, Wilma, they're keeping that to themselves. We'll follow this story and pass along information as we receive it. Reporting live from Mirrors Lounge parking lot, I'm...

Ace turned the TV off. He knew the dead soldier's name. David Wallace. As he'd watched the reporter, his anger had grown. He picked up his gun and pointed it at the TV set, finger on the trigger, adrenaline coursing through his veins, wanting to blast the TV into oblivion. He got a grip and calmed himself, realizing it would only bring him unnecessary attention.

With the safety back on his Glock and his tension under control, he thought, *Who could have known about my plans, that I was going to take these guys out and in what order? It was only written down once, and that was back in Savannah in my locked room. No one was ever in that room except me. Unless . . .*

The thought hit him like a lightning bolt. Angelina Valentine, his former landlord, had some electrical work done after a utility worker came by and said they'd had a power surge in the area of her home. They needed to do a home inspection. He hadn't been home at the time and thought it was bogus. But it was Angelina's house. Besides, by the time he was home, the deed was already done. The man had been in his room. *He couldn't have seen those plans...could he?*

Chapter 17

The phone call from Nancy Brown of the Marine Corp's Anti-Terror Unit took Major Maurice Alexander by surprise. He had instructed his aid to direct all such calls to the Base Commander's office, but Brown had insisted on speaking with the Major. The conversation made him less than comfortable.

"I'm sorry, Ms. Brown, but all inquiries relative to the murders of Wesley, Dempsey, and Aims will be handled by the base Commander's office. I don't have any information for you," He wished that he could hear what Nancy Brown had to say, but officially, he couldn't get involved in the matter. He'd been given a direct order by the commanding officer at the academy that he was to take no action on the inquiry from the Anti-Terror Unit. He did, however, have a question for Nancy Brown.

"Ms. Brown, why is the Anti-Terror Unit and the police department of Grand Forks, North Dakota, interested in the murder of three Air Force Officers, two of whom were retired?"

"Well, Major, I could tell you, but I'd be aiding and abetting in your violation of a lawful order." She paused a moment, then continued. "What if we were to keep this conversation and any future conversations to ourselves? Could we come to a mutual understanding? You wouldn't have to act on the information unless you were given the go ahead to conduct your own investigation. If you learned something that would help in apprehending the killers, you could come forward at the right time and earn a few points with the base commander."

If he was caught violating a direct order, he could be court-martialed. It most likely wouldn't come to that, but why take the chance? He was on the fast track to lieutenant colonel and would most likely get a cherry assignment for his next transfer. But the thought there might be something significant coming out of a major murder investigation intrigued him. Besides, the colonel had given him a directive that basically said 'Do not do your job.' That had to be a violation of some kind. If the investigation were a simple job, then his office could have handled the details in no time. There had to be something big that was being kept under the radar. Now, he cursed himself for shredding the file.

"Alright, Ms. Brown…"

"Nancy. Call me Nancy, please."

Alexander smiled. "And you can call me Moe." There was a moment of silence. "So, Nancy, why the interest?"

"First, you and I have to agree this is just between the two of us for the time being. We'll reveal all of the pertinent details to others with a 'need to know' when the time is right. Agreed?"

He had a lot more to lose at this point in his career than Nancy Brown, but he wanted to know the big secret the commander was keeping. "Agreed."

"The Anti-Terror Unit isn't interested in this case as much as I am personally." This revelation surprised Alexander. Nancy continued, "I don't mean I have a personal stake in the matter, just that I was in NCIS when a series of murders took place near military bases in Virginia, North Carolina, Georgia, and North Dakota a few years ago. I was the lead investigator on a parallel case."

"So what does the murder of these men have to do with the murders two years ago?"

"It's a long story. Better sit back and relax."

Nancy told him the story of Bobby Garrett and Rebecca Lippert, two scam artists who had taken a bunch of young military men, a multi-million dollar insurance company, and the United States government for a long, expensive ride. She went into some detail about her and Joe McKinney's involvement and how they chased the duo over half the country.

When the story appeared to end with the death of Bobby and Rebecca, he asked, "I still don't get the connection. So these two are killed and the scam and the murders come to an end. What am I missing?"

"As one famous radio announcer would say, 'And now the rest of the story.' One other person was killed that morning at the apartment complex. Her name was Abbie Glover. We're trying to figure out what role Abbie Glover played in this whole scam, but whatever it was, she charged our apprehension team when we tried to arrest Bobby and Rebecca. She was gunned down as she ran at the team."

"This is all very interesting, but we're still missing the connection to the three murdered officers," Moe said.

"I'm about to get to that. Abbie Glover had a son, Ace. We don't know for sure if that's his real name or a nickname, but he's about twenty years old, blond hair, and a real charmer. He was apparently at the scene the morning his mother was killed, but he was able to slip away without being seen. He made the trip from Virginia to North Dakota in three days and somehow convinced Colonel Milton Chester to meet him at an abandoned missile silo."

Alexander said, more to himself, than Nancy, "What could a twenty year old kid use to convince a full bird to meet him alone at a remote location? It had to be something big."

"We don't know yet, but we're closing in on some possibilities. That was one reason that we sent the inquiry. We were hoping to find some connection between the murders of Milton Chester and the three officers."

Moe glanced up as his assistant, Asiamarie Vance, walked into the office and laid a brand new manila folder on the desk in front of him. She flipped the folder open, exposing the stack of forms inside. They were bright white and in pristine condition. He touched the first sheet in the stack, still warm from the copier. His assistant turned and left the room, closing the door behind her.

Major Alexander looked down at the top page in the folder. It was the first page of the inquiry from the Marine

Corps Anti Terror Unit, the same one he had shredded the previous day. The folder was thicker than the original inquiry.

The silence on the line lingered so long that Nancy asked, "Moe, you still there?"

"Uh, yeah Nancy. I just received some new information. I need to look it over, then I'll call you back."

"Okay."

***

By the time Airman Goff had finished talking, Detective Banks wanted to buy Goff dinner and a case of beer. The airman had responded he couldn't take any gratuities, that he'd done it because he had to get it off his chest. According to Goff, it wasn't right that the Air Force brass was putting a gag order on its people. There was no explanation why, just that it was in the best interests of the Air Force. Goff told Banks and Hansen that it sounded more like it was in the best interests of covering somebody's behind.

The detectives went back to the police station to write up their notes on the interview with Goff, being careful to leave the Airman's name off the official report. No sense getting the kid in trouble for doing the right thing.

They had barely asked the tall, slightly chunky airman a single question when he dove into a monologue about the strange goings on at the base.

"For one, Colonel Chester was wound tighter than a fiddle string when he left the base the day he was killed. I was just walking past his assistant's office when he growled something at Major Hull about having business off base and that he wouldn't be back until morning. When Major Hull asked about his appointment that was scheduled in less than twenty minutes he more or less shouted at her to cancel it. He stomped out of the office and nearly ran me down. I said, 'Pardon me, sir.' He just sneered at me and kept going. He was in a real hurry, that's for sure."

Banks asked if he saw the colonel after that and Goff said no, then he continued his long spiel. "After the colonel turned the corner I looked in on Major Hull. She looked worried, almost in tears. I asked her if she was alright and she said yes, but I could tell, she really wasn't. She was white as a sheet. The colonel shouldn't have snapped at her like that, especially in her condition. I mean, she was already emotionally wired."

Banks and Hansen looked at each other. Hansen shrugged.

Goff continued, "I didn't know if she was taking the colonel's comment personally or if it was something else. She was always so steady, I mean, no emotion, almost like a machine. Then for the last month or so before the murder, she was a wreck. It's like her entire personality changed. Even her eating habits changed. I know because I always did the meal runs for the colonel and the major, well, and half the staff at HQ."

"Was Major Hull seeing anyone? We know from the background information we received from the base she wasn't married, but did she have a boyfriend, fiancé, or anyone significant in her life?"

Goff hesitated. Then he looked directly at Detective Banks. "No, sir…but she did have a fling with the colonel."

***

Banks' phone rang. He reached for the phone and tipped his coffee cup over. Luckily, it had just a little cold brew left in the bottom. He tossed a handful of paper towels over the spill and reached for the phone, retrieving it at the beginning of the fifth ring.

"Grand Forks PD, Banks."

"Hello Bill. How are things going in Grand Forks?" Nancy Brown said.

Banks smiled. He'd been about to call her with the different bits of information from Airman Goff. He hoped she had something for him in return. "Hi, Nancy. To what do I owe the pleasure?"

"Well, I have some information for you. Colonel Chester, General Wesley, Colonel Aims, and Colonel

Dempsey were roommates at the Air Force Academy. Apparently, they were tight back then."

Banks' smile broadened. "That's very interesting. They apparently stayed close throughout their careers."

There was a pause on the line, as Banks wondered why they had been murdered. It couldn't be a coincidence. It had to be the same killer or killers. Though why the difference in the murders? Colonel Chester had been killed at close range with a handgun in a very personal, sadistic way. He'd been shot several times with the obvious intent to maim and inflict pain. The others had been killed with single, accurate shots from a concealed location.

Banks broke the silence. "Did you know that Colonel Chester's assistant was transferred? She was given an assignment at the Air Force Academy. She wasn't married and it's rumored that the only guy she ever went out with was Colonel Chester. And we think she was pregnant."

There was a pause as Banks allowed Nancy time to process this information.

Nancy asked, "Have you contacted her at her new command?"

"Not yet. We tried to reach her, but she wasn't available. When we asked when she might be available, they were non-committal. Either they have a large number of personnel or they were stalling. Any chance you could use your connections in DC and track her down?"

"Let me do some checking. Maybe I can pull a few strings."

Chapter 18

As soon as Wilson Brush emerged from the missile deck hatch of the USS *Nevada*, he knew he was in for a scorcher of a day. After being under the ocean for over four weeks in the controlled environment of the great ballistic missile submarine, stepping into the hot, humid conditions of southeast Georgia was breath snatching. He hadn't realized just how oppressive the heat would be, especially on the black deck of the submarine. It was as if the black paint absorbed the sunlight and converted it instantly to intense, radiant heat. His pores oozed within a few steps of the gangway.

An Instrumentation Technician in Engineering, Wilson felt lucky to be getting off the ship so quickly. Usually, the Nukes were the last personnel to get liberty.

Wilson looked out at the pier and saw his friend, Doug Farrell, standing among the wives waiting for their husbands, mostly crew members from the forward part of the ship.

Doug had also been on the USS *Nevada,* up until his discharge from the Navy just three months earlier. He'd been looking forward to moving to Florida near his parents and starting his job search there, but his parents were killed in a car accident on Interstate 4 near downtown Orlando just two weeks before his discharge. Doug's life and plans were on hold until his parent's estate was settled.

"Hey, Doug, how're you holding up?" Wilson stuck out his hand, then put his free arm around Doug's broad shoulder. They embraced briefly.

When they stepped back, still shaking hands, Doug said, "Hey, Wilson. I'm hanging in there. I'm kinda getting over the shock. It's helping to keep busy with the estate stuff."

Wilson's face tightened. "It has to be rough. I don't know what I'd do…."

Doug's smiled looked forced, "Let's not talk about it for now, okay?" Wilson smiled and nodded. Doug continued, "How about we head to that new wing place in Kingsland?"

Wilson had been thinking about where he'd like to go when he got off the ship. He'd decided he needed to go to a certain bar near the base; Tommy's where he'd met Tanya Walters, aka Rebecca Lippert.

The first time he'd laid eyes on her, she'd been sitting at a booth in Tommy's, alone, looking as if she was waiting for a friend. In reality, she'd been waiting to find a gullible sailor so she could get her hooks into him. That sailor had turned out to be Wilson Brush. When she was finished with him, he was broke and broken hearted. In the end, even knowing what she'd done to him, he was still in love with the young woman. He was able to put his feelings aside long enough to help NCIS bring her and her boyfriend down. Now he wanted to put the whole episode behind him, once and for all. That, he believed, would require a visit to the place where it all started.

Wilson looked his friend in the eyes. "I want to go to Tommy's."

Doug's entire six–foot-six-inch tall, muscled frame sagged. Several seconds passed before he spoke. When he did, he sounded incredulous.

"Wilson, you're my best friend in the world and I'll go along with whatever you decide. But why, why, why do you want to go to that place? Nothing good can come from it."

Wilson forced a smile, then took a deep breath. "I have to. I need to know I'm really over her. When we get there, we'll have a shot and a beer, then we can get out of there. So, I know when we leave that place, I'll be able to move on with my life."

Doug shook his head. "Okay, man, your call. One shot, one beer and we're done. But don't even look at any women while we're there. That place is bad luck for you."

He smiled. Wilson shrugged.

***

They walked into Tommy's and had their boilermakers. There were just a handful of people in the bar at 2:30 in the afternoon, and only one was a woman. She was the wife of a Masterchief Machinist Mate from one of the other ships. She held a lit cigarette the entire time they were in the bar, causing a haze to hang in the air, and she spoke with a low, heavy smokers voice.

The visit to Tommy's was exactly what Wilson needed. The place now had an entirely different atmosphere than when he'd met Rebecca Lippert and gone star-struck. There was no magic in the air. On the contrary, Wilson felt out of place. He was happy to leave the bar and head with Doug to the new wings and sports restaurant in Kingsland.

**

Once the afternoon was finished, Doug dropped Wilson off at his new apartment. He'd moved away from the one that he and his 'bride' had shared for just a few weeks. The place held too many bad memories. After Rebecca's death, he always felt like she was there in the apartment watching him. It was a creepy feeling, one that he couldn't shake. He lost hours of sleep, fearing she would somehow reappear and crawl into bed with him.

Once, he'd awoken with a start. He'd had a dream that felt so real that he'd thought Rebecca had curled up beside him, massaging his hard erection. When he awoke, he'd found that he'd ejaculated in his sleep. He never spent another night in the apartment and he never had another dream about her again.

Wilson opened the door to his apartment, then picked up the stack of mail lying on the floor under the mail slot. Tired, and a bit buzzed from drinking most of the afternoon, he figured most of the stack was probably junk mail. He made a circuit of the apartment, checking that no one had broken in since his departure on the USS *Nevada*. Everything looked as it had when he left so he set his alarm clock, stripped off his clothes, and went to bed naked. It was only 8:45 PM. But he had to report to the ship early the next morning so he wanted to get a good night's sleep.

The harsh sound of the alarm roused Wilson at 4:00 AM. It took him a moment to realize he was in his own apartment, in his own bed. He'd had a dream he was back in

East Liverpool, Ohio, with his father, fishing on the Ohio River. He rarely remembered his dreams, but this one remained in his consciousness even after he awoke. He smiled and decided he needed to call his dad and let him know that he was okay...no...better than okay. He was finally over Tanya and ready to get on with his life.

He showered, dressed, and fixed a pot of coffee. While he waited for the pot to finish brewing, he leafed through his mail. Most of it was junk. Some were bills, but most of those were just statements since he had automatic withdrawal to ensure his utilities and rent were paid while he was out to sea. One postcard encouraged him to take control of his future and open an electronic investment account. He smiled. *With what, my good looks?*

Then he came to an envelope with no return address that had his apartment address handwritten in black ink. The thick envelope was a standard business size. Wilson frowned as he flipped it over in his hands. He grabbed the flap and ripped it open, grabbing the contents, then dropping the envelope on the kitchen counter.

The coffee maker made a spurting sound. Coffee was almost ready. Setting the contents of the package aside, he pulled a mug from the cupboard and filled it. He settled on a barstool and picked up the contents of the envelope again. There was a standard letter size paper with a short handwritten note, and several clippings from a newspaper stapled together at one corner. He carefully unfolded the newspaper clippings and read the headlines. "Three Dead in Early Morning Apartment Shootout."

With no small amount of dread, he read the newspaper account of the shootout that occurred two years ago outside Dean Gray's apartment. Wilson remembered that morning all too well. He was there with the apprehension team when his wife, Rebecca aka Tanya, her boyfriend, Bobby Garrett, and Rebecca's mother, Abbie Glover were killed. He shook his head. *Rebecca Lippert.* He said it over and over again to remind himself she was a con artist, a scammer. She'd scammed him and many other young men. He'd thought he was through with his feelings for her, but someone had played a cruel trick on him, sending him this story, ripping his heart from his chest yet again.

The handwritten note brought him back to reality. It read, 'You can't just walk away. You're going to pay, just as Becky did, with your life.'

Wilson set the note down on the counter alongside the article and took a deep breath. He was tired of feeling blue, of blaming himself for what the woman had done to him. *No more. I'm through being a victim. Come and get me if you think you can. Coward.*

Chapter 19

The scent of fresh brewed coffee and banana bread filled the Grand Forks Police Department. A newly hired patrolman's wife had baked the bread and sent it in with her husband. The office received fresh baked goods two or three times a week ever since the kid was hired. The entire loaf was already devoured, leaving a bare plate and crumbs. William Banks had gotten his slice as soon as the plate hit the table by the coffee pot. He had a call to make and he knew the loaf would be gone if he didn't stake his claim early.

The call was a long shot at best, but he figured he had nothing to lose, so he sat forward in his office chair, dialed the number, and waited. He fully expected to get a piercing tone in his ear that the number had been disconnected. So when a stately female voice answered after the fourth ring and said, 'Vivian Moore,' he was taken a bit by surprise. He paused a moment to form his reply.

"Ms. Moore?"

"Yes."

"I'm sorry. I was trying to reach a Mrs. Chester."

Silence followed. Banks was afraid he'd dialed the wrong number and that Vivian Moore, whoever she was, had disconnected the call. He waited and thought he heard breathing on the line.

Finally, Ms. Moore spoke. "Who are you?"

Banks snapped out of his momentary funk. "My name is William Banks. I'm a detective with the Grand Forks Police Department. I'm trying to locate Mrs. Vivian Chester."

"Well, hello Detective. I never thought that I'd hear from you people again."

The woman's voice exuded confidence. He pictured her as being in her late forties, with hair colored to a mature, dark blonde. He imagined she was in good shape, but not naturally thin. Then he looked at the Milton Chester murder file a bit closer. Vivian Ashton Chester was the name of the murdered colonel's wife. He stumbled for his next words, then said, "So, are you Vivian Ashton Chester?"

"I was, but I've recently remarried. It's a good thing that you called now. My husband and I are moving. The phone is set to be disconnected day after tomorrow. We're leaving Grand Forks Tuesday for South Carolina."

Banks wasn't sure if her assessment of his call being a good thing was true or not. "Congratulations on your marriage. Is your new husband military?"

"No, no. He's a sales consultant for a contracting company that does business with the military. We're moving so he can be closer to his family.

"Now, what can I do for you, detective? I'm sure you didn't call to chat about my family."

"Well, Ms. Moore, this is probably a tender subject, but we're looking into your former husband's murder. We've had some new, related developments."

"Please, call me Vivian. You're referring to the murders of Wesley, Dempsey, and Aims? I half expected someone would call about that."

Banks thought that she would continue talking about the three Air Force Officers murdered in Florida, but she paused, maybe not knowing what information to volunteer or wanting Banks to lead the inquiry. He waited just a bit longer, until the silence became awkward.

"I take it, by your comment, that your former husband and the three Air Force officers were friends?"

"I think they were more than friends. I think they were co-conspirators of sorts."

Both of Banks' eyebrows rose. "How so?"

"They'd been friends since the Academy in Colorado Springs. They roomed together, had most of their classes together, graduated together, even dated some of the same women. After graduating, they got together nearly every year to go on a week-long golf outing. They did more than golf, that's for certain, but they always came home to their wives afterwards."

"Where did they go and what kinds of 'things' did they do on these outings?"

"They liked South Carolina near Myrtle Beach, sometimes Orlando, and St. Augustine. On a rare occasion, they'd go to the Panhandle of Florida and Alabama, but only once or twice that I recall. What did they do? You know, guy things. They'd golf during the day. At night, they'd hit a few bars, a few restaurants, a few 'gentleman's' clubs. The boys thought we didn't know about that, but they charged drinks and cash advances and 'private entertainment' as if we wives didn't know what that meant. While the boys were gone 'golfing,' we ladies would do our thing."

"Did you and the other wives get together during that week?"

"Oh, no. We knew each other, but we weren't close. We socialized when duty called, mostly military events, but those were few. No, we did things with our own friends. Rich Aims' wife, Sally, got together with her college friends and spent the week shopping and bar-hopping. Jane Wesley visited her mom and dad for the week. They were getting on in years and she felt it was a good opportunity to visit and check up on them. Her dad has since died. Vicky Dempsey went to her hometown, but she never did say what she did there. The Dempseys were an odd couple. Both quiet and intense. They always seemed strung a little tight for my liking. But Milton was a little like that, too."

Banks would have let her talk on as long as she liked, but she stopped at that moment.

"Do you know of anything, or do you have any ideas on what might have gotten the four men murdered?" he asked.

Banks heard a tentative tone in her voice when she answered. "Are you asking because you think the murders in Florida might be connected to Milton's murder? I mean, these men would have a little fun once a year, but to my knowledge they never did anything illegal or that would cause someone to be so angry with them they would murder any one of them, much less all four."

Banks had no desire to cause this woman any anxiety, especially when she was trying to start a new, happier chapter in her life. But this might be his last opportunity to question the former Mrs. Chester about her husband and his activities. So he pressed on, trying to think of ways to pose his questions with kid gloves.

"I'm going to ask this question in a way that may seem accusatory, but-"

"Detective, my husband was murdered. I've already been questioned at length about our relationship, any difficulties we may have had, any secrets, any drugs, you name it. You can ask me any questions you like in any manner you like. You don't have to sugar-coat it. I have nothing to hide."

Her direct, matter-of-fact tone took Banks by surprise.

She continued. "We did have some difficult times in our marriage, especially close to the end, just before he was killed. He wasn't faithful. I was, even though I had plenty of reason and opportunity not to be. Milt was a bastard, no doubt. But he took good care of me financially, though there were times we were short on money when we shouldn't have been. At the time, I thought he might have a gambling problem, but I never found any evidence. So I'm not sure where the money went. I just figured he was out with some bimbo, blowing his wad and our cash."

Banks heard her take a deep breath. "Early on, I tried to confront him about it. He always had an explanation. Most of the time it didn't wash, but I just put up with it. If I had to do it over, maybe I'd take a different tact."

Just as Banks was about to ask another question she said, "His mother seemed to sense that I wasn't happy, and there were times when I thought marrying him was a mistake. She would talk with me about my options, calm my fears, point out he wasn't such a bad guy. That I was doing fine, that things would get better. They changed, not necessarily for the better, but I stuck it out anyway."

Banks was satisfied she had nothing to do with her husband's murder. Based on what she'd said, he was also pretty sure she wasn't close enough to the wives of the other three officers to have an opinion on whether or not they were capable of murdering their own husbands, or having it done for hire. From her description, they were off doing their own thing during the 'golf' outings, so he didn't even head down that path.

He was about to thank Vivian and end the call when she said, "By the way, I have several boxes of Milton's old stuff. School records from the academy, grades, letters from instructors, some official records, stuff like that. Would you be interested in them? If not, they're headed to the landfill."

***

Banks and Hansen loaded the last of the six copy-paper sized boxes into the trunk of the Grand Marquis, thanked Vivian Moore and wished her well in her new marriage. They briefly looked through the boxes, just to get an idea of the types of papers and documents in each. They didn't expect to find a detailed note by Milton Chester that said he suspected he and his friends were in imminent danger of being murdered, but there was plenty of history in the six boxes that, when reviewed and put in logical order, might yield some clues that had been overlooked before.

Once back at the station, the detectives commandeered an office and pulled papers from the boxes, arranging the contents by date, earliest first, most recent last. They were just what Vivian Moore had said: school papers from the academy, notes from classes, graded papers, fitness reports, personal mail, notes and cards from Vivian while they were dating. Some of the paperwork from school was in binders and spiral notebooks. Some were loose, individual pages. The letters from Vivian were still in their envelopes, cards from her for birthdays and holidays were in a stack, the envelopes apparently discarded. It was going to take hours to go through the six boxes, and probably a few days to look for detailed clues. The good news was that this was all new information, some of which might corroborate things they already knew. Certainly, there was a chance they would learn something new.

It took nearly an hour just to get the papers lined up in chronological order. Now came the hard part.

Banks asked Hansen, "Where do you want to start?"

Reid scratched his head. "How about if I start in the middle and work to the most recent. You start with the old stuff and work to where I started, then I'll go back to the beginning. If we find anything, we can take notes. Then we compare notes and fill in our timeline."

"Sounds like a plan."

It also sounded like they'd be bored to tears within the hour, but Banks had a feeling there was a gold nugget of information in all this paperwork. He only hoped their eyes wouldn't be so glazed over by tedium they'd miss it.

Chapter 20

Anxiety and fear crept into Pat McKinney's dream. The air smelled like rain, thick with a fine mist, so thick it looked like fog. It was dark, early morning, predawn. The apartment complex was asleep.

Pat looked to his left, then to his right. Everyone was in the right place, but a sense of dread hung over him. His arms felt leaden, his legs like they were moving through water. He had difficulty keeping his 9mm raised and level, like someone or something was pulling the weapon down.

Wilson Brush was to his left, his brother Joe to his right. Nancy Brown was next to Joe, two others were beyond her. The entire team moved in slow motion towards the apartment complex. They were concentrating on the common area in front of several apartment doors. There were mail boxes, a stairway, a fire extinguisher box, and several outdoor lights. No windows faced the common area. All of the windows for the individual apartments faced the parking lot.

Pat looked up at the windows and thought he saw faces. He tried to focus to see who would be looking out on the team as the raid progressed. He saw his son, Sean in one window. He waved at Pat or maybe his Uncle Joe; Pat wasn't sure. He tried to take one hand off his gun so he could signal Sean to duck his head down and stay out of sight, but his hand wouldn't move. He wanted to shout at Sean. He wanted to warn him that he could be in danger. He couldn't. Yelling would send a clear warning to their targets. He looked up one last time, thinking he could finally get his hand free. When he looked up, Sean was no longer in the window, but Sean's sister Anna was, smiling at her dad, waving. *They should be in bed. Why doesn't Diane have them in bed?* He started to panic. When he looked up again, the window was dark; Anna's face was gone.

Pat took a deep breath, thinking the danger had passed. His attention turned back to the team. His arms again felt heavy as he tried to move forward. But the harder he tried to catch up, the further behind he fell. The apartment building faded away, getting smaller in his field of vision. He pushed forward, his feet moving, step after step after step. His shoes stuck to the ground as if thick mud had formed on the bottom, caking, gaining weight each time he lifted a foot.

The apartment suddenly disappeared along with the apprehension team and everything else. Pat found himself standing on a polished white floor in a room...or a gymnasium...or just a wide open space; he couldn't tell because he saw no walls, no ceiling, no sky, no doors or windows, nothing but white as far as he could see. He still carried his gun, but now it was weightless, as if it were made of plastic or something even lighter. His shoes were clean, also weightless. The air was clear with a slight scent of floor polish, the industrial strength type they used in military base office buildings and barracks. He was still wearing the NCIS vest over the Kevlar vest.

He should be scared, but he wasn't. All of his teammates had disappeared, the apartment, gone. Then he remembered his children in the window and that he was afraid they'd be caught in the crossfire and injured, or worse. Why had Diane let them look out at the scene? She knew it was dangerous.

"It was dangerous for you, too."

It was Diane's voice, but where had it come from? He looked up at the bright white above him. To his left and right there was nothing but endless white.

"I'm back here, Pat, behind you. I'm always behind you in everything you do. Don't you know that?"

Diane's voice was quiet and soothing and sensuous. He turned slowly and faced the direction from where her voice had come. There was nothing except endless white.

"Diane. Where are you?"

In a soft, far-away voice, she replied, "I'm right here, Pat, beside you. I'll always be at your side, no matter what."

Again, Pat looked in every direction, but saw nothing except the white void. He picked up a different scent now, Diane's favorite perfume. Faint at first, then it grew stronger. A slight breeze blew directly at his face. He closed his eyes, expecting his eyelids to block out the white, but they didn't. The vast expanse of white remained. Fear welled up in his mind.

He asked Diane, "Why can't I block out the white?"

She answered in her soft, soothing tone, "You don't want to block it out. If you do, the darkness will engulf you, swallow your soul. You won't survive it. Just stay with the light and be happy. I'm here with you. As long as we're together, and we will be forever, as long as you don't allow the darkness in."

Pat smiled. He believed she was right. All he had to do was stay with Diane; stay in the light and out of the darkness.

His smile grew as he relaxed his arms down to his side, still holding the gun that remained as light as a feather. He walked in the direction of Diane's voice, but something was wrong. His feet again grew heavier with each step. The bright white that had surrounded him began to change, first to a lighter white, then a dull gray, gradually to multiple colors. Diane called out, sounding more distant than before. He kept walking towards her voice. She sounded like she might be in distress. He ran. As he did, his feet grew heavier, the imaginary mud once again caking up on his shoes.

Diane's voice turned to shouts. "Help! Help me!"

"I'm coming, sweetheart! I'm coming! Hold on!"

He raised the 9mm pistol. It felt like a lead brick once again. He didn't understand what was happening. Up ahead he saw the apprehension team coming into view. He gained on them even though he felt as if he were running in water. Then the apartment building came into view and the air again smelled of rain and pine. They ran straight at the apartment entrance. He had been here before, in this exact spot under these exact circumstances. He knew what was coming next and braced for the muzzle flashes.

But they never came.

Behind him, he heard Diane's soft, soothing voice again.

"Hey, tough guy. Looking for a good time?"

Pat turned one hundred eighty degrees. As he did, the pure white returned all around him, but this time Diane was there, five feet from him, in a tiny, pink negligee, looking sexy as hell. Pat smiled at his wife, his mind totally removed from the imminent firefight.

She held out her arms. "Come here. I've got something special for you."

"I can see that. Can it wait for a couple more minutes? I'm about to be in a shootout with some bad guys."

"Oh, I think they can wait."

Diane walked up to Pat, unzipped his NCIS vest, worked it off his shoulders and dropped it to the side. Then she roughly un-tucked his tee shirt, and pulled it over his head, catching the sleeve on the 9mm that Pat still held. She dropped the tee on top of the NCIS vest on the ground. Pat got chills as Diane reached for the straps that held the Kevlar vest in place.

Pat frowned. This wasn't right. He was about to be in a gun battle and Diane was removing his armor, his protection. He looked over Diane's shoulder and froze. In the distance there was a woman running at them. The white that had surrounded them was again turning dark. Soon, the white turned to a parking lot with a large center grassy area, a gazebo and picnic tables.

Diane continued to loosen the straps on the protective vest. Pat felt the lower straps come completely loose. Diane then moved to the upper straps. He again looked over her shoulder. The woman was closer now, still running at the two of them. He looked back over his shoulder but didn't see a soul. When he turned back, the woman was even closer. Pat saw her face now. He'd seen it before. It was contorted in rage, focused on one goal, to kill him. It was Abbie Glover.

Pat grabbed Diane's wrists and calmly said, "Stop."

"Come on, Baby. Let me get this off."

This time Pat said it with a little more force, "Diane, stop."

But Diane kept working on the upper strap, determined to remove the vest.

Abbie was only thirty feet away when she raised her gun and pulled the trigger. The flame seemed to shoot out of the barrel of her gun for ten feet. Then a bullet emerged from the flash. It moved in slow motion, about two feet per second. Pat estimated he had less than ten seconds to save Diane's life. He grabbed her wrists and shouted, "Stop! The bullet is coming!"

Diane just laughed and tried to pull free. Her laughing angered Pat. Didn't she realize the danger? He looked past her and the slug was now just ten feet behind her. As he watched, the bullet closed the distance, now within just a few feet. He had to act.

He grabbed her by the arms and threw her aside. When he did, the bullet kept coming, closing in on his chest. He looked down as it hit him, dead center of his chest. It stopped like a cartoon prop and dropped straight to the ground.

He sat up straight in bed, panting, drenched in sweat, eyes wide open, his and Diane's bedroom dark, but coming into focus. From the floor beside the bed, he heard a rustling. He turned and saw the top of Diane's head as she slowly picked herself up off the floor.

He rolled to his left and jumped down beside her. "Oh, my God, Diane, I am so sorry. Are you alright?"

"I'm pretty sure." She held up her arm and looked at her elbow as best she could. "I think I have a rug burn."

Pat jumped up and turned on the bedroom light. He looked at the clock. It was 4:00 AM. He put his hands on his forehead and rubbed his eyes with his palms as he knelt down next to his wife.

"That must have been some dream for you to throw me out of bed. I was trying to wake you up. I wish I had a tape of some of the stuff you said."

He thought of Diane in his dream in the tiny negligee. "I think I'm glad that you don't." He paused for a moment. "Are you sure you're alright?"

"I'll live." She touched his cheek. "So, tell me how Abbie is going to kill you. She's dead."

"I don't know. She's gotten into my head." After a few seconds, he said, "I'm afraid my nightmares are coming back."

She put her arms around his neck and pulled him close, whispering in his ear, "We'll get through it. Just relax now. You'll be fine."

They had an early morning of intense passion before they both nodded off to sleep.

Chapter 21

The loud, staccato pops made Pat jump, but as Sunday morning, July fourth progressed he settled down and got used to the fireworks around the neighborhood. By 11:45 AM, the midday sun beat down on his and Diane's Dunnellon, Florida home. Their children, Sean and Anna, were in the swimming pool where they'd been for nearly two hours. They had been joined by their cousin, one year old Danielle and their Aunt Lisa. From the lanai, Uncle Joe, Nancy Brown, William 'Hatch' Hatcher, Pat, and Diane kept a watchful eye in the direction of the pool. Pat, Joe, and Hatch drank beer while Diane and Nancy sipped Moscato wine. All of them wore swim suits and tee shirts. It was hot and humid in the lanai, but the ceiling fan kept the air moving so that it was somewhat comfortable.

The conversation ranged from their last cookout to Brian Purcer and the Hot Licks' upcoming concert schedule. Finally, it came to the topic of the recent murders of the three Air Force Officers on a St. Augustine, Florida golf course. Diane, not wanting to participate in this particular part of the conversation, excused herself to prepare the side dishes and appetizers for the cookout.

Nancy looked at Hatch, Pat, and Joe in order then said, "There's a pretty fair chance that whoever killed Milton Chester also killed the three officers at the golf course, but there are too many differences in the murders to make a connection."

Pat and Joe both raised their eyebrows. It had been two years since the colonel's murder. The person they believed to be the murderer had not been seen or heard from since then.

Hatch said, "Now, boys, just let the lady finish before you get all fidgety. There's a bunch of reasons why some folks are thinkin' this way."

They both turned their hands up in a gesture that said, *Okay, convince us.*

Nancy continued. "We sent an inquiry to the Air Force Academy in Colorado Springs to get some background on Aims, Dempsey, and Wesley. It turns out that they roomed together all the way through the program. They had one more roommate."

Pat took a swig of his beer. "Milton Chester."

Nancy nodded. "The inquiry was supposed to be handled by the Tenth Security Squadron at the Air Force Academy. The Commander there is Major Maurice Alexander. It turns out that the office of the Commanding Officer received the inquiry and decided to handle the communications. Major Alexander was ordered to stand down."

Pat and Joe made a face. Joe said, "That's odd. Why wouldn't the CO let the security staff do their job?"

Pat was looking at his kids in the pool. He chimed in, "Cover-up?"

Joe asked, "Why keep secrets now? All four of them are dead."

Nancy asked, "Remember the Tailhook Scandal? That was back about ten years ago. Maybe there was something going on at the Air Force Academy long before that and the Air Force doesn't want it brought to light. A lot of careers could be at risk. Motive for murder, though?"

"Could be, but murder's a pretty big step. Who would risk it?" Joe said. "Maybe someone's career was ruined. Maybe they're back to take out the people they feel are responsible."

Pat glanced at his brother. "Or maybe someone high up the chain is taking care of a few loose ends, people who could name names."

Nancy shook her head. "That doesn't seem likely. We know the gun used to kill Kevin Reardon was the same gun used to kill Milton Chester. That same gun was also used in the murders of all those guys coming out of boot camp along the southeast. Why would the academy have any interest in those poor kids?" Nancy took a deep breath, then a long drink from her long neck beer. "Then there's two years when nothing happens that we know of, but now these three officers get whacked out in the open on a golf course in broad daylight. They had this close friendship with Milton Chester. There's nothing else in their files that give any reason for anyone to kill these guys. It wasn't a robbery or a terror attack, regardless of what those nitwit congressmen said. These guys were so unimportant that we're surprised they made it as far as they did in their careers."

Pat was watching the others for their reactions. He was usually the first one to ask probing questions so he could gather all the pieces of the puzzle. He shifted his attention towards the pool, watching Sean and Anna splash each other. Then Sean ducked underwater to look for something in the pool's depths.

Pat set his empty bottle down. "There're too many ties back to Chester. And it all goes back to the academy. I know it's a long time to hold a grudge, but maybe there's a good reason why. Maybe someone was in prison or Leavenworth or they've been married with a normal life that they wanted to protect their family and they couldn't just go out and kill three people in public."

The last comment drew eye rolls from Joe and Hatch. Nancy didn't flinch.

Nancy looked at Pat. "I agree there are too many ties to the academy to ignore, but you also can't dismiss the inconsistencies. The gun used to kill the officers in St. Augustine was a semi-automatic rifle with 7.62mm ammunition. Milton Chester was killed with a 9mm handgun. So, why the change? My people think there are different killers. But there are lots of holes here. We're missing some big pieces."

Pat felt the wheels turning, bits and pieces of the conversation coming back, old memories of the boot camp murders bouncing against the facts of the recent murders.

Hatch asked Pat, "So, Sherlock, what can ya tell us that we ain't already figured out?"

Pat smiled. "Maybe the killer lost his gun and had to get a new one. Maybe he opted for a more powerful weapon."

"Or maybe it's not the same person doing the killing?" Joe's tone lacked his normal sarcasm when talking with his brother. "I mean, Nancy has a point. Just because there are ties with the colonel, it doesn't mean we're looking at the same killer. It's an interesting theory about some military brass or someone, maybe in politics by now, wanting to protect their backside."

Pat looked towards the trees behind their house. Similarities between the cases were non-existent. The locations were different. An abandoned missile launch complex versus a crowded golf course in the middle of the day. The weapons of choice were different, too. Milton Chester had been killed at very close range, indicating passion, rage, a personal grudge. The three officers were shot from a distance. That meant either indifference or a lack of need for the victims to see their executioner and therefore know why they were being killed. As far as the killer was concerned, there wasn't a need for personal satisfaction. Their prey just had to be dead.

"So far I've got nothing," Pat said. "Sounds to me like two different killers. But I don't think we can ignore the connection. There has to be some tie, some common thread that links the murders. I still think it's a revenge killing." Pat looked around at the faces looking back at him. He could see their thoughts churning through the possibilities. "What could possibly cause a person to lay low that long before you retaliate? I mean, you have to hold a grudge a long time to wait two years before you come at somebody for revenge."

Joe glanced at his brother. "I don't know, Pat. How about murder? How about rape? Maybe someone did something to their family that caused them to go temporarily insane." Both Pat and Hatch grimaced at his comment, but Joe continued, "How about maybe being away in the military for years? And what if this guy was in prison for a couple years, rotting away in a cell, not able to act on his rage? Maybe all that pent up hatred is now being unleashed?"

Pat knew first-hand that holding a grudge had no time limit. What Joe said was true, but the example he used was far too personal. Except for the prison stint, his brother was describing the McKinney's situation to a 'T' when they had gone after their former business partners. He was also describing Hatch and his quest for vengeance against the men who had killed his parents and his little sister.

Hatch asked Pat, "So, if this is all tied together and this is a vengeful killin', how is this guy or guys different than a couple guys that I know, includin' the one I see in the mirror every day, if I had a mirror, that is? I don't want you to think I'm above it all, by any means."

Pat caught Nancy looking around, probably to see if Lisa, Diane, or the children were within earshot of the conversation.

They all took a deep breath and sipped their drinks. After nearly a minute of silence, Pat tried to defend what they had done as just, but Joe and Hatch shook their heads.

Joe said, "You don't know what the shooter, or shooters, went through to push him or her to kill those officers or Milton Chester, or our boot camp brothers. We don't need to know why they're motivated. It would be better to know where they're going next. Or if they're finished."

Nancy turned the conversation back to the murder investigation. "Banks and Hansen seem to think all these murders are linked through a common person or event. When we went to Grand Forks, we went there to investigate Becky Lippert and Bobby Garrett. Remember that we thought the trip up there was out of place, out of character. There had to be a reason for Bobby and Becky to make it. Maybe they were the common link? The real question is: why were they up there in the first place? What drew them there? My guess is Milton Chester is that link. Somehow, he's the central figure in all this."

The group sat silent for a minute, drinking. Pat rubbed the scar on his chin. There were quite a few things they knew for certain. The same gun was used on Milton Chester and the boot camp grads. A pen was used and discarded at each scene. A dark van was observed leaving the boot camp murder scenes but that was recovered, so it was no longer of concern. That still left many holes in the investigation.

Nancy asked, "What were the biggest unanswered questions about all the murders?"

Joe took the first one. "If it is the same shooter, where's he been for two years?"

Pat chimed in, "Why a different gun?"

Joe rubbed his square chin as Pat, still rubbing the scar on his chin, stared off into the tree line over two hundred yards behind the house.

In the distance someone lit off a full pack of firecrackers. They popped and snapped for about ten seconds.

Hatch broke the silence. "How does a nineteen-year old kid get a colonel to meet him at a remote, abandoned location? Whatever it was, it had to be a pretty powerful incentive."

"Drugs, guns, something illegal that went wrong?" Joe tossed out.

Nancy said, "I'd think it would have to be something more powerful, maybe more personal than that. No one ever remembered Colonel Chester meeting with anyone like this before. According to Airman Goff, the colonel's staff assistant, Major Hull, was an emotional wreck when the colonel left for that meeting. Maybe the kid had something big on the colonel. One other thing, we haven't been able to talk with the major. She was transferred to the academy some eighteen months ago. For some reason we can't get her on the phone.

Pat was thinking down the same line as Nancy. Whatever enticed the colonel to the missile site, and ultimately to his death, had to be very personal and persuasive, information that could potentially ruin a career. The types of activities that could ruin a military career were many, but a nineteen year old kid wouldn't have access to information like that, would he?

A realization hit him. What had caused him and Joe to take drastic actions to get revenge against their former business partners? Someone did something so heinous to a member of their families that they took matters into their own hands. To get the colonel out to that site, the killer had to have proof that the colonel did something to his family. The only family that they knew about was Abbie Glover, the woman that Joe shot and killed at the apartment complex. That was Pat's second epiphany. Joe might be next on the killer's list.

Before Pat could tell Joe, Hatch, and Nancy about his suspicions, Diane came out to the lanai with the telephone. Holding the phone against her tee shirt so the caller couldn't hear, she looked at Pat. "For you."

"Who is it?"

Diane shrugged. "A guy named Art Gray. He seems pretty upset."

Pat recognized the name. He stood and took the receiver and walked into the house to get some privacy. Moments later he came back out to the lanai, his face tense and serious.

"That was Art Gray, Dean Gray's dad. Dean was murdered yesterday."

Chapter 22

The coffee was strong, just the way Harold Trent liked it. That was the only good thing about his breakfast. The eggs were over-cooked and the hash brown potatoes were still cold in the center of each small cube. To add insult to injury, the wheat toast was cold and stale. He liked his eggs sunny-side up and runny. He liked his hash brown potatoes cooked until they were slightly brown on the side of each piece of potato and cooked all the way through. *At least they used redskin potatoes. There's no excuse for these eggs though. I'll just leave a lousy tip. It ain't the waitress' fault, but she needs to give the cooks hell. I told her what I wanted and she didn't deliver.*

Harold Trent sat in a diner, simply named *The Diner,* on Fort Jackson Boulevard approximately one half mile outside the main entrance to Fort Jackson in Columbia, South Carolina. The place had a capacity of seventy-five patrons according to the placard on the wall near the entrance. Today about fifteen people sat at tables and another three perched on barstools at the counter. Half the crowd was reading the morning paper.

The décor was old greasy spoon late 1950s, with an overdose of patriotism centered heavily on the Army and the role they played in the region. So many pictures of men and women in battle dress, carrying M-16s and a variety of other weapons lined the walls that you could barely see the red paint behind them. Interspersed with modern military men and women were pictures and paintings of the Army throughout the history of the United States. Pictures of the Civil War era were mostly of Confederate soldiers. A large portrait of General Robert E. Lee graced the entrance to the diner. There wasn't an open space for another frame anywhere in the place.

The waitress approached Trent's table. She smiled and asked in a deep southern drawl, "Need a refill on that coffee, hon?"

Trent didn't say a word. He just pushed his cup in her direction. She refilled it while her jaw worked on a piece of gum. When she finished, she asked, "Is there anything else I can getcha?"

Trent just eyed her up and down with a look that could have been interpreted a hundred different ways, none of them friendly. He shook his head slightly and looked back down at his copy of *The State*, Columbia, South Carolina's daily newspaper.

The headlines said something about the challengers that Texas Governor George W. Bush was likely to face for the Republican Presidential Nomination. Another story announced the USS *Nimitz* would embark on a goodwill cruise to the Mediterranean Sea. Trent smirked and snorted at the thought as he chewed a mouthful of half-cooked hash browns. He dropped his fork on the plate, making sure it made a loud noise to show his displeasure with the cook. He flipped the newspaper to page three, saw the story headline in the crime section of the paper and smiled.

Man Shot and Killed Outside Local Bar
Police Mum on Suspects

A US Army soldier was shot and killed outside a bar near Fort Jackson Friday, July 2. Sergeant David Wallace was found with a fatal gunshot wound to the chest. He was declared dead at the scene by the Medical Examiner's office. Mr. Wallace was formerly from Hickory, North Carolina and recently returned from his second tour of duty in Iraq.

The article was brief. It contained little detail except that, at present, they were still investigating and they would not name any suspects. Trent's smile widened; he was certain no one would be looking for him. As far as the local authorities knew, he didn't exist.

Finishing his coffee in two quick gulps, he tossed a five dollar bill on the table for a meal that was billed at $4.79. Nobody from the diner was around, which was disappointing, because he wanted to catch the reaction from the waitress when she found her lousy tip. He'd just have to get his kicks somewhere else today.

He looked across the street at the *Econo Lodge*. Ace Glover had checked into room 212, which Trent could clearly see from his window seat at the diner. Ace had not come out of his room the entire morning. Trent wondered why he was staying holed up in his room. It was nearly 10:40 AM. Most people, even night owls were rising, getting breakfast, showering, and getting on with their days.

Noticing movement from the second floor of the *Econo Lodge*, Trent turned his head in time to see Ace leave his room and head towards the stairs. When Ace came out of the stairwell and headed for the lobby, Trent relaxed. If Ace was checking out, he had plenty of time to head for his truck. He noticed Ace didn't have any bags, so most likely he was heading down for the continental breakfast, but he watched the lobby door for another ten minutes. When Ace didn't come out, Trent waved down the waitress and pointed to his coffee cup. She 'accidentally' spilled coffee on the table so the hot brew spilled onto his lap.

She said in a mock apology, "Oh, sorry, hon. My mistake."

Trent cursed and quickly began to wipe up the coffee on his crotch as the waitress retreated to her station. After a few moments trying to clean off the embarrassing stain, he sat back down. At least he had a half cup of brew left. *The waitress better not pass this way again or she'll be sorry.*

His attention went back to Ace. Trent knew he planned to head for Southeast Georgia today. There was a certain ship that had come back to port carrying a certain petty officer named Wilson Brush. If all went well, tomorrow was going to be the worst and last day of Wilson Brush's life.

***

Ace awoke at 9:45 AM, stripped off his underwear, started the shower, and jumped in. The hot stream of water felt good against his skin, reviving his senses, washing away the layer of crud from the previous evening. What a night it had been, nearly getting caught with a silenced pistol, the murder weapon from so many killings. Maybe it was time to discard the gun and get something new. Not a bad idea, but he liked the Glock. It had served him well and if he was caught with it during the commission of a murder, what difference did it make? He'd be on the hook for murder anyway.

He toweled off, brushed his teeth, shaved, and performed his morning ritual of rubbing down his body with a body lotion made for men. The women seemed to like it, so who was he to deprive them?

After he dressed, he peeked out the window, drawing back the curtain slightly to see what kind of day would greet him. It was sunny with few clouds in the sky which meant that it would be hot and humid, a good day for a drive to Kingsland, Georgia. First, he needed a good breakfast. There was the diner across the street, which the front desk recommended if you didn't want to take advantage of their continental breakfast.

As he looked out the curtain, a feeling of déjà vu overtook his senses. Something familiar caught his eye, but he couldn't place it for a moment. Then it hit him. At the diner, a beat up pickup truck was parked at the outskirts of the cracked pavement of the parking lot. The same truck he'd seen the night before at the *Mirrors Lounge*, where he had hoped to find David Wallace. Then a realization came to him like a bolt of lightning. He'd seen the truck at least once before, in St. Augustine, Florida, in the parking lot of the Slammer and Squire Golf Course.

He let the curtain fall back into place, his thoughts racing. Could the FBI be tracking his moves, spying on him, trying to catch him while he was executing his plan? Were there bugs in the walls, listening to his conversations? *That's just silly. I don't talk to anyone, even myself, unless I'm at a bar.* Then he realized that he only stayed at most hotel rooms for a single night. He moved around so much it would be impossible for any law enforcement agency to set up bugs where he stayed. By the time they got a court order, he'd be on to the next hotel. Besides, they wouldn't use an old, beat-up truck for surveillance. They'd be in a non-descript van with all kinds of recording equipment. No, that truck was someone's personal vehicle, someone without a lot of money or any connection to law enforcement. *Whoever it is, they're following me and that has to stop.*

Ace tucked his wallet into his pants pocket, picked up his keys, and removed the Glock 9mm from the drawer next to the bed. He didn't bother with the silencer. It was in the trunk of the car which was in clear line of sight of the diner. If someone was watching, they would see him open the trunk and remove the small box. Besides, he didn't plan on using the gun this morning. That was for tomorrow, for a guy named Wilson Brush.

Opening the door to the hotel room, the heat hit him right away. He closed the door behind him and turned to the railing, pausing to make sure that anyone watching would see him leave his room. He headed down the walkway to the stairs that led to the office area of the hotel, where the remnants of a continental breakfast were available until 11:00 AM. He entered the lobby, stopped and looked around for a doorway to the rear parking lot of the hotel.

The clerk noticed him looking. "Something I can help you with, sir?"

Ace looked her way. "No, just forgot something in my car."

He headed for the door to the rear parking lot. Once outside, he jogged east on the sidewalk and exited the hotel property into a wooded area. He walked another fifty yards, then turned towards Fort Jackson Boulevard where he was concealed from view by anyone sitting at the diner or in the diner's parking lot.

Mid-morning traffic on the four-lane road was heavy. Ace got to the edge of the street and had to wait nearly a full minute before a break in the traffic allowed him to cross to the diner side of the road, but nearly one hundred yards past the parking lot. As he walked back in the direction of the diner sweat beaded on his forehead. His shirt clung to his back and chest. He kept his eyes on the diner parking lot.

When he came within fifty feet of the lot, he slipped into the wooded area that bordered the parking area to the east. Footing on the ground among the trees was tricky. Tree roots snaked out in all directions, but it was cooler under the shelter of the tree's thick canopy.

He made his way parallel with the road again and stood at the edge of the parking lot within a few feet of the old pickup truck. There was no doubt it was the same truck he'd seen on the two previous occasions. Whoever owned the truck most likely was in the diner. But why? Was he being followed? If yes, then by who? Ace thought for a moment. *The shooter.*

No matter. Whoever it was, they were going to have a hard time following him now. He snuck up to the truck to make sure no one was lying on the seat in the cab. He peered through the driver's window behind the seat of the truck, looking for a weapon, thinking that, if it was the shooter, there would be a rifle in the cab. *That's silly. He'd have to be a complete idiot to leave the murder weapon in plain sight.* After ensuring that he was alone, he removed the valve cap for the front, driver's side tire and loosened the valve stem core until he heard a constant stream of air. In just a matter of minutes and the tire would be flat.

Satisfied, Ace retraced his steps. By 11:10 AM he was back in his room, packing his bag and heading for the lobby to check out.

* * *

At the edge of the diner's parking lot, Shawnda Hull sat in her beat up Toyota Corolla, overheated, miserable, and depressed. Sweat ran down her back even though her car was in the shade with the windows rolled down. The heat and oppressive humidity drained the energy from her entire body and mind. To make matters worse, she replayed the telephone conversation from two nights ago in her mind until she could hardly stand it. She missed her son, Trevor, missed his voice, his pudgy cheeks, and that million dollar smile. The time and distance between them was tearing her apart.

If only circumstances hadn't torn her away from her little boy and her duty as a major in the Air Force, she'd be with him now. The big question was, when she got back, what would her punishment be for going AWOL. For an officer, being absent without leave, the penalty would be stiff, possibly years in confinement. Most definitely she'd be stripped of her rank and dishonorably discharged.

But no punishment could be greater than the time she would have to spend away from her precious Trevor. For that blunder, she was gravely sorry.

Sitting in the heat of a South Carolina diner parking lot watching for movement from the *Econo Lodge* was driving her deeper into depression. She was on the verge of packing it all in and heading north, home to her son, home to face her father, to kiss her mother. Then she would turn herself in to the nearest Air Force base and face the punishment she knew she deserved. She had taken the oath and failed to uphold it. But then she saw Ace Glover open the door to his hotel room and head into the lobby. Fifteen minutes later, he surprised her, emerging from the wooded area next to the old pickup truck, just fifty feet from her car. The truck looked familiar. She thought she may have seen it before, but there were thousands like it on the road, especially in areas where there were a lot of home-grown landscaping companies.

Why was he checking out the trucks interior? Finally, Ace crouched down by the front driver's side tire. Then she heard the air escaping. Shawnda ducked down in her seat when Ace stood and looked around the parking lot. As quickly as he showed up, he was gone back into the wooded area and out of sight, leaving Shawnda wondering just what he'd been up to.

Chapter 23

The task of wading through the boxes provided by Vivian Moore, the former Mrs. Chester, was mind numbing. The vast majority of the papers were classroom notes from Milton Chester's years at the Air Force Academy. A number of personal papers, such as cards and letters from his then girlfriend, Vivian Chester, and copies of numerous official forms rounded out the contents. Nothing of consequence was obvious.

Banks came across a sealed envelope simply labeled "*Trent.*" He had already placed it in the pile of inconsequential papers when he frowned because the envelope had apparently never been opened, the flap on the end in pristine condition. He scratched his head, grabbed a letter opener from his desk drawer, picked up the envelope and sliced the end.

The envelope contained two sheets of notebook sized paper. The first was an official looking form. The form listed Harold Trent as being Absent Without Leave, a violation of Article 86 of the Uniform Code of Military Justice." *Banks frowned. Who the hell is Harold Trent and why does Milton Chester care?*

The second sheet of paper was a handwritten note with only one sentence. "If Trent shows up, there's gonna be trouble. We'll have to deal with it immediately." It was signed with the initials "MC. With copies to AW, RA, and CD."

"Hey Reid, check this out. Any idea who Harold Trent is?"

Hansen read the documents. "Nope, but I'm thinking that we should be watching for that name. If Chester thought that he might cause trouble for him and his buddies, we should keep that in mind. Maybe Templeton or Barnes know something more."

Banks and Hansen took a break from looking through Milton Chester's boxes. They reviewed pictures of the original timeline from the two-year old Kevin Reardon murder investigation and had it recreated on the whiteboard next to their desks. They added the new information provided by Airman Goff. The original timeline had ended with the murder of Colonel Chester. Immediately after his death all contact with their military sources ceased. If Goff hadn't chased them down the afternoon of the interviews with Air Force personnel, they wouldn't have had anywhere else to turn. The interviews, on the whole, had been useless.

Airman Goff contacted the detectives in violation of direct orders from the commanding officer at the base. He put his career in jeopardy. It was either very courageous or very stupid.

The conversation with Goff had been most enlightening. The day prior to the detectives' interviews with Air Force personnel, Goff was assigned to clean the conference room behind Colonel Templeton's office and prepare it for an afternoon meeting. He was just about to finish the setup and empty the trash when he heard the colonel's phone ring, followed by the booming voice of the colonel, saying that he would take the call in his office. Goff heard only Colonel Templeton's side of a phone conversation as he greeted Colonel Barnes by name.

The conversation was tense from the start. Templeton was defensive, saying things like *I hated Chester and his buddies. They nearly ruined my career.* Goff said that even in the conference room he could hear Colonel Barnes' voice ranting into Templeton's ear.

Templeton, normally in complete control, was flustered by whatever Barnes was saying. It was as if he had something to hide, though Goff couldn't imagine what it might be. Templeton seemed like such a boy scout. The airman said he'd be real surprised if his commanding officer had been involved in anything more than a friendly poker game because he was so by-the-book.

When the conversation ended, Templeton uncharacteristically slammed the phone down in its cradle. He stormed out of the office, telling Major Sanders that he'd be out for at least an hour and to move any appointments necessary.

Banks asked Hansen, "So, do you think he went off to cool down after a dress down from a peer? Why would he take that from someone of the same rank without giving it right back?"

Hansen had been thinking the same thing. The way Goff described it, the call was a one-way conversation with Barnes delivering the message and Templeton taking it like a dog who had just crapped on the living room carpet. "I agree. I wouldn't have stood for that unless somebody had the goods on me. If I had to fall in line because of something that was being held over my head, I might, but that would have to be one ball-buster of a reason."

Banks rubbed his chin and felt the stubble already starting to stick out of his face, like one hundred grit sandpaper, well on its way to eighty-five grit. Maybe Chester and his pals had bullied the colonel back at the academy. He was such a geek-looking guy, even in his early forties that Banks could imagine what he'd looked like back in his academy years.

"So, is Templeton a new connection to the two murders?" Banks said.

"Maybe we should return and put a little more pressure on the Colonel? Maybe throw in that we've sent an inquiry to the academy and we're finding some interesting dirt on the colonel and his friends," Hansen said.

Banks sat thinking for a moment. "I wonder if Colonel Barnes might have something to hide. Would she be calling Templeton on the carpet to try and shut down any investigation? Remember what Nancy Brown said when she tried to contact the security squadron at the academy? They were blocked from getting involved in the inquiry by Barnes.

"I think we're getting closer. Why else would everybody start getting panicky? Maybe if we keep digging we might hit pay-dirt." Banks continued, "Let's finish getting the timeline filled in with Goff's information, then we can put together a letter to the academy security squadron and let's make sure the Commanding officer knows about it."

Hansen smiled, his square chin jutting out, exaggerating the dimple in the middle. He filled in the whiteboard with the phone conversation from Barnes to Templeton. Then they added Goff's initials in code so no one would know where the information came from. Last, he added a question. *Who is Harold Trent?*

As they finished filling in the last remarks on the timeline, the fax machine whirred. Hansen walked over and picked up the stack, seven pages total. They were from Philip S. Miller Public Library, Castle Rock, Colorado. Hansen frowned. He couldn't place the city of Castle Rock, then called across the squad room to Banks, "Bill, any idea where Castle Rock, Colorado is?"

"Nope. Why?"

"Because we just got an anonymous fax from the library there."

As Hansen read the cover page, his eyebrows lowered as his face turned into a frown. Then his eyebrows shot up. The more he read, the more his frown turned upside down into a smile. If what he was reading was true, then contact with the Air Force Academy Security Squadron Commander was essential.

Hansen handed the cover sheet and the first page of the fax to Banks. He then continued to read the second page and scanned the third. The fourth through the seventh pages appeared to be from an investigation folder similar to the ones they used at the Grand Forks Police Department. The copies were bright white paper, but the reproduced pages obviously had been handled quite a lot. Smudge marks from finger prints and stains from drinks and food particles showed up on the copied images. They were from twenty-five or more years ago based on the dates in some of the entries. Banks had finished reading the second page and reached out to get the third page from Hansen when he saw his partner's face. Hansen smiled and handed the fax over to his partner. Banks read the page and looked up. His mouth was open, but no words were coming out.

A "smoking gun" had just dropped into their laps.

***

Nancy Brown dialed Bill Banks' number at the Grand Forks Police Department. Banks picked up on the second ring.

"Banks."

"Bill, this is Nancy Brown. We've got some developments that you need to know about."

"This must be my lucky day. We just got a fax from Colorado. If this pace keeps up we could solve a few murders by dinner."

Nancy smiled at the exaggeration but thought that it must be good news. Then she frowned remembering the news she had to deliver. "I'll go first. Dean Gray, one of the guys victimized by Becky Lippert, was murdered Friday."

"Damn." He paused then asked, "What do you have on it?"

"Not much. But a 9mm was used and no one saw much of anything. It was in the middle of the day. Most everyone in the apartment complex where he lived works at that hour. The ones who don't are night-shifters and were asleep."

"How many other names were on your victims list?"

Nancy had the list in a folder on Hatch's desk. She pulled it up and looked at the paper. "Just two others that are still alive. David Wallace, sergeant in the Army, and Wilson Brush, petty officer on the ballistic missile submarine USS *Nevada*."

"Do you know where these guys are now? If you know, so does this Glover kid, assuming he's the shooter."

"We're tracking that information down now, but since I'm no longer active duty I have a lot less pull than I did before. I'm working the military angle through my boss at the Anti-Terror Unit. Colonel Warner is making the official inquiries."

Banks was silent until Nancy wondered if the call disconnected. "Bill, you still there?"

"Sorry about that, mind was just working a little overtime, that's all. We've got to get ahead of this Glover kid, if he's the gunman."

"So what about your news?"

"We just got a fax from Colorado. It's anonymous from a library about forty miles north of Colorado Springs. It appears to be pages from a suspect's file or a military personnel file. The name on the file was Milton Chester."

He had Nancy's full attention.

"It was a written reprimand for participating in activities contrary to the code of conduct that each cadet was sworn to uphold. Specifically, he was reprimanded for hosting a party where liquor was served."

Nancy wasn't impressed. She'd been to a few parties herself where cadets, soldiers, and sailors got a little out of hand. That was nothing new. She was about to ask what was the big deal when Banks continued.

"It turns out that there were at least two minors at the party, one of which was a female, a girl really. Her name wasn't mentioned in the report, but there were several accompanying pages, one of which named the young woman. I'd make you guess but her name was Abigail Glover. She was fifteen years old at the time."

Nancy smiled. The missing link, but still not a bombshell. She was a minor at a booze party. There had to be more.

Apparently, Bill Banks read her silence and decided to give her the really big news. "It turns out that a number of the men at the party had their way with Abbie because there was an official inquest into the men's activities. The Security Squadron Commander wanted to charge the men involved with rape."

"Why didn't they?"

"Because the commanding officer of the base put a stop to it and sealed the records of all the cadets involved."

Nancy frowned, actually getting angry about a crime that happened decades ago. The bastards had destroyed Abbie Glover's life. She'd been used and abused and the men who did it were never brought to trial. "Why would the C.O. cover up such a horrific crime?"

"Because the commanding officer at the time of the incident was Lieutenant General Alton Chester, father of the late Milton Chester."

Nancy's jaw dropped.

"That's not all," Banks said.

"There's more?"

"Oh, yes, ma'am. The other three men involved in the rape? Our three murder victims; Wesley, Aims, and Dempsey."

"You're kidding me."

"I'm not done. We also have a birth record here for one Rebecca Glover, a.k.a. Rebecca Lippert. She was born to Abbie Glover in early 1971. Abbie was fifteen at the time and gave the baby up for adoption." A pause. "In the fax one of the pages was a DNA test. It proves that Rebecca's father was none other than Milton Chester."

Nancy's head was spinning with the flood of new information. Without time to write down the details and try and see where these new pieces fit, it was just too much too fast to make sense of it all.

"Why would Ace travel across the country to kill Milton Chester? He wasn't even born then. Chester isn't his father. Or maybe he is. No, that wouldn't make sense at all. Would he have done it to avenge his mother and his half-sister?"

"Let's hope we can catch up with him and ask before he kills anyone else. Did you want me to forward these faxes to you?"

Nancy looked around at Hatch's office and realized he didn't have a fax machine. "Not right now. I'm in Moniac, Georgia. They apparently don't have fax machines here yet."

"I'd make a joke about Moniac, Georgia if I wasn't living in Grand Forks, North Dakota. Best to leave that one alone."

Nancy smiled. "When I get back to civilization I'll call and you can fax it to me at my office. I don't want to leave anything like that lying around too long."

"One more thing. I'd let the other two guys on your list know they should be cautious until we catch Ace. With Dean Gray's murder, I'd say those guys are in real danger."

"Already on it, Bill."

***

Less than an hour later Colonel Sheila Warner called with the news of the murder of David Wallace. Nancy frowned. "At least Wilson Brush is out to sea right now."

"Don't you wish? The *Nevada* is in port for an unexpected visit. I can't tell you the particulars because we're not on a secure line, but he's on dry land."

Shit. "I'd better try and find him then."

Nancy disconnected the call just as she heard a knock on the door of Hatch's cabin. She moved to a window with a view of the front porch. Wilson Brush, in the flesh, was standing on Hatch's front porch standing next to some other big guy. They were sweating through their tee shirts, looking around at the surrounding swamp of the Hatcher estate.

Chapter 24

Shawnda Hull had watched as Ace disappeared into the wooded area next to the restaurant parking lot after flattening the old pickup truck's tire. She continued to watch as he reappeared at the lobby door to the *Econo Lodge* across Fort Jackson Boulevard only to disappear again into his room. After just a few minutes he came out onto the second floor walkway with a small suitcase in hand. He was leaving, that much was clear, but he didn't appear to be in much of a hurry. He moved slowly along the second story railing, glancing at the diner. He had a smile on his face.

The bright sun was high in the sky. Even though her car was in the shade, a glare from several cars in the hotel's parking lot was in her eyes. She forgot about giving up the chase and heading for home. She now had Ace in her sights.

The air from the tire. Why did he sabotage the truck? He must know the owner. She looked more closely at the truck and thought that she'd seen it before...but where?

The glare changed. Ace's car was backing out, turning in the direction of the exit of the hotel parking lot. Shawnda panicked and grabbed for her keys on the passenger seat. She looked up and saw Ace's car turn right out of the hotel parking lot towards Interstate 77. She put her keys in the ignition just as a scruffy looking man ran out of the diner and headed for the pickup truck. As he rounded the rear of the truck heading for the driver's side door, he stopped and looked at the front, left tire. It was still spewing air but it was running low, the rim nearly crushing the tire into the worn pavement.

Shawnda started her car, hoping the man wouldn't see her. That was easier said than done as she had to drive right past him to exit the diner's parking lot. But the man continued looking at the tire. He moved closer, picked something up off of the ground and looked at it. Then he looked closer at the tire, reaching out as if he could fix the leak by magic. Whatever he did stopped the air flow, or maybe it was just out of air, but the noise stopped abruptly. He continued to kneel by the tire. This was her chance.

She eased the car into gear and headed for the exit. Fifty feet from the truck, the man stood up, his attention still on the tire. Thirty feet. Twenty feet. Then with ten feet to go, the man turned and bolted out in front of her car. She slammed on the brakes, her front bumper on the driver's side stopping just inches from his knees. He lost his balance and leaned over, putting his hands on the hood of her car.

"Watch where the hell you're going. You trying to kill me or something?"

Shawnda's anger flared but she stammered, not knowing what to say in reply. This jerk actually believed it was her fault he wasn't watching where he was heading, but the combination of fear and impatience kept her from saying anything. She stared back at him, waiting and hoping he would move on.

Instead of moving he looked at her for a long, uncomfortable moment. Recognition came over his face. Fear started to fill her from the inside out, her chest constricted, her arms and legs stiffened, and her face grew pale. Her foot, twitching with nervous energy, nearly stomped down on the accelerator. After what seemed like an eternity he moved across her path and headed back towards the restaurant. He looked back over his shoulder once then continued on, breaking into a jog.

Taking a deep breath she stepped on the gas and headed out onto Fort Jackson Boulevard. She was startled by her ringing cell phone. When she answered, the tense voice of Airman Adam Goff said, "Major, I just wanted to let you know that, in case you didn't know, Ace is heading east on I-26."

Shawnda Hull, sighed. "Adam, you can call me Shawnda. I'm not in your chain of command anymore. And thank you for helping me. You're putting yourself and your career in jeopardy, you know."

After a pause, Goff replied, "Yes Ma'am, but you need the help. Whatever it is you're doing, it must be important to you. I'm happy that I can help. I just...I mean...I'm worried about you and your son." After another brief pause, Goff said, "Shawnda, you call me if there's anything else I can do. And Ma'am, be careful."

With tears in her eyes, she said, "Thank you Adam. I will. You watch your back." She hung up as she headed east towards the interstate hoping to gain ground on Ace. She had a full tank of gas. At least that much was in her favor. She took the ramp a bit too fast and ran onto the shoulder, spitting up stones, causing the car to bounce on mounds of dirt on the edge of the pavement. She regained control and accelerated, merged with southbound traffic without further incident. Perspiration broke out on her forehead and ran down her backbone and chest. *Jesus. Get control of yourself. You're an Air Force officer for crying out loud.*

Shawnda made the interchange with Interstate 26 and headed east towards Charleston. She believed Ace planned on taking Interstate 95 south to the submarine base at King's Bay. If Goff was right, Ace planned to track down a sailor who was briefly married to his half sister. Wilson Brush was supposed to be at sea, but the USS *Nevada* was in port for emergency repairs and was expected to remain there for several days. Brush might not get off the ship for any length of time, but if he set foot off the base, he'd be in danger. She had to warn the young sailor of Ace's plans. Her original plan to film him in the act of some crime was pure folly. Besides, her heart wasn't in it anymore. Just hearing her son's voice over the phone the previous night had ripped her emotions to shreds. She felt empty inside. Her mother was right; she had more pressing responsibilities, like raising her son. The longer she remained absent without leave, the longer it would be before she could be with her son.

Shawnda's mind wandered, tired as she was from lack of sleep and her long surveillance of the hotel from the parking lot in the morning heat. The rumble of the warning grooves that separated the traveling lane from the shoulder of the interstate jarred her out of her dreamy state. The car in front of her, a red, aged Dodge Dart traveled less than fifty-five miles per hour while the rest of the traffic pushed eighty-five, including Shawnda. She braked and looked for an opening in the passing lane. No such luck. Less than ten feet from the Dart's tail she yanked the steering wheel to the right, felt the warning grooves vibrate the car as she maneuvered onto the shoulder. As she flew past the Dodge, she glimpsed an elderly man behind the wheel, staring straight ahead, either unaware of the chaos around him or too scared to take his eyes off of the road.

Just as quickly as she'd jerked the car to the right, she whipped it back into the traveling lane, now with a bit of space between her and the car in front of her. She stole a glance in the rear view mirror and saw cars swerving into the passing lane to avoid hitting the old man. With a deep breath, now wide awake, Shawnda asked herself again why she was on this quest. Originally it was for justice for her child's father. Now, she wondered if it was worth the effort.

***

Ace made the Interstate 95 south interchange and cruised along at eighty miles per hour. He would need to stop for gas soon, probably at St. George, where he could get a bite to eat and grab a beer. If that guy in the truck was trying to follow him, an unexpected stop might throw him off track. On the other hand, getting that tire fixed and pumped back up was going to take some time. Maybe he should continue to Kingsland and get a hotel there. Then he could do a little surveillance on that friend of Wilson's, Doug Farrell. No doubt, when Brush's ship was in port, he'd hook up with Farrell.

Ace thought about the man in the pickup truck. In the last week, Ace had been all over the southeast, from Savannah, Georgia to St. Augustine, Florida, back up to Norfolk Virginia, then to Columbia, South Carolina. He'd seen the truck on at least three occasions in different states. *Coincidence? Maybe in the movies, but not in real life.* Besides, the man had killed that bastard, David Wallace. It was logical to assume he also was the shooter in St. Augustine, Florida. Ace hadn't heard any news on Dean Gray, but it wasn't much of a stretch that he'd also killed Gray. If he could confirm Gray's murder, there would be no doubt that this guy was taking care of business…his business. In Ace's eyes, that just wasn't right.

He decided he'd continue on to Kingsland and follow his original plan. Wilson Brush was next on his list. Then it was on to Florida.

In just over an hour, he'd pass by Savannah. *Maybe I should drop in on Angelina and surprise her. She might be upset that I borrowed a little cash. I could try and sweet-talk her a bit.* Ace thought about Angelina's platinum hair and her shapely, surgically sculpted body. He smiled. In his head he heard her voice in that heavy southern, drunken drawl, "Ace, be a darlin' and fetch me anotha glass of wine. Oh, and put anotha bottle in the wine chilla. Then come rub my feet. They ache so bad."

By the time he came out of his trance, he was pushing ninety and his fists were wrapped tight around the steering wheel. In the heat of the early afternoon, he was passing cars and trucks like they were standing still. Taking deep breaths, Ace backed off the accelerator until he was again cruising at eighty. He relaxed a bit, checking his mirrors for South Carolina State Troopers. A minute later, he spotted a trooper sitting in the median, timing traffic headed south. Too close for comfort. *I guess dropping by Angelina's isn't such a great idea after all.*

***

Harold Trent was spooked. The woman in the beat up Toyota or whatever it was, stared right at him. Did she know who he was? She certainly didn't look like she was part of any military investigative team, but she did have a military look about her. *Maybe I'm paranoid. If she was following me, she would have called in the dogs. No. She was just some stupid civilian, nothing more.*

Trent ran into the diner and looked in the entry for a pay phone. He needed the yellow pages to find a tow service, and hoped they could come with a truck that had an onboard compressor. He also worried the tire would be forced off the rim since the air was so low. He didn't have any change. Popping his head inside the diner's interior doors, he asked the person at the cash register if she had change for a dollar so he could use the phone.

She looked at him with a smirk and said, "Sorry. I'm fresh out of change."

The waitress who had waited on him, the one he'd stiffed with the lousy tip, came up next to her and glared at Trent. Her coworker asked, "Y'all wouldn't have any change for this poor guy, would ya'? Looks like he's got himself an emergency."

She didn't even reply, just turned away from Trent and walked back to the server's station. The first waitress said, "Well, looks like none of us here have any change, mister. Why don't y'all try across the street at the hotel? Maybe they can help."

Trent glared at the young girl, but only for a moment. He had more pressing matters. The tire had to be fixed and he had to get on the road and catch up with Ace.

The vision of the lady in the Toyota kept coming back to him. Where had he seen her before? No time to dwell on that. He ran out of the diner and across the street to the *Econo Lodge*. Maybe he'd have better luck with someone he hadn't insulted.

Chapter 25

Nancy yanked the door open. "Get your asses in here."

The young men moved past her into the living room of Hatch's cabin. She looked down the long, gravel approach, the only means to get to the cabin on two or four wheels, then immediately shut the door behind them. She closed the curtains at the front cabin window, then motioned for Wilson and his friend to move to the eat-in kitchen.

Nancy's face was serious and tense. "What the hell are you two doing here?"

Wilson, in a highly sarcastic tone said, "Hi, Ms. Brown, nice to see you again, too. How the heck are you?"

Nancy cracked the slightest of smiles. "I'm fine, Wilson."

She turned to Wilson's friend. "You must be Doug Farrell. I'm Nancy Brown."

Nancy stuck out her hand and shook Doug's with a firm grip. Doug was giving her a brief once over with his eyes, trying not to be too obvious, but it wasn't working. He smiled. "Nice to meet you. Should I call you Nancy or…"

"Nancy's fine." She shook her head then asked, "Anything to drink, maybe an ice water?"

Without waiting for a reply, she grabbed two tall glasses and filled them with ice from the only modern appliance in Hatch's log cabin, a side-by-side refrigerator-freezer. She filled both with water and set them on the table.

She turned to Wilson and said, "I have to tell you that it's a real surprise seeing you here."

Wilson smiled. "Not half as surprising as it is to see you here. Where's Hatch?"

"He didn't say where he was headed when he left, but I'm thinking he's looking for you. Or he might be at Doug's, figuring that's where you'd head first when you got into port."

Wilson's brow furled in a confused look. "Why would he be looking for me? I'm supposed to be at sea. As a matter of fact I have to be back to the ship at six in the morning. We're only in port long enough to get a motor shaft replaced, then its haze gray and underway again."

Wilson took a long drink of water, then set his glass on the table. Doug did the same. Nancy looked from one to the other. "You have no idea what's happening, do you?"

The two young men glanced at each other, then turned back to Nancy and shook their heads.

She looked right at Wilson. "The best place for you right now is at sea. I hate to bring up a sore subject, but remember the older woman who was killed at the apartment in Norfolk? Abbie Glover?"

Wilson frowned. "The one who charged us as we were moving in on Tanya and Bobbie at the apartment? I mean, Becky and Bobbie?"

His face took on a pained expression. "Yeah, I remember all too well. I still see Tanya in my dreams, whether I want to or not. Some of the guys on the ship make fun of me because I toss and turn in my sleep. I guess I make some strange sounds." Wilson paused for a moment. "In those damned dreams...nightmares really. I see her alive and happy. Then I see her sprawled out in that damned entryway at the apartment. It's really vivid, too. I can smell the rain and the pine scent from the trees, and I can see the lightning flashes lighting up the sky. I can smell the blood, too. How weird is that?"

Nancy kept her expression neutral. Seeing someone die in such a violent, senseless way, especially someone for whom you had strong feelings, was traumatic. She knew that image would be ever embossed into the depths of his brain. Over time the image might fade, the feeling might dull, but it would never go away.

Nancy wasn't sure how to tell him he was in danger. But if she didn't, and he was killed, she'd never be able to live with herself. He could stay at Hatch's cabin tonight, then head straight for the ship early in the morning. He'd be out of sight and safe. Hatch and Nancy could deliver him straight to the pier and make sure he safely boarded the ship.

She asked, "Do you want the good news or the bad news first?"

Wilson went to the refrigerator and refilled his glass. He took a long drink of cold water, then set his glass on the table. "Let's have the good news I guess."

"You're still alive."

Wilson stared straight at her. "Is that supposed to be funny, because it missed the mark."

Doug Farrell gave Nancy a slightly contemptuous look. "What's that supposed to mean? I mean, is someone dead?"

Nancy, with a dead serious expression said, "Several someones, five so far." She turned to Wilson. "Do you remember Joe McKinney and me talking about David Wallace?"

Wilson nodded.

"He was shot and killed outside a bar in Columbia, South Carolina."

Wilson's face turned to a frown.

"And Dean Gray, the guy who lived in the apartment where Rebecca, Bobbie Garrett, and Abbie were killed? He was killed in his apartment in Norfolk the other day."

Wilson's expression was now a blank stare.

Nancy continued. "You probably don't remember us talking about Colonel Milton Chester. He was murdered at an abandoned missile silo about 2 years ago. We're not even counting him, but he had three buddies who were in the Air Force Academy with him. They were gunned down on a golf course in the middle of the day earlier in the week. We don't know why or what the connection is to the other murders, but somehow they're all linked."

Nancy knew she had Wilson's full attention, but he still looked confused. "Two of these guys were married to Tanya, Rebecca, Charlene, whatever her name was. We think that the killer is coming after anyone who had personal contact with her."

Wilson asked, "But why?"

"That we don't know. Maybe he believes he's avenging her death. Maybe he thinks her "husbands" abused her. Maybe he was jealous, who knows? But we do know that the pattern, if it's followed, leads to you. You're one of the few left we know of who had direct contact with her." She paused. Doug took a long drink from his glass, finishing the water. "This shooter started in St. Augustine, Florida then went to Norfolk. From there he came down to Columbia. Now it's a relatively short drive from Columbia to Kingsland, Georgia. It only makes sense, if any of this makes sense, that you're next."

Doug asked, "How would he know that Wilson's ship is in port?"

Nancy stood and walked to the refrigerator. "Either of you want a beer?"

They both nodded and said, "Sure."

Nancy grabbed three longneck Bud Light's and set them on the table. They twisted the tops off in unison and took a long pull on their beers.

She and Hatch had discussed this very question and had no good explanation. Hatch had said it wasn't all that difficult to get one of the wives of the crew to talk, but they didn't really know anything until right before the ship returned, usually less than forty-eight hours. There were other ways to find out, but none was very easy.

Nancy said, "I'm not sure the killer knows the ship is in port. It's just the next logical stop, unless he plans to skip you and head for his other targets."

The two men's eyebrows rose simultaneously. Wilson asked, "Other targets?"

***

Hatch had been south of the King's Bay Submarine Base at Tommy's Bar. Tommy's was a favorite hangout for submarine sailors just in from sea or heading home on their off duty days while their submarine was in port being prepared for going back out on patrol. He asked the bartender if he'd seen Wilson or Doug, then asked if anyone from the USS *Nevada* had been in today. The man said he'd seen a few crew members, but not Wilson or Doug. He knew them both on sight, but didn't start his shift until 1:00 PM. So they may have been in earlier. Hatch thanked the man and headed out to his car.

Hatch sat thinking for a few minutes before starting his car and heading west. Maybe they went right to Doug's place. That way, Wilson could get a shower and change into something more appropriate for the hot day.

It was only a ten minute drive to Doug's apartment in Kingsland, Georgia. Hatch hoped that, if they were there, they locked the door behind them. They had no idea danger was hot on Wilson's heels.

Chapter 26

At 1:45 PM Ace was on Interstate 95 south, passing Exit 109 just inside the Georgia border northwest of Savannah. The sun was high overhead, the sky a bright blue. There were just a few white, wispy clouds that looked like stretched out cotton balls, the white strands so thin you could almost see through them. The traffic was not too heavy, but not too light. The driving was easy and Ace had time to think of other things besides dodging crazy drivers who were in too much of a hurry. Two fighter jets maneuvered low on the horizon to the east, the sun glinting off of the surface of the aircraft as they made sharp turns in the sky over the ocean.

Ace wondered what it would be like to be in control of such a powerful aircraft, high above the chaos caused by mankind. He imagined he could see hundreds of miles in all directions from the cockpit of a jet. He'd never flown, but he decided he would add that to his bucket list. He wondered if flying a jet aircraft would be as much of a rush as pulling the trigger of a 9mm Glock, snuffing the life out of some bastard who didn't deserve to breathe the same air as his family. He shook his head, clearing away the dark vibes attempting to strangle his mind.

He had a strong urge to get off the interstate and drive past the home of Angelina Valentine. So strong, he pulled over to the right hand lane, thinking he would take Interstate 16 east and head into Savannah. At the last minute he came to his senses and decided the risk was too great, that Angelina would have him arrested the moment he pulled into her driveway. He drove on, heading south towards Kingsland. Only an hour-and-a-half, if he didn't make any other stops. He didn't need gas, and he wasn't real hungry after going through the drive-thru of the McDonalds back in St. George, South Carolina.

His first stop in Kingsland would be at the apartment of that friend of Brush's, Doug Farrell. He was out of the Navy now, but once a squid, always a squid. Just like that asshole, Bobby Garrett. Ace smiled at the thought that Bobby was dead, then his smile slowly turned to a frown realizing that in dying, Bobby had gotten his poor half-sister, Rebecca killed; used her for a shield like a coward, like all the guys in her life treated her. *Don't worry sis, the job's nearly finished. If I could just get the job done myself before the bastard in the pickup truck steals all my thunder.*

Ace's mood took a downward turn. Who was this guy, the one doing his job and what was his motivation? *I swear if he kills one more of those bastards I'm gonna kill him. I might do it anyway, just for him sticking his nose in where it doesn't belong.*

Ace decided to stop and stretch his legs. He spotted a *Speedy* gas station sign high over the trees at Exit 90 and pulled in even though the tank was just over half-full. When he finished topping off his tank, he went inside to pay cash so he didn't leave a credit card trail. He grabbed some snack food, a couple bottles of water, and a newspaper. Within fifteen minutes he was back on the interstate heading south again, the snacks and newspaper in the passenger seat.

As he cruised down the highway, he glanced over at the paper's front page. July 5, 1999. It had been less than one week since he'd left Angelina's in Savannah and headed for Florida. As much as he hated the way she treated him, he missed her. His mother had been his companion, nearly twenty-four hours a day, seven days a week before she'd been killed. When she was taken from him, it left a gaping hole in his heart. He yearned for companionship and hated it when he was alone. He craved human interaction, though he wasn't too much into conversation about current events, the latest gossip, or psycho analysis. He just liked being in the vicinity of people, or at least one person.

The drive to North Dakota after his mother had been gunned down had been the most painful three days in his life.

That was saying a lot because his childhood was full of painful moments. Several times in the Plains States he'd pulled off the highway and sat, his eyes so full of tears he could barely see the lines on the road. When the job was done and Colonel Chester was on his way to hell, Ace had felt some relief. But it had been at that moment he'd realized just how alone he really was.

Ace snapped out of his funk. He'd been thinking so long and hard about his personal problems he'd nearly missed Exit 3 for Kingsland, Georgia. He pulled off the highway at the exit ramp between stands of high pine trees, then turned west. He let both driver and passenger side windows down, letting the humid air flow through the car. The air was fresh, the scent of pine strong as he headed towards town.

As he drove along the roadway at the posted thirty-five miles per hour, he took in the nice homes and businesses. Life here seemed ordered, the houses well kept, painted and clean, the grass trimmed and green. New, small trees were mixed in with older trees, some covered in Spanish moss. Ace drove nearly a mile into town then turned left on Grove Boulevard. He passed a park with four baseball fields grouped so that the fields would look like a four leaf clover from the sky. Every field was busy with kids in tee shirts and blue jeans sporting baseball gloves or bats as their coaches pitched batting practice or hit ground balls.

The Colony Pines apartment complex where Doug Farrell lived was just south of the fields. From the southern-most parking spaces for the ball fields Ace could keep an eye on the apartment complex entry. He looked at the note paper he pulled from his pocket. It was so worn the creases in the slip of paper were torn, the writing smeared to the point where it was difficult to make out the characters.

It didn't matter. Ace had memorized Farrell's apartment number, 17D. Ace was in luck. Apartment 17D was right in front of one of several open spaces in the parking lot for the baseball fields. Ace pulled in and turned off the engine. He let the seat back just a bit, then grabbed the newspaper, preparing for what promised to be a long afternoon and possibly a late evening.

He scanned the front page, then the second and third pages, skipping the editorials. A story in the police blotter section caught his attention. *No Suspects in Murder of Wealthy Widow, Gloria Mason's Killer Still a Mystery.*

Ace frowned. The last time he'd seen Gloria Mason, Angelina Valentine's very close friend, was at the bar the night he left Savannah. *Angelina must be distraught.* He read on and determined that her body was found the very evening, or actually, early morning that he'd left Savannah. When he'd last seen her she was alive and well.

Ace shifted in his seat. Bypassing Savannah was a good call. *Could this have been that guy in the pickup truck? Nah. Why would he?*

* * *

William 'Hatch' Hatcher passed under the Interstate 95 bridge heading west on East King Avenue. This area was a bit too congested for his liking. He was used to the quiet of the swamp surrounding his log cabin in Moniac. It was just a short drive away, but to Hatch it seemed like a different universe.

It's not like Kingsland, Georgia was a major metropolis; it was just that the area was growing rapidly with the commercial development surrounding the Kings Bay Submarine Base. Since his discharge from the Navy at this very base, the population of the surrounding area had exploded. It seemed like money was flowing in from everywhere to capitalize on the government's rising investment in the base.

Hatch made the left turn onto South Grove Boulevard, driving past the baseball parks. The young kids were learning their skills on the ball field, guided by the amateur instructions of one or more of the boys' fathers. It was as American as it gets. Kids learning the game played by some of their heroes like Hank Aaron, Mickey Mantle, Al Kaline, and Sandy Kofax. Then Hatch realized most of those kids wouldn't recognize any of those names. They'd want to hear about Chipper Jones,

Andruw Jones, and Greg Maddux. He was getting older. That was a sobering thought.

Many of the kids on the field had just been born when Hatch joined the Navy. Now they were out playing ball, approaching adolescence. He had vowed he'd never bring a child into this world. But watching the kids on the ball fields, he wondered if he hadn't made that vow at a time when his thinking was jaded by his personal tragedy.

Hatch turned his attention back to the Colony Arms Apartment complex ahead on his left. Something caught his eye in the parking lot of the baseball diamonds and he decided to drive past the complex and do a U-turn.

On the way back towards the ball fields, he saw it. A white, non-descript sedan, the same one he'd seen in North Dakota at an abandoned missile site, sat in the parking lot of the baseball fields. It faced the apartment complex with a direct line of sight to apartment 17D, Doug Farrell's apartment. He looked closer and saw the blonde man sitting in the driver's seat.

Ace Glover.

Hatch turned right into the parking lot and slowly approached Ace's car. There was an open parking spot right next to his on the driver's side. Hatch decided it was time for a little fun.

He backed his Silver Taurus into the parking spot next to Ace's car, making sure his windows were down. He eased the car in far enough so that his window and Ace's were right next to each other. Hatch killed the engine and turned his attention to the kids on the ball diamonds.

He glanced left and noticed Ace had his head buried in a newspaper, all but ignoring him. Ace's car was facing away from the fields in the opposite direction of Hatch's.

After several minutes of sitting there, nearly within arms' reach of each other, Hatch said in a loud voice, "Alright, Jimmy, way to go." He paused. "Keep going, you got it, alright."

He turned to Ace and said in his heavy southern drawl, "That's ma boy, Jimmy. He's the star of the team this year."

At first, Ace didn't acknowledge Hatch had said anything. He looked Hatch's way briefly then went back to the newspaper.

Hatch then said, "Come on, Jimmy. Hustle it down there. At a boy."

Then in Ace's direction, "He's the fastest kid on the team, too." He paused to see if he had Ace's attention. When Ace didn't turn his way Hatch asked, "Which one is yours?"

Finally, Ace gave in, "He's out there on one of the fields on the other side. There's no parking over there so I just park over here."

"Yeah. That's one thing 'bout the fields here. The design's not so great. I mean, they coulda put parkin' pretty much all the way round the complex, but some city planner didn't use his head."

Ace looked at Hatch for a bit. He looked dumbfounded, seemingly not knowing how to reply.

"Name's Hatch. That's what folks call me anyway."

"Ace."

Hatch was surprised when Ace used his real name, but he kept his face cheerfully neutral. "So Ace, what do you do? You know, for work?"

"I'm a handyman. I fix things, mainly electrical and electronic stuff."

Hatch noticed him glance at the complex, towards Farrell's apartment. "Somebody you know?"

"What? No, I thought I saw something moving over there." He pointed to a gray squirrel digging in the ground. "I think that squirrel caught my eye."

"It's funny, but I know a dude who lives in the complex. We was in the Navy together."

Ace asked, "What's the guy's name? Maybe I know him."

"He's a big 'ol boy. Name's Doug Farrell. Folks call him Dougie. We was on the *Nevada* together. We're both out now. He just got out a short while ago." Hatch paused, looking for any reaction, but Ace kept a poker face, not letting on that he knew Doug Farrell. "Last I heard he was in Florida for a week or so."

It was a gamble playing that last line, especially since Farrell could pull up to his apartment at any time. Worse, he could have Wilson Brush with him, but he needed to see how much Ace Glover knew. If he didn't know too much, maybe he'd give up on Wilson and move on to his next target.

Hatch, not getting any reaction from his comments, turned his attention back towards the baseball fields. He shouted, "Good catch Jimmy." Then to Ace he said, "We used to practice for hours ever' day when I was in port. That's why I got out. I missed my kid somethin' fierce. Do you know what it's like to miss someone so much you would change your life completely to be with 'em?"

Ace's expression finally cracked a bit. Hatch knew he'd struck a nerve. Ace suddenly straightened, started his car, then backed out. He left the parking lot a little faster than necessary, especially with all the kids milling around.

Hatch smiled and opened his cell phone. He dialed Nancy's cell phone. She picked up before the second ring.

"You'll never guess who I just talked to."

She replied, "You'll never guess who I'm sitting with."

They said at the same time, "You go first."

Chapter 27

"Yes, ma'am, I can wait."

The voice on the line asked if he'd rather call back, that it might take a while to get through to Colonel Barnes, but Bill Banks preferred to stay connected. If he remained on the line it would be easier to get the colonel's full attention. If he gave up and called back he might never get through.

After about nine minutes, the attendant came back on the line. "The colonel will speak with you now, detective."

With that, the line clicked and a woman's voice, clear and sharp, came on the line. "Detective Banks, what can I do for you?"

"Thank you for taking my call, Colonel. I'll be brief. We're trying to reach Major Shawnda Hull. We understand she was transferred to the Academy a year-and-a-half ago. We need to interview her with regards to a murder investigation."

There was a long silence on the line, so long that Banks thought they might have been disconnected. Then Colonel Barnes said, "I'm afraid that an interview with Major Hull won't be possible at this time."

Banks was already perturbed by the lack of cooperation from the Air Force. He'd run into road blocks at Grand Forks Air Force Base. Then when trying to contact other interviewees who had been transferred, they were either on duty or "deployed." All sorts of obstacles were being thrown up to thwart any progress in their investigation. He was in no mood to get the run–around again.

"Colonel, I hope I don't have to go over your head to—"

"There's no reason to go over my head, Detective. Major Hull is not here. In fact, we don't know where she is because she's AWOL. Has been for over eighteen months."

Banks jaw dropped. He reached for his coffee cup and took a sip. The swill in the bottom of the cup was cold and nasty. He swallowed it anyway. For the briefest of moments, he didn't know how to react. He'd been in touch with Colonel Templeton and his staff at Grand Forks. They had to know that Major Hull had gone off the reservation. Why hadn't they said anything? Even Airman Goff didn't reveal that Shawnda Hull had disappeared.

Maybe she'd been threatened by the killer and was in hiding. Or maybe she was already dead.

"Detective?"

"Yes...sorry. I was thinking. Do you have family contact information for Major Hull, a husband, parents, siblings?"

Colonel Barnes was again silent long enough that Banks was becoming impatient. He said in a firm voice, "Colonel Barnes, five military personnel have been murdered in the last week. We're getting a lot of, what I would call, interference from the military. It's in your best interest and the best interests of the Air Force that you cooperate with us so we can find the bastard killing your people. It could very well be that Major Hull is a target of the killer. Now, you can help us or you can sit back and watch the bodies pile up. Which will it be?"

The colonel sighed and said, "Okay, Detective, but I'll have to get one of my staff working on it. Leave your number with my assistant. She'll contact you when we get it together."

"Thank you, Colonel."

"And Detective, it isn't that we don't want to help. We're busy and we're short staffed, just like everyone else. What I'm saying is, don't expect a call in the next ten minutes."

"Fair enough, Colonel."

To Banks, the colonel's last line sounded like another stall tactic. How long would it take to pull up a computer file or open a filing cabinet and pull Major Hull's file? After all, she was AWOL and probably at the top of a lot of people's lists.

***

Shawnda Hull turned left on South Grove Boulevard and noticed the kids practicing baseball. It was late in the Little League season, so these were probably teams preparing for the playoffs. As she drove slowly past the fields, a white sedan turned onto the street heading in her direction, moving much too fast for an area crawling with kids. Then, as the car approached, she saw the blond hair. It was Ace.

A chill ran down her spine. Was she again too late to catch Ace in the act? Had he killed again and was fleeing the scene?

She accelerated, looking for any sign of where Ace might have just been. But what? A body? Maybe a screaming woman or a crowd of people calling for an ambulance? When she didn't see anything obvious, she yanked on her steering wheel and turned into the parking lot intending to do a u-turn. As she tried to back out onto the street, a car horn blared close behind her. She looked in her rear view mirror and saw a car close to her bumper. She waited for the car to move. When it didn't, she pulled forward, hoping to drive in a quick circle in the parking lot and head back out onto South Grove Boulevard and catch up to Ace's car. As she completed the turn and angled back to the exit, the car that had been behind her again blocked her path. She slammed on her brakes, her tires screeching loud enough to make everyone's head turn in her direction. She was going to lose Ace if she didn't get on the road in a hurry. She laid on her horn, trying to get the man to move his car, but he made no attempt to clear out of the exit. There was no other exit from the parking lot unless she drove over the sidewalk, tree lane, and curb.

The man in the car blocking her path opened his car door and headed towards her. Shawnda was confused. Why the hell didn't he just move his damn car so she could get on the road?

He slowly strode up to the driver's side of the Toyota and in a deep southern drawl said, "Hello, Shawnda, or would y'all prefer Major Hull?"

She nearly panicked when this total stranger addressed her. He held up his hands and said, "Now, calm down. I'm not with the military and I'm not with Ace. I do believe that we need to talk though."

***

Hatch and Shawnda Hull sat together at a picnic table by the baseball fields, but far enough away from the crowd so no one could hear their conversation. They sat in the shade under the canopy of an ancient live oak tree where Spanish moss hung in long gray strands from thick branches that extended out from a massive center trunk. The breeze couldn't be called cool, but it did offer some relief from the afternoon heat.

Hull listened while Hatch explained his interest in Ace, and that he knew about the recent murders of Aims, Wesley, and Dempsey in St. Augustine. He told her Dean Gray and Sergeant David Wallace had also been killed, and that he and others working the case knew that Ace wasn't the gunman.

Shawnda told Hatch that she knew Ace hadn't killed the three officers, but she hadn't known for certain about the other killings.

Hatch asked, "How long have y'all been followin' Ace?"

"About the last six months. It took me almost a year to find out where he was. When I left Grand Forks I came east to be with my folks and to have my baby."

"Didn't the Air Force come lookin' for ya? I mean, it wouldn't be too tough figurin' that y'all would head for your folks."

"They did. My dad put me up in an apartment close to home under a different name. He hated doing it 'cause he's retired Air Force. Thought I should turn myself in right away. I'm going to do that when this is over."

"So when did ya learn where Ace was holed up?"

"I have a friend in Grand Forks. He's kind of a nerdy guy, knows computers inside and out. He has another friend who's even more of a geek than him. But they know a private investigator in Savannah, Georgia. They helped track Ace down.

"Y'all's friend wouldn't be Airman Goff, would it?"

Hull just stared at Hatch. How could he know about Airman Goff? And what else did he know?

"Yeah. Adam Goff, the lovable creampuff. He's in love with me, I think. But I guess he's just too nice of a guy for me." She paused then continued, putting the conversation back on track. "When I found out Ace was in Savannah, I came right down here and started to watch him." She paused. "It was tough because he didn't really do anything for the first couple of months. Then he started hitting the clubs. That was tough, too, because he only went to the expensive clubs and I couldn't afford to get in. I didn't understand what he was doing. He was living with a wealthy widow, but he was going to clubs, picking up women and giving them a line of bull shit, like he was some poor guy who'd run into a streak of bad luck. They were actually giving him money, lots of money," Shawnda said.

Hatch thought for a moment, looking up at the beautiful old oak trees with their expansive, thick branches. He could think of only one reason why Ace would have been accumulating cash. He left his live-in lover and was heading out on his own on a mission and he needed cash for tools. The tools Ace needed were guns to continue his killing spree.

"How were ya living up there? I mean, y'all had to have livin' expenses, like food, an apartment, utilities, other bills."

"My mom kept my bank account filled when I needed money. I think Dad knew, but he had to put on this front that he didn't approve. I mean, he really didn't approve, but I think he just ignored what my mom was doing for me. It goes against every fiber in his body, you know?"

"Yeah. I think I understand." Hatch paused then asked, "What were ya figurin' on doin' once ya found him? I mean, why didn't ya just call the law?"

"I guess it's because I really didn't have proof of anything."

She told him about her plan to film Ace in some illegal act and turn it over to the police.

He smiled, but it was a sad, half-smile. "Y'alls awfully lucky that other fella didn't kill ya'. Ya know, whoever that dude is, he's killed a bunch of folks already. Y'all know who I'm talking about, don't ya'?"

She flashed to the guy with the pickup truck in the parking lot of the diner in Columbia, South Carolina. It had occurred to her he might be involved somehow, but the shooter? She'd been so intent on trying to implicate Ace in something criminal that she'd lost sight of the fact she might actually be in danger.

"I didn't care if it was dangerous. I just know Ace killed Milt."

"Ya mean y'all's boss, Colonel Chester, right?"

She smiled, but her smile had a deep sadness about it. Hatch could tell that her heart ached. He had surmised that she was in love with Milton Chester and the look on her face only confirmed his suspicions.

"Yeah, my boss."

"Miss Hull, ma'am, it ain't none of my business, and y'all can tell me to take a hike, but is the late colonel your son's daddy?"

Her jaw dropped just enough to show her astonishment.

Hatch watched her expression and could easily read that she was becoming skeptical of his intentions. He needed to get her to a safe place and get her back home where she was out of harm's way. The way she was operating she was bound to get hurt or killed.

Hatch said, "I have an idea. How 'bout we let y'all talk with someone else who knows just how dangerous this situation is for ya? I promise she isn't in the military and we're not going to try anything sneaky. After we're done, we'll let y'all decide your next move. Deal?"

Shawnda thought about it, then slowly nodded. Her will to fight was running on fumes. Maybe she could get home to see her son before she had to face the music.

Chapter 28

Nancy frowned when she heard a car badly in need of a muffler coming up the access road to Hatch's cabin. It surprised her because there was only one inbound road surrounded by swamp and cypress trees. She had expected to hear Hatch's quiet Ford Taurus, the only sounds being the popping of twigs under his tires. Grabbing her forty-caliber Smith and Wesson out of her purse, she glided towards the window closest to the southernmost point in the cabin. She pinched the end of the curtain and moved it slightly, just enough to see Hatch's Ford Taurus coming up the drive. It was only then she spotted the source of the noisy muffler, an older model white Toyota Corolla. A redheaded woman sat in the driver's seat. It took Nancy a moment, but then recognition flooded in. She said quietly to no one in particular, "Major Shawnda Hull. What on earth are you doing here?"

Wilson Brush, hearing Nancy's voice asked, "What was that?"

"Nothing. We're having all kinds of visitors today, that's all."

Nancy retreated to the couch and placed her pistol back into her purse. She returned to the door and opened it just as Hatch and Major Hull walked up.

Hatch, seeing Wilson and Doug Farrell sitting at the kitchen table put on a big smile and said, "Well, if it ain't Tom and Jerry, or is it Mutt and Jeff?"

He walked up to the two men who each gave Hatch a bear hug. All three wore smiles as bright as day.

Hatch said, "It sure is good to see y'all, especially alive and well."

Wilson replied first. "You, too Hatch. This is quite the place you have here."

Hatch waved him off. "It ain't bad for a country boy like me. But it ain't no palace. Did Nancy give y'all the tour? It takes about ten seconds 'cause what ya see is what ya get."

He swung his arm like a game show host towards Shawnda. "Nancy has already met our guest of honor, but I'd like to introduce y'all to Major Shawnda Hull, United States Air Force. Miss Shawnda is currently on leave of absence from said Air Force, but plans to return real soon."

Hatch turned towards Shawnda. "Miss Shawnda, I am pleased to introduce y'all to Mr. Wilson Brush," he pointed towards Wilson, "and Mr. Douglas Farrell. Wilson here is active duty Navy stationed aboard the mighty USS *Nevada*. Dougie is now ex-Navy, but was also stationed aboard the *Nevada*."

Shawnda held out her hand in a nervous gesture and said hello to both men.

Hatch, ever the gentleman asked, "Miss Shawnda, may I interest you in a drink of some sort?"

Again nervously, "Water, thanks."

Hatch headed towards the kitchen, talking over his shoulder as he went. "The Major is going to tell us a little story, so I want y'all to listen closely to what she has to say."

Hatch noticed the shocked expression on Major Hull's face. He nodded to Nancy, giving her the go-ahead to take charge of the discussion. He figured she wasn't going to play nice with the Major.

In a rather stern voice she said, "Major, I take it that right now, you are AWOL from the Air Force."

"Yes, Ma'am, I am. I'm planning to turn myself in immediately after I go to my parent's house and see my son. I'll be doing that as soon as my business is done here."

"And what is your 'business' here?"

Hatch gave Nancy an approving look as he delivered Shawnda's ice water, which he set on a cypress coaster on the coffee table made from a three inch thick slice from a large cypress tree.

Major Hull hesitated, took a deep breath, then looked resigned. She picked up the glass of water and took a long drink, wiping her mouth with the back of her hand.

"I've been following a man named Ace Glover. I believe he killed Colonel Milton Chester two years ago in North Dakota at an abandoned missile silo. I want to make sure he's arrested and tried for that murder."

Nancy continued without a beat. "So you're willing to throw away a promising military career to follow a murderer around the country? Why is this so important to you? I know he was your boss, but it seems a bit extreme to be hunting down his killer...unless there was more going on than a professional relationship."

Nancy and the three men watched as Shawnda's officer demeanor started to crack. When Nancy had started in on her, Shawnda had maintained a stone faced look, stoic and unwavering. As Nancy continued to question her judgment, her chin began the slightest quiver. Then her lips turned down and her eyes began to tear up. Without being asked, Hatch handed her several tissues...and the flood gates opened.

***

Harold Trent had lost nearly forty-five minutes getting his tire pumped back up before he could head out on the interstate. As he hit mile marker twelve just ten minutes north of the exit for Kingsland, St. Marys, and the Kings Bay Submarine Base, he tried to channel his thoughts and concentrate on Ace. He had a good idea where Ace was headed and the tracking device on Ace's car would make finding him easy, but his thoughts kept getting sidetracked by the red-headed woman in the beat up Toyota. Had he seen her before? If yes, where? She had the look of a military officer and that scared him a bit. But if that were true, why was she driving around in that beat up piece of crap? The way she'd been sitting at the back of the parking lot at the diner, maybe she was part of a police surveillance team that was looking for Ace. If true, then Ace was in deep trouble and needed his help. That was a big if, though, because they could have taken Ace at the hotel. Why chase him all the way to southern Georgia?

Trent turned off the highway and headed towards the submarine base, then he turned right at the roadway just before the main gate. As he approached the turn, his nerves went haywire when he spotted the uniformed Marine guards standing post at the entrance. If he were stopped for any reason, his life as he now knew it would be over. He wasn't living the life of luxury, but it beat the hell out of life in a military prison. They hadn't caught up to him in over twenty-five years so chances were he was long forgotten. But the military machine had long memories and held a grudge for people who crossed the line.

Making the turn east along the southern fenced border of the base, the scent of pine was strong enough to mask the slight odor of rotting vegetation from the Crooked River.

After five minutes, Trent pulled his truck into the parking lot of Tommy's Place, a bar favored by sailors coming home from sea, particularly those who had no wife or children to greet them. It was also one of the first stops of men coming off long duty days during refit, when sailors and contractors readied the ship for heading back out to sea. After a long duty day followed by a normal day's work, it was a convenient stop outside the southern gate of the base.

Trent waited in the bar entry for a moment, allowing his eyes to adjust from the bright sunlight to the artificial light of the bar room.

The bar was a large, single room with about a dozen tables and an equal number of booths along three walls. The fourth wall was consumed by a long mirror behind an excellent collection of liquors, from bar brands to top shelf labels. An older man worked behind the bar, drying a glass with a dish towel, then setting it on a shelf hidden under the dark, polished bar.

Trent scanned the faces in the small crowd. No one looked his way for more than a split second, except the blond man in the booth all the way across the room. Ace Glover sat alone, nursing a beer, apparently deep in thought until he saw Harold Trent standing at the door. Recognition flashed in Ace's eyes momentarily then he glanced back down. Trent walked to the bar and ordered two long necks from the old man, then headed right to the booth where Ace sat.

He placed one of the bottles on the table in front of Ace. "Mind if I join you?"

"Free country."

Ace kept staring at his beer bottle, then lifted it to his lips and drained the last swallow. He set the bottle aside, picked up the bottle that Trent had just delivered and took a long pull. He set the bottle down as Trent slid into the booth across from him.

Ace said, "You're the one."

Then he looked Trent in the eyes. "Why are you looking at me like you don't know what I'm talking about? You're the guy from St. Augustine and Columbia and a couple other places. The pickup truck. You drive that beat up truck."

Trent couldn't run from it any longer. Ace had called him on it. He'd followed the young man for years. He'd known this day would come, even wanted it to come. He had tried to make it happen many times before, but chickened out, hadn't been able to go through with it. That was back when Ace's mother was still alive.

Abbie. His dear, sweet Abbie. Well, she wasn't really all that sweet. In fact she'd kicked Trent out, made him leave the two of them so she could pursue a life with that prick, Bobbie Garrett. *That ended well, didn't it?* That bastard had left her for Becky. He had left her and her young son penniless to fend for themselves while he and Becky went after their fortunes. Trent guessed karma had kicked in and evened that score, but Abbie had paid the price. Now he had to protect her son—their son—from the same fate. He had to tell Ace the truth about their relationship. It was past time. He just hoped it wasn't too late.

***

The phone rang a few minutes after 6:00 PM. Pat and Diane McKinney were just clearing the dinner dishes from the table when Pat answered, "McKinney's."

"Do y'all always answer the phone like that?"

"Hatch, how the heck are you?"

"Well, Patrick, it's too bad you and your brother aren't here. I have a cabin full of crazy people. Y'all would fit right in."

Pat smiled. "Who's invaded the swamp?"

"I'll start with Nancy. Then there's Wilson Brush, Dougie Farrell, and someone that you'll never guess in a million years."

"Okay, I'm not going to try."

"Do you remember your brother Joe talkin' about Colonel Milton Chester's assistant at Grand Forks Air Force Base?"

"Are you talking about that red headed major..." He snapped his fingers a couple times. "...Hull, right? Sharon Hull?"

"Very good. Except its *Shawnda* Hull. She's just told us some very interesting facts about Colonel Chester we didn't know."

Pat waited.

"Well, aren't ya goin' ta ask me?" Hatch said.

"Sure Hatch, what–"

"Don't interrupt me. I'm on a role. Colonel Chester and Major Hull had a bit of a thing going. It turns out the major was pregnant with his child when the colonel was killed."

Pat whistled into the phone. "That's big. Is she still in the Air Force?"

"Yes, barely. She's AWOL right now, but we're fixin' to get that straightened out, as much as it can be straightened out. Ya see, she's been followin' our killer all over hell and high water. But she's headin' back to her folks in Virginia in a few hours."

"So, if she's in southern Georgia, then Ace Glover is, too. And he's looking for Wilson. So have you got the doors and windows barred yet?"

"Why would I do that?"

"So Ace can't get at Wilson."

"Funny you should say that. I spoke with Mr. Ace Glover earlier today. Said he was watchin' his kid play ball, but he was facin' Dougie Farrell's apartment."

There was a long pause, then Pat said, "I think you should start at the beginning."

Chapter 29

Harold Trent took a long gulp of beer, set the bottle down on the table, then took a deep breath. It was time to come clean with his son, Ace Glover. But now that the moment had come, he had a hard time putting his thoughts in order. The speech he'd practiced thousands of times, the one that would put the past behind them so that they could live out their lives as father and son stuck in his throat. Maybe this was a mistake.

Ace sat across from him, staring with icy gray eyes. In them, Trent saw years of pain. Ace's eyes weren't dead, but they had seen death more than once. A chill ran up Trent's spine and he took another long pull on his beer, delaying the inevitable.

Ace finally broke the ice. "So, just who the hell are you and why are you here?"

Trent set his beer down again and took another deep, nervous breath. He shook inside, worried about his first words, what they would sound like to this kid who'd never had a father figure in his life.

Trent cleared his dry throat. "I knew your mother, Abbie. I actually met her about twenty-five years ago, before you were born."

Ace's expression didn't change. He kept staring.

Trent went on. "I was in the delivery room when your half-sister was born. Your mother gave her up for adoption."

Ace sneered. "How do I know you're telling me the truth? Anybody could find that out. Of course she gave Becky up for adoption. She was only fifteen; she had no money, no future." Ace stared at Trent. "Why were you there?"

"The Air Force. They ordered me to watch. They wanted to make sure the baby was born, the adoption was completed, and that your mother would never see the child again."

He paused, looking away from the weight of Ace's steel glare. He picked up his beer and took another long drink, emptying the bottle, hoping when he looked up again, Ace would be looking around the bar or out the window or anywhere but at him. When he finished his drink, he looked back across the table. Ace's eyes again locked in on his, pulling on his soul.

Ace said nothing. He just continued to stare at Trent, his eyes unblinking.

Trent continued, hoping to break the tension and establish some kind of bond before he told him about their biological relationship. "Your sister was adopted by a real nice couple. It looked like that was going to work out…but your mother was a mess. I gave her an envelope with some cash. That-"

"You want me to tell you the rest of the story?" Ace said in a quiet voice filled with barely controlled anger.

Ace trembled slightly as he spoke. Trent wished they were someplace private. He feared Ace would explode in rage and start yelling right here in front of nearly two dozen witnesses. Trent nodded, and hoped as Ace told his story, the tension would ease.

"My mother moved east, got an apartment in Norfolk. She figured she could make a living there. Her mom kicked her out after she got pregnant. So what else could she do? She had ten grand to make a new start. But it turned out she was about as good with money as she was at picking men."

Ace took a deep breath, but his eyes never left Trent's face.

"When she got to Norfolk, some guy showed up and helped her out for a while. She stayed with him for a little over five years. Then she got pregnant again and the bastard left her high and dry. My father."

Ace's stare grew harder and deeper. His face turned red, the anger welling up from deep inside.

He leaned forward and continued in a very low, cold voice, nearly too quiet for Trent to hear. "My father...what a joke. He never so much as acknowledged that I was alive."

Ace finally turned his gaze away for just a moment. It seemed he was looking around the bar to see if anyone was listening. He snapped his glare back towards Trent, burning a hole deep into his eyes. "Mom said he was dead, that he died a long time ago. I think that's the only lie Mom ever told me. She was hoping I'd forget him, you know, think about other things she thought were more important. But I know he's alive." He paused again, the stare more intense, his face twisting as if he'd bitten into something sour. "If I ever find that bastard, I'll kill him with my bare hands."

Harold Trent's throat went dry, the chill racing up and down his spine. He shivered. It was good that Ace had picked up the story before Trent could blurt out he was Ace's long lost father, but he had to set the record straight. Abbie had told him to leave, that she didn't deserve him, that he needed to get away from her. She was bad luck and anyone who stayed around her was somehow contaminated, their lives turned upside-down.

It didn't matter what Ace thought. Now was the time to tell him the truth. If Ace decided to kill him right here in the bar, so be it. Trent wasn't long for this life, regardless of the outcome of this meeting anyway.

All his life, he'd rarely made the right choices. Sometimes it was fate, other times it was a conscious decision. This time he didn't have a backup plan, something he could pull out of his bag of tricks and use to weasel out of this conversation. He thought about ordering another round of beers to give himself more time to think, but decided enough was enough. Calm came over him as he realized the moment was upon him.

In a low, clear voice Harold Trent said, "Ace, I'm your father."

***

Pat wasn't sure what he was going to tell his wife Diane about the mail he had just received, since she was the one who'd retrieved it a few minutes ago. When he opened the thirteen by nine inch envelope and read the headlines on the newspaper clippings it contained, he knew who had sent them. At least, he thought he knew.

The articles came from several different newspapers in major cities in the southeast and a couple from South Dakota. They were stapled in chronological order, the oldest date on top, the more recent towards the bottom. Pat leafed through the stories, reading far enough to understand they were accounts of murders that had happened over two years ago, the deaths of Rebecca Lippert and Bobby Garrett.

The stories didn't stop there. There were several articles from the Grand Forks Herald on the murders of Sergeant Kevin Reardon, the first murder that pulled Nancy Brown and Joe McKinney into the investigation, and Colonel Milton Chester. The story on Milton Chester was just a reiteration of the fact that the murder had not been solved.

The next series of articles described the murders of Private Edward Sharp, Richard Wallace—father of David Wallace, and Private Leonard Skiff, the young Marine assigned to assist in finding Bobby Garrett and Becky Lippert. Each of the men was killed by the same weapon, therefore, most likely by the same person. The newspaper had yellowed somewhat, belying the age of the articles.

Besides the faded pages were two articles that appeared new. The first was from the *Virginian-Pilot*, the Norfolk area daily paper. It described the murder of Dean Gray in his apartment. The story even noted the apartment was the scene of a deadly gun battle two years ago in which federal agents shot and killed three people, two of whom were accused of defrauding the federal government. The third was thought to be an accomplice. The article noted there were no witnesses to Gray's murder.

The second was from *The State*, Columbia, South Carolina's daily paper. The story had been cut out of the paper so that the date was showing, *July 5, 1999. Yesterday.* The article described the apparent murder of David Wallace, an

Army Sergeant who was facing a court martial for the murder of two Afghan civilians. Again, there were no witnesses, but the bartender and several bar patrons gave a good description of a person at the bar who left about the same time as the victim. A police search didn't turn up anyone matching the description.

Pat thought about the intended message of the clippings. *No one can catch me...and you're next.* He rubbed the scar on his chin, a habit he had picked up shortly after he got out of the hospital where a doctor had removed a nail from his jaw, then stitched up the hole it left.

His first concern was for his family. The last thing he needed was some deranged murderer to break into his house and put his family in harm's way. His second concern was his brother and his family. He had a one year old baby girl and a wife he adored. He had to call Joe and warn him.

As if on cue, Pat's phone rang. He answered.

"McKinneys."

"Ditto."

"Hey, Joe, I was just going to call you."

"About the newspaper articles?"

Pat was dumbfounded, then realized Joe had received his own package. "Yeah, exactly. Does Lisa know about them yet?"

"No, but it's only a matter of time. She doesn't miss much. She handed me the envelope and asked if I knew what it was. At the time, I had no idea. I'll give her about five more minutes before she's in here asking what it is."

"I know what you mean. I figure Diane is going to beat that time. We better get our stories straight."

Just then, Diane walked in with a glass of ice water. She handed it to Pat then asked with an accusatory tone, "Which story is that, sweetie?"

Pat hesitated. "Joe, about that story? Lisa's going to know the truth in about ten minutes. That's right after Diane gets rid of my body."

"Aw, shit."

Pat heard Lisa's voice in the background on Joe's end of the phone, "What are you swearing about?"

"Pat, I've gotta go. Hopefully we'll be alive later to talk about this."

"Yeah, hopefully."

***

Forty-five minutes later Diane and Lisa were talking on the phone. Neither woman understood how their husbands managed to get drawn into such predicaments.

"Do you ever regret marrying Joe?" Diane asked.

"No, not for a minute. He's such a great father, and he's very good to me. It's just weird I guess. I kind of like the adventure, but now with Danielle in the picture and another one on the way, I just wish things would settle down. I worry sometimes, about the kids."

Diane was quiet for a moment. "There was a time when I really thought about taking the kids and leaving Pat. I was worried sick about the kids getting hurt. Now, I hate to say it, but I'm kind of used to it. Is that scary or what?"

Lisa sipped her coffee, "Yeah, it is. I think we need to have a talk, the four of us, about this whole situation. What do you think?"

"When we go shopping tomorrow, let's figure out how we're going to pin Pat and Joe down on what they're going to do about this Ace Glover character. They'll both be at your house when we get finished. If we don't like their plan, we can give them our advice."

"I think they need more than advice."

"When I give Pat advice, he knows the consequences of not taking it."

Lisa agreed. "Sounds like a good plan."

Chapter 30

Angelina Valentine realized Ace wasn't coming back. It had been fun while it lasted, but it was time to move on. Part of moving on involved cleaning out Ace's room. Since he'd spent most of his evenings in Angelina's room, his room was seldom used. The closet and dresser drawers were full of untouched clothes. She hadn't wanted to disturb anything in case this whole mess was a misunderstanding. She would not believe he had anything to do with the murder of her close friend, Gloria Mason. There were still no solid leads, but Ace was still the only person of interest.

She made her way up the wide, winding staircase, then down the hallway to Ace's room. The police had been there with a search warrant, which they hadn't needed since Angelina would have let them search to their hearts content. They didn't make too big of a mess, but, they didn't clean up after themselves. She'd seen the cop shows on television and had expected worse. After she packed up Ace's wardrobe in large trash bags, she planned to call the local Goodwill. After all, she had no use for his clothes.

Before she started bagging all of Ace's belongings, she sat at the foot of the king sized bed, looking around the huge guest room with its white ceiling and trim, the gray walls with the veins of white running over the surface, and the few expensive paintings hanging where the decorator said they should. The floor length curtains were pulled back to let in the light that managed to stream through the tall oaks and the multitude of Spanish moss hanging from their branches.

Angelina took deep breaths, finding in each one just a hint of the aftershave and cologne Ace wore. The scents were gifts from her, gifts that, in his haste to escape, he'd left in the medicine cabinet in her bathroom.

She lay back on the bed, feeling the silky smoothness of the comforter that had been thrown back on after the police officers had yanked it off, then tossed it aside before they'd searched under, on, and around the bed-frame and mattresses. Thankfully, they hadn't damaged any of her belongings.

She closed her eyes, inhaled deeply again, and imagined Ace lying next to her, his warmth emanating from his body as he eased closer. Her lips curled up in the slightest of smiles, as she remembered the first night she'd knocked on his door, then came into this very room wearing a sexy, silky robe and nothing else. He had taken charge and she had let him. For a young man, he seemed experienced, knowing what to say, when to breath close to her neck, how to caress, easing her slowly up the hill, building to great heights of pleasure. As she thought about that night, she moved slowly, sensuously on the comforter, not touching herself, but allowing her thoughts to coax her along the path, up the slow, easy incline where Ace had guided her. Her body warmed. In her mind she saw Ace moving around her, the tingling in her breasts pronounced. Heat rose along the center of her being as her mind and body merged. She grasped the comforter, fighting the urge to touch herself.

The shrill sound of the phone pierced the fantasy. Her eyes popped open and she stared at the ceiling as the phone rang again. She let it ring a third time before she sat up in bed, rolled towards the night stand and reached for the phone.

She cleared her throat. "Hello."

No one answered. There was sound, like the wind echoing over the receiver. The caller might be at an outdoor pay phone or on a cell phone outside. She heard breathing, but no voice.

"Hello?"

Again, no response.

"I'm hanging up now."

And she did. She shook her head, angry that a phone call had disturbed her daydream. Pushing her blonde hair behind her ears, she resumed gathering and bagging Ace's things. It was tedious work for someone who had a maid service, but she wanted to do this herself. It was one last personal, nearly intimate act she could do with her ex-lover. *I should be mad as hell with him for stealing that money, but he must have had a good reason to take it. Hell, he could have helped himself to a lot more.* Angelina shrugged and set to work, opening drawers and stuffing bags full of shirts, jeans, shorts, socks, and underwear. She sealed each bag with a twisty, then headed for the closet.

The deep, walk-in closet was nearly the size of a bedroom in most homes. The fourteen by twelve foot space was custom fitted with three separate dressers for shoes, sweaters, spare wallets, and assorted men's accessories, nearly all of which Ace had never worn. He was content in his cargo shorts, golf shirts or tee shirts, and sandals or leather deck shoes. Angelina never once saw him wear one of the nearly three dozen ties that hung neatly at one end of the closet.

A handful of suits and dress pants had been pulled from their hangers during the search and were strewn on the closet floor. Most of the remainder of the clothing still hung undisturbed. She moved to the first row of dress shirts, all of which had been washed only once, when they were removed from the store wrapping.

As she continued bagging the clothing, her thoughts lapsed back to a time she and Ace were out to dinner. They had run into a number of Angelina's friends from before her husband's death. Their attitudes towards her had been cold, but she'd introduced Ace in a gleeful way, letting them know she was moving on with her life, that she was through playing the grieving widow. She still had plenty of life to live and she wasn't going to waste a minute.

For his part, Ace played along. He had pretended to be in love with her, a line that almost had her believing that he did. Maybe in his own way he had fallen for her. It couldn't have been just her money. He had access to a fortune and he'd taken a fraction of that amount. But why had he left? She knew he had secrets, the way he avoided specifics about his past. He never let on about where he was born or who his parents were. He always changed the subject, or redirected those questions to her, asking about her past or her family history. In the end, she realized that he knew everything about her, and she knew precious little about him.

She worked her way to the shoe dresser where drawers contained dozens of pairs of dress shoes. These were in such pristine condition she was certain he'd never worn a single pair. She pulled the top drawer completely out of its slot and dumped the shoes on the ground. *Someone at the Goodwill is going to strike the jackpot with these. One hundred and fifty dollar shoes for a song.*

She moved to the next drawer and dumped those shoes on top of the first drawer-full. At first, the gallon sized zip lock bag didn't register. She thought it might be a sleeve for shipping paperwork. After she set the drawer down on the floor, bottom up, she realized that the bag had been taped on the drawer recently. Through the clear plastic bag, Angelina saw papers with Ace's handwriting.

***

Lisa handed Joe the telephone. When he covered the mouthpiece and quietly asked her, "Who is it?" she shrugged her shoulders, held out her palms in the universal gesture of 'I have no idea.' Joe noticed she didn't look happy.

He turned his attention to the cordless phone. "This is Joe."

A sensuous, nearly sultry voice with a very strong southern accent said, "Joe McKinney. Y'all's voice sounds just as I expected."

Joe's bewildered look wasn't lost on Lisa as she turned and left him alone in the family room. He couldn't place the voice.

"Mr. McKinney, we've never met, but I believe y'all may be in danger. Do y'all have a brother named Patrick?"

This is just a bit too weird. "Miss, before I answer any questions, how did you get this number and what this is about?"

Joe heard the woman swallow some kind of drink. Then she said, "This is about a young man I've come to know quite well. Or at least I thought I knew him. He lived with me for a while, but has since left."

He wished she'd get to the point. He was about to tell her to do just that when she continued. "Does the name Ace Glover ring any bells?"

Joe was surprised, but he'd expected the day would come when he heard about Ace Glover again. "I've got a lot of questions for you about Ace, but first, I don't even know your name."

"Angelina Valentine. Ace was my house guest for some time here in Savannah. He did...odd jobs around the grounds and the house for me."

The way she delivered the last line made Joe feel like he was being seduced over the phone.

"Ms. Valentine, I..."

"Please, Joe, call me Angelina."

"Okay, Angelina. Maybe we should start with how you met Ace."

She explained how she and Ace met at Trader Joe's, how her husband had been killed in an automobile crash, and how Ace helped her through a rough time. She admitted she'd fallen in love with him, but knew it wasn't going to last just by the way Ace had been acting. He'd been getting nervous, antsy, and ready to move on. She'd started to see through his lies, but hadn't wanted to throw him out.

"I could tell there was something else on his mind all the time. No matter how hard I tried to, how should I say it, distract him, his mind was always somewhere else, someplace dark."

Joe said, "Go on."

She took another sip of something. "Our lovemaking, well, it was getting strange. He was less intimate and more...mechanical. It was like a chore to him in the months before he left. Then when he did leave, he took a sum of money.

Not as much as he could have, but enough to get him by for another year or so. Or enough to do a specific task."

Joe raised an eyebrow. "What do you mean by a 'specific' task?"

"Ace left in a hurry, in the middle of the night. I was asleep at the time. He took just a handful of clothes and the money. I left all his things alone until just today. I figured that he isn't coming back so I decided to clean out his things and give them to Goodwill or the Salvation Army. Anyway, I found some papers and other things that he'd hidden. The papers have information on several people. He made a list of people that, according to what he wrote down here, he believes destroyed his mother's and his sister's lives. Several of the names are lined through, like maybe they aren't a problem anymore, but your name and that of your brother are still on the list."

Joe listened without interruption. His mind was working overtime, trying to determine what questions he should ask next.

"Angelina, the names that are scratched off, can you still read them?"

"Why yes, I believe so. Just a moment, let me look." There was a pause on the line. When she came back she said, "The first name is Kevin Reardon, then Edward Sharp. Bobbie Garrett is next. He has two stars next to his name, like he was especially important. Then Milton Chester. He has three stars and his name is circled multiple times, like Ace was angry when he did it. All those names are crossed off."

Joe asked, "What are the other names on the list?"

"There's Richard Aims, Adam Wesley, Carl Dempsey, David Wallace, Wilson Brush, Dean Gray, Nancy Brown, and y'all and y'all's brother, Pat."

Joe knew that over half the names on the list were already dead, recently murdered. Ace was busy, on a killing spree, supposedly to avenge the deaths and abuse of his mother and half sister. He didn't need to tell Angelina any of this, but she wasn't finished.

A Lifetime of Betrayal   209

"There's more. Apparently Ace was stalking y'all and y'all's brother for a bit. Maybe stalking's too strong, but he had pictures of y'all's wife, y'all's brother's wife and children, and some notes about y'all's daily routines."

Joe was speechless. How had this lunatic gathered all this information without him or Pat noticing?

"Joe, y'all still there?"

"Yes. Can you tell how old the information is? I mean, is anything dated?"

"No, but have y'all recently moved? There's some notes about y'all moving from an apartment into a new home. Does that help?"

That bit of information let Joe know that Ace had been tracking his movements around two years ago, shortly after Milton Chester was murdered. He wondered why Ace hadn't continued working down his list back then. Maybe money was an issue and Angelina was the answer to that problem.

"Yeah. Yeah it does." Joe paused. "Is there anything else?"

"I don't believe so." The line was silent for a moment. "Joe, y'all need to be careful. I hope this is helpful."

"Angelina, thank you. If you hear from Ace, be cautious. He's killed at least nine people already. If he finds out you've helped us, you might make it onto his list. And if you hear from him, please let me know."

"I will Joe. Good luck." In a deliberately sultry voice she said, "If y'all wasn't a married man…Well, I'll just leave it at that."

The line disconnected. Joe knew he and Pat couldn't afford to sit back and wait. They had to take immediate action.

Chapter 31

Harold Trent stared at Ace, even as Ace's face changed from a dark, deadly stare to a broad smile. Was this all a big joke to him? Did he believe it wasn't possible Trent was his real father? Or was he pleased that God had smiled upon him today, delivering the person he most wanted to kill, right into his clutches? Trent was confused. It wasn't at all the reaction he'd expected.

Then Ace laughed. Quietly, at first, then growing louder as Ace leaned back in the booth, no longer looking at Trent, his hands flat on the table as if to keep his balance. The laugh lasted nearly a full minute. Trent shifted from confusion to frustration, then to concern. Surely other patrons were looking at them. Finally, Trent's face turned red with anger.

In a low voice, he said, "Hey man, knock it off."

Ace leaned forward and wiped his eyes, watering from the long laugh. "Okay, Dad, whatever you say." He paused then continued, "You're the boss."

He started to laugh again, this time, keeping his eyes directly on Trent, mocking his attempt at parental authority. Trent got the message. *You can't tell me what to do. You saying you're my biological father means nothing.*

Trent glanced around the bar. No one looked their way, at least, they weren't staring, but he knew that he and Ace had to get out of there or trouble would soon follow. He looked back at Ace. "Let's go somewhere else and talk. I have more I want to tell you."

"Sure thing, Dad. Whatever you say."

Trent got angrier each time Ace opened his mouth. Maybe he deserved it, maybe he didn't, but regardless, a bar was not the place to hold this conversation.

He motioned Ace towards the door and got up. He dropped twenty dollars on the bar as he passed. When he turned around and looked back at the booth, Ace still sat there, staring straight ahead at nothing in particular. The forced smile was gone. His face was contorted and red. He looked angry and alone, as if he'd lost his only friend in the world. Trent had hoped to fill Abbie's shoes, but his plan was off-track after just a few minutes. If that was the only reason for this meeting he would be okay with that, but the subject of the real mission hadn't even had a chance to surface. He turned and walked out the door to the parking lot and stood alone in the late afternoon sun. He could still recover, but he needed Ace to participate. He leaned against the bed of his truck, pulled out a cigarette, and lit up.

The temperature outside was starting to drop from the mid-eighties as the sun headed lower in the cloudless western sky. It would be a few more hours before it made it to the horizon. The night would be hot and humid, like most nights in southern Georgia. Trent hoped his hotel room had good air-conditioning.

It took two more cigarettes, but Ace finally made his way out of the bar. He walked right up to Trent who stood up straight, blowing smoke out of the side of his mouth before he dropped the butt and stepped on it.

When he looked up from where his cigarette butt was crushed on the gravel, all he saw was a fist. Ace hit him hard in the jaw with a straight right jab. Trent went down hard on his back, his right elbow and shoulder taking the brunt of the fall. It wasn't the hardest blow he'd ever taken, but he saw stars. Though he felt a welt forming on his jaw, he was more worried about his shoulder than his face.

He looked up at Ace whose expression was again without emotion. He stood straight, staring down at Trent, not making any further aggressive moves.

The bartender came to the door and surveyed the scene. "Everything alright out here?"

Trent, still on the ground yelled back, "Yeah. I just tripped, that's all."

Apparently making sure that the business wouldn't be sued, the bartender asked, "Okay, then. Nobody's hurt, right?"

Trent staggered up. "No, I'm fine. No problem. Everything's cool."

The bartender went back inside. When he was out of sight, Trent grimaced a bit as he felt his elbow, his hand wet with blood from the oozing strawberry scrape. It would leave a scab about the size of a silver dollar. That was no big deal. Then he rubbed his shoulder. The pain was worse just to the right of his chest. He hoped it wouldn't cause any problems with his shooting.

Ace was still looking at Trent with that blank look, like a dog you didn't know and weren't sure if it was safe to pet him; or if you did, he'd reach out and bite your hand.

Trent said, "Okay, I deserved that, but not for what you think." He rubbed his shoulder again. "Can we talk now?"

***

"Can we talk about this, now?"

Lisa's question changed the mood of the evening in an instant. Pat and Diane had joined her and Joe for an evening of gin rummy around the card table in their lanai.

The brothers looked at each other.

Pat said "We, Joe and I, think Ace Glover sent those newspaper clippings. We also think he killed a couple of people recently, like within the last week."

Diane turned to her husband, "So, McKinney, when were you planning to tell us?"

"Sweety, we're all McKinneys here."

"Yeah, but you're the only one on the witness stand right now."

"Okay, okay. We didn't want to alarm you two, plus we didn't have time to even discuss it before you found out about the articles. So there really wasn't any other option."

Diane, in her best mock attorney voice, said, "We've got some crazy killer on the loose and apparently he's looking for the two of you. So, what are we doing about this?"

Joe answered. "Whoa. *We're* not doing anything. Pat and I are going to take care of this. You and Lisa are going to stay out of this guy's sights."

"And how are we going to do that?" Lisa said. "We have lives, too. Are we just supposed to hide in a cave somewhere while you two heroes go charging off to find this guy? Do you even have a clue where he is right now?"

Joe glanced at Pat, who gave him a slight shoulder shrug that said, 'She's got you there. You're on your own on this one.'

Pat said, "We know Hatch spotted Ace in Georgia near the Kings Bay Sub base. He was trying to find Wilson Brush. We know Wilson is safe at Hatch's place in Moniac. Hatch and Nancy plan to take him back to the base tomorrow morning and make sure he gets back to the ship in one piece. If Ace is still there trying to get to Wilson, then we have a little time to plan. If not…"

Diane, without a trace of emotion, said, "The truth is that this lunatic could be sitting in front of the house right now."

That thought had crossed Joe's mind. Since Hatch hadn't called, they were safe, at least for the time being. Joe had his gun loaded and ready, as he knew Pat did, just in case Hatch couldn't reach them.

Sensing his brother was at a loss for words, Joe said, "Listen, Hatch and Nancy are on top of this. They know where Ace is and they'll let us know if he leaves the area. Before this guy gets to the Florida-Georgia border, we'll know it."

Diane and Lisa both looked skeptical.

Pat said, "Okay, here's what we should do. I'll call Hatch and see if he has a fix on Ace. If he does and Ace is still in Georgia, then we know we have at least three hours separating him from us. Agreed?"

Heads nodded around the table.

"Then we let Hatch know he can't let Ace out of his sight and he should contact the local authorities about our suspicions, that he's the killer of five men in the last week." Pat said.

"They're going to want evidence before they can get a warrant. How do we manufacture that?" Joe's question caused Pat to pause. He rubbed the scar on his chin while Joe watched the wheels in his head spin. Then a smile lit up Pat's face.

"We've got lots of evidence, or at least NCIS does. If we can convince the brass to assist in the take down, they have all the evidence from the murders two years ago. But all this is going to take a little time. Maybe Hatch and Nancy can help by contacting the locals. Nancy can also contact Colonel Griggs, the commanding Officer for NCIS at Camp Lejeune."

Joe thought this might just work. Then the brothers looked at their wives. Lisa and Diane looked only slightly less skeptical, but it was a step in the right direction.

Chapter 32

Hatch and Nancy Brown sat in Hatch's Ford Taurus outside Tommy's Tavern at dusk. A bright, multi-colored glow from neon beer signs bounced off the windows of the vehicles in the parking lot. At the moment, only one of those cars interested them.

Ace Glover and Harold Trent never went back inside the bar. They had sat in Ace's rental car in the parking lot for more than an hour. Apparently, they had a lot to talk about.

Hatch asked, "So Miss Nancy, you wanna make out?"

Nancy smiled. What else could they do? They'd been sitting in the car for nearly two hours, first watching the bar, then watching the car. It was worse than watching paint dry. She turned to Hatch, leaned over, grabbing his face between her hands and laid a serious lip lock on him. After several seconds she pulled back with a loud smacking sound which nearly made Hatch's ears pop.

"Will that hold you over until later?"

Hatch's eyes widened in mock surprise. "I'm not sure I can hold out that long. We may have to jump in the back seat and…Dag nabbit. Of all the times they choose to stop all the chit-chat."

Nancy turned back towards the parking lot as Harold Trent exited Ace's car on the passenger side, closing the door behind him.

Hatch fastened his seat belt. "I guess I'll have to get a rain check on that back-seat lovin'."

Nancy reached across the seat and squeezed Hatch's right thigh. "That should hold you over."

As Harold Trent stood watching, Ace started the car and sped off, spitting gravel from the front wheels as he accelerated. Whatever had passed between them had not ended well.

Nancy asked, "Okay, Einstein, what do we do now since we had to come in the same car?"

Hatch smiled. "I guess that ends our romantic moment for this evenin'."

He thought Nancy's sarcasm was pretty funny, since she had always been such a serious-minded person.

They both watched as Harold Trent shuffled towards his beat up pickup truck. Even in the relative darkness of the parking lot, Hatch could see the demeanor of a beaten down man.

"We're goin' ta follow that fella right there."

Nancy looked puzzled. She clearly didn't understand why Hatch had chosen to follow Trent instead of Ace.

"Here's why. According to Miss Shawnda, that man right there was in Columbia, South Carolina watchin' Ace from a diner across the street from a hotel where Ace was stayin'. She said she watched as Ace gave this poor guy a flat tire and hauled his butt outta there in a big hurry. Ya followin' me so far?"

Nancy nodded.

"Now, outta the blue, he catches up with Ace without knowin' where he's goin'. That's a pretty good trick…unless you've got help of some kind. Like maybe a trackin' device?"

"How can you be so sure? Maybe he just knows where Ace's next targets live and work. It would be simple enough for him to find someone in a small town like this."

"Yeah, maybe after a day or two, but not within an hour of arrivin' in town. Just too coincidental, don't you think?"

As they sat talking about the probability that Harold Trent had a tracking device on Ace's car, the beat up old pickup truck came to life. It was misfiring and in need of a muffler. It pulled out of the parking spot, jerked one time as the engine misfired badly again, then pulled away quickly as Trent gave it some gas.

Hatch started the Taurus. "Showtime."

He was about to head out behind Trent's pickup when he saw a set of tail lights at the edge of the parking lot. From a parking spot beneath the trees an old, white Toyota Corolla headed towards the exit. As the car passed them, both he and Nancy saw the unmistakable face and red hair of Shawnda Hull. Apparently, her plans to head north had changed.

"This is going to make trailin' either of these guys a whole lot harder. It'll be like the Moniac Fourth of July parade – literally. We only have four vehicles in the parade in Moniac, which is pretty much everybody in town," Hatch said.

Nancy just shook her head and smiled.

***

Ace turned right onto Point Peter Road, passing St. Marys airport on his right. The sun had just set beyond the runway amid light clouds, bright orange at the horizon, turning to a deep pink semicircle. Ace found it hard to concentrate on his driving with so many distractions, from the disturbing meeting with Harold Trent to the simple, beautiful sunset that tugged at his heart. It reminded him of times at one of the trailer parks where he and his mother had lived when he was a boy of five or six. She would tell him to go play before her live in boyfriend came home from work, or more likely, home from the bar. She didn't want Ace to see them argue. More times than he could count, he sat on a swing at the playground watching the sun go down until it was dark. Alone, he had watched many sunsets from that park. Since then beautiful sunsets only caused painful recollections of a tough life with his mothers' abusive boyfriends.

He turned his head back to the road just in time to see a stop sign. He slammed on the breaks. His tires screeched, as the car came to an abrupt stop, just short of nosing into the intersection. He shook his head and took a deep breath. *Wake up Ace.* He thought about the illegally modified AR-15 and numerous weapons that he had in the trunk of the car, especially the one used in several murders. He spun the wheel to the right, easing out onto Osborne Road. After about a mile heading west, Osborne turned into East King Avenue which passed under Interstate 95.

The man who claimed to be his biological father spoke of Abbie Glover in such an affectionate way that Ace almost believed that he loved her. Several times, Trent had brushed tears from his eyes. It was all very convincing, except that he had left her high and dry right before Ace was born. If he was so in love, so devoted to his mother, why had he left her – and his unborn child – to fend for themselves? A man who was truly in love, truly devoted, would have found a way to make it work, to convince Abbie that she needed him. But he gave up and left her at a time when she needed him most. He left before he ever laid eyes on his own flesh and blood. *What kind of father does that? If he was so interested in my well-being why hadn't he shown his face before now?*

Trent claimed he was trying to protect Ace, to keep him from killing any more people. That's why he was staying ahead of Ace, taking care of the problems, the people who had ruined his life. Trent didn't understand this wasn't his business; this was Ace's problem to deal with. Ace had asked why Trent thought it mattered. Ace had already killed several people and there was no redemption for him. *There's no statute of limitations on murder.*

The discussion got heated a number of times before Ace told Trent to stay away and let him take care of his own family problems or, biological father or not, he'd be dead. Finally, Ace told him he should leave and not look back. He never wanted to see Trent again. Blood didn't matter, even if he was telling the truth, which Ace still doubted. Even if they were related, they would never be father and son. That ship had sailed long ago.

Ace pulled up to the Colony Pines apartment complex, then parked several spaces down from Doug Farrell's apartment. Wilson Brush had to show up sometime. It didn't matter when. Ace had time on his side.

He looked around the parking lot, then at South Grove Boulevard from where he'd just come. He heard Harold Trent's pickup truck even before he saw it make the turn into the parking lot at the opposite end of the baseball diamonds where Ace had encountered the guy named Hatch. He shook his head. *Just one more obstacle to remove.*

***

Shawnda Hull watched as Harold Trent parked his truck in the parking lot of the baseball fields in Kingsland. There were no other cars around that she could see in the rapidly darkening dusk sky. A mercury vapor light blinked on, a copper colored glow becoming brighter after several seconds of warming up. It cast an eerie light that reflected off the glass of the scorer's booth where the four baseball fields came together.

She started to panic when she realized a decision was imminent. In a parking lot devoid of any vehicles except Trent's and hers, she was a sitting duck. He might recognize her from earlier in the day at the diner. Hell, he'd seen her face from about four feet away when he had nearly sprawled out on the hood of her car. She had to keep driving past, as if she belonged in one of the apartments beyond the ball fields. She turned into the Colony Arms apartment complex where she parked in an available space. Since there was nowhere for her to go, she leaned her seat back, closed her eyes, and began to think.

She was exhausted and depressed. What made her think that she could outsmart Ace? Now this other guy in the pickup truck was involved somehow. Then there was Hatch and Nancy Brown. Who knows? Maybe a dozen cops were watching?

Her mind drifted to her son and how much she missed holding him, watching him. Every minute she spent here in Georgia or anywhere away from her child diminished the now slim possibility that she would see him grow up, learn new things, at home or school. At this rate, she'd be lucky to be out of military confinement in time to see his senior prom.

Tears flowed onto her cheeks. Before long her face was soaked. She wiped her eyes with a tissue and blew her nose, then threw the tissue on the floorboard on the passenger side of the car. Moments later, exhaustion took over and she was fast asleep.

***

Harold Trent saw the white Toyota Corolla leave the parking lot at Tommy's behind his truck. He'd seen it earlier in the day at the diner in Columbia, South Carolina. Why was this woman following Ace? There had to be some connection.

Trent parked as far away from any of the parking lot light posts as possible. When the first light blinked on, he was satisfied he was out of any direct light, so that anyone looking would not be able to easily identify the make and model of his truck.

He tried to keep his eyes on Ace's car, about a dozen cars away from the white Toyota, but he was tired and hungry. He hadn't had anything except snacks since breakfast at the diner. His stomach growled. The interior of the truck was too hot for comfort, so he rolled down the driver's side window. He leaned over to the passenger side door and rolled that window down as well. A nice breeze rolled through, giving immediate relief.

He sat up and leaned his head back on the head rest, relaxing for just a moment. His eyes popped open with a start and he rubbed them with both hands, trying to clear out the dry film. Across the parking lot at the apartment complex, Ace's car still sat, just as it had when he had dozed off. The Toyota was still there, too.

A mosquito buzzed near his right ear and he swatted at the sound.

He wondered if Wilson Brush had come to his friend's apartment yet this evening or if Ace was going to strike out. He looked at his watch. Ten minutes to midnight.

The voice near his left ear startled him. "You should've listened when I said I didn't want to see you around anymore."

Ace's voice sent a chill down Harold Trent's spine. He turned to Ace, intending to explain why he couldn't leave. All he saw was a bright flash, then nothing at all.

Chapter 33

Tap, tap, tap. Shawnda wondered, What was that noise? Where did it come from? It seemed close, but it was all around her—like in a dream. That's it. I'm having a dream.

The dream had come on suddenly. It felt like a sauna, the humidity overpowering, as if she were drowning in her own sweat. The odor was strong, like one of the bums that she'd encountered outside the dumpster at the diner in Columbia.

Tap, tap, tap. There it was again. This time it sounded like the electronic pilot on a stove, more of a click than a tap. Then she heard someone speaking in a low, muffled voice. It sounded like a warning, a warning that she couldn't hear over the background noise of…what…a train rumbling past on tracks? No, that wasn't it. A thunderstorm rumbling as it approached? Possibly. She saw a man now, off in the distance, drifting closer, the background a hazy gray-white, like a mist; the same hot, humid mist that surrounded her, drowning her.

Another *tap, tap, tap,* but this time louder, like *pop, pop, pop*, like distant gun shots. As the man came closer, his features showed more definition. He was dressed all in white, his blonde hair a bit long, but model perfect. He held something dark in his right hand. His left hand held a notebook, a small pocket sized flip pad. His movements flowed in slow motion. He glanced at the notebook and spoke. The words came out in a slow baritone, "It's your turn." He pointed the gun directly at her.

Shawnda Hull jerked awake at the loud tap on her car window. She stared straight ahead for a moment, getting her bearings down. When she saw the buildings through the car windshield, she realized she was sitting in the parking lot of the Colony Arms apartments. Half a dozen mercury vapor lights lit up the parking lot around her car. Another light tap on the driver's side window caused her to jump and look that way. Hatch and Nancy Brown stood next to her car. Hatch giving her the universal sign to roll her window down. She turned the key in the ignition, pressed the button and the window slid down with a jerky motion, sticking in spots where the track had worn unevenly.

With a smile Hatch asked, "Didja catch a nice nap there, Miss Shawnda?"

Shawnda stretched and yawned, still a bit freaked out by the dream. Wondering how Hatch and Nancy had found her, slowly realizing they had caught her in a lie. She'd said she was headed back to Virginia, but here she was in Kingsland, Georgia.

Hatch said, "I hope y'all's rested because it's goin' to be a long day, especially if the local cops find out you were camped here, within a hundred yards of a murder scene."

At first Shawnda looked confused, then her expression changed to panic. "Where? Was it Wilson?"

Hatch's smile was almost imperceptible. "No ma'am. Wilson is just fine. He's back on board the Nevada. Dougie is fine, too. He just went upstairs to get some sleep before he has to work later this morning." He paused then said, "They spent much of the night in a couple of nice, warm, comfortable beds. What was ya thinkin', followin' Ace and that Trent fella'? Take a look in your rear view mirror. Tell me what you see."

In her mirror, she saw police cars and an ambulance. The pickup truck that had been following Ace was in the middle of the commotion. In the dim, early morning light, several police officers stood near the truck, talking amongst themselves.

Nancy turned to Shawnda and, in a tone that had a hint of military authority said, "Major Hull, you are leaving today for Virginia. We're going back to Hatch's where you are getting a hot shower, a change of clothes, and a good breakfast, then you're leaving for home. If we have to escort you all the way, we will. Is that understood?"

Shawnda Hull was defeated. She was fatigued from not eating or sleeping right. Her stress level was through the roof, and her emotions were torn to shreds. Hearing Nancy's command, her lower lip quivered, her eyes watered, and she leaned her head against the steering wheel and began to cry in loud, long sobs.

Hatch looked at Nancy, and whispered, "I believe that we're going to book a flight for Miss Hull. She's in no condition to drive."

Nancy nodded.

Hatch leaned down through the window of the Toyota. "Miss Shawnda, We're going to get you on a flight today. Y'all can leave the car at my place and I'll see to it that it gets back to Virginia in the next few days. After y'all get cleaned up, y'all can call the son and the folks and let 'em know y'all'll be home later today."

He said to Nancy, "I'll drive Miss Shawnda's car. Y'all can drive mine. Now's a good time to head outta' here, don't ya think?"

Nancy nodded. Shawnda, calmer now, moved to the passenger side and Hatch squeezed into the driver's seat. He had a hard time adjusting the seat back to where it was comfortable for him, but they finally got on the road.

When they passed the pickup truck, they couldn't see much due to the truck being surrounded by cars and people. They did see that a team of paramedics was placing a body in a black, plastic bag on a gurney. Shawnda's jaw dropped as tears again flooded her eyes. *Is this my fault? Could it have been me that was killed?* She wept in earnest.

Hatch turned to her. "This ain't your fault. Your only concern should be your son. Everything else? It just ain't important. Understand?

***

The question of the day was, *Where was Ace?*

Hatch flipped open his cell phone and hit the speed dial for Pat McKinney. When a groggy sounding Pat answered,

Hatch said, "Wake up sunshine. I have good news and I have bad news."

Pat yawned loudly into Hatch's ear. He said, "Let's have the good news first."

"Well, I lied. There ain't any good news. Ace is missing. Before he left, he shot and killed the guy who was followin' him."

Pat was instantly wide awake, trying like the devil not to wake his wife.

***

Back at Hatch's cabin, after a breakfast of bacon, eggs, hash browns, and coffee, he and Nancy Brown sat quietly at the kitchen table. The dirty breakfast dishes were pushed towards the center of the table. No one was in the mood to clean up. The sun was now well above the horizon, sending streaks of light through the cypress trees and thick Spanish moss, dust particles illuminated in the rays of light. Hatch's mind wandered, thinking he should get an air purifier. Then it was back to the botched tailing job. Inwardly, he cursed himself for allowing Ace to escape their surveillance, but there was no sense reliving the evening. It was now history.

Nancy was deep in her own thoughts, probably going over every detail of the previous evening, trying to figure out what they could have done differently. Neither was in the mood to talk.

Shawnda Hull was in the shower in the main bathroom cleaning several days' worth of funk from her body. Hatch had already purchased the airline ticket for her trip back home to Virginia. This time, they were going to make sure she boarded that jet before they turned their backs on her. Nancy had laid it on thick, threatening to call in her connections at NCIS to take her to the Navy brig. In the end, Shawnda had broken down, pleading to be allowed to go home first to see her son. They listened as she spoke to her parents, telling them she would be home later in the day. Finally, they saw the slightest hint of a smile and Hatch was pretty confident she was headed home.

The sound of running water in the shower stopped, snapping Hatch out of his thoughts. He ran a hand across his face, then glanced at Nancy. "I guess I really hosed that whole deal up. You said we should take separate cars and you were right."

Nancy laid her hand across Hatch's. "You can't predict the future. How could you have known Ace was going to go after Trent?"

"History. That's how. He has a history of killin' people who get in his way. Trent was gettin' in his way."

Hatch shook his head in disgust. He was angry with himself for not anticipating what was going to happen. Because of that, a man had lost his life. It wasn't that Harold Trent was a pillar of society. Under the right circumstances, Hatch might have done the same thing, but he wasn't sure exactly what Ace's circumstances were.

The deed was done. The time for self reflection was over. They had a job to do. They had to stop Ace before he hurt their friends, the McKinneys, and Ace had a big head start.

***

In a room at a Holiday Inn Express just outside of St. Augustine, Florida, Ace's attempt at sleep was fleeting. He tossed and turned, sleep coming in small stints as his mind replayed the look on Harold Trent's face over and over again. He didn't feel any remorse at the murder. After all, Trent had stolen from him. He'd stolen his ability to get justice for his mother and half-sister, Rebecca.

He dozed off briefly then saw his mother's face. She smiled at him, and he smiled back. Then a vision of Rebecca came into the scene. She screamed at his mother…their mother. When he started to intervene, she turned on him and screamed. He awoke with a start, looked around the hotel room, which looked like dozens of other hotel rooms in which he'd stayed, then laid his head back down.

Eventually, sleep finally won out. He gave in to a deep slumber until mid-afternoon. He thought for a moment about what day it was, then smiled. It really didn't matter. It was time to get moving. He had to take care of business in Central Florida.

Chapter 34

The phone rang several times before Joe reached over, fumbled with the receiver, and got it to his ear. He and Lisa had been napping in each others' arms. They had grabbed an opportunity to make love while their daughter, Danielle, slept after her afternoon feeding.

He took a deep breath before answering in a voice that was a little too sleepy, "Hello."

"Did I wake you?"

Joe recognized Bill Banks voice, yawned, then said, "Not really, I just dozed off for a minute." He paused. "What's up?"

"We received some information about an incident that may have some bearing on the current murders."

Joe was immediately interested. He threw back the sheet from his side of the bed. "Can I call you back in three minutes?"

"Sure."

Joe pulled on a pair of shorts and slippers, then headed to his office on the other side of their home in Winter Garden. He wanted to let Lisa sleep as long as possible without being disturbed. They'd both had no idea raising a child was going to be such a drain on their energy.

He punched in the number for Banks' extension in Grand Forks. Banks picked up on the first ring.

"We received another fax from that library north of Colorado Springs. We're still not sure who's sending them, but I've got to tell you, it stinks of an Air Force cover-up."

Joe flashed back to when he and Nancy had encountered resistance from the Air Force Office of Special Investigations in Grand Forks. Banks and Hansen had run into the same issue of trying to run an investigation blindfolded.

Every time one of them got close to a piece to the puzzle someone would move that piece just out of reach. It had been frustrating.

"What did these mystery faxes say?"

"Back in 1971, Milton Chester, Richard Aims, Adam Wesley, and Carl Dempsey were all cadets at the academy near the end of their junior year. There was a party where things got out of hand. They were accused of raping a fifteen-year old girl and then just dumping her off a few blocks from her home. Nothing was done until the middle of the next semester. Now these guys are seniors and looking at graduating and starting their military careers. Following so far?"

"Sure. Go on."

"In October, 1971, there's an accusation that one of the female cadets is having an affair with another female cadet. The cadet is brought in for questioning. She denies the allegation, but during questioning makes a comment about knowing of a real crime that had taken place earlier in the year, and she brings up the party and the rape. The officer in charge of the investigation into her alleged misconduct decides to look into the matter. He gets the names of people this female cadet knew were at the party and starts to question them. The allegation is starting to look pretty solid. So he decides to take the allegations to his superior for formal charges. That accusation is brought to the attention of the base commander and is immediately quashed, all the evidence and transcripts of the interviews sealed."

That took Joe by surprise. "Why the hell did they do that if everything looked solid?"

"Because the base commander at the time was Colonel, soon-to-be-General, Alton Chester, father of Cadet Milton Chester."

Stunned, Joe listened to the silence on the receiver as a million thoughts raced through his head. His first question, "So what happened to the female cadet who reported the rape?"

"She went on to have a very successful career. In fact, she's the current commanding officer at the Air Force Academy, Colonel Melinda Barnes."

"Holy shit! No wonder Major Alexander isn't getting any cooperation from her office. She wants this to stay buried. I wonder if some bargain was made to keep her quiet about the rape."

"No doubt. But that's not all. There's another player in this mess. It seems that the reason the young girl was at this party was because she was invited by another cadet. According to the transcripts, he thought she was eighteen. He brought her with him so he would fit in with the other cadets who had girlfriends. This guy was apparently kind of immature. I think kids today would call him a geek, something like that. Anyway, he started drinking and passed out. When that happened, the other four took his "date" into a bedroom and raped her."

"These guys were real bastards," Joe said.

"I'm not done."

Joe couldn't imagine what more they could have done, but he kept listening.

"So, this other cadet, the one who brought the under-aged girl, was passed out. These guys hauled his ass up to the room where the girl was near passing out now. They threw him on the bed next to her, stripped off all his clothes and posed him next to her. Then they took a series of pictures of the two. I guess they thought it was funny at the time. A few weeks after the party, the pictures started showing up in his room. He freaked and went to a friend of his, another cadet, someone he trusted. It happened to be the female cadet who was alleged to have had this lesbian affair. She went to the four cadets and told them to knock it off, that she wanted the negatives or she would destroy their careers before they started. Apparently they stopped sending the photos, but she never got the negatives."

Joe asked, "So who is the guy in the photos?"

Banks hesitated for a second, then said, "That would be Colonel Templeton. He's the current commander of Grand Forks Air Force Base."

***

Since Diane McKinney's mother-in-law was watching their children, Sean and Anna, Pat and Diane took a trip to Winter Garden to spend time with Joe and Lisa and their daughter Danielle. It was Lisa's regular grocery shopping day. Diane tagged along.

Lisa pushed Danielle in her stroller as they made their way through the local Publix Supermarket. Diane pushed the cart as they stocked up for the Fourth of July barbecue. Lisa checked off each item from her list as she dropped them into the cart. They talked quietly about Pat and Joe, and how this latest investigation was drawing them in like a magnet to steel.

Diane said, "Every time Hatch calls, Pat gets more engrossed in the details of this case."

Lisa replied, "I know what you mean. That detective from Grand Forks calls Joe nearly every day. Joe tried to keep his distance, but since he and Pat received the newspaper articles, he wants to know as much as he can about this Ace Glover. And the call from that Angelina Valentine woman didn't help. Ever since then, he's been on edge, back to his old super-serious attitude. He figures knowing where this guy is gives him an edge. He says it's our best defense right now. At least until they catch him."

They rounded the corner in the area that contained dairy products. They were both looking at gallon jugs of milk, trying to read the smudged sell-by dates when they heard a man's voice behind them. They turned to see a young, blond man picking up Danielle's sippy cup from the floor, then handing it back to the baby girl who was smiling back at the man.

"She sure is a cutie. I saw her drop the cup. I wasn't sure if you heard it fall."

Lisa smiled at the man and said, "Thanks. You're right, I didn't hear it." She looked down at Danielle. "Say thank you to the nice man."

Danielle just smiled, taking a quick drink from the cup. Lisa looked at the man. "Thanks again."

She turned back to the task of scrutinizing the dates on the milk. During this entire exchange, Diane watched the man from the corner of her eye, trying not to be obvious. When Lisa turned back, the man had an odd smile on his face, almost like a smirk. She noticed he looked directly at Lisa's behind, not that that was odd for a man, but this look was different. He wasn't admiring her figure. When he took a quick look in Diane's direction, her eyes met his and his expression changed to one of annoyance. He held Diane's eyes for just a moment, then turned and disappeared.

Diane thought, *Something's off with that guy.*

She wanted to call Pat, but what would she tell him? That some young guy was helpful and gave Danielle her sippy cup back after she dropped it? Or that she had a bad vibe from the guy? She wasn't going to say anything to Lisa at the moment, but maybe once they were in the car, she'd ask if Lisa had gotten the same impression.

Lisa turned to Diane and surprised her by saying, "Did that guy give you the creeps or what?"

"I was thinking the same thing."

"Did you see the way he was looking at me? I was watching in the mirror behind the milk jugs. What a weirdo. I'm calling Joe. When we leave, we need to watch for him."

They continued their shopping. Diane couldn't believe how calm Lisa was under the circumstances. She wondered if this guy could be the one who'd sent the articles to Pat and Joe. The killer, this Ace character, was supposedly in Georgia just last evening. The trip to Winter Garden wasn't that long, but how could he have found them, determined who they were and followed them in such a short period of time? It didn't seem at all likely to Diane, but why take the chance.

When they were just about finished loading Lisa's cart with groceries, they stopped close to the entrance to the pharmacy where there was a relatively quiet and secluded spot. Lisa hit the speed-dial button on her cell phone for Joe.

In a calm voice, Lisa said, "Hi, Sweetie. I think we have a problem at the grocery store." She told him about the encounter at the dairy aisle. She described the young man in as much detail as she could remember.

Joe listened until she finished, then said in a tense voice, "We'll be right there."

***

Ace thought about Lisa McKinney's ass as he sat in his rental car in the parking lot of the plaza across the street from the Publix Supermarket. His car was wedged between two other non-descript foreign cars so his Chevy blended right in. From where he sat, he had a clear view of the main entrance doors. He'd be able to see them exit and watch as they made their way to Lisa's mini-van. *She sure is hot, especially for a mom. Too bad she's wasted on that ex-Marine asshole.*

The evening was beginning to cool by Central Florida standards. At least he wasn't sitting in the sun soaking his shirt with sweat.

Her sister-in-law was pretty hot, too, though not quite as stunningly beautiful. Pat's wife had seemed to be a bit too curious. Maybe he could use that to his advantage. If she thought they were in danger, she might call her husband to rescue them. That would be a real bonus. *This trip could be a test run. If those bastards scramble to protect their wives, that would make them easy targets. The best way to get to a man is through his woman.*

Dusk was approaching, though true darkness wouldn't be for nearly an hour or so. The green Publix sign above the store blinked on and the parking lot lights started to come to life. *Time to sit back, relax, and see what happens next.*

As if on cue, Joe and Pat McKinney showed up and parked close to Lisa's mini-van. When they got out of the car, Joe started walking towards the store. Pat stayed near the car and the mini-van.

Ace got a chill. *Could I take out the one brother while he stands right there out in the open?* He started his car and headed for the exit that would take him directly into the parking lot across the street. As he sat at the light, he opened the center compartment between the driver and passenger seats and removed the silenced Glock. The light turned green and he drove directly across Route 50 into the Publix Parking lot, turning right, slowly driving to the lane where Pat stood by his car. Just as he was about to turn down the lane, he spotted a Winter Garden Police car near the store entrance. Lisa, Diane, and Joe were coming out. They waved to the police car, then continued on into the parking lot.

Could they have called the cops and requested an escort or was it just coincidence that the cop was there? Regardless, with a smooth motion, Ace straightened out the steering wheel and continued on to the next parking lot exit. He eased the Glock back in the compartment and headed out onto Route 50.

He cursed his luck this time, but it was probably better to plan this move instead of taking the brothers down on a spur of the moment impulse.

Next time, they wouldn't be so lucky.

Chapter 35

When Joe saw Lisa in the store he gathered her up in his arms. He held her tight for nearly a full minute before Diane cleared her throat. He released his wife and turned around to see Diane scanning the space around them. When Joe turned his head to see what she was looking at, he noticed nearly everyone in the store was looking at them.

He smiled and shrugged. "I guess we'd better go."

Lisa said, "So much for keeping a low profile."

Joe grabbed the stroller and headed towards the door, the two women following. When they got to the parking lot, Pat briefly kissed and hugged Diane. Lisa put Danielle into her car seat. Then everyone helped load groceries into Lisa's mini-van. Joe moved to the driver's seat, Lisa to the passenger side. Pat and Diane followed them in their car. Joe watched his wife, stealing glances as he drove down Route 50 towards home.

She looked calm, but Joe saw her taking note of everything she saw. She kept glancing into the back seat to check on their daughter, then out the back window to see if any vehicles were tailing them. She also looked at the drivers of cars closest to their mini-van.

Joe asked, "So tell me about this guy in the store."

Lisa thought for a moment, then said, "Blond, handsome, young, about twenty-three, give or take a year. He was charming, smiling the entire time, but not fake. It seemed natural on him."

"What about his height and weight?

Lisa closed her eyes. In a quiet monotone, she said, "Six-feet-one inch, One hundred seventy-five pounds, square shoulders, strong but not powerfully so." She opened her eyes. "If he killed all those people a few years ago, he's a complete psycho. How can you be so outwardly calm and friendly…"

She didn't complete her thoughts. Instead, she reached back and took Danielle's sippy cup. Danielle began to cry, but Lisa didn't return the cup. She pulled out a zip lock baggie, dropped the cup inside, and put it into the baby tote with their daughter's other supplies.

Joe looked at her, his face tense with understanding. "Keep an eye on her. If there was a problem, we'd probably already know it, but it's better to be safe.

Lisa's face, which moments ago was calm and collected, now showed signs of the tension that comes with worrying about your child. For only the second time since they'd met, Joe saw tears forming in Lisa's eyes. The first time was when her father passed away from a massive stroke. This time he knew she was frightened by the thought of a stranger getting that close to their daughter.

Danielle kept crying. Lisa stretched her arm back, grabbed up a tiny, stuffed bear, then slipped it into her daughter's arms. The bear was a gift from her cousin, Anna. When Danielle saw the bear, she stopped crying immediately. She grabbed the bear and gave it a big squeeze, the glow of a big smile returning to her face.

Joe turned to see the tension leave Lisa's face, her tears from tension turning to tears of relief and joy. Everything was going to be alright.

He turned his attention back to driving, but he couldn't stop thinking about the encounter in the store, his anger building, thinking the best way to stop Ace from harming his family was to kill him. If that's what it took to protect his family, Joe was up for the task.

Lisa's description matched what they knew about Ace. Joe wondered what they could do to confirm his identity, but at the moment he had to get his family home safely. Once there, he and Pat would talk through their options.

Then they needed to talk with Hatch and Nancy to see if they had any ideas on how to get ahead of this guy. Until they did, they were all in danger.

***

Trailing Joe's minivan, Pat tried to remain calm. He rubbed the scar on his chin with one hand while steering with the other. The man in the store was probably Ace, but he had to be sure.

Pat was afraid what this episode might do to his and Diane's relationship. She was growing weary of the danger these situations brought on the family. He hated placing his family in harm's way fearing that one day, Diane, Sean, or Anna might get hurt.

Pat noticed Diane looking around in a near panic. He wanted to tell her the danger had passed, but he didn't believe it himself. A deranged killer was on the loose in their midst, and had the balls to walk right up to his wife in the middle of a crowded grocery store without any fear of being recognized. In fact, it appeared he wanted to be recognized, to send a message: *I can get to you and your family any time I want.*

The trip took less than fifteen minutes, but it was an intense fifteen minutes. They unloaded the groceries, closed and locked the door behind them, then sat in Joe and Lisa's lanai. Lisa prepared a meal for Danielle then asked Joe if he could help with dinner. Diane immediately offered, but Lisa said she needed to talk with Joe alone for a few minutes. Diane took a deep breath and said okay.

When Joe left to help with dinner, the tension that had built up in Diane's body and mind deflated. She sank into the chair where she sat and started to cry. Pat immediately went to her and knelt in front of her.

"Are you alright?"

She leaned forward and hugged him, then held him tight. "No, Pat, I'm sorry, but I'm not alright. I'm scared. We need to get home so I can be with the kids."

She was right. They needed to get home and relieve his mother of the responsibility of watching Sean and Anna, especially if Ace got the crazy idea to go to their house. He held Diane a little tighter. "Let's go tell Joe and Lisa we're heading home. They'll understand."

***

They were on Route 91 to Dunnellon, Florida in less than fifteen minutes. Exhausted by the tension of the day, Dianne soon fell fast asleep. An hour later, they were home, Diane hugged their children tight, thanking Emma McKinney for watching the kids for the last couple of days. Emma had left a nice dinner in the refrigerator for them. All they had to do was toss it in the microwave and grab a couple of drinks.

After they finished eating and Diane and Emma were in the kitchen cleaning up, Sean went to his dad and quietly said, "Dad, can I talk to you, in private?"

Sean's face was stone-cold serious, as if the weight of the world was on his shoulders. "Sure, son. Let's go." The two men, thirty-year old Pat and eight-year old Sean headed to Pat's office for a man-to-man talk. Pat had a good idea what was on his son's mind.

Sean sat in one of the guest chairs and Pat sat next to him in the other. "Why so serious?"

Sean took a deep breath. "I think you should teach me how to shoot. I know Uncle Joe offered, but he can't unless you give him permission. I think it's better if you teach me. That way, Uncle Joe doesn't have to worry about it."

Pat got off of his chair and knelt in front of his son on one knee, looked into his eyes and asked, "Sean, why is this so important to you?"

"Because I can tell something bad is happening. Somebody is trying to hurt you and Uncle Joe."

Pat couldn't hide his surprise, but he quickly changed his expression to one of confidence. "Listen, son, your Uncle Joe and I know how to take care of ourselves. You shouldn't be worried about us." Then the harder question, "What makes you think Uncle Joe and I are in danger?"

Sean hesitated, then said. "I heard Gramma talking with Mom on the phone last night. Gramma thought that I was sleeping, but I wasn't."

Sean lowered his head as if he was sorry for doing something wrong. The look tugged on Pat's heart. Sean had been doing so well in the pool, acting like an eight-year old kid, something he'd never done before. He'd also written in his journal, getting his feelings off of his chest. Now, based on one side of a telephone conversation, he was back to his serious-beyond-his-years mode again.

He needed to do two things for his son. First, he would teach him how to use a gun, starting with gun safety. Second, he had to stop Ace. Once Ace was gone or locked up, their problems would be over. At least, he hoped that was true.

Pat's throat tightened as he gathered his thoughts. Struggling to keep his voice clear and steady, he said, "Sean, you didn't do anything wrong. Listening in on your grandma's conversation isn't bad. Being concerned for your Uncle Joe and me isn't bad either. Don't beat yourself up over that. You're a good kid. Your mom and I both love you very much. Always remember that."

Next was the tough part, because he and Diane hadn't agreed on whether Sean should learn to handle a gun. "I'll start teaching you about using a handgun tomorrow. I have to talk with your mom first, but I think she'll say okay as long as we take it slow. Before you can actually shoot one, you have to know how to handle it."

Sean just nodded. Most boys hearing these words would jump for joy. Sean took the news like he was about to learn how to use a new tool on the job. Just another step in life.

"We'll study how guns are made, gun safety, and how to handle a gun." He paused. "It's important for you to know that with guns, in the real world, there are no do-overs. If someone is killed, they're really dead, no second chances. So safety is extremely important. Understand?"

"Yes, sir."

"That's good. I have to talk with your mom now. Are you okay with this plan?"

"Yes, sir."

"Okay. Let's go swimming tomorrow morning."

Sean smiled. Spending more time with his son was one thing Pat wished he could do over. He opened his arms and gave his son a big hug, trying to squeeze the fear out of him.

When he let go, Sean continued to hang on. He whispered in his dad's ear, "I love you Dad."

"I love you, too, son."

Sean let go and left the office without another word.

Chapter 36

The only sounds in the office of the Commander of the 10th Security Forces Squadron were the loud hum of the ballast in the fluorescent light fixture in the ceiling, the shuffling of paper on the commander's desk, and the squeaky springs of the government procured office chair. As with most government offices, the light fixtures emitted enough lumens to light a small stadium. In the commander's office, the walls had recently been painted bright white. The fresh paint odor was still strong. Coupled with the overpowering fluorescent lights and the reflection off the highly polished floor, the walls had an eerie blue hue.

Major Maurice Alexander was exhausted and the bright lights put a strain on his tired, red eyes. Sleep had eluded him. Anxiety hounded him. It was like being trapped in a room where the walls closed in, but you couldn't see them move. When you looked at one wall, it stood still. Turn to look at the other, and it was closer than it had been just seconds before, but it too looked stationary.

For his next move, he was supposed to report to his superior, but she would become the focus of what would undoubtedly be a major investigation. So the question remained: who should his contact be?

The Air Force Academy was a grand institution. Next to West Point, it was arguably the most renowned military training facility in the country, perhaps in the world. A few graduates from Annapolis might argue the point, but it would be a difficult argument for them to win. It was never easy to air dirty laundry about such an institution or the people in charge. It was even more difficult when that person was your boss in the chain of command.

In order to maintain the integrity of the institution, standards were set high; rules were strict and had to be followed. Not just for the cadets who dreamed of becoming Air Force Officers, but for the staff as well. Especially the staff. Where possible, they had to exceed those standards so as to be an example to the impressionable young officer candidates. If they saw staff cutting corners on the rules, it meant it was okay for them to bend, even break the rules.

Currently, Major Maurice Alexander was the man enforcing those rules. He had never before been as mindful of the weight of his position as he was now. Before he'd left his house this morning, he'd looked at himself in the mirror and asked the reflection looking back, "Do you have the balls to do what you swore an oath to do?" The reflection hadn't blinked. He was obligated to uphold the laws of the land and the rules of the Air Force Academy, and he would honor that obligation.

Three criteria had to be met. Number one: Was the evidence that he held a legal document that could be used against the suspect? Number two: Did the documents contain information that clearly violated the Uniform Code of Military Justice? Number three: Was the evidence in the documents obtained legally and therefore admissible in court martial proceedings? If any one of these criteria was not met, then there was no case and he had to place these documents under seal, then determine if the documents were acquired legally. If not, he had to pursue charges against the person who had supplied them, his administrative assistant, Technical Sergeant Asiamarie Vance.

He had been up late, reading and rereading the information in the official report on the party that had happened over twenty-eight years ago. If they were still supposed to be sealed, then it wasn't legal for him to have the documents in his possession. He worried about the ramifications of a report that should have remained buried for all eternity. The fact remained, he had them and they contained a lurid tale.

First, he had to find out how Vance came to possess them. The nature of her answers was crucial in determining the legality of their existence outside of a locked vault and sealed envelope.

It was only 6:30 AM. She wasn't expected until 7:00 AM, so he was surprised when he heard the door to the outer office open. The door to his office was open, and he saw her at her desk, preparing for her day.

Technical Sergeant Asiamarie Vance worked hard and performed her job with a high degree of skill, efficiency, and accuracy. She was so proficient that when Major Alexander moved to the 10th Security Squadron, he requested that Asiamarie transfer with him. His request was honored.

As she put her handbag in the lower right hand drawer of her desk she said, "Good morning, sir. Is this coffee any good? I can make a good, fresh pot if you like." She smiled and moved to the inner office door. "Have you had breakfast yet? I was going to grab something from…" Her voice trailed off when his tired, bloodshot eyes met hers.

"Come on in, AV, and close the door."

"AV" was a nickname that Maurice had given her a few years ago when he got tired of saying "Sergeant Asiamarie."

Quietly, she said, "Yes sir." Maurice motioned to one of the guest chairs in front of his desk. She took a seat, smoothing out her uniform skirt as she did.

He took a sip of coffee, made a face as if he'd tasted a lemon, shook his head, then set the coffee cup down. "When we're finished here, you need to deep six that pot of coffee and make one that's drinkable."

She smiled. "Yes sir." Then the smile faded.

"Before I tell you what this is about, I need to tell you that your answers to my questions are strictly between you and me…for now. It's extremely important you are completely honest. You can't hold anything back, is that clear?"

Almost too quiet for Major Alexander to hear, she said in a voice with a slight quiver, "Yes, sir."

"And you can't be a wimp about this. Understand?"

Louder now, she said, "Yes sir."

"How did you come into possession of the files surrounding the party at the apartment of Cadet Milton Chester?"

Asiamarie took a deep breath, then tried to clear her throat.

Alexander looked at her and asked, "Do you need a glass of water?"

Asiamarie nodded.

The major returned with a glass of water and handed it to her. He was surprised to find her near tears and tense. She was always so calm and collected, but this topic had the potential to create a very public, very high profile scandal. She'd probably figured that out and was worried about whether she would be charged with a crime for holding these files.

She took a long drink then set the glass on a coaster on his desk. He sat in the chair next to her, a look of concern on his tired face.

She took a deep breath, stared at an imaginary point on the front of his desk, and began again, this time in a clear voice. "I was in the Air Force for just over a year and was stationed here at the academy. There was a disciplinary inquiry going on that was kept below the radar. Only a handful of people even knew it was being conducted."

"This was the Chester, Aims, Dempsey, and Wesley inquiry?"

She glanced at him, then turned her head back towards his desk. "Yes, sir. I worked for the 10th Security Squadron back then, too. This office was handling the preliminary questioning. We had seven witnesses. All were questioned and transcripts written up. They were being assembled for a formal inquiry. I was ordered to stay after work one afternoon and make copies of the transcripts and other forms associated with the investigation."

Her voice got dry and raspy. She paused, then took another long drink of water. After a deep breath she continued. "My boss, Major Reicker told me to make two extra copies of the files. He told me I needed to keep one copy in the safe in the office and put the other copy in a safe place off academy grounds. He said a safe deposit box would be best and I shouldn't divulge the files location for any reason until I was ordered. I never received the order. Major Reicker was killed in a car accident later in the week and his replacement had no idea the copy existed."

Maurice's eyebrows tightened. *A car accident?* It sounded like something out of a movie.

"AV, just so we're clear, the car accident was just that, a car accident, right?"

"Yes, sir. Nothing suspicious was found, except the timing of the accident."

"So, why did you decide to bring out the copy of the investigation now?"

She turned in her chair to face him and said with conviction, "Because there's been too much dirt shoveled to cover up this mess. I used to be proud that I was in the Air Force. I worked hard to get where I am today. I made something of my life. My mom said it would never happen, but I did it. With all this going on, how can we be proud? We're working harder at hiding the truth than we are at holding people to the standards we push on these new cadets at every turn."

At that moment, Maurice knew he could make a case for the legality of the documents.

"Thanks, AV. I think things will work out fine." He smiled. "How about making us a decent pot of coffee."

She didn't smile but stood and said, "Yes, sir, coming right up."

Chapter 37

Stale cigarette smoke clung to everything in the lounge behind *ABC Liquors* on US 436 on the south side of Apopka, Florida. Tar residue yellowed the normally white fluorescent lights that ran along the back of the bar under glass shelves holding a wide variety of liquors. A thin cloud of smoke drifted towards the exhaust fan at the far end of the bar.

The bartender, a tall man in his mid fifties with a day's growth of white stubble on his leathered face, dried recently washed beer mugs, then set them on a drying mat behind the bar. Seven patrons kept him just busy enough this Thursday night that he didn't have time to read the evening edition of the Orlando Sentinel Star.

Ace Glover sat at one corner of the bar, facing the back door that led to the liquor store, angled so he could keep an eye on anyone coming in from the parking lot. He'd been sitting at that spot for over an hour, sipping a beer, and sulking. The rush he'd felt after killing that fool, Harold Trent, was long gone. His mood cycle was on the deep slide down and he hadn't yet hit bottom. He was smart enough to avoid shots of whiskey or gulp his beer. Who knew how deep into depression he would have gone had he not kept his head, gotten a decent dinner, and disciplined himself not to go off the deep end?

Ace just wanted to be left alone, and this hole in the wall bar was the perfect place. The mug in front of him was within an inch of the bottom when the bartender approached and grunted more than asked, "Nother'n for ya?"

Ace nodded, then downed the last of the nearly warm liquid. Just as he set the empty mug down the bartender set a fresh beer in its place, then cleared away the empty. Ace picked up the fresh mug, raised it towards the bartender, and took a sip. He figured he could make this beer last about half an hour.

Ace had a lot on his mind. He missed Angelina Valentine more each day. Distance and time had softened the hard feelings he'd had when he left. Savannah was only about four to five hours by car from where he sat. But it was late on a Thursday night and he'd already had two beers. Besides, he had come to Central Florida for one purpose. He needed closure, to put balance back in his life, the yin and the yang. Someone had taken something precious from him. It was time to balance the scales of justice.

They killed my mother and sister. I should make them suffer the way I suffer every day. I should take something from them that they love. That would be far more painful than a bullet to the head or the chest. Joe and Pat's wives were beautiful women. Surely the brothers felt blessed. *They would feel equally cursed if their wives were suddenly taken away, wouldn't they?*

"Hey, partner, everthang okay?"

The bartender stood right in front of Ace, looking into his face with as much concern as a weathered old bartender could muster.

Ace replied, "Yeah. I'm fine. Just got a lot on my mind."

"If y'all want to tell me 'bout it, I'm here. That's what bartenders are for, that an' gettin' yer drinks." Ace noted the scars on his face, and that his top front teeth were chipped, probably from a fight some time back in his youth. The man asked, "Y'all got women troubles? They's usually the cause."

That brought the slightest smile to Ace's face. In a way, it was women troubles. His mother had let men treat her like a doormat. Then there was his half-sister, Rebecca. She'd had the same problem. There might have been hope for her, but the McKinneys put an end to that.

Ace, not trusting his words even with the few beers he'd drunk, didn't want to talk about himself. "How'd you get that scar? Looks like that was a nasty cut."

"Yeah, it was, but y'all know what they says. 'Y'all should see the other guy.' I smacked his head so hard that he don't talk right no more. Got hisself a permanent headache."

The bartender smiled slightly and only the right side of his lips seemed to work. Ace figured that the blade, whenever it happened, must have cut into some of the muscles on his face.

"I like your style. You just can't let people screw with you. You gotta stand up for yourself." Ace raised his glass to the man and took a drink. "You married?"

"Twice. First time wasn't even outta high school. AnnieMae Richards. Purdiest girl in school. I was on the football team. Hell, she got pregnant in 'leventh grade. My daughter is thirty-four now and has a couple of her own kids. Anyways, that only lasted 'bout eight months. She got all bitchy about money and me gettin' a job. Hell, only thing y'all can do 'round here is work in the greenhouses. Pay sucks and it's hotter'n a firecracker in there. Anyhow, it didn't work out. She left me. She married some guy who owns a couple greenhouses. She's doin' okay.

"My second wife tried to shoot me. So I left. I liked livin' a whole lot more than I liked her anyways."

Ace smiled and the bartender gave him a half-smile back. He looked Ace in the eyes and stopped smiling. "Name's Tom. I been here 'bout twenty years, tendin' this bar. I seen and heard most everthang. I'm purty good at readin' most folks and I can tell ya, y'all need a friend. If y'all want to talk, I can listen and never repeat nuthin'. So just what're y'all runnin' from?"

Ace's expression got serious. He took another deep gulp of his beer, nearly finishing the last half in one swallow. "Tom, get me another beer and a round for the bar. I'll tell you a story.

After three hours and more beer than Ace could remember, he told Tom about his life. He left out the parts about murdering men in cold blood, but left little doubt in

Tom's mind that he had doled out punishment to those he felt deserved it.

One of the men playing pool overheard part of Ace's story and said 'bullshit' under his breath. Ace didn't look his way. It wasn't worth his time or energy to bother with the punk.

Tom turned to the pool player. "Skip, y'all just mind y'alls game. Ya hear?"

Skip made some dismissive noise, then turned back to the game.

Tom turned his attention back to Ace. "I told y'all I'd keep this chat 'tween us. I gotta tell y'all sumthin' though. Y'all told me a lot tonight. What scares me is what ya ain't told me and I don't want ta know anythang more. But if y'all don't stop now, an' I mean right now, this thang that's buggin' ya is gonna be the death of ya."

Ace heard every word the older man said. He even connected with some of it. But, in the end, not one word swayed him from his goal.

"Tom, thanks for letting me bend your ear, and for the advice. But..." Ace lifted his mug and drained the last ounce of beer in one gulp..."I'm already dead."

He stood, threw another forty bucks on the bar and said, "Another round." He moved his finger in a circle at the other patrons then turned and walked out to the parking lot.

Chapter 38

Shawnda Hull's heart ached. Her brain told her to stop chasing her lover's killer. Leave that to the professionals. At the same time, she wanted to take matters into her own hands and make sure the job was done right.

As other passengers piled into the seats of the Boeing 737 jet, the fuselage appeared to shrink, the walls closed in. It seemed there were more people crowding the aisles than the plane could hold.

The tightness started in her chest. She had difficulty drawing a breath, her heart thumped like a bass drum, her ears pulsed with the rhythm. She leaned her seat back as far as it would go and covered her ears with her hands, but the thumping and drumming increased. The faces of the people around her drifted in and out of focus as they stuffed oversized carry-on bags or backpacks into the overhead compartments.

As the last passengers settled, Shawnda took several deep breaths. The strong scent of perfume combined with assorted body odors assaulted her nose. Her chest tightened further. She snatched up her purse, and after several attempts to speak, asked the elderly woman in the aisle seat if she could move past her. She gave Shawnda a look of disgust, then after a moment's hesitation, she unbuckled and turned her knees to the left, allowing Shawnda just enough room to get past her and into the aisle.

Working her way through the maze of bodies, Shawnda made it within ten feet of first class when a flight attendant approached her. "Ma'am, please take your seat. We're preparing for takeoff."

Shawnda took deep breaths, trying to force enough oxygen into her lungs to relieve the shortness of breath. The tightness worsened. She opened her mouth to speak, but her throat was dry. She pointed towards the front of the plane with her left hand while shaking her right hand. Finally, she managed to choke out, "I have to get off the plane...right now."

Shawnda shoved past the attendant who made no attempt to stop her. From the galley by the cockpit, another flight attendant stepped into the aisle. She took a deep breath, put on her brightest smile and moved towards Shawnda.

"Ma'am, can I help you?"

Shawnda shook her head and kept moving, still gasping for air, trying to ignore the attendant. Her heart beat quickened and sweat glistened on her forehead. She cleared first class and turned left, where another attendant was preparing to close the airtight door. Shawnda shouldered her way past the woman and pushed the door open just enough to squeeze through.

As the attendant inside the jet tried to grab Shawnda by the arm, she leaped across the three foot gap onto the moving gangway, stumbling as she landed. The man operating the gangway grabbed her by the arm, pulling her to safety. He started to ask her if she was okay when she broke free of his grasp, then ran for the doorway to the terminal. She didn't slow down until she reached it.

After several minutes, her breathing slowed to normal. She boarded the shuttle bus to Budget Car Rentals and leaned back for the ride. She hoped and prayed she had enough room on her credit card for a two day rental.

Her mind was made up. She would take matters into her own hands. Now all she needed was a gun.

***

Colonel Melinda Barnes was surprised by the request for a meeting by Major Maurice Alexander. She had ordered him to drop the investigation into the backgrounds of Wesley, Aims, and Dempsey. If this was the purpose of his visit, she would charge him with insubordination. No junior officer in her chain of command would violate a direct, lawful order and get away with it.

On the other hand, maybe his visit was for a totally different matter. After all, he was a man of integrity and not likely to disregard her directive. He knew the consequences. He'd seen what happened when a male subordinate thought he could get the better of her because she was a woman. That former officer was forced out of the Air Force after her scathing performance review left him without a future in the military. Certainly that was engraved in Major Alexander's memory banks.

As she waited, she worked through the stack of reports in her inbox, signing several in a mindless frenzy, trying to clear the clutter from her desk before the next stack came in. Over the years she'd learned how to scan the important papers for key information before signing. Other, routine papers were signed without a second glance.

As she perused a report on the grade point average of the recently graduated class, her administrative assistant buzzed her.

"Colonel Barnes, Colonel Templeton is on line one, ma'am."

She frowned, then pressed the intercom send button. "Thank you, Sergeant."

She picked up the receiver and pressed the button below the blinking red light. She and Templeton had agreed they would have little or no contact while the investigation into the murders of the three Air Force officers was in progress. It would either die for lack of evidence or the killer would be caught. There was no reason for her or her counterpart at Grand Forks to be concerned...unless they brought attention to themselves.

"Gene, this better be damned important."

Colonel Eugene Templeton took a deep breath. Even with his deep, radio talk show voice, he sounded like a kid trapped on a school playground getting bullied for his lunch money.

"Mel, he's dead."

Melinda Barnes frowned. "Who's dead?"

"Trent. Harold Trent. The guy who—"

Colonel Barnes stiffened. "Not over the phone. Don't say any more. When I leave the base today, I'll call you at home. Be there by six." Then she hung up.

God, he is such a wimp. Why the hell is he talking about Harold Trent? He hasn't been seen in twenty-five years or more. She shook her head, trying to clear the negative thoughts seeping into her brain. She didn't have time for this. Major Alexander was scheduled...

A buzz from the intercom. "Colonel, Major Alexander is here for his appointment."

After a slow, deep breath, Colonel Barnes said, "Send him in."

***

The door to the colonel's office opened. Major Maurice Alexander, in a sharply pressed, light blue button shirt with dark blue slacks entered the office, his cover under his left arm. He wore a serious, no nonsense expression.

Colonel Barnes wore an equally serious expression. When she spoke her voice was crisp, conveying a message that she didn't have time for a casual visit and idle chatter.

"Major, I have a very busy schedule. What's this about?"

Maurice Alexander had taken his deep breaths outside the office so that he didn't have to in front of the colonel. He knew that she was an expert at exploiting weaknesses in character and he wasn't going to allow her the opportunity to throw him off track. The timing of his visit to her office couldn't have been better. Hearing the colonel's administrative assistant buzz her with the incoming call from Colonel Templeton boosted his confidence that he was on the right track. He plowed ahead.

"Colonel Barnes, my office has evidence that a number of Air Force cadets were involved in the rape of a young woman at a party."

She stared at him for a moment. "Major, your department handles these matters. Why are you wasting my time?"

Major Alexander's expression didn't change. Not a single muscle in his face twitched, contracted, or moved. There was no smile. No fear. No outward emotion.

"I'm here to inform you that I will be presenting evidence to your superior regarding your actions on the night of April 30, 1970. That was the night you and Colonel Templeton aided four other cadets in the rape of an under-aged civilian girl named Abigail Glover."

Alexander's stare didn't waiver. He hadn't blinked and his voice stayed steady and clear. There wasn't a crack in his composure, even as Colonel Melinda Barnes' own face grew red with anger.

Before she could get a word out, Alexander continued, "I will also present evidence that you blackmailed the base commander, Colonel Alton Chester, the father of one of the cadets involved in the rape."

Barnes' gaze remained steady on the major's face. In a smooth, swift motion, without looking away from the major's face, Colonel Barnes punched the intercom button on her desk. "Sergeant, hold all my calls."

"Yes, Ma'am."

Her face was nearly back to its normal color but remained stone-like. "So, Major, what would possess you to barge into my office and make such a ridiculous claim?"

Chapter 39

The interior of Pat McKinney's twenty-four foot by fifty foot detached garage was clean and organized. The first floor space was divided into three separate rooms. A service door opened into a twelve by twenty foot space. Two interior doors opened into two other rooms. A thirty by twelve foot workshop was on the left. The other room was fifty feet long by twelve feet wide with a bay door at both ends.

In the large bay near the center a stairway led to a second floor room that extended the entire length of the garage. The room was only nine feet wide and seven feet high, the height restricted by the pitch of the roof. One end of the room was fortified with steel plates fronted by a wall of dense foam. The other end had a set of tables divided into two stalls. Markings along the ceiling were set at five feet intervals beginning at forty-five feet at the far end, down to twenty feet at the closest point. Two cables, both controlled by an electric pulley system, ran along the ceiling the length of the room. A clamp held a frame used to affix targets to the cable. A spring loaded switch turned on a motor that moved the targets down the length of the garage to the desired distance from the stalls and back again. It was Pat's private firing range.

Diane had insisted that Pat insulate the garage with sound proofing material so the neighbors couldn't hear the reports from the gunfire and complain about it. Now, with Pat teaching Sean how to handle a gun, she wanted that privacy even more.

Pat had built the garage as part of his mental rehabilitation after he was shot in the chest in Norfolk, Virginia. The Kevlar vest had saved his life, but the mental toll had been far greater. Nightmares plagued him until he concentrated on the design and construction of the ultimate garage. His brother Joe had helped with the construction, but the design was all Pat's, except the tool and gun cabinets. Those were Diane's idea.

Pat and Sean stood side by side in the second floor of the garage, both quiet and in deep concentration. Pat's brand new dark black Sig Sauer 9mm lay disassembled on a white cloth in one of the firing stalls. The parts were in the approximate position of where they would be if the gun were fully assembled, but in an exploded view. The scent of the original oil from the disassembled weapon filled Pat's nostrils. His gun cleaning kit sat to one side, ready for use when it came time to reassemble the weapon.

The previous day, Pat had gone over basic gun safety and explained why it was absolutely critical he follow the rules. Sean was so intent on learning how to use a gun that he listened to his dad's every word. He was a young man, a boy really, on a mission.

One by one, Pat picked up a part and asked Sean its name and its purpose. It was a long process, but an effective one.

Pat lifted a part.

"Barrel."

Another part.

"Recoil spring."

Another.

"Firing pin spring."

Another.

"Grip Safety."

Sean identified the parts as fast as Pat could grab them. He had already disassembled and reassembled the weapon three times, the last time without instructions. Pat knew his son was anxious to actually shoot the gun, but he wanted to be certain Sean had a good understanding of how it worked mechanically. That Sean was learning quickly was an understatement, which, on one hand, pleased Pat. On the other hand, Sean was much closer to reaching a point from where there would be no return. Once Sean fired the Sig, he would be on the road to becoming a gun enthusiast. It was just the way he was wired. He got on a topic and he couldn't let it go.

Pat and Diane thought he had Obsessive Compulsive Disorder, but when they described his personality traits to a psychologist, he'd told them that their son would probably grow out of it. When they had the pool installed, it appeared as though the doctor might have been right. Now they had their doubts.

"Okay, Sean, put the Sig back together. Before you put the slide in place, be sure to oil the points where I showed you. Leave the clip out."

Sean assembled the weapon perfectly, lightly oiling the slide points, making sure not to over-lubricate, all while keeping the business end of the weapon facing away. Pat was impressed. Even though the gun was obviously not loaded, Sean was already developing good safety habits. When he finished, Pat reached into his pocket and placed a box of fifty 9mm target grade bullets on the white cloth.

Sean looked at the box, not moving, his facial expression not changing, waiting for his father to say the word.

Pat knew he was anxious. He saw a vein in Sean's temple pulsing with the excitement of the moment. He wasn't going to violate any rules and one of the rules was that you didn't do anything on impulse while working with your weapon.

"Okay, son. Here's the deal. You've read how to load the clip and you've watched me a few times. The spring in the clip is a bit powerful, so it's going to be tough the first couple times until you get used to it. Understand?"

"Yes, sir."

"Alright, open the box and slide the tray of bullets out. Put it on the bench."

Sean did as instructed, the flat surface of the shells facing upward, most of the brass of the shell hidden by the plastic case.

"Now take the clip and one bullet and load it."

Pat watched as Sean struggled a bit with the spring pressure. Offering his help would only aggravate his son, so he kept his mouth shut and watched as Sean worked against the spring pressure to load the first round. Finally, he slowed down and methodically forced the round into the clip, letting spring pressure lock the round into place.

A smile spread across his face. He reached for another round and repeated the process. The second round went in much easier, the third easier still. When he got to the eighth round, he struggled a bit as the tension from the compressed spring started to fight back, but he managed to get the bullet in place. The clip held fourteen rounds, but Pat had instructed Sean to load only ten. That was plenty for his first lesson.

Holding the clip in his left hand, Sean looked up at Pat with anticipation. Pat took a deep breath. "Remember what I taught you. Go ahead and put the clip in the pistol, but don't chamber a round. Wait until we have our safety gear on. Okay?"

"Yes, sir."

Pat noticed the nervous smile on Sean's face. This was the big moment.

***

After half an hour of slow, methodical practice and instructions, the live fire portion of the lesson was over. Sean had done exceptionally well. At first, his pattern on the target was spread out and to the lower left of the bull's eye. After some careful instructions, the pattern tightened significantly. By the final ten shots, Sean's target displayed a tight pattern only five inches from the center. He hit the bull's eye twice and had centered the cluster on the target. He was ready to continue shooting, but Pat told him that it was time to stop and clean the weapon. With a serious expression, Sean nodded, cleared the weapon and began the cleaning process for the fifth time in just over an hour.

As Pat watched, a smile slowly spread across his son's face. He was pleased with his first live fire lesson. Pat was proud, but apprehensive. On one hand, his son had learned a great deal about gun safety, and the potential danger that guns presented when not handled properly. He had also learned how to shoot correctly, with a careful, steady aim.

On the other hand, Sean was now hooked on guns. Pat could tell as he watched Sean manipulate the weapon with great care there was no turning back. He would want to shoot whenever Pat had free time.

Diane would never understand and most definitely not approve. She would go along to get along, but she would never agree that this was a good idea.

***

Sunlight streamed through the gap in the curtains and hit Ace directly in the face. He tried to remember the name of the flea-bag joint. *The Sunset Motel or the Seashell...what the hell. It doesn't matter.* He tried to move his head to avoid the light, but that just made his head pound. The beer had flowed too freely for too long. He was paying the price now. Still lying in bed, he rolled to his left. The digital clock on the nightstand blinked 5:23, as if power had been lost overnight. *Shit, that can't be right. It's too light for early morning and I couldn't have slept until late afternoon.*

The room smelled faintly of damp, musty carpet, and stale smoke. He rolled over in bed pulling the pillow over his head to block the sunlight. The angle of the sun made him think it was around mid-morning. It couldn't be noon or the sun would be more directly over head.

He dozed off again for another twenty minutes. Finally, the stream of sunlight was out of his eyes to the left of his head. He sat up, his head pounding, punishing him for drinking so much. He leaned over, groping for his watch on the nightstand. Blinking the floaters out of his eyes, he strained to see the hands. 11:10 AM. Time to move. *A hot shower, some coffee and a good breakfast, and I'll be as good as new.*

Ace had a big day ahead.

***

Hatch drove south through Apopka on U.S. 441, then turned right on Clarcona Road towards Ocoee and Winter Garden. He was heading for Joe and Lisa McKinney's house, hoping he and Nancy would get there before Ace...if that was Ace's destination. They were in Hatch's Ford Taurus, a car that Ace knew since their encounter at the baseball fields in Kingsland, Georgia.

Hatch was familiar with Apopka as long as they stayed on the main roads, but once they turned onto Clarcona Road, he needed directions.

Nancy studied the map, tracing roads with her right index finger. It didn't help that the map was nearly ten years out of date. Apopka had grown significantly since Hatch's last trip to Orange County. Nancy had never been there.

"It looks like you stay on this road until you get to Silver Star Road. Then take a right."

Hatch thought for a moment. "Silver Star Road. Joe and Lisa used to live in an apartment complex on Silver Star. It's near Hiawassee Road."

"Yeah. Clarcona runs roughly parallel to Hiawassee. But Winter Garden is to the west. It shouldn't be but about twenty minutes from here. Just guessing."

"Y'all's probably close. Do y'all have their address?"

In a tone of mock astonishment, Nancy said, "I thought you did." Then she held up the paper with Joe and Lisa's address and smiled.

"Y'all's evil," Hatch said.

"Seriously, I just hope Ace doesn't figure out where Joe and Lisa live. When Joe's wallet was stolen, he was still living at the apartment."

Hatch kept his eyes on the road as it curved around one lake, then circled back around another lake on the other side of the road. "I'm afraid our boy Ace is a bit smarter'n that. I'm just glad we got Miss Shawnda out of the way. She don't need to mess her life up any more'n it already is."

Nancy nodded just as the first raindrops hit the windshield. The rain was early today.

Chapter 40

At 11:30 AM on July 9, Joe and Lisa's kitchen still held the aroma of coffee, bacon and eggs, and grits, though breakfast had been finished and cleaned up several hours earlier. Concerned about Ace Glover's whereabouts, Joe, Lisa, and Danielle had skipped their two mile trek around the neighborhood. Instead, they opted for some leisure time in the pool.

After drying off and changing back to street clothes, it was lunchtime. It was also their first experiment at allowing their little girl to feed herself. Lisa, obsessive about being neat and tidy, literally had to sit on her hands the entire time Danielle ate. Despite her initial shock at the colossal mess her daughter had made, Lisa finally laughed before beginning the cleanup, praising her baby girl for the effort.

Joe came in the front door, heard the laughter, and strolled into the kitchen. He took one look at his daughter's food covered face, shook his head, and chuckled. He leaned over and kissed his wife on the cheek, congratulated her for her self control, then kissed his daughter on the top of her head, the only spot on the girl not coated with goo.

In the stack of mail Joe held, one package stood out from the usual combination of regular arrivals, a standard 5x7 inch soft pack envelope addressed to Mrs. Lisa McKinney. There was no return address and the address label had been typed.

Joe laid the envelope on the counter alongside the rest of the mail. "There's a package for you. It feels like a small box inside."

Lisa was busy teasing their daughter, rubbing the tip of her nose with the washcloth, speaking in a sing-song baby voice, "That's my girl" then pulling the cloth away. Each time she did, Danielle laughed. Joe smiled. He was amazed at the transformation of his wife from a serious, career woman to one hundred percent motherhood since she'd discovered that she was pregnant. He worried it might someday hit her that she'd given up on her dreams to devote her life to her child and husband. He'd seen it before and wondered if there was anything he could do to make sure it didn't happen to Lisa. Clearly, though, it would be some time before that question was an issue. For now, he would simply enjoy his time with his family. He wondered how he had been so lucky in love.

Lisa looked up from cleaning the last bits of lunch from Danielle's face. "Who's the package from?"

"Don't know. No return address. Maybe it's from your secret admirer."

"Hmm. I wonder which one." She gave Joe a teasing smile. "I'll check it out in a bit. I have to get this little monster cleaned up."

Lisa picked their daughter up out of the high chair and disappeared for ten minutes. When she returned to the living room, she set their daughter, now dolled up in a pretty dress, in her playpen, surrounded by stuffed animals.

Joe was enjoying a cold glass of iced tea when Lisa walked up to him smiling. She held a heart-shaped gold locket, approximately one inch tall by three-quarters of an inch wide attached to a delicate gold chain. The heart had small, intricate designs engraved on the front that looked like rose buds in the early stages of bloom.

"Isn't this beautiful?" She cupped the locket in her left hand, the thin chain dangling behind. "It must be from Mom. Maybe she ordered it from a shop in Savannah."

"How do you know it's from your mom?"

She flipped the locket over showing Joe the inscription. "It says 'A Mother's Love' on the back. I have to call Mom and thank her. I wonder why she'd send it this time of year. Maybe she's feeling a little lonely since heading back home."

Lisa grabbed the cordless phone, sat next to Joe and punched in a series of numbers. Joe heard the muffled voice of Lisa's mother when she answered.

"Oh, Mom, you wouldn't believe the mess she made today."

Mother and daughter spoke of baby Danielle and her adventure at lunchtime. Lisa described all the things that baby Danielle had learned since the last time they spoke.

"So, Mom, the reason I called, I want to thank you for the beautiful locket."

Joe noticed his wife's mood change from surprise to confusion, then to concern. When she hung up the phone, she turned to Joe. "Mom said she didn't send me the locket."

***

After Lisa and her mother said their goodbyes, Lisa inspected the locket with greater scrutiny.

The gold locket caught the sunlight reflected into the lanai from a stainless steel grill on the patio. Lisa looked closer at the heart. A small clasp held the locket closed. She brought the locket to her face and opened it. Two pictures, both black and white, were snapped into place on the inside of both halves. Confused, she thought the pictures might be generic shots, like those used in new frames while they sat on department store shelves. But these pictures looked like a Kodak or Polaroid snapshot.

The left hand picture showed a woman with light hair, a thin face, a smile that appeared forced and out of place. Even in the tiny shot, Lisa sensed sadness, a feeling the woman had endured a hard life. The smile was little more than a prop to project the image she was happy to be in the picture, that life wasn't as bad as the truth the rest of her face gave away.

When she looked at the picture in the right side of the locket, it took her a moment. She gasped as the stark realization hit her.

Joe asked, "What is it, babe?"

***

Diane McKinney had just finished her lunch and was opening the small stack of mail on the table in the breakfast nook. She came to a soft-pack envelope, the type used to send fragile mail. She wondered what kind of come-on the package contained since there was no return address. *Interesting.* Using a plastic letter opener with a razor embedded in between a hand grip and a pointed tip, she sliced the end of the envelope and tipped it, spilling a small box onto the table.

When she removed the beautiful gold locket from the package, she knew right away that it wasn't cheap. The fine, delicate chain appeared to be fourteen carat gold. The locket itself was beautifully engraved with rose buds. Flipping the locket over, she read, 'A Mother's Love' professionally scripted. This wasn't from *her* mother. They weren't that close and her parents didn't have the financial means to buy a gift like this. They gave practical gifts, like kitchen utensils or clothing, but never anything like jewelry or make-up.

Then she wondered if Pat's mother, Emma might have sent it. She looked at the postmark. Savannah, Georgia. Not Emma. She never bought anything mail order without first laying eyes on the merchandise. Emma always did a thorough inspection of all her purchases. It was almost a ritual.

Diane opened the locket, looking at the picture of the woman on the left, then glancing at the picture on the right, a picture of the young Ace Glover. Which meant the woman was Abbie Glover.

She dropped the locket. It landed on the opened envelope, then slid onto the table. A chill ran down her spine, then throughout her body. Fear seized her, then anger followed. She hollered, "Pat, get in here!"

The *tick tick tick* of a cheap clock on the wall filled the silence as Pat ran into the room.

"What's the matter, dear?"

She was silent for a moment, then stabbed a finger at a gold locket. "This…is…what's the matter, Pat. This locket. The fact that this lunatic knows where we live, knows our names. Who knows what else he knows?"

Pat picked up the locket from the table and looked at the pictures.

"I have to call Joe."

As Pat reached for the wall phone in the kitchen, it rang. He cursed and picked it up on the second ring. After a moment, he said "I know. Diane got one, too. They sound identical. We have to get the cops involved." It must have been Joe on the other end, Diane thought.

Then Pat said, "I think we need to let Hatch know he should get down here as quickly as possible."

After Pat hung up the phone, the couple continued to talk about the locket and the message it implied. Diane whispered, "I think he's planning to hurt our children."

Pat took a deep breath and whispered back, "I'm afraid you're right, but we're not going to let that happen."

After a few moments, Diane's fear subsided, replaced by resolve. She was not going to let this crazy bastard get to her children.

Chapter 41

"I'm sorry gentleman, but this has to be quick. I have a staff luncheon in fifteen minutes. What can I do for the Grand Forks Police Department today?"

Detectives Banks and Hansen looked at each other, then Banks cleared his throat. "Call your sergeant and tell her to cancel it because you won't have time for that."

Major Jean Krantz, Officer in Charge of the Air Force Office of Special Investigations, frowned. She reminded Banks of his seventh grade math teacher, the scariest woman he'd ever met…until now.

"This better be good. What is so damned important that you'd come to my office without an appointment, then tell me that I need to clear my calendar?"

Banks pulled a briefcase onto his lap and extracted the papers that had been faxed to the Grand Forks Police Department the previous day.

"We have copies of a file that were faxed to our office. The file is from an investigation that took place back in the 1970s. May I?"

The look on Major Krantz' face could have stripped paint off the walls. For a moment, he thought that she was going to call in the MPs and have them thrown in the brig.

"I'm to clear my calendar for a twenty-five year old investigation? You've got about ten seconds to convince me that you both shouldn't be thrown bodily from this office!"

Banks stood and laid the pages on the desk in front of her. Then he explained how they had come into possession of these documents. It took less than one minute for the major to understand why she had to not only cancel lunch, but clear her calendar for at least two days. Her office was about to get very busy.

Major Krantz, punched the intercom button, "Sergeant Spindel, get in here."

When Spindel entered the office, Major Krantz glared at him. "Cancel the luncheon and all my appointments for the rest of the day. Inform the brig that they have to hold Briggs and Stratton a few days longer."

Banks gave Hansen a sideways glance at the names of the two detainees. He was afraid to smile in case Major Krantz caught him and decided to toss him in along with the small engine pair.

She continued, "Let the JAG office know the session for later today has to be postponed until next Tuesday at the earliest. Also, cancel all my appointments for Monday. One other thing, Sergeant Spindel, except for the people you have to contact regarding their appointments, *do not* speak a word of this to anyone. Is that understood?"

In a hurried, nervous voice, Spindel responded, "Yes, ma'am."

Without another word, he pivoted and left the office, closing the door behind him. Krantz turned back to the detectives.

Banks returned to his seat and waited as Major Krantz reread the documents he'd laid in front of her. The more she read, the more her face twisted and her jaw tightened. A crimson tint appeared on her cheeks and spread to her earlobes. Banks swore he could feel the heat rise in the room as Krantz neared the boiling point.

Finally, after reading the documents for the fourth time, she looked up at Banks, then at Hansen, then back to Banks. "Gentlemen, if I read these documents correctly, Colonel Templeton is in deep shit."

The detectives walked the major through the evidence they'd received via fax from a staff sergeant at the Air Force Academy. It detailed crimes committed over twenty-five years ago by Cadet Eugene Templeton and at least five other cadets. Four of the suspects were now dead, possibly in retaliation for that crime. Only Templeton and Colonel Melinda Barnes were alive.

Banks removed his lightweight blazer and tossed it over the back of the office chair where he'd been sitting. His white shirt was beginning to show moisture at his armpits from the tension caused by the review of some very damaging evidence for Colonel's Templeton and Barnes.

Reid Hansen sat quietly for most of the meeting. He would occasionally inject a comment, filling in minor details that Banks had skipped over.

A slight sheen of perspiration formed over the top of Major Krantz's lip. Her forehead glistened from a thin layer of sweat. She took a deep breath, then leaned back in her leather office chair before swiveling and gazing out the window that over-looked the landing strip.

Banks could see the wheels turning in her mind. She was probably thinking not only of this case, but of her own future. He knew the case was full of land mines. One false move and she'd be shot down in flames. He had to somehow convince her that she needed to take immediate action. It didn't matter if the crime had taken place twenty-five years ago or a hundred years ago, the suspects needed to be arrested, charged, and tried. At the very least, they were accessories to crimes which had no statute of limitations.

Without looking at Banks, Hansen said, "Jean."

A thin smile worked its way onto her face. It was nearly undetectable, but it was there. Banks turned to Hansen and cocked an eyebrow as if to ask, 'Isn't that a bit personal?' But he managed to keep his mouth shut and let his partner go with it.

Slowly, Major Krantz swiveled her chair back to face the detectives. "So tell me Reid, do I need to be worried about this so called evidence that you two have dropped in my lap?"

Keeping a deadpan face Detective Hansen said, "You can count on the evidence. There was a question about whether it was valid to use in a military tribunal, but that question has been asked and answered. The files were supposed to be sealed.

Before I tell you anymore, this would be more appropriate coming from a fellow Air Force Officer." He paused, then continued, "I think you should call Major Maurice Alexander at . . ."

". . . the 10th Security Squadron at Colorado Springs. I know Mo very well. And I trust him. I'll do that, but if you're telling me you've already discussed this with him then I know these files are legit."

Major Jean Krantz was convinced. It was going to be an ugly Friday at Grand Forks. When the news broke the base commander was being arrested, it was going to hit the fan in a big way.

***

"You can't go in there. The colonel said that she was not to be disturbed."

"Stand down, Lieutenant. Take a seat and do not touch that intercom or you will be charged with obstructing official business."

Major Maurice Alexander opened the door to the office of Colonel Melinda Barnes. He walked in with his head held high, his uniform pressed to perfection. He looked like he'd just come from a photo shoot for the cover of Air Force Times. If all went as planned he might very well make the cover, but that was far from his mind. His goal today was to lock up a criminal.

Colonel Melinda Barnes stood behind her desk, talking on the phone when the major and two chiseled MPs opened her door without her permission. She shot the major a look. He could almost feel the heat from the glare.

Into the phone, Colonel Barnes said, "I have a meeting that I apparently forgot. I'll call you back later."

Major Alexander started to speak, but Colonel Barnes cut him off. "Major Alexander, let's get this straight right now. I am a colonel in the United States Air Force. I've not been convicted of any crimes and I demand that you respect me for the position I hold. The next time you enter this office you will use proper protocol. Is that understood?"

Major Alexander stood, stone faced, not saying a word. The tension in the room rose with each passing second. This wasn't a case of busting a couple drunken airmen at a bar. He was about to take a full bird colonel into custody. And it appeared the colonel wasn't going to go down without a fight.

Finally, a slight smile formed on Alexander's face. He wasn't falling for her power play. He had a job to do.

"Colonel Barnes, you are under arrest for being an accessory to the rape of Abigail Glover, who at the time was a fifteen-year old minor. You have all the rights afforded you by the Uniform Code of Military Justice. Do you understand…"

***

Major Jean Krantz tried to call her friend, Mo Alexander before driving over to the headquarter building at Grand Forks Air Force Base. His assistant said that he was not in his office and she didn't know when to expect him back. Krantz drove her car, followed by two MPs from the Air Force Office of Special Investigations. They, in turn, were followed by the detectives' car from the Grand Forks Police Department driven by Bill Banks. Reid Hansen rode shotgun.

Banks grinned as they moved along in the small convoy. He stole a glance at Hansen. "So what's the deal with being on a first name basis with Major Krantz?"

Hansen smiled as he looked out the window at the Air Force housing units. He turned back to Banks. "If I tell you, you can't say anything to my wife, okay?"

"Awe, geesh. What the hell did you do?"

Hansen shook his head. "It isn't what you think. Well, that's not really true. It is what you think, but not how."

He paused for quite a while. So long in fact that Banks said, "Well?"

Finally, Hansen said, "I went to school with her older brother. High School. She was quite a bit younger than me but when I got back from 'Nam, she was over eighteen. Well, she looked over eighteen anyway. I'm actually not sure if she was, but I'd just got back from over there, you know, and I was horny as hell."

Hansen's smile was wide. Banks had a smirk on his face.

Reid continued, "Anyway, it was a one-time thing. We really didn't have anything in common. She was against the war and listened to country music. I was hard core rock-n-roll. So we went out one more time and decided that it wasn't going to work."

"Is that when you started dating your wife?"

"Well, sometime around there. I gotta tell you, she was a lot cuter back then, but she was just as ornery."

Banks chuckled at that. "It's a damn good thing you let that one go. She'd have had you for breakfast, lunch, snack, and dinner."

They pulled into a visitor's spot at the front of the headquarters building and met Major Krantz and the two MPs by their cars. Banks and Hansen were a bit tense, but in good spirits. The major and her MPs wore serious expressions. They all headed towards the main entrance.

***

From his office, Colonel Templeton saw the cars pull into the parking lot. He called to his Administrative assistant, Major Blaine Sanders. "No visitors for the next hour. I have a lot of work to do. Can you please meet the group that is coming at the front lobby and get rid of them?"

In her deep voice she replied, "Yes, sir."

She reached the lobby just as Major Jean Krantz, the two MPs, and Banks and Hansen walked through the front door.

Major Krantz spoke first. "Major Sanders, is the colonel in his office?"

"Yes, he is, Major, but he asked that he not be—"

A loud bang echoed throughout the building. All six of the occupants in the lobby knew the sound of an AN1911 forty-five caliber pistol.

***

As the Air Force Rescue Squad wheeled the gurney with the black vinyl body bag down the hall, Banks and Hansen stood against the wall, their good mood destroyed by yet another death related to Milton Chester. Majors Krantz and Sanders were talking quietly in the outer office by Sander's desk. Krantz was trying to determine what, if anything, Major Sanders knew about the events of nearly a quarter century ago at the Air Force Academy. The two MPs were dismissed to head back to their office. The crowd that had formed outside the colonel's office had dispersed. Everyone in the building was told to return to their jobs, and they would be questioned later about the turn of events that day. It was expected that few, if any would know more than the fact that they'd heard a gunshot and that it appeared to have come from the colonel's office. After about fifteen minutes Major Krantz joined the two detectives.

"I'm pretty sure Blaine knew nothing about what Templeton had done. She did say that he's made several calls to Colonel Barnes at the Air Force Academy, and that he turned into a blithering idiot when talking with her."

She smiled for a second. Hansen asked, "What?"

Krantz said, "Blaine called him a pussy. Kind of funny coming from her. She's kind of a dick." Her smile grew wider.

Banks thought, *Real damn funny. Guy isn't even cold yet.*

Chapter 42

The drive west on Florida's State Route 50, then north on State Route 471 allowed Ace plenty of time to think. He had passed through Clermont, Groveland, and Mascotte and was on a stretch of road that was still relatively primitive, a condition that was rapidly disappearing in the Sunshine State. He had time to reflect on everything that led to this moment in his life. The drive to Dunnellon had a calming effect, as if he was near the culmination of a lifelong goal. As he drove along in the bright sunshine, he rolled down the windows allowing the hot, humid Florida air to blow through the car. Sweat formed on his back from the heat trapped between his body and the driver's seat, but he didn't mind. His thoughts were all on scores that had to be settled. Realizing that he might not live to wipe the slate completely clean, he concentrated on the next name on his list: *Pat McKinney.*

He wasn't jealous of the McKinney's or anyone born with a silver spoon in their mouth, but he wondered why he'd been dealt the sorry hand he now held. Born to an unwed mother who spent her time being abused by lousy, low-life bastards, whose only goal in life was to drink and get laid. His mother had all but invited them to take out their frustrations on her. She'd tried her best to shield Ace from the abusers, but some still managed to take out their anger, or in some cases, their pleasure, on him when he was a child. Some had made it a sport to abuse mother and son.

Even though his mother, Abbie Glover and half-sister, Becky Lippert, had only spoken face to face five or six times, Becky had obviously inherited all of her traits. The pattern of abuse should have stopped with Abbie if environmental factors were the only influence at play, but Ace's half-sister had her mother's genes. It was the only explanation for Becky's abuse at the hands of her boyfriend, Bobby Garrett. She had many opportunities to leave him, but opted to stay. Ultimately, that decision had ended her life.

At the bar in Kingsland, Harold Trent had claimed he treated Ace's mother like a queen. Ace hadn't believed him. Trent was like all the other abusers and deserved to die. Ace wasn't even born when Abbie threw Trent out, warning him to never come back. At least, that was Trent's story. Then he'd said he was Ace's biological father. Was it true? Had he killed his father in that parking lot in Kingsland? *No matter. He was no father to me.* Ace searched his heart and mind for even a tinge of remorse, but found none. The fool hadn't listened to his repeated warnings to leave well enough alone, to leave vengeance to its rightful owner. Just another name crossed off in his notepad.

Earlier in the day, he'd driven around Joe and Lisa McKinney's neighborhood, an upscale subdivision on the outskirts of Winter Garden. The homes were in pristine condition, landscaped to perfection, though Joe and Lisa's grounds weren't as spectacular as some of their neighbors. Still, Ace was impressed. The house stood on what appeared to be an acre-plus of ground with a bright green lawn, a few palm trees, and a number of shrubs near the house in a stone covered bed. He didn't begrudge the McKinney's their success. He didn't know if it was Joe's shots that had killed his mother, but that didn't matter. He'd been on the apprehension team, the team that killed his mother and half-sister, and that placed Joe at the top of Ace's hit list. His brother, Pat, shared that place.

When Ace had cruised the neighborhood, he had noticed a car parked on the street several doors down from Joe and Lisa's house. The only car parked on the street, it looked out of place in this posh neighborhood. As he approached the car from behind, he noticed a young, red-headed woman in the driver's seat.

It can't be. But how could she know?

Even with just a quick glance from a poor angle Ace recognized the red hair, the rounded cheeks, and the pale complexion. Major Shawnda Hull. She no longer drove the beat up Toyota, but a white Chevy Cavilier. *Probably a rental.*

At that moment, Ace thought about stopping right next to her and blowing her brains out. It would serve her right. But she hadn't done anything to his family.

He had kept his cool driving past the car, keeping his face turned away from the young woman. He didn't know how she knew, but somehow she was a step ahead of him and waiting to do what…stop him from avenging his mother's rape and murder? Why would she care?

There was no need to hang around here. He was too easy to spot on the street in this neighborhood. If you drove anything less than a Lexus, you were out of place. The neighbors were, no doubt, taking note. Someone may have already called the cops on Hull. Joe McKinney would have to wait for another day.

That had been over half an hour ago. He was approaching Dunnellon, just twenty-five miles away. Even though he knew the street address, he hadn't pinpointed the exact location of Patrick McKinney's house. That should be easy enough. How many Patrick McKinney's could there be in Dunnellon?

No matter. It was approaching noon on Saturday, July 10 and the sun was already punishing anyone spending time under its rays. Ace pulled his car off the road at a convenience store in Wildwood to fill up on gas and grab a snack. After ten minutes, he was back on the road on State Route 44 feeling better after a sub-sandwich and a cola. All in all, things were looking up.

***

Joe McKinney picked up the phone on the third ring. It was his neighbor two doors down.

"Hey, Joe, do you know the lady in the white Chevy watching your house?"

Joe had no idea what Willy Carson was talking about. He carried the phone to the window. Sure enough, a white Chevy Cavalier sat in front of his neighbor's house, but the driver was obviously looking at Joe and Lisa's house. Even from over two hundred feet, Joe knew it was Shawnda Hull.

Joe told his neighbor thanks, then ran out the front door to the street directly towards Shawnda's car. She started the car and pulled away from the curb. He stepped to the middle of the road, holding up his hands. She sped up and tried to swerve around Joe. He moved to block her. She slowed a bit, still trying to get around him, but Joe kept blocking her path. He hoped she wasn't cold hearted enough to run him down, but she kept trying to angle around him. When she was within thirty feet, he made a final move, stepping to the left. Shawnda slammed on her brakes, leaving a track of rubber several feet long, stopping less than three feet in front of him.

He yelled at her to turn off the car's ignition. When she did, he ran to the driver's side door and leaned in, grabbed the keys, then yanked them from the ignition.

Joe crouched down, looking in the window at the subdued Shawnda Hull who was now crying. He needed her to calm down and get control of her emotions. He needed information and he needed it fast.

"Major, what are you doing here?"

She tried to speak, but the words got lost in a sea of emotional gibberish. Joe felt sorry for the woman, but he had no time to waste.

He yelled, "Major, get it together. Why are you here?"

After a moment, she stopped crying. She told Joe she had been tracking Ace, that she figured Joe was his next target. She also said she thought she'd seen him drive by but wasn't sure.

"When was that?"

Major Hull hesitated. "About fifteen minutes ago. I thought he'd come back, but he hasn't."

Maybe Ace had seen her here on the side of the road and took off. Maybe this target was too conspicuous with the major sitting at the curb. As to what Ace might do next. *I'd move on to my next target.*

Damn. He's going after Pat.

Chapter 43

The phone rang seven, eight, nine times. No answer. Joe tried dialing again, but got the same results. He smacked the cell phone against his leg in frustration. Either no one was home at Pat's house or they were all out by the pool. There were other possibilities, but Joe didn't want to think about them. He ran into the house and told Lisa he was heading to Pat and Diane's. It was 11:40 AM and he could make it there by 12:40 if he hurried.

After Joe's brief explanation of the possible danger, Lisa simply said, "Go! I'll keep trying to call from here."

Joe grabbed his 9mm and headed for his Jeep, his cell phone in his pocket. He hit speed dial for Hatch as he sped out of his driveway. Hatch picked up on the second ring.

"Yo."

"Hatch, this is Joe. We might have a big problem."

"Shoot."

"I think Ace is going after Pat."

Joe told him about Shawnda Hull sitting out in front of his house and that she thought she'd seen Ace. Hatch was shocked. He and Nancy had personally seen Major Hull to the airport for her flight home. How she'd managed to get to Central Florida that same day, he had no idea. That was an issue for another day.

Hatch asked, "So, how soon do ya think Ace will make it ta Pat's?"

Joe thought for a moment, then said, "He may be there in about forty to forty-five minutes. I tried calling the house but there's no answer."

"Y'all sure Ace couldn't have made it there already, right?"

"Yeah, I'm sure. He was just in front of my house twenty minutes ago." He paused then asked, "Where are you now?"

"Nancy an' me are on Silver Star Road near Ocoee. I can make it ta Pat's in about an hour, I think."

If Ace stopped for any reason or if he staked out the house, Joe, Hatch, and Nancy might get there before Ace made his move. "Alright, we'll all head there. I'll try to reach Pat and warn him. You just drive."

Hatch simply said, "Yup."

***

Joe tried calling Pat's house continuously as he drove. He'd let the phone ring twenty times before hanging up and redialing. *Damn it, Pat. Pick up the damn phone!* He noticed the battery on his cell phone was being drained with the repeated attempts. *Shit, Shit, Shit! One last time.*

After three rings, he heard a click and said, "Pat?" He waited for a second then asked again, "Pat, you there?"

Silence. He looked at his phone. The battery was dead. *Shit!* Joe pitched the phone into the passenger side footwell and pressed the accelerator. Seventy-five in a fifty-five mile per hour zone, and the car felt like it was crawling along the two lane state highway. He nearly lost control on a curve on State Route 44, catching the back tire on the passenger side on the lip of the road. He took a deep breath, then backed off slightly. Over the next minute he eased the accelerator down again, adrenaline pumping through his body.

I hope Lisa gets through.

***

Hatch and Nancy narrowly missed getting pulled over by a Highway Patrolman as Hatch accelerated over the speed limit before leaving the Bushnell town limits. They were now just four miles behind Joe, wondering if Joe had managed to reach Pat.

Hatch said "I think we better try to call Pat. The more people who try, the better chance someone will get through."

Nancy dialed Pat and Diane's number. The phone rang fifteen times before she hung up.

"No answer."

"I think that's good news…but maybe not."

Hatch, Nancy and Joe had about twenty-five minutes to go, *if* they didn't get stopped and *if* they hit the traffic lights just right in some of the towns south of Dunnellon. *Damn, I hope they're not home* Hatch thought. He pressed the accelerator a little harder.

***

In the city of Dunnellon, Ace Glover slowed at the intersection of East Pennsylvania and Wekiva Circle. The directions he'd gotten from the store clerk at the convenience store were apparently wrong. The kid had said to turn right at the Spanish style apartment building, but that was Wekiva Circle. Quail Run Drive was supposed to be on the left after about a quarter mile. Wekiva Circle didn't have an intersection with Quail Run. He looked around, spotting an old man heading towards him, walking a tiny dog, one of the types that movie stars carry in their purses. He wondered what self respecting man would own a dog like that.

When the man came close he rolled down the passenger side window. "Pardon me, sir. Can you tell me where Quail Run Drive is located?"

The man leaned over and looked at Ace. "Do I look like a road map?" Then he turned and said to his dog, "Come on, Margaret."

Ace was stunned, then ticked. He yelled out the window, "Screw you, old man. And your punk-assed dog." He did a u-turn and headed back to the convenience store where he parked, entered the store and asked the clerk again about Quail Run Drive.

"Like I said before, go down East Pennsylvania and turn left after the Spanish style apartment onto Camp Drive. It'll be on your left. Then turn left onto Mockingbird Drive, and left again on Quail Run."

Ace was about to argue with the clerk and tell him what a jerk he was for giving him wrong directions before, but he decided he had more important things to do. Within three minutes he was turning left onto Quail Run Drive, looking for the home of Pat and Diane McKinney.

***

Joe was making the curve on North Florida Avenue just south of Dunnellon. He approached the intersection with West Dunnellon Road. The light turned yellow. He gambled he could make it. When he hit the intersection, the light turned red. He nearly hit a young couple, swerving at the last minute, missing the young woman by a foot. In his rearview mirror, he saw them gave him the finger. Then he focused on the last stretch of roadway before the intersection with Pennsylvania Avenue. *Four minutes to go.*

***

Hatch and Nancy hit the lights just right, and closed the gap between them and Joe. They couldn't raise Pat at home. *Maybe that was good news, but in reality it wasn't a clear sign of anything.*

Hatch flipped open the center console and checked to make sure his Glock 9mm was there and ready, safeties off. It was. Nancy opened her purse and did the same. She took a deep breath. *Come on Pat. Answer the phone, please.*

She hit redial. The phone rang fifteen times. She hung up the phone for the last time as Hatch pressed hard on the accelerator as they approached Pennsylvania Avenue.

***

Pat and Sean were in the pool getting a real workout. Pat would throw the colored rings into the deep end and Sean would dive to retrieve them as Pat timed his dives. Sean was trying to beat his best time of eighteen seconds, but just couldn't seem to break that mark.

Finally, he said "I have to use the bathroom."

"At least you're not peeing in the pool."

"Dad, it's number two."

Pat smiled. "Well hurry up. You can't do that in here."

Sean laughed, then headed into the house after drying off a bit.

Diane and Anna were out shopping for new outfits for Anna's cousin Danielle. Her birthday was coming up and they wanted to get something special for her.

Pat did one full lap in the pool, then got out and toweled off. He stood next to the pool wondering where Ace was. He hadn't heard from Hatch, and he figured that was a good sign. But he worried that Ace might give Hatch the slip. He decided to call his friend for an update, just to ease his mind.

He walked over to the edge of the covered patio, picked up his glass of iced tea and was about to take a sip when he noticed the ice had melted completely. He tossed the contents onto the lawn, then turned towards the patio door that led to the kitchen. He stopped dead in his tracks. The barrel of a dark black 9mm pistol hovered a mere six feet from his face. Behind it, the ice cold stare of Ace Glover came into focus.

***

Two minutes, just two minutes, that's all. Everything's fine. Joe told himself, willing the car to go faster down East Pennsylvania Avenue. He almost missed seeing an old man step out onto Pennsylvania with his miniature dog in tow. Joe slammed on the brakes. The old man stopped in the middle of the road and started yelling at Joe that he should watch his driving.

Instead of arguing, he threw the Jeep into reverse and backed up twenty feet, slammed the gear shift back into drive, then drove up onto the curb to get around the still cursing old man.

***

Hatch and Nancy spotted Joe's Jeep making the left turn onto Camp Drive. As they accelerated down East Pennsylvania, an elderly man standing in the middle of the road raised his fist at Joe's speeding car.

Hatch said, "I wonder if Joe insulted his little dawg."

Nancy didn't smile.

Hatch wiggled his fingers at the old man as he sped around him, leaving a safe distance between him and his dog and their car. Seconds later he turned left as he followed Joe's skid marks on the street.

***

Sean finished his business and was heading back out to the pool when the phone rang. He walked into the kitchen and answered, "McKinneys."

Sean heard his Aunt Lisa sigh. "Hey, big guy, is everything okay there? We've been trying to call for quite a while."

"Hi, Aunt Lisa. We've been out in the pool. I've been diving for those colored rings. You should see me. I'm down to eighteen seconds now."

"That's great Sean. You're a great swimmer. Is your dad there?"

"Yeah, just a minute. He's still outside."

Sean placed the hand set on the counter and headed to the patio door. He yelled, "Dad, Aunt Lisa's on the phone!"

***

Pat's heart sank when he heard Sean yell. He watched as his son approached the patio door. His heart pounded as adrenaline flooded his body and his brain shifted into overdrive.

Ace instinctively turned his head towards the voice. His gun shifted just enough to the right for Pat to make his move. Two quick steps, and Pat pushed off with his right leg, launching himself like a rocket at Ace, hitting him square in the chest. Ace pulled the trigger as he fell. The report sounded like a cannon under the roof of the covered portion of the patio.

Pat butted Ace's face with his forehead, catching him between the nose and cheek, not hard or square enough to cause any damage, but it clearly hurt. Pat grabbed at Ace's wrist, for the hand that held the gun. He needed to stay on top of Ace, keep his full weight on the younger man, try to wear him out.

Ace maneuvered with his legs, trying to get Pat on his back. He pressed the ground with his legs, twisting and arching his back until he had Pat nearly turned on his side.

Pat knew it was only a matter of time before Ace flipped him over. He had to get that gun away, make sure Ace couldn't use it. *Sean. I have to protect Sean.*

In a desperate move, he let go of Ace's body and grabbed Ace's wrist with both hands. He yanked the arm to his face and bit Ace's hand, hard, right below the thumb. His teeth sank into the soft flesh, drawing blood, the copper taste filling his mouth.

Ace's grip loosened. Pat freed one hand, snatched the gun, then threw it as hard as he could towards the pool. It landed in the deep end with a splash.

***

Sean saw the bad man with the gun pointed at his dad. For a moment, he panicked and didn't know what to do, then he thought, *I have to stay calm and get the gun.* He ran to the phone and said, "Aunt Lisa, a bad man is here. I have to go." Sean hung up the phone.

Sean raced down the hall into Pat's office and opened the safe where Pat kept their guns. He pulled out his gun with one hand, then a clip. He checked that the clip was full, pointed the barrel away from himself, then slapped the clip in place. He jacked a round into the chamber and checked that the safeties were on. In less than thirty seconds from the time he entered Pat's office, he was back at the patio door.

***

After Pat threw Ace's gun in the pool, Ace twisted on top of him, then punched him in the face, stunning him. Shaking his sore hand, Ace darted towards the pool. He spotted his gun right between the shallow and deep ends.

Pat leapt to his feet and lunged. He hit Ace square in the lower back, and both men tumbled into the pool. Ace grabbed Pat around the neck and shoved his head underwater.

All the hate and rage built up over the years flooded Ace's mind. He held Pat's head under the water, felt his body begin to grow slack. He would finish Pat off, then head back to Winter Garden.

"Let my dad go!"

Ace turned to see Sean pointing a pistol at his head. He continued to hold Pat's weakening body under water.

Sean yelled, "Let him go now!"

Ace noticed the boy's shaking hands and smiled. "You won't shoot me. You don't have the guts, kid."

***

Sean's hands sweated. The bullet was chambered, the safeties off. All he had to do was pull the trigger to send a bullet into that bad man's head. But he had a hard time keeping the gun steady.

The report was deafening. It knocked Ace backwards, his grip around Pat's neck loosened, blood from the exit wound filled the area of the pool behind Ace.

Sean whirled and saw Uncle Joe holding a smoking gun. Joe kept his gun trained on Ace's now limp body as he hurried down the shallow end steps towards his brother.

He said, "Sean, go call 911 and tell them we need an ambulance and the police. Go, do it quick."

Sean took a fearful look at his father as Joe pulled him above the pool's surface. Hatch and Nancy came into the back yard and jumped in to help Joe pull Pat from the pool. Sean took one last look at his father's pale white body,   then   ran to the phone and dialed.

"911, what is your emergency?"

Sean yelled, "My Dad's hurt real bad. I think he might be dead."

Chapter 44

Two dozen patrons at the graveside service stood solemnly as family members came forward and placed flowers or special mementos on the casket. Oppressive heat punished the small crowd. Thankfully, the gravesite was under the canopy of several large southern oaks. Even in the shade the mourners waved programs to fan themselves.

Diane McKinney looked around at the crowd. She listened to the muted conversations. Joe, in a light gray sport coat and slacks stood stone-faced next to Lisa who held Danielle in her arms. Lisa wore a light summer dress.

Lisa leaned over to Joe and whispered, "When we get home, I'm stripping down naked and jumping straight into the pool."

"I'd say that's not real appropriate for this solemn occasion." He paused then smiled, "But I plan to join you."

Emma McKinney standing next to Joe, whispered, "You know, God is watching you two." She turned forward to face the casket again, a thin smile on her face.

Diane looked at her son, Sean, who stood at his grandmother's side, locked into his too-serious-for-an-eight-year-old mood. He had shown signs over the last few days of breaking out of his funk. She knew it had been a difficult period for him. Joe and Hatch had both taken him aside and talked to him about the incident by the pool.

Anna held Sean's hand. She had told Diane that she didn't really want to be at the cemetery, but as long as her family was there, she would be there, too. She looked around and smiled up at Danielle who waved back at her cousin.

Diane held Anna's other hand. She smiled down at her daughter then up at Danielle. She thought for a moment about how lucky Joe was to have such a beautiful family with a new addition on the way. Lisa wasn't exactly glowing in the summer heat, but she was excited at the prospect of becoming a mother for the second time. Anna and Sean were looking forward to having a new cousin.

Diane looked back at the casket then around at the crowd that had shown up for the funeral. She was surprised at the number of people at the gravesite. She hadn't shed a single tear during the service.

Pat stood on her left, balanced on his crutches, tears in his eyes. The cast on his left leg obviously made him very uncomfortable. When he'd knocked Ace into the pool, he'd hit his leg just below the knee on the concrete ledge. It had snapped like a twig.

"What are you crying about?" Diane whispered to her husband.

He whispered back, "Poor Aunt Sylvia. And this damn cast is killing me. One minute my leg itches like hell, the next it feels like it's on fire." Pat paused for several seconds then whispered, "I'll miss Aunt Sylvia. She was always so nice to Joe and me when we visited her in Sandusky."

Diane rolled her eyes. "Did you visit her often?"

"Not really. Dad used to force us to go there when we were kids. I remember she used to open a can of Seven-Up and split it between Joe and me. When we asked for another glass she would say, 'Get a glass of water. That pop's not good for you. And we have such good water here in Sandusky.' Then she'd scowl at us and walk away. She was mean and old even back then."

Diane smiled at the story. She'd never heard that one before, but there were many other Aunt Sylvia stories that Pat and Joe had shared at family barbeques. Diane hooked her left arm around Pat's right, being careful not to make him lose his balance.

Her mind drifted to the chaotic scene that had greeted her the week before when she and Anna had returned from the store. Two ambulances, three Dunnellon Police cars, three cars she didn't recognize, and Joe's Jeep were scattered across her lawn and driveway. One ambulance was being loaded with a gurney, a man strapped in. At first, she hadn't recognized Pat, white as the sheets wrapped around most of his body. She had screamed just as Joe, Hatch, Nancy, and Sean rounded the side of the ambulance. Joe grabbed her in a bear hug and tried to calm her, reassuring her that Pat was going to be alright. She calmed a bit and went down on one knee and hugged Sean, picked him up and squeezed him tight.

The next four hours were a blur. Hatch and Nancy took Anna and Sean into the house. Lisa had been frantically calling the house and Joe's cell phone with no luck. She called the Dunnellon Police Department and told them about Sean and the bad man. When she called Pat and Diane's house again, Hatch had answered and told her what had transpired. Joe, with Diane in his passenger's seat, followed the ambulance to the hospital. Pat was in the emergency room several hours, hospital staff ensuring that his vital signs stabilized and he was breathing on his own. They set his broken leg and placed a temporary cast on it, then kept him overnight for observation, since he'd been underwater for a fairly long stretch. Pat had no idea how long he had been unconscious.

In the end, there was no brain damage, though Diane asked the doctor how he knew for certain, given Pat's obvious pre-existing lack of brain function. Everyone got a good laugh from that one, but Diane barely cracked a smile.

After the doctors determined Pat was physically, mentally, and emotionally out of the woods, Diane sat alone in his room while he slept. She wondered if this was the end of her husband's past returning to haunt him…and his family. Would she ever leave Pat to protect her children? Sean had come dangerously close to killing a man. Granted, the man was trying to kill his father, but that was beside the point. Prior to this incident, it was only Pat whose life was in danger. Where would it end? Or was this the end? After more soul searching, Diane decided she could never leave Pat. After all, she loved him with all her heart.

***

Several weeks had passed since the attempt on Pat's life. Diane remained concerned with Sean and his mental state. After he'd gone to sleep one evening, she took his journal and read the entries from the past few days. Her heart ached reading the turmoil her son wrangled with over his hesitation to shoot Ace Glover while Ace had tried drowning his dad.

I don't know if I could have done it, I mean killed that man. I was shaking and sweating and the gun was so heavy, not like when Dad and I practiced. If Uncle Joe hadn't killed him, my dad might be dead now. Uncle Joe thinks I would have done it, but maybe it would have been too late. He told me it isn't easy to kill someone. It looks easy on TV and in the movies, but I know it isn't like that. Dad told me that when he was teaching me that it isn't easy to kill and he was right. I think if I had to do it over, it might be easier. Maybe I'll never know.

Uncle Hatch said I should be proud of myself, that I've got nothing to be ashamed of. He said to keep practicing shooting, but more important, always remember to do what is right. He said as I grow up it will be easier and easier to know the difference. I hope he's right.

I'm just glad my dad's okay. I don't know what I'd do if he died and I could have saved him.

Tears welled up in Diane's eyes. Her son had seen too much for such a young age.

***

Back at Joe and Lisa's house, the women and children beat the heat of the sweltering day by jumping in the pool. As soon as Sean hit the water he played with his cousin's diving rings. Before long he was laughing and splashing as he had when Pat and Diane first got their pool. They smiled at each other, believing that Sean's remedy for anything that ailed him was going to be a swim in the pool.

Pat, Joe, and Hatch each cracked a beer and touched the necks together in a toast. Soon the conversation settled on their recent adventures.

Hatch said, "I spoke with Shawnda Hull. She finally made it home after our half dozen attempts to get her there. She's gonna face court martial. The Air Force is lettin' her spend a few days with her child so long as it's under her dad's supervision. He told 'em she'd be there for the proceedings."

"Pat's eyebrows shot up. "That seems awfully kind of them. Does she have any idea what the punishment will be?"

"She said she expects to spend at least a few months in the brig and be dishonorably discharged. Said she didn't care. She was just happy to be home with her son and not trailin' Ace all over the country." He turned to Joe. "She said to thank ya for killin' Ace. She figures justice was served."

Joe said, "I spoke with Detective Banks yesterday. He and Major Alexander up at the Air Force Academy exchanged notes on the cases against Colonels Barnes and Templeton. It seems this whole mess started when they took Abbie Glover to a party at Milton Chester's apartment when he was a cadet. After they raped her and she got pregnant, Chester's old man began the cover-up. If Alexander's assistant hadn't kept those files, this whole thing would have been swept under the rug. They'd have gotten away with a whole list of crimes from rape and kidnapping all the way down to obstruction of justice. Plus, Barnes used what she knew to move up in the ranks faster than her male counterparts. She wasn't planning to stop at colonel either."

Hatch said, "So let me get this straight. Y'all's telling me that Barnes and Templeton supplied the underage Abbie to the four cadets and she was s'pose to be Templeton's date? That was it? Why'd he blow his own brains out?"

Joe sipped his beer. "Banks thinks the guy was just a nerd. He couldn't get a girlfriend his own age so he picked up younger girls who were easily impressed, then supplied them to other cadets to get on their good side. He was just trying to make friends and fit in."

"That's one way to do it," Pat said. "Or you could do other cadets' homework. That would be better than accessory to rape. That's what he was facing. I just don't think he could handle the guilt or the possibility of going to Leavenworth."

The three were silent for a while, then Pat asked, "Why did Ace kill all those other guys, you know, his sister's 'husbands?'" He used his fingers to put quotes around the word husbands. "As far as we know, most of those guys treated her like a queen."

"I doubt we'll ever know the answer to that one," Hatch said. "He must have hated any man that came near his mother or sister. Everyone on the list that he was carrying either raped his mom, was married to Becky, or was involved in the raid on Bobby and Becky."

Joe picked up the thread. "Banks found out more about that Harold Trent guy, the guy killed by Wilson's apartment. Turns out he was an Air Force officer at the academy. He worked directly for Commander Chester. He was assigned to make sure Abbie left town after delivering the baby. Turns out that Milton Chester, the commander's son, was Becky Lippert's father. Trent felt sorry for Abbie. He went AWOL and followed her around the country trying to get to know her and protect her from the freaks she normally picked up."

"Why would he do that?" Pat asked.

"Y'all ain't real bright, are ya? He was in love, man. He fell for Abbie. Keep goin', Joe. Pat'll catch up in an hour or so." Hatch smiled at Pat.

Joe continued, "So Trent manages to get together with Abbie and, as luck would have it, Abbie has a little baby boy named Ace."

Pat, with an astonished look said, "No way!"

Joe and Hatch answered in unison, "Yes, way!"

"So Ace killed his own father?"

Joe said, "Yepper, and you thought you had a rough childhood."

Pat looked at Hatch as if he wanted to ask a question then looked away.

Hatch smiled. "Y'all want to know why I followed Ace all the way across this great country, then stood by and let him kill a man in cold blood, then didn't tell anybody except y'all two. Am I close?"

Pat smiled. "Well, yeah. You could've stopped Ace right there."

Hatch shrugged his shoulders and raised his beer for another swig. "I didn't know who was the bigger bastard, Ace or Chester. Who am I to judge? It's not like I'm gonna get canonized in the church anytime soon." He took another drink. "Besides, I had a date with Miss Nancy and I didn't want to stand her up." He smiled.

The men fell into silence. Pat was deep in thought, rubbing the scar on his chin when Joe asked, "What's got you all twisted up?"

"I'm just trying to figure out who else might want to screw up our lives."

"I hope nobody."

"I sure hope you're right."

Hatch smiled. "Y'all'll be bored to tears within a week."

Pat looked at the crutches leaning against his lawn chair, then felt the center of his chest where a bullet from Abbie Glover's gun had struck the Kevlar vest that saved his life. As he thought about the different situations Joe, Hatch, and he had faced over the years, he reached up and rubbed the scar on the left side of his chin. Looking over at Anna and Sean splashing each other in the pool, he smiled. He turned towards his wife. She was in the shallow end of the pool talking with Nancy and Lisa, who was holding baby Danielle, and subconsciously rubbing her belly.

He turned back to Hatch and Joe. "You know what? I think I'm ready for a little of that boring life."

Pat, Joe, and Hatch touched the necks of their beers again. Pat said, "To a boring life!" They all smiled, then took a long pull on their beers.

###

McKinney Brothers Suspense Novels

A Lifetime of Vengeance
A Lifetime of Deception
A Lifetime of Exposure
A Lifetime of Terror
A Lifetime of Betrayal

Peden Savage Suspense Novel

Drug Wars

Non-Series Suspense Novel

Under the Blood Tree

Pete 'P.J.' Grondin, born the seventh of twelve children, moved around a number of times when he was young; from Sandusky, Ohio to Bay City, Michigan, then to Maitland and Zellwood, Florida before returning to Sandusky, OH. It was there that he met his future bride.

After his service in the US Navy in the Nuclear Power Program, serving on the ballistic missile submarine, USS *John Adams*, Pete returned to his hometown of Sandusky, OH where he was elected to the Sandusky City Commission, serving a single term. He worked as an Application Process Specialist in the IT department of a major electric utility until his retirement in 2015.

His current novels in the McKinney Brothers series are *A Lifetime of Vengeance, A Lifetime of Deception, A Lifetime of Exposure, A Lifetime of Terror, and A Lifetime of Betrayal.*

His first novel in the Peden Savage series is *Drug Wars*. His first non-series suspense novel is *Under the Blood Tree.*